By Nicole Edwards (cont.)

The Devil's Bend Series

Chasing Dreams

Vanishing Dreams

The Devil's Playground Series

Without Regret

The Pier 70 Series

Reckless

Fearless

The Sniper 1 Security Series

Wait for Morning

Never Say Never

The Southern Boy Mafia Series

Beautifully Brutal

Beautifully Loyal

Standalone Novels

A Million Tiny Pieces

Inked on Paper

Writing as Timberlyn Scott

Unhinged

Unraveling

Chaos

Naughty Holiday Editions

2015

Fearless

A Pier 70 Novel
Book 2

Nicole Edwards

Nicole Edwards Limited
PO Box 806
Hutto, Texas 78634
www.NicoleEdwardsLimited.com
www.slipublishing.com

Cover Image: © Oleksandr Nebrat | 123rf.com (front cover image - 13515462); © wrangel | 123rf.com (back cover image - 34596028)

Ebook Image: © magenta10 | 123rf.com (formatting image - 14284060)

Cover Design: © Nicole Edwards Limited

Editing: Blue Otter Editing **www.BlueOtterEditing.com**

ISBN (ebook): 978-1-939786-62-3
ISBN (print): 978-1-939786-61-6

Gay Romance
M/M interactions
Mature Audience

Table of Contents

Dedication

This book is dedicated to the one person who makes me feel as though I can do anything in this world. Colt Edwards, you are my rock and I always feel safe jumping when I know you're there to catch me. I couldn't do this without you. I love you!

Prologue

Fifteen years ago

"DON'T MOVE. STAY *right* where you are."

Dare held as still as possible, although it was the complete opposite of what he wanted to do. Not moving wasn't an easy task when the pleasure was slamming through him, making his eyes cross.

Still, he managed.

Barely.

This position—lying on his side, facing the television with the man of his dreams flat against his back, body curled around him, penetrating him right where he needed him— fuck if it didn't feel good.

So-o-o good.

"Noah..." Dare endured for only a few torturous seconds, willing his boyfriend to move his hips a fraction of an inch, just enough to brush that spot that made Dare see stars.

"Hmm?" Noah's breath was warm against the back of Dare's neck.

Fearless

Dare inhaled deeply, Noah's strong arm banding around him, holding him against his tense body. Dare's skin felt two sizes too small as the heat of Noah's chest pierced him. It was the second time today that he'd found himself at Noah's mercy, but fuck if it didn't feel like the first time … ever.

Every time felt like the first time when it came to Noah.

They'd been lying on the couch, watching a movie for the past hour, spending a lazy Sunday evening at Noah's apartment. As was the case anytime they found time to be alone, Dare's body had been humming with anticipation, his mind half-ass in tune with the television. Right up until Noah had started stroking Dare's dick, then his gray matter had gone offline completely. The only thing his nineteen-year-old brain cared about was being fucked into oblivion.

Even though that impromptu hand job had lasted far less time than Dare would've liked, he hadn't minded at all when Noah had reached over him to retrieve the lubricant on the end table, shoved Dare's shorts down, and then guided his lubed cock right into Dare's eager ass.

He only wished Noah would get on with it, because if he didn't, Dare was going to go insane.

"Not ready to come yet." Dare loved the gravelly sound of Noah's voice; it reflected his apparent effort to hold back. "Feels too damn good."

"It'll feel better … if"—Dare thrust his hips back with every word—"you … fuck … me."

"Aw, fuck yes, baby." Noah groaned. *So sexy.* "Beg me, Dare." Noah's command was followed by a gentle bite on the sensitive skin of Dare's shoulder. "You know how much I love it when you beg."

He'd beg, all right.

"Please…" Dare moaned, then laughed. "Just fuck me already."

Noah thrust his hips forward. "Ahh, fuck. Too good."

Dare's ass clenched around the thick intrusion, his own cock rock hard and in need of some attention. "Assume you mean me and not the movie?"

"Fuck the movie." Noah's hand tightened on Dare's hip, a rumbling growl following his words.

"Thought it was *me* you were fucking," Dare teased, pushing back against Noah so that Noah's cock slid deeper inside him. "Fuck yes," he hissed when Noah's dick pressed against that mind-numbing spot.

"That what you want?" Noah's words were strained.

"Yeah…" *Fuck yeah.* It was what he always wanted. Anything Noah wanted to give him, Dare was more than willing to take.

Noah shifted so that he was kneeling behind Dare, his hands roughly jerking Dare toward him so that he didn't dislodge his cock from Dare's ass. Dare didn't put up a fight, bending until he was right where Noah wanted him, on his knees, one shoulder pressed into the cushion, using one hand to balance.

Noah slowly pulled back, holding Dare's ass cheeks firmly, then guiding himself home, filling Dare once again. He could feel the heat of Noah's gaze as he watched while he penetrated him. The idea of Noah so caught up in watching sent another tremor racing through him.

Dare's hand closed around the edge of the cushion, the sweet penetration sending shards of sensation all over him. He loved these moments, loved feeling Noah inside him. But it wasn't enough.

"Quit fucking with me." He needed more friction.

"You're in too much of a hurry."

"Only 'cause I wanna fuck you before I come."

"Mmm."

Dare knew Noah would like that.

"So get on with it." Dare thrust back against Noah, trying to take him deeper.

"Hold still." Noah smacked Dare's ass. Hard.

"Oh, yeah." Heat bloomed on his skin, and he briefly wondered if he would like being spanked. Never hurt to try. He teased Noah by glancing over his shoulder and winking. "Spank me again."

Noah chuckled, as Dare wanted him to.

"I'm gonna *fuck* you. That's what I'm gonna do."

And that was exactly what Noah did, slamming deep, making lights dance behind Dare's closed eyelids while electricity fizzed beneath his skin.

Tightening his grip on the couch cushion and putting one hand on the arm to hold himself in place, Dare gladly accepted Noah's punishing thrusts, relishing every second of it. Noah impaled him over and over, faster, harder, deeper, until Dare feared he would come.

Biting his bottom lip, he held off until Noah roared his release, the heavy weight of him falling against Dare's back, crushing him into the cushions. Dare didn't give Noah much time to recover before he wrestled him onto his back, then grabbed the lube bottle that sat open on the coffee table. Within seconds, he was slicked up and ready, slowly driving himself into Noah as he stared down at the man he loved.

"Hot." *Scorching.* God, it felt so good being inside him. Dare hissed, inching deeper inside Noah's ass. "So fucking hot."

Noah pulled his knees in close to his chest, allowing Dare to lean over him, their eyes locked.

"Have I mentioned how much I love you?" Dare pumped his hips slowly as he fucked them both to ecstasy.

"You have..." Noah nodded, the unmistakable connection between them solidifying. "Fuck, that feels good... But you can tell me again."

Dare held Noah's dark gaze, slowing his pace. Suddenly, the moment shifted from fast and frantic to something much deeper, much more intense.

Yeah, he loved Noah with every ounce of himself. They'd been together for a little over two years, practically lived together since he stayed with Noah most of the time. And with every passing second, Dare fell deeper and deeper for the man. Hell, he wanted to spend the rest of his life with him, never imagined being with anyone else.

"Wanna feel you come inside me."

Dare barely heard Noah's whisper, the thumping of his own heart loud in his ears. He managed a nod, forcing his hips forward, then back. Holding himself up with one hand, he used the other to push a lock of Noah's thick, dark hair from his face, never breaking eye contact as he repeated the thrust and retreat.

"I love you, Noah." Dare felt his heart constrict at the same time that electrical spark ignited inside him. "Gonna come... Fuck." Dare pumped his hips as he was assaulted with pleasure so intense he thought he might pass out. "Love you so much."

"I love you, too." Noah's hand gripped the back of Dare's neck as he stared up at him. "Now come for me, babe."

And that was exactly what Dare did.

Half an hour later, after they'd cleaned up and restarted the movie back to the part they'd lost interest at, Dare found himself lying on the couch once again. This time he was behind Noah with his arm tossed over him, curled up against Noah's bare back, fingers gliding slowly up and down Noah's stomach. Dare was drifting, trying to stay awake, but it wasn't easy.

Fearless

The only thing keeping him conscious was the pressure on his brain. All of the thoughts weighing down on him. Things he'd tried to talk to Noah about for some time now. Things he knew Noah didn't want to talk about. But Dare couldn't hold back anymore. He needed answers, needed to know where this was going.

"Why don't I move in here?" Dare muttered, attempting to keep his voice soft, words gentle.

Despite the delivery, Noah tensed and a sharp pain pierced Dare's heart. Unfortunately, in the position they were in, there was no way Noah could've hidden his reaction, which meant the conversation was going to take place, even if Dare no longer wanted to discuss it. That simple flex of Noah's muscles was all the answer he needed.

Noah didn't want him. Not permanently.

"Never mind." Dare sucked in air as more pain lanced him. Nope, he changed his mind. He didn't want to talk about it. "I'm still high from the sex."

"Probably." The rumbling vibration of Noah's laugh made Dare's insides go cold. "Makes you think crazy shit, huh?"

Crazy shit?

Ouch.

Dare didn't respond. He couldn't. His throat was tight, and it felt as though there were a lead weight on his chest, suffocating him.

Knowing Noah, he expected Dare to simply drop the subject as he usually did. They'd been together for twenty-five months (yes, he kept track), and things had been going great between them. As far as Dare was concerned, it wasn't too farfetched to think they should officially move in together, start planning for their future.

There was only one major problem with that.

It didn't seem they were on the same page.

Fuck. They *had* to talk about this. It was inevitable. No way would Dare be able to sleep unless they hashed it out. Deciding there would be no better time than now, Dare shifted deeper into the cushions behind him, then forced Noah onto his back so Dare could see his face.

"Where do you see this going?" The words were blunt, sure, but that was because Dare's stomach churned with nerves and he suddenly felt sick.

"See *what* going?" Noah was playing dumb, evidently.

Swallowing hard, Dare forced the words past his parched throat. "Us. I know it's not just the sex that's so great between us."

"But the sex *is* pretty fucking good, huh?"

It was obvious Noah wanted to change the subject, but Dare wasn't going to allow it. Not this time. "Do you love me?"

Noah met Dare's gaze, a deep line forming in his forehead. "Of course I do. I've told you that."

"Then what's the problem?" Dare didn't understand. If they loved each other, why the hell shouldn't they make this official?

Noah repositioned so that he was looking at Dare more fully. Dare didn't move, waiting for an answer that would cause this to all make sense.

"You're only nineteen, Dare."

"Ah, good." Dare attempted to rein in his anger. He took a deep breath and … failed. "Glad we're both aware of that. I thought for a second you forgot."

Seriously, Dare thought they were long past the age thing. In the beginning, when they'd met and Dare had been only seventeen, he'd understood Noah's reasons for wanting to wait before they had sex. Somehow, they'd endured three and a half months before they had sex for the first time, on Dare's eighteenth birthday. They'd taken things slow, done things right. And now... He was getting tired of his age always being Noah's issue.

"Dare..."

"No." Dare jerked back, the pain ricocheting through his insides. "I don't need you to remind me that I'm nineteen and that you're twenty-three. When you had your dick in my ass, or mine in yours, our ages didn't seem to be an issue."

"They're *not* an issue." Noah's retort sounded almost believable. "The age difference isn't the problem."

"Then what is?"

Noah jerked away, sitting up and thrusting his hands through his disheveled hair.

Dare moved away from him, getting to his feet and pacing the floor. It pissed him off that this was how the conversation always went, and in the end nothing would change, but Dare wasn't backing down now. "Are you seeing someone else?"

Noah's head snapped up, his mouth gaping open. "No, I'm not fucking seeing anyone else. Goddammit, Dare, why the fuck would you ask me something like that?"

"It's the only logical answer I can come up with. You don't want me to move in here, yet you can't give me a reason. Maybe there *is* someone else."

Noah got to his feet and moved toward him, the hard lines on his face softening. "No. There's no one else. I love you. Only you. I thought I'd made that pretty damn clear."

Dare's stomach tightened painfully. This was not going the way he'd hoped it would.

"Look..." Noah cupped Dare's cheek and forced him to look at him. "Things are good between us. I don't see any reason we should rush it."

"Rush it?" Dare frowned. "We've been together for two fucking *years*."

"I know. And you're only *nineteen*."

"Why do you always say that?" Dare's anger was making his face heat. "It's always about my age, but I don't fucking understand. If I were twenty, would that change things? 'Cause in a few months, that'll be the case. What excuse will you use then?"

Noah's gaze hardened. "You're too damn young to think about settling down with anyone."

"No! *You* don't get to do that. You don't get to blame this on me. No one gets to tell me what I am and am not ready for. *I* get to do that. And honestly, I want more than this." As the words came out, his throat tightened around the ball of emotion lodged there. "I'm talking forever."

Noah stared at him, jaw tight. "Babe, you're just a kid. Forever's a long damn time."

Dare took a step back, the force of those words like a punch to the gut.

A kid?

He couldn't breathe from the agony that filled his insides. It felt as though there were a band on his chest, slowly tightening, squeezing the life from him. It was a physical ache, and it threatened to take him to his knees.

"Dare... Come on. I don't wanna fight with you."

They shouldn't have to fight about this. They should've been on the same page. Two years was a long damn time to be with someone, to give every piece of yourself ... yet, it seemed Dare was the only one who'd come to terms with that.

Yet Noah called *him* a kid.

Fearless

Standing there in the shadows of Noah's living room, the light from the television flickering across Noah's handsome face, Dare knew what had to happen. He'd spent the past two years falling deeper and deeper in love with this man, but this wasn't the first time they'd had this argument. And as far as he could tell, they didn't seem to be getting any closer to making this a permanent relationship. No matter what Dare wanted.

As far as he was concerned, he'd fought the good fight. He'd gone after what he wanted, to no avail. And truth be told, he was tired of fighting. They obviously wanted different things.

"You're right." Dare moved closer, allowing Noah to wrap his arms around him. He gripped Noah tightly, burying his face in Noah's neck, fighting the tremor of emotions that rumbled in his chest. Dare breathed him in, memorizing the fresh scent, the warmth of his skin, the firmness of his arms surrounding him.

"You ready for bed?" Noah pulled back and looked at him.

"Yeah, sure." He wasn't, but it sounded good. Dare took a deep breath and stepped back.

"Good. I'm exhausted. Come on." Noah took Dare's hand, the subject dropped just like that. "I wanna hold you."

With his heart cracked open and bleeding in his chest, Dare followed Noah into the bedroom. He crawled into bed, slid beneath the covers, and allowed Noah to hold him.

For the last time.

One

Saturday, May 28th
Present day

"WHAT TIME DOES your flight leave tomorrow?"

Dare Davis glanced up from the iPad screen—where he'd been playing WordBrain, of all things—to see Cam standing at the main counter.

Giving his friend a quick once-over, Dare had to admit he was impressed. The guy didn't look nervous or in a panic, yet the countdown to D-Day was on. T-minus five days until Cam Strickland and Gannon Burgess would tie the knot, officially hyphenating them.

Strickland-Burgess.

Or was it Burgess-Strickland?

He grimaced, realizing he'd never asked.

Burg-land it was.

Dare grinned at his friend. "Aww, isn't that sweet. You worried I won't be there to watch you profess your undying love?"

"I'm not worried that you *won't* be there." Cam smirked, clearly brushing off Dare's snide comment as he had since they'd made the big announcement. With a devilish gleam in his eye, Cam's grin widened. "I'm more worried that you *will.*"

Ha ha. Funny. Dare chuckled. For the past couple of weeks, Dare had received a couple dozen warnings—from everyone—that he was not allowed to pull any pranks before, during, or immediately after Cam and Gannon's wedding. In fact, they'd sworn him off any type of prank until early June—as if outlining the time frame mattered at all to him. Of course, Dare hadn't actually planned to do anything drastic—at least not until Cam had mentioned it. Multiple times.

Now, he wasn't willing to make any promises.

When Lulu—the three-year-old golden retriever who was as much a part of the marina as ... oh, say, the lake—came over and rested her head on Dare's knee, he gave the dog's head a scratch.

Dare looked at Cam. "I get into Orlando at one thirty in the afternoon." *And then he had to travel to Port Canaveral.* He smiled when Cam frowned, already knowing what Cam was thinking. "And before you freak, I *will* make it to the ship before it leaves. I swear."

Because everyone who could run the day-to-day of Pier 70 Marina would be on that ship to celebrate Cam and Gannon's nuptials, the four of them had worked the schedule so that Dare would be the last one to leave, ensuring they had coverage right up until the last possible minute. Since they would have to close the marina for tours for eight straight days—the week that included Memorial Day weekend—it had been the only logical thing to do. And though Teague had said he would stay back and man the place while everyone else went on the seven-night cruise to the Bahamas, Dare had simply smacked Teague on the back of the head and told him not to be a dumb ass.

They would all be present and accounted for on D-Day, no matter what.

Luckily, one of Cam's father's friends was willing to pitch in and cover the place in case of emergencies, as well as take care of Lulu, while they were gone. Everything else would have to wait. It was rare, but there were some things that were more important than work. Love and marriage and baby carriages apparently qualified.

The visual of Cam pushing a baby stroller made Dare chuckle to himself.

"What's so funny?"

Dare shrugged off Cam's question.

"Shouldn't you be heading to the airport?" Dare glanced at the clock, then back to Cam. It was only nine in the morning, but Cam and Gannon, as well as most of the others who would also be boarding the ship tomorrow, were flying to Florida today and staying in a hotel overnight.

"Gannon's got it covered." Cam grinned.

"So, that means Milly's running point and making sure y'all get where you need to be?" Dare knew how this worked.

"Yes, that's what I meant."

Of course it was. Milly Holcomb, Gannon's assistant *slash* best friend *slash* maid of honor, was on her game, all right. She'd been so busy these past few months getting things ready for the wedding that Dare hadn't seen her since February, though he'd had many text conversations with her. Including the one from last night, when she'd all but threatened to castrate him if he didn't show up on time.

"And the best man?"

"Packed up and ready to go."

Spinning around in his chair, Dare found the source of the voice. He saw Roan Gregory—a.k.a. the best man—walking in the back door, wheeling a suitcase behind him.

"Ooh, spiffy." Dare looked Roan up and down.

"What?" Roan frowned as he looked down at himself. "Because I'm wearing jeans?"

Dare grinned. Their preferred uniform at the marina was shorts and a T-shirt—year round. Sometimes just shorts. "Nah. Because your shirt has those little round things. What're they called?"

The line in Roan's forehead deepened. "Buttons?"

Dare nodded, smirking. "Yeah. Those. Nice touch."

Watching Roan, Dare tried to determine if there was any trace of the confused emotions the man had admitted to having all those months ago when Cam and Gannon had first started dating. Although Roan's personal life hadn't picked up—at least not that Dare knew of, anyway—it seemed as though Roan had realized the error of his ways. The man hadn't been in love with Cam as he'd said he was. Instead, he'd been worried that he would lose his best friend.

Didn't look to be the case anymore. Thank God.

Probably helped that Gannon had all but hired Roan on to be one of his most trusted beta testers for his upcoming video game releases, ultimately feeding Roan's gaming addiction. Dare figured it wasn't easy to have a grudge against the guy who provided your fix.

Cam cleared his throat. "Anyone seen Teague? Or Hudson?"

"Did you know…?" Dare tapped his finger on his lips, casting a quick glance at Cam, then Roan, and back again. "I read somewhere that there are more than sixty-one thousand Americans airborne over the United States in an average hour? I'm thinking y'all should be part of that number in the very near future."

Cam flipped him off, grinning from ear to ear.

"Could you just go get on a plane?" Dare grumbled, still smiling. "You're supposed to be relaxing, getting your muscles prepared for that ball and chain you're gonna drag around with you for the rest of your life." Dare widened his eyes as he looked from Cam to Roan. He put his hand over his mouth. "Oops. Did I say that out loud?"

Cam barked a laugh. "Fine." Cam looked at Roan. "You ready to head to the airport?"

"Whenever y'all are." Roan's confidence wavered, his eyes sliding to Dare. "You sure you can handle this place for a day?"

It wasn't the first time he'd stood sentry over the marina, but Dare pretended to consider that. "I read somewhere that there were, like, a hundred and thirty-four million houses in the United States a couple of years ago." He glanced at Cam as he explained. "Yes, the article was old, but still offered valuable information." Dare tapped his finger on his chin as he smiled. "And if I remember correctly, there were something like one point three million house fires that year." Dare met Roan's gaze. "That means statistically there's less than a one percent chance that—"

"I get it," Roan groused, a grin tugging at his mouth. "Just don't catch the place on fire."

Dare offered his best smile, all teeth. "I'll try not to. Now, if you don't mind"—Dare motioned toward the iPad— "I've got a game waiting to kick my ass."

"See you tomorrow." Cam offered a two-finger salute as he shouldered his bag.

"You can count on it."

He watched his two closest friends walk out the front door, Gannon coming down from the upstairs apartment to join them. Dare laughed when the alarm sensor sounded *after* they were out in the parking lot. "Lulu, someone's gotta fix that thing."

Lulu lifted her head from where it now rested on the floor near his feet, but didn't appear at all impressed by the conversation. Not that Dare had expected her to be. For all intents and purposes, their guard dog was more of a living, breathing floor decoration.

For a few minutes, Dare stared out the front door, watching as Cam loaded their things in Gannon's Lexus and then drove away, the car spitting gravel behind it, taking his best friends off to the airport. He couldn't help but smile at the thought.

Sometimes it was hard to believe that Cam had settled down and was about to get married.

"Married, Lulu. Burg-land. Can you believe that shit?" He kept his eyes on the parking lot as he mumbled to the dog.

Honestly, Dare had never considered getting married. Well, not since that one time many moons ago... So, yes, technically there had been one point in his life when he'd thought he might join the land of the hyphenated, legally *or* hypothetically. But he'd quickly learned that all parties involved needed to be on the same playing field to make a relationship.

Unfortunately, Dare had only *thought* he'd met that guy. Turned out that hadn't been the case at all. And since that fateful day when he'd finally accepted that he was the only one looking for a happily ever after, he'd stopped wishing for it. So much so that he hadn't had a relatively serious relationship in...

Hmm. It had been a while. Damn. A long fucking time, that was how long it had been. In fact, it had been fifteen freaking years since he'd last had an actual relationship.

Not that he had any intention of thinking about that now. He needed to tie up the loose ends here at the marina so he could head out first thing in the morning and celebrate with his friends.

"Come on, Lulu." Dare eyed the snoozing dog. "Let's get some tools. I've got an idea on how to fix that door sensor."

"GOOD JOB OUT there today."

Fearless

The sound of heavy-booted steps had Noah Pearson looking up to see Detrick Miller, the captain of Station 45, as he passed through the room.

With a nod and an exhausted smile, Noah reclined in the worn leather chair, staring up at the flat-screen television mounted on the wall in front of him. Behind him, he heard the murmur of conversation, along with the distinct click from the Ping-Pong table being used in the recreation room.

Captain Miller was referring to the four-car pileup they'd assisted with a short while ago, pulling a frantic mother and two small kids out of a crushed compact that had been precariously close to going through the guardrail.

It'd been one hell of a morning already and it was just getting started. That, combined with the fact that he'd doubled up on his roofing jobs this past week, meant he was now running on pure adrenaline. Although Noah would've preferred to sleep away the rest of the day, there was a subtle hum of energy beneath his skin, making it nearly impossible to relax. He was tempted to head to the weight room. Do something to burn off some of the minutes counting down until he was out of there for the next two weeks, but he couldn't seem to drag his ass out of the chair.

Two solid weeks.

He still couldn't believe he was taking some time off. In the event they didn't get a call, he would be at the fire station for—he glanced at his watch—at least twenty more hours. Then, off on a cruise to the Caribbean for eight days, followed by a week of catching up on some z's.

Closing his eyes, Noah took a deep breath. How he'd allowed his stepsister, Milly, to manipulate him into going on this excursion was beyond him. And by manipulate, he meant use her womanly wiles (otherwise known as a smile) to get him to agree.

Truth was, Noah was happy that Milly's boss had found the love of his life. For months on end, Milly had gone on and on about how Gannon was finally happy and she couldn't wait for him and the guy he was marrying to seal the deal. Because Noah had only met Gannon twice, he hadn't paid too much attention to her ramblings, but he appreciated her excitement.

However, the invitation had blindsided him.

It wasn't that he and Milly were all that close. His mom had married her dad three years ago, and during that time, they'd spent a minimal amount of time together, mostly an impromptu dinner with the parents or the occasional holiday meal. Other than that, they shared a few texts to check in from time to time, but for the most part, Noah didn't see or talk to her much.

Probably because he worked so much. When he wasn't working a shift at the station, he was running his roofing business.

First and foremost, Noah was a firefighter, and he lived for his job, having been on Engine 45 for the better part of the last thirteen years. Becoming a firefighter had been his lifelong dream, and it kept him on his toes, which was all that he cared about. He'd learned long ago that keeping busy was the best way to avoid what was lacking in his life.

His last semi-relationship—more like friends with benefits—had detonated more than five years ago. He hadn't been interested in repeating that anytime in the near future—his track record with relationships was rocky at best—so his social life was on the fritz. Which explained why he spent so much time at the station with the guys he considered family. They were easy to be around, so it wasn't a hardship.

"Pearson!"

Fearless

Sliding one eye open, Noah nodded his chin in a silent affirmation that he was awake as Captain Miller passed through the room once more, this time on his way to the kitchen.

"S'up?" Noah met the captain's dark gaze.

"Now that I think about it, aren't you supposed to be on vacation?"

"Tomorrow," he confirmed. If a seven-night cruise with his stepsister and her friends could be considered a vacation, then yes. Personally, Noah saw it as more of a favor, with the bonus of an all-expense-paid boat ride attached. The week following would be vacation.

Since the day Milly had told her father about the trip, Larry Holcomb had been worried that his sweet baby girl—Noah knew Milly, she was mischievous and lighthearted, but sweet? Nah, he couldn't see it—was going off into the great unknown without a chaperone. Didn't seem to matter that Milly was thirty-one years old and had been on her own since she'd graduated from college at twenty-one. Larry was definitely a little overprotective of his daughter, at least from what Noah saw.

He still remembered the night he'd been roped into going. He and Milly had been having dinner with the parents while she filled everyone in on the upcoming trip. Out of the blue, Milly had mentioned it would be nice if Noah went with her, that it would make her feel more at ease. An unabashed manipulation if he'd ever heard one.

Of course, Larry had thought that Noah going along with her, to keep an eye on his baby girl since it was clear her best friend would be otherwise occupied getting married, was a brilliant idea. He had even offered to pay for the trip. Noah remembered the way Milly's eyes had widened, her smile radiant as she'd pleaded with him to say yes. And because she'd asked so nicely, he hadn't been able to tell her no. So, rather than work, Noah was being forced to relax.

His phone chimed and he fished it out of his pocket.

Speak of the devil.

The text read: *Please tell me you're not planning on backing out on me.*

He wondered how many times she'd said that in the past two months. Eight? Nine? Twenty?

Not planning on it. Flight leaves in the morning.

Yay. Gonna need someone to drink with. Gannon's a hot mess.

Noah grinned as he typed, *The guy's getting married. What did you expect?*

Married. That was a word that sounded strange, even in his head. Not once in his life had Noah given serious consideration to settling down and getting married. Sure, he'd dated a few guys who had potential, but only once had he actually given it a fleeting thought—definitely not serious, though. Granted, at the time, he'd been young and stupid, so he'd done the only thing he'd known to do. He'd laughed off the idea of a happily ever after, effectively sending the only man he'd ever found himself in love with running for the hills.

Noah tried his best not to think of that time in his life. He'd been barely twenty-three, and settling down hadn't even crossed his mind. Sure, now, at thirty-eight, there had been a few times in the past couple of years that he'd wondered what it would be like. Perhaps it would be nice to come home to someone occasionally, rather than an empty apartment.

His phone chimed again.

Oh, and there's someone I want you to meet.

Noah frowned.

Milly had mentioned setting him up with someone a while back, but he had adamantly refused, hoping she would get the hint. Noah didn't have problems finding guys on his own, thank you very much. He definitely didn't need his stepsister setting him up with her friends. That was a recipe for disaster on all fronts. What if Noah didn't like the guy? Or vice versa? The last thing he needed was to upset Milly, even if she was simply trying to do a good deed—her words.

Still not interested, Milly.

Noah stared at his phone, waiting for her response. It finally came.

Oh, but you will be, trust me.

With a heavy sigh, Noah was about to give her a long lecture on why he didn't want to be set up when another text came in.

Flight's about to leave. Gotta run. Be prepared to relax and have fun for a few days.

Knowing she wasn't going to listen if he rehashed his many reasons for her minding her own business, Noah typed: *That's the plan.*

It was his only plan, actually. He would be boarding a ship, not knowing a soul other than Milly and Gannon, so he figured he'd have plenty of time to himself. And since he hadn't taken a vacation in too many years to count, Noah was secretly looking forward to it.

Not that he had any intention of letting Milly know that.

Two

Sunday, May 29th (the next morning)

DARE GROANED AS he popped open one eye to find the sun shining through the blinds in his small apartment. Since it was all one room, that little bit of light filled up the whole space.

This was bad.

The sun should *not* be that bright.

Not yet.

"Son of a bitch." He rolled over, reached for the nightstand, and found his phone. He gave a quick peek at the screen. "Aww, hell."

At that exact moment, his phone chirped. Rubbing his eyes, he pulled up the text.

If you're still in bed, I'm going to personally kick your ass.

Milly.

Great.

Not for the first time, Dare was grateful he was gay. He couldn't imagine getting on a woman's bad side and dealing with her wrath indefinitely. Dealing with Milly on a part-time basis was stressful enough.

Fearless

He tapped out two words—*I'm awake*—then dropped the phone onto the mattress beside him.

In an instant, he was out of bed and on his way to the shower, forcing his boxer briefs down his hips and letting them land somewhere on the floor along the way. He'd overslept and now he had less than fifteen minutes to get presentable and out the door.

After a quick piss, he flipped on the water in the shower, then turned on the water in the sink, purposely ignoring the reflection staring back at him.

Rushing out of the bathroom while the water warmed, he headed for his closet. Opening the door, he yanked on the chain to turn on the single bulb above his head. It flickered once, then came on. With a bright white glow casting everything in a harsh light, Dare stared at his options in clothes. On one side of his closet, he had at least forty T-shirts, most of them white with some logo or another on the front. The other side had a variety of shorts—athletic, swim, cargo.

None of which he was looking for.

Pushing his comfortable attire out of the way and ignoring those that fell from the hangers, Dare finally found the last pair of jeans he owned, along with a forest-green polo shirt. He shook them in a weak attempt to remove some of the wrinkles. To this day, he couldn't remember why he'd bought either—if he had to guess, Grams had forced him to—but he was pleased he'd had the forethought.

A couple of weeks ago, Roan had convinced him to go shopping to buy clothes for the cruise, during which Dare had argued profusely. For one, Dare made a point to avoid shopping at all costs. He'd read somewhere that there were around 109,500 shopping centers in North America—all of which were on his *I'm-not-gonna-go-there-if-at-all-possible* list. And two, they were going on a freaking cruise. Shorts and a T-shirt seemed quite logical.

But *no-o-o*, Roan had insisted that Dare also have jeans and shirts without holes in them.

Nitpicky bastard.

Despite his aversion to more clothing, Dare had bought what Roan had insisted he get. And all of that was packed in his suitcase, still with the tags—in the event he didn't wear them, there was no reason he couldn't take that shit back. That was his motto.

Passing back through his bedroom, he tossed the clothes on his bed, glanced at them, then picked them up again. Maybe the steam from the shower would help smooth them out. With hangers dangling from his fingers, he then went into the bathroom and hooked the hangers on the towel bar.

Ten minutes later, he was shaved, showered, and dressed in the clothes that still looked as though he'd pulled them from the back of his closet ten minutes ago.

Eh. It had been worth a shot.

Five minutes more and he was in his truck, heading to the airport, praying he had everything he needed. He patted his pocket, confirming he had his wallet and his phone—the only two things he really needed as far as he was concerned.

Yep. Both there.

He took a breath for what felt like the first time that morning. It was a damn good thing he didn't have to do shit like this often. He was quite content with his regular routine of rolling out of bed, yanking on shorts and a T-shirt, then making the three-minute drive from his apartment to the marina.

"Good thing you're my best friend, Cam." After sharing his thought with his truck's interior, Dare turned on the radio and put his foot to the floor.

Fearless

The drive to the airport took less time than he'd expected, which allowed him to make up a few minutes but still didn't give him much of a buffer. He found a spot in short-term parking, grabbed his suitcase, and made a beeline for the doors.

"Cam, I hope like hell you appreciate this, man," Dare mumbled to himself after he checked his luggage and made it through security—thirty-three minutes later.

Jesus.

As though his best friend heard him, Dare's phone vibrated once, signaling a text.

Praying it wasn't someone intending to give him a hard time, Dare pulled it from his pocket as he double-timed it toward his gate, squeezing between the slower-moving people.

I assume you're on the plane.

Not Milly. Or Cam.

Roan.

Dare stared at the screen and tapped out a response as he maneuvered through the crowds lined up at the other gates.

Of course I am.

Smiling to himself, he kept moving.

You overslept, didn't you?

Okay, so maybe he was a little predictable.

Rather than give them anything more to worry about, Dare responded with: *It's all good. I'm on my way. See y'all in a few hours.*

Then he tucked his phone back in his pocket and prayed like hell he made it on time.

Because if he didn't, there would be hell to pay.

And he was pretty sure hell's name was Milly Holcomb.

WHEN HIS SHIFT was over, Noah headed for his apartment. It'd been a slow night, and he had managed to get a couple hours of sleep, figuring he'd grab a couple more on the plane. The short drive gave him a few minutes to plan out his morning, which he did for the twentieth time since yesterday. As had been the case for most of his adult life, he wasn't the type to leave anything to chance.

Once inside his small, one-bedroom apartment, Noah dropped his bag on his bed, careful not to wrinkle the comforter. He set out unpacking it, putting the clothes where they belonged—clean in the drawer, dirty in the hamper—then tossed the bag on a shelf in the closet. On his way out, he grabbed the clothes he would wear to the airport, which he'd already picked out, ironed, and had lying on the small chest in his closet.

Twenty minutes later, he was shaved, showered, dressed, and ready to go, leaving him a solid hour before he needed to head out. After putting away the few dishes he'd hand-washed the night before last, then taking the trash down to the dumpster, Noah pondered what to do with the rest of the time. Rather than start a load of laundry and pace the living room to count down the minutes, he opted to go, hoping to beat the mad morning rush—if there was any such thing—at the airport. He'd heard security could be a bitch, and Noah was nothing if not prepared. Or he tried to be, anyway.

Fearless

He made it from his apartment to Austin-Bergstrom International Airport in record time. Even managed to make it through security and to his gate with plenty of time to grab a breakfast taco and coffee, which he did, eating it while he waited in the empty area that would soon be filled with passengers ready to embark on their destination.

Sometimes being prepared was lonely as shit.

Glancing around, he noticed only one other person was there—a guy in a suit tapping away on a laptop while holding a phone to his ear. He seemed a little out of place on a Sunday morning, but, from experience, Noah knew that work didn't always wait for a weekday.

While he sat patiently, he sent his mother a text to let her know he was leaving, checked the baseball scores on his phone, and then shot a quick text to Milly, giving her an update. It was that or wait for her to text him half a dozen times. The woman was a little uptight, and Noah only hoped that once everyone was on board the ship, she would relax some. If not, what was the point of this trip, anyway? Well, other than two people getting married.

His phone vibrated.

I wish everyone was as prepared as you.

If Milly only knew he'd arrived more than an hour early.

Grinning, he looked up to see that another passenger—this one female—had joined him and the suit.

Noah messaged Milly back: *Everything cool?*

Other than my fear that the ship will leave and half the wedding party will still be on dry land?

Yes, other than that.

Noah took a breath, then relaxed in his chair, watching as more people began to arrive at his gate while it seemed the floodgates had opened and the airport was beginning to buzz with anxious travelers. He did not envy those who were running to their destination. That shit would make him crazy.

Then again, his OCD probably made most people nuts. Along with being unorganized, being late was one of his pet peeves.

His phone vibrated again.

I think it'll all be fine. At least I hope it will. Have a safe flight and I'll see you when you get here.

Will do.

With that conversation out of the way, Noah leaned his head against the window behind him and closed his eyes. He had nothing to do but wait for them to announce they were boarding, so he figured now was as good a time as any to catch another power nap.

Three

Six hours later

DARE HAD FINALLY fucking made it, and now he was out of breath as he stepped into the banquet room Milly had instructed everyone to meet in when they arrived on the ship. As he tried to slow his heart rate, he grabbed a napkin from an empty table and dabbed the sweat from his forehead. Stupid-ass jeans. If he'd been wearing shorts and flip-flops, he wouldn't be sweating.

He scanned the place, smiling and nodding at the familiar and some not-so-familiar faces, trying to appear casual and not as though his heart was about to beat out of his chest. Not for the first time today, he was thankful that it took a lot to get him rattled; otherwise, he would've been a hot mess at this point.

Dare dabbed the napkin against the back of his neck. *Technically, you are a hot mess.* Okay, true, but not the way he'd meant.

The fact that he'd boarded his plane at the last possible second, managed to *finally* get transportation to the port (which had only taken a little more than an hour), then painstakingly worked his way through the ridiculously long check-in process in order to get on this damn ship had left him feeling somewhat frazzled.

He was beginning to think that whoever said the benefits of travel were almost immediate hadn't actually been anywhere. Dare recalled the statistic he'd read recently: *After only a day or two, eighty-nine percent of people experience significant drops in stress.* Had anyone considered that *getting* to your vacation destination *doubled* stress levels? So, if he did the math correctly, the reduction actually didn't even get you back to the one hundred percent.

Great. That didn't help him to relax at all.

But he knew what would…

To kick this off, a little alcohol would go a long way toward settling his nerves.

As he weaved his way toward the bar, Dare shot a grin to Cam's sister, Holly. *That's right. I'm here.* Although he hadn't missed a single scheduled event in his entire life, he knew that everyone had been worried that he wouldn't make it—because not everything could go smoothly for the wedding, right?

And okay, yes, maybe he wasn't the promptest person in the world.

Or the most organized.

Whatever.

He had arrived on time. So any mishaps … they weren't on him.

Fearless

Now that he was here, Dare was having a hard time wrapping his head around the fact that Cam and Gannon were officially tying the knot in a few short days—on this fancy cruise ship, no less. Not that it wasn't long overdue or anything. Those two were perfect for each other. In a weird, opposites-really-do-attract sort of way. Ever since the two of them had started this game of slap and tickle—as Grams liked to call it—in the marina office nearly a year ago, they'd been playing kissy-face. It was about damn time they made it official.

And here Dare was with at least two dozen of their family and friends, all of whom had probably arrived two hours ago and were already settled in while Dare had stowed his suitcase with the concierge so he could make an appearance before Milly's head exploded.

Speaking of Milly… He glanced around, looking for her.

"What's up, pretty boy?"

Dare spun around when he heard the familiar voice.

It would appear that she'd spotted him first. Then again, he wouldn't put it past her to have had him microchipped for this occasion.

Milly stood there, hand cocked on her slender hip, holding a clipboard, looking as dazzling as ever in a short red sundress with her blonde hair piled on top of her head, lips a rich ruby red. Her light blue eyes lit up when he met her gaze.

"Pretty boy?" Dare hugged her to him when he approached. "Ruggedly handsome, sure. Devastatingly good-looking, I can see. But *pretty*…?"

Her lips curved up into a grin, eyes dancing with … *hmm*. That looked a lot like relief. Had she really thought he wouldn't make it?

"Look at you." Her smile brightened as she slid her hand over his smooth jaw. "All grown up."

It was true, Dare hadn't seen Milly in a few months, but he wasn't sure he'd go so far as to say he was all grown up. At thirty-four, he wasn't quite ready to grow up. He'd been through that phase once in his life—a long, *long* time ago—and he had the scars on his heart to prove it. He had no intention of going through that again, so he'd settled on planning to be a kid for the duration.

However, if she was referring to the fact that he'd used a razor that morning, was dressed in something other than shorts and a T-shirt—and yes, wearing shoes—then okay, fine, he was all grown up.

"Where're Cam and Gannon?" He peered over the heads of the others to see if he could find the happy couple.

Milly checked something off on the paper on her clipboard before responding. "If I had to guess, Cam's probably seducing Gannon to keep him from overthinking the fact that we're on a boat."

Technically, they were on a ship—*a ship could carry a boat, but a boat couldn't carry a ship*—but Dare didn't correct Milly.

Everyone knew that Gannon wasn't keen on the idea of boats—or ships, or water in general—but they were also aware that Gannon would pretty much do anything for Cam, which, Dare assumed, was how Cam had talked his future husband into this.

"I wouldn't doubt it." He met Milly's eyes. "Gannon did look a little green yesterday. And that was *before* they left Texas."

"Green?" Milly chuckled. "Are you kidding? He's more like an overripe avocado at this point."

"Oh, yum." Dare cringed. "Have you seen anyone else yet?"

While most of the others had spent the night seeing what a difference a stay could make at Embassy Suites, Dare had come straight from the airport. Apparently, they'd been smart in their planning and he'd been ... rushed.

Time to change that, he thought.

No better place to chill than on a ship in the middle of the ocean.

Gannon, no doubt, didn't agree, since, according to Milly, he currently resembled Kermit the Frog's twin brother.

"Roan and Teague left to take a quick tour of the boat, see what trouble they can get into," Milly noted, then nodded across the room. "Hudson is over at the bar with his plus one—who is quite yummy, I have to admit. And I saw Mr. Strickland, Holly, Keith, and the kids when I was on my way here. Oh, and my stepbrother's around here somewhere."

"Your stepbrother?"

Milly's smile was impish. Ever since Gannon and Cam had gotten together, Milly had been teasing Dare that she wanted to set him up with her stepbrother. And here he'd thought he had dodged that bullet by telling her he wasn't interested in a relationship. Granted, this was Milly. He'd learned she was as hardheaded as they came.

"I needed someone to accompany me on this big ol' boat." To go along with her fake southern-belle drawl, Milly's eyes reflected every ounce of feigned purity she could apparently muster.

"I thought that's what *I* was here for." He puffed out his chest purposely.

They'd become friends over the course of the past year, and Dare enjoyed spending time with Milly. She was fun and relatively easy to talk to, even if she was a tad nosy. Okay, more than a tad. A *lot* nosy.

"Who said you weren't?" Again, she offered him those big, innocent eyes.

God, this girl made him laugh. She definitely wasn't innocent.

"You need a drink." Taking her hand, Dare tugged her toward the bar.

"Or you mean *you* need a drink?"

"That, too." He needed more than a drink if he was going to have to dodge Milly's stepbrother this trip. The only thing he could picture was a pimply-faced, twenty-something with Coke-bottle glasses, a pocket protector, and greasy hair. Video game chic, he thought it was called.

On top of that, Dare couldn't help but wonder what in the hell she'd told the guy about him. That he was interested? That he couldn't wait to get a controller in hand and duke it out with him?

Fuck, he hoped not. He tried to keep his video game obsession on the down low, thank you very much.

Somehow, when Milly had brought the subject up, Dare had always managed to deflect, not wanting to know anything about the guy. And to this day, he hadn't so much as learned her stepbrother's name. He had to admit, he was pretty good at avoidance when need be.

But he hadn't been lying when he'd said he wasn't interested in a relationship. And dating—whether one or more times—could potentially lead to a relationship. Therefore, Dare was abstaining. Indefinitely. One-night stands were more his forte. And even those were few and far between.

"Apple martini for the lady," Dare told the bartender. "And I'll take a Rolling Rock."

The bartender nodded, then turned away to retrieve their drinks.

"You're cute when you're flustered." Milly patted his arm.

"Me? Flustered?" Dare snorted. "Not a chance."

"There's my stepbrother now," Milly announced, loud enough for half the room to hear.

"Wait. *What?*" Dare spun around, looking in the direction she was facing, but he didn't see anyone he didn't recognize.

"See? Told you. Cute when flustered."

Dare turned back to her, scowling as he did. "Not funny, Holcomb."

"On the contrary." Milly's grin widened and she looked incredibly pleased with herself.

"What in the world am I gonna do with you?" Knowing she was teasing him allowed him to relax somewhat.

Roan and Cam both had informed him that Milly was a female version of him. Only, he didn't see it. The more he was around her, the more he had to wonder just how wrong they were. And if they weren't wrong, then... Surely they were wrong. He wasn't that obnoxious, was he?

"There he is." He heard the smile in Milly's voice.

"No way." She couldn't fool him twice. He kept his attention on the bartender. "Not falling for it again."

"Hey, Milly."

Dare's entire body went rigid at the sound of that voice. It was deep, raspy, and ... eerily familiar.

A cold chill slowly trickled down his spine.

There was no way.

Milly's hand landed on Dare's forearm, tugging him around. He managed to keep his back straight as he slowly pivoted.

"Dare, I'd like you to meet my stepbrother, Noah Pearson. Noah, this is Cam's friend, one of the other owners of the marina, Dare Davis."

Son.

Of.

A.

Motherfucking.

Bitch.

There was no possible way this man could be Milly's stepbrother. Definitely no pimples, no pocket protector, no glasses. Doubtful he even owned a video game controller.

Nope, this was a big, brooding, sexy man.

With intense brown eyes.

Eyes that Dare had once stared into when…

A strange ghosting pain echoed in his chest, one he remembered all too well from his past.

Fighting the urge to rub the ache away, Dare stood there, rooted in place. Doing his absolute fucking best not to let on that, at one time in his life, this man had single-handedly ripped Dare's heart right out of his chest.

And then drowned it.

WELL, THERE YOU have it.

The world as Noah knew it ceased to exist, and suddenly he found himself stepping into a time warp. Only, he doubted there had been a disruption in the space-time continuum.

At least not today.

Unfortunately, he didn't seem to be dreaming, either.

And this dark-haired, hazel-eyed, *absurdly* handsome man might look disconcertingly similar to the guy Noah had once been head-over-heels in love with, but he certainly wasn't *that* guy. Sure, he looked the same, only older, rougher around the edges. He even had the same eyebrow twitch that Noah had always found oddly adorable, but there was something different about him.

The fifteen years that had separated them was likely it.

Noah swallowed as reality sank in.

It *was* him.

Dare Davis.

How the hell had this happened? How had they ended up here of all places?

It looked as though six degrees of separation wasn't as absurd a theory as he'd once thought.

Noah hoped he didn't look as off-balance as he felt, but he couldn't be sure. The way Dare was staring back at him as though he were planning how he intended to toss him overboard told Noah that he was equally shocked. Not that he could blame the guy. Standing less than two feet away was the one man Noah had never thought he'd see again. Not after…

"Noah." Dare's greeting carried an icy chill.

"Dare." Noah nodded, mocking his tone, refusing to look directly at Milly, though he knew his stepsister was already trying to figure this one out.

Good luck with that.

"You two know each other?" Milly questioned curiously.

Noah spared her a quick glance, noticing the way her gaze flipped from one to the other, her mouth hanging open. She looked as stunned as he felt. Thankfully, unlike her, he'd managed to keep his mouth closed. He hoped.

Regardless of how he looked, Noah didn't know how to answer Milly's question, so he returned his attention to Dare.

Yes, they knew each other, but it had been years since he'd seen Dare. Many, many years.

"Fine," Milly huffed, her tone firmer this time, "it's pretty obvious you do, so let me dumb it down a bit. *How* do you know each other?"

"It was a long time ago." Dare narrowed his eyes at Noah before turning around to face the bar when the bartender appeared. "But not nearly long enough."

For some reason, that spiteful remark pulled a smile from Noah. The fact that Dare was unhappy to see him didn't surprise him one bit.

Noah glanced at the drinks being placed on the bar in front of Dare. The apple martini would be for Milly; he knew that much. When she wasn't chugging wine like water, his stepsister was a huge fan of those fruity drinks. And the Rolling Rock … same old Dare. If he recalled correctly, Noah had been the one to introduce an underage Dare to that particular beer.

If Dare's drink selection was any indication, some things hadn't changed with the blast from Noah's past.

He allowed his gaze to stray to Dare when the man turned back around and handed Milly her drink. Noah casually took him in from head to toe, doing his best not to let the heat that consumed him show. Just as it had been all those years ago, there was an instantaneous physical attraction that Noah couldn't deny.

Dare was casually dressed in a forest-green polo that brought out the green in his hazel eyes, a pair of faded Levis that showcased his long legs, and a pair of brown leather Rockports that looked as though they'd never been worn.

No doubt about it, the guy still had it going on. Fiercely.

Those sexy, rugged features had been what had drawn him to Dare in the first place. Dare was the modern-day gay equivalent of a Greek god. Still. Long and lean, he oozed sex appeal with his crooked smile (which was noticeably absent at the moment) and bedroom eyes. And for the twenty-five months they'd been together, the sex had been … off the fucking charts.

Dropping his gaze to his feet, Noah took a deep breath. He certainly wasn't going to think about that now. Definitely not with Milly likely scrutinizing his every facial muscle, still waiting for an explanation.

Milly cleared her throat.

Noah lifted his gaze to Dare's, noticing the way he was clenching his teeth, the muscle in his jaw flexing, the tick in his eyebrow making his left eye twitch.

Yep, still fucking adorable.

Okay, so maybe some things had changed. He was still long and lean, but gone was the skinny guy Dare had once been, and in his place was a thicker, more muscular, damn sexy man with a determined glint in his eyes. Seemed as though the past fifteen years had been good to Dare. Very good. And he still had the same intriguing eyes, same short, brown hair—though it seemed lighter than before, probably from all the time he spent in the sun, since, according to Milly, the guy owned a marina.

"So which one of you is gonna fill me in?" Milly was still staring as she sipped her drink. "And you should both know right now, I'm quite adept at torture. So either spit it out or I will drag it out of you."

Noah didn't know how to explain their history together. Didn't even know if he should.

"Hey, Mill."

Milly and Dare both turned to face whomever the disembodied voice coming from over Noah's left shoulder belonged to. Noah took a step forward, a tad closer to Dare, before he turned and faced the man who was responsible for saving the day. Though, now that he saw who it was, he was, ironically, *also* the man responsible for this—whatever this was—by association.

"Gannon," Milly greeted, her eyes smiling along with the rest of her as she shifted so that she could include Noah in the conversation. "You remember my stepbrother, Noah."

Gannon nodded, then held out his hand.

Noah returned the gesture. "Good to see you again, Gannon. And congratulations."

"Thanks." Gannon blushed, a move that was noticeable due to the unusual paleness of his skin. "I'm just ready for it to be over."

"What? The wedding?" Milly chuckled. "Or the boat ride?"

"It's not so bad right now." Gannon glanced between the three of them. "I'm not sure I'll feel the same when this thing's moving or when we're miles away from land."

"You'll be fine," Milly assured him. "Just think, Cam will keep you busy."

Gannon nodded. "Speaking of..." Gannon's gaze hopped between the three of them once more before landing back on Milly. "I'm gonna go find him."

Noah wondered if Gannon felt the tension or if he simply wanted to go find his future husband.

"I'll go with you." Dare took a step forward, his shoulder bumping Noah harder than was necessary. On purpose, no doubt.

Milly instantly placed her hand on Dare's chest. "Nope. Uh-uh. You stay here. *I'll* go with him."

Noah noticed Dare's frown.

Before Milly left, she came to stand directly in front of them both. "You two better play nice."

Noah had every intention of playing nice. How else would he play? It'd been fifteen years ... which was the equivalent of ancient history as far as he was concerned.

"Oh, and do me a favor." Fortitude replaced the amusement in her bright blue eyes.

Noah lifted an eyebrow, waiting for her to continue.

"Don't let me stumble upon the two of you naked anywhere. If you're gonna get naked, take it back to your cabin."

Dare snorted.

Noah smiled.

Leave it to Milly to lighten the mood. Or try to, anyway.

The thought of Dare naked…

Definitely not what he needed to be thinking about.

A quick peek at Dare once more and Noah noticed he was still sulking. He didn't need to wonder why the man wasn't happy. Looked as though, for some, a decade and a half wasn't long enough to forgive and forget. It was clear Dare didn't want anything to do with him.

Not that Noah understood that exactly. From what he remembered, their breakup hadn't been Noah's fault. If his memory served him correctly, Dare had been the one who'd walked away.

In the middle of the night.

When Noah was asleep.

Once Milly left, Noah spared another quick peek at Dare to find him scowling, his eyes leveled on Noah's face.

"Why are you here?" Dare hissed, his voice low.

Noah grimaced. "Because Milly invited me?"

"You're tellin' me it had nothing to do with me?"

For a brief moment, he felt like laughing, but then he realized Dare was serious. Noah's face heated, his anger igniting. Lowering his voice, he took a step closer to Dare, getting right up in his face—ignoring how damn good Dare smelled. "How the fuck would I know you'd be here? I haven't seen you in fifteen fucking years."

Not that he'd kept track. Much.

Dare's eyes narrowed, his mouth opened, then snapped closed.

"How do I know *you* didn't have something to do with this?" Noah added, unable to refrain. "Maybe *you're* the one who told Milly to invite *me*."

Dare moved another step closer, and they were almost touching, chest to knee. "I had no fucking idea you were her stepbrother. Last I remembered, your parents were still married and you were an only child."

True. He had been. But a lot of shit had happened since then. Shit Noah did not want to think about today or any day, for that matter.

"I was," Noah confirmed. "Right up until the day Milly's dad married my mother, three years ago." What he didn't say was that his dad had *died*, fucking Noah's world up beyond repair.

And yes, maybe this was one hell of a coincidence.

Didn't mean Noah had a fucking clue how to deal with it—or get away from it, for that matter. They were stuck on a boat for the next eight days.

The only positive … it was a big fucking boat.

Four

DARE KNEW HE needed to get his shit together. Being an asshole certainly didn't suit him.

Or maybe it was the clothes he was forced to wear.

Or both.

He took a deep breath, trying to fight off the overwhelming emotions that swamped him. It had been more than a decade and a half since he'd last seen Noah, but standing here now, it felt as though that devastating day he'd lost the only man he'd ever allowed himself to love had been yesterday.

But it hadn't been.

And technically, he hadn't *lost* Noah. A search party had never been issued because he'd known right where Noah was. Dare had simply walked away. And Noah ... well, he hadn't cared enough to come after him.

Swallowing hard, he stared back at the blast from his past who had somehow ended up on this ship. For a brief moment, he worried he wouldn't be able to handle being in close contact with Noah for any length of time. Not after...

He needed to remember that he was fifteen years older now. Far wiser than the nineteen-year-old punk he'd been back then when he'd allowed Noah to break his heart.

He wasn't that guy—or *kid*, as Noah had called him—anymore.

He was a grown-up.

A civilized adult.

Okay, maybe not civilized, but an adult, nonetheless.

Which meant he could *act* civilized if he had to.

Right?

Knowing better than to get lost in the past, Dare forced a smile. "Gotta go chat with some people. Have fun."

"I plan to," Noah replied as Dare walked away, but Dare managed not to turn around and ask him what that meant.

He didn't want to know.

Dare found Hudson standing in the far corner, sipping what appeared to be something strong. Lucky bastard. Shaking off the past few minutes, Dare nodded toward him and asked, "Why do you look pissed?"

Hudson grinned, then signed back, *I was going to ask you the same thing.*

Rolling his eyes, pretending he wasn't pissy, Dare said, "Looks like my past caught up with me. What's your excuse?"

Hudson shook his head and drained the rest of his drink.

That was when Dare followed Hudson's line of sight, coming to rest on Teague, who was … yep, blatantly flirting it up with one of the waiters.

Not surprising.

Dare glanced at Hudson once more, then back to Teague, unable to contain his laugh.

Hudson waved a hand in front of Dare's face, getting his attention.

Why are you laughing?

"Why are you pouting?"

Hudson's green eyes narrowed, and he flipped Dare off, making Dare laugh louder.

"I thought you brought a plus one? Why're you worried about Teague?"

Hudson's grin was slow and wicked, causing Dare to watch him closely.

"Who's the plus one?" Dare was far too curious not to ask.

My brother, AJ. Hudson's grin widened. *Just don't tell Teague that. I'm pretty sure he already assumes otherwise.*

Based on the way Teague was glaring in their direction, that was likely a safe assumption. Not to mention, it was just like Hudson to lead the kid on and make him think that way.

Those two were something else.

It would be quite easy for Hudson to snag Teague if he wanted to, Dare knew. The hostility between those two … it was tightly wrapped in a bubble of sexual tension, tied with a bow made solely of desperate, undeniable attraction. Only, it seemed that both Hudson and Teague weren't aware of that. Or if they were, they were pretending otherwise. Which amused Dare.

Hudson nodded his chin in the direction behind Dare. *Who is the hot guy staring you down?*

Dare shrugged. It was better than lying, at least.

Hudson smiled. *Right. At least you didn't deny he's hot.*

"Whatever." Dare lifted his beer to his lips.

Okay, so this hadn't been the greatest idea in the world. Of all people, the man who couldn't speak was the one giving him shit.

Needing some air, Dare turned to Hudson once more. "If anyone's lookin' for me, tell them I'll be back."

Hudson nodded, and Dare tossed back what was left of his beer, set the empty bottle on the table, and made a beeline out of the room. He didn't stop until he'd made it to the deck, the sun beaming down on his head, the scent of saltwater filling his nostrils. Only then did he take a deep breath, stretching his arms out in front of him as he gripped the rail and bent over, dropping his head between his shoulders and staring at the ground.

Noah Pearson.

Of all the people in all the world, how was it that Noah was Milly's stepbrother? And how was it that he'd never once heard Noah's name mentioned?

Oh, yeah. Because Dare had changed the subject every damn time.

Stupid.

"Stupid, stupid, stupid."

"You okay?"

A firm hand landed on Dare's back, causing him to bolt upright, turning to see Roan standing beside him.

"Never better, why?" Yep, he was fairly certain that was a squeak that had followed his response.

Roan smiled. "Yes, and you sound it, too."

"Thanks."

"Pre-wedding jitters?" Roan baited.

"Something like that." More like he was tempted to jump off the side of the ship and take his chances in the water. Didn't matter that the ship hadn't left the port yet.

"Let me guess." Roan leaned back against the rail and crossed his arms over his wide chest, giving Dare his full attention. "It has something to do with Milly's stepbrother."

Dare glanced over. "How'd you know?"

Roan smirked. "I didn't. Not until now."

Rolling his eyes, Dare couldn't help but laugh. Leave it to Roan to turn the tables on him. It really was good to see his friend back to his normal self. For the longest time, Dare had thought they'd lost Roan's sense of humor completely.

Didn't look to be the case. Though it could use a little work.

"Spill." Roan nodded, crossing one ankle over the other as though he was settling in for a long story. "How do you know him?"

"What makes you think I do?"

Roan cast him a sideways glance. "I've known you a long damn time, and never once have I seen you quite so shaken by a man."

Yeah, well. Noah wasn't just any man. He was only the man Dare had thought he would spend the rest of his life with.

Oh, how he'd been so wrong.

"Just a guy I dated." Dare tried to sound nonchalant. At least he didn't squeak.

Roan laughed again, and once more, Dare weighed the dangers of launching himself off the side of the ship. Since he doubted he would survive without breaking a few bones—or even his neck—he decided he had no choice but to suck it up.

Especially when the horn sounded, announcing their departure for sea.

Great.

Just. Great.

"I think I'm gonna go get unpacked," Dare told Roan. "I'll see you at dinner."

Roan nodded. "If you need to talk…"

"I know." Dare appreciated that his friend offered, but he wasn't planning to do anything of the sort.

He was here to have fun.

That—along with pretending Noah didn't exist—was the only thing he planned to do.

AFTER WATCHING DARE disappear, Noah had been tempted to follow him, though his common sense told him that wasn't a wise idea. So, rather than make a fool of himself, he had remained right where he was.

At the bar.

With a drink.

Now he was on his second.

While he'd attempted to drink away the last half hour, he'd kept an eye on the people in the room, listened to them talk amongst themselves, everyone seemingly ecstatic about the upcoming wedding, but more so about the fact that Cam and Gannon had insisted on taking a cruise.

Yep, eight wonderful days on the open water, forced to be with the same people, unable to get away…

Suck it up, Pearson.

While everyone else was having a good time, the only thing Noah wanted to do was find Dare and confront him. About what, he didn't know yet, but he was almost certain that by his third or fourth drink he would have a good idea.

So yes, two drinks in and he was feeling a little looser than before. His mind wandering to things better left alone. For example, the day—or rather, night—Dare had disappeared from his life without so much as a note. And okay, maybe Noah hadn't been completely caught off guard because of the falling-out they'd had when Dare had suggested they take their relationship to the next level. But surely he had deserved some warning.

A good-bye would've been nice, too.

Seemed Noah had come full circle, right back in the presence of the man who had flipped his world on its axis, making him fear his future. Which was ironic in itself. At the time, Noah had been twenty-three and fearless, ready to conquer the world. Only, one man had proven him wrong.

His fear of a future with Dare hadn't been because of any problems they'd been having. And not because he hadn't thought that he and Dare would've had a good life, either. There had been a possibility. Their relationship had been solid, or so Noah had thought. But at the time, Dare had been nineteen. In Noah's mind, that was far too young to be settling down.

Never had it occurred to him how serious Dare was at the time. The guy hadn't exactly been known for his maturity. The Dare he knew wasn't the responsible one, he was the jokester, the life of the party, the guy who was always pulling one prank after another. It'd been charming, but not something that had Noah thinking long-term thoughts.

And still, he'd thought about Dare frequently over the years, wondering what he was doing, where he'd gone. But not once had he set out to find him. After the initial anger had worn off and he'd stopped hating Dare for leaving him and for the subsequent events that had followed, Noah had hoped that Dare had done something with himself, found someone to settle down with, fall in love with…

Who said he hadn't?

Okay, so that thought took Noah by surprise. Just because Dare had been shocked to see him certainly didn't mean he was single and ripe for the picking.

The mere notion of Dare belonging to someone else did not sit well with Noah.

Great. Now it seemed the sea air was making him crazy.

He glared down at the empty glass in front of him. Yes, he would blame it on the drinks.

"So, Milly tells me you're a firefighter."

Noah turned to see Cam Strickland, the man he recognized from the wedding invitation picture as Gannon's muscular, tattooed other half.

Smiling, he held out his hand to Cam. "Nice to officially meet you."

"Same goes." Cam shook Noah's hand and grinned. "Can't tell you how happy I was to hear Milly would have a chaperone on this trip."

Noah chuckled. He could only imagine. "And yes, Austin Fire Department," Noah explained.

Cam nodded. "Rumor has it you know Dare."

"Rumor has it?" Noah chuckled. "Or Milly said?"

"Is there a difference?"

Cam had a point. "No, I guess there's not."

"Well, I'm glad you could make it, regardless."

"You might be the only one." Noah thought about his interaction with Dare.

"Who? Dare?" The lack of concern in Cam's tone made Noah feel marginally better.

Cam leaned against the bar, his elbows on the scarred wood as he faced the room.

Noah turned to see what Cam was looking at. "If I had to guess, Dare's currently plotting a way to shove me overboard. And make it look like an accident."

"I wouldn't doubt that." Cam laughed. At least someone could. "But he'll get over it. He doesn't hold a grudge for long."

Fifteen years is a long damn time. And clearly Dare was still holding one, or so it seemed.

Fearless

The subtle shift beneath his feet told Noah that the boat was moving, which meant there was no turning back now. Unless he was planning to take a long swim or hijack a life raft, he was in it for the long haul.

"Shit," Cam rumbled, standing up straight. "I better go find Gannon before he disappears. See you at dinner?"

"Definitely." If he wasn't passed out by then.

When Cam left him and the bartender asked if he needed another drink, Noah waved him off. The thought of getting shit-faced was appealing, but the last thing he needed to do was get drunk tonight. That wouldn't go over well with anyone. And since he was still contemplating finding Dare and seeking some of the closure he'd been wanting for the past decade and a half, it was the safest thing to do.

Not that anything about this trip was safe.

Especially not with Dare Davis on board.

Rather than give in to the temptation, Noah pushed away from the bar and went in search of Milly. She'd met him on the ship when he'd arrived, and they'd stashed his suitcase in her cabin so she could introduce him to a few people. Now, he wanted a few minutes to get settled before dinner.

"Hey," Milly greeted, turning away from a group of people when he approached. "Where's Dare?"

Noah shrugged. "I need to get my suitcase out of your cabin so I can find mine and get unpacked."

Milly nodded, then grabbed a key card out of the little clutch purse in her hand. Two key cards. "Here's mine and here's yours. You're in 21218. Same floor as me."

Noah took both key cards from her and repeated the number in his head. "Thanks."

"Don't be late for dinner," he heard her call out as he sauntered off.

Was it him or was there a hint of mischief in her tone?

Fifteen minutes later, Noah had retrieved his suitcase from Milly's cabin and was headed down the narrow corridor to his own. He counted down the numbers until he found 21218, as Milly had said.

He swiped the card and pushed open the door, only to come to a jarring halt when he saw...

"What the fuck?" a deep voice bellowed from inside the cabin.

Yeah, his thoughts exactly.

With the door open, Noah peered back at the number once more, just to make sure, although he already knew he was in the correct cabin because the key card had unlocked it.

"You have got to be kidding," he muttered to himself, watching as Dare planted both fists on his hips and squared off with him from across the room, which was only a few feet away.

"No. No way," Dare snapped. "One of us is in the wrong cabin."

Noah smiled, unable to help himself. Rather than stand in the hall and argue with Dare, he stepped into the small cabin and allowed the door to close behind him.

When Dare grabbed his cell phone from the vanity counter, Noah knew he had to say something.

"What are you doing?" He moved farther into the room and parked his suitcase against one wall while he cast a cautious glance at Dare.

The space wasn't very big, roughly one hundred and twenty square feet, which, for two people, felt like a shoe box. Especially when it was obvious that one of those two people was hostile.

"Calling Milly. She's gonna have to get me another cabin."

"Don't be ridiculous." Noah crossed his arms over his chest and faced Dare. "What? You want to piss her off right before the wedding?"

Dare's hazel gaze lifted to meet his. "And you're okay with this?"

Noah glanced around. There were two twin beds, a narrow couch, what someone considered a desk, as well as a small bathroom and what he assumed was a closet. Yeah, it would be very close quarters for seven nights, but it was doable. Not like they had to sleep together or anything.

Heat curled low in his gut and his dick twitched.

They would *not* be sleeping together.

Noah cleared his throat, dropped his arms. "It'll be fine."

Dare shook his head. "I'll bunk with Roan."

"Suit yourself. You can be the one who makes a scene, not me."

Dare dropped his phone on the counter with a loud clatter. "Fine," he huffed. "If you're good with it, I'm good with it."

Yeah, he sounded like he was good with it.

Noah glanced up at the small window above the bed. They had a nice, albeit limited, view of the ocean, but it wasn't the view he was looking at. He was trying to determine if Dare would be capable of shoving him out of that little round hole.

Not likely.

Noah sighed, then crossed his arms over his chest again. "Look—"

"Nope. No lectures. No way."

Yep, hostile. Just like Noah had thought.

Another grin found its way on Noah's face, but from the looks of it, that pissed Dare off. "Think of it this way"—Noah kept his eyes on Dare's face—"it's not like we'll be in this room much."

Only to sleep.

Together.

Shit.

This was not at all how he had envisioned this trip going.

Five

DARE SAW THIS playing out one of two ways.

One, he called Milly up and told her to find him another cabin or put him in with Roan so that he wouldn't have to endure spending even one extra minute alone with Noah. Or two, he sucked it up and pretended that Noah's presence didn't affect him.

The first way would make him look like a little bitch. The second ... well, he feared that the second would definitely be the harder of the two. That was taking into account how upset Milly would be if he raised a stink about his accommodations, even though he was pretty damn sure she'd played a big part in this clusterfuck.

Shit.

He was so screwed.

But if Noah could do this, then so could he. Hell, he could do it better.

"Fine." Dare glared at Noah, trying to sound unaffected by their sleeping arrangements. "Which bed do you want?"

"You were here first," Noah responded immediately. "You pick."

"Fine." The single word popped out again, and Dare realized that was one word he needed to drop from his vocabulary. "The left."

Noah nodded and moved to the twin bed on the right. Not that it really mattered which bed he chose. They would still be close enough to touch.

The thought sent a frisson of awareness coursing through him.

No. Not awareness. Dread. That was definitely dread.

Or not.

Dread didn't usually make his dick hard.

Damn it.

Unable to look away, Dare watched as Noah easily lifted his suitcase and set it on the bed, unzipping it and then unpacking it with care, sliding his clothes into one of the drawers beneath the vanity, moving to the bathroom and stowing stuff in there, then returning to zip up the suitcase and put it away.

Before Dare knew what was happening, Noah was pulling off his shirt.

"Shit. What the hell are you doing?" Dare blurted, eyes locked on the hard muscles of Noah's well-defined back.

Noah cast him a glance over his shoulder. "Changing. What does it look like I'm doing?"

Dare noticed the smirk.

Asshole.

Fine. Two could play that game. They hadn't nicknamed him Double Dare for nothing.

Dare immediately pulled off his own shirt, dropped it on the floor.

Noah chuckled as he turned around.

And there they stood, both of them shirtless.

The first thing Dare noticed was that the man a few feet away from him did not look anything like the guy he'd once been in love with. This version of Noah was fucking ripped.

"Nipples pierced, huh?" Noah said, his dark eyes dropping to Dare's chest.

Dare peered down at the silver rings piercing his nipples—his *hard* nipples. It was the metal that did that. Really.

He ignored his traitorous nipples and looked up at Noah again.

"Tattoo, huh?" Dare countered, admiring the fire department symbol that was tattooed on Noah's left pec.

Noah glanced down, then back up to meet Dare's eyes as his hands slid to the button on his jeans, beneath the dark trail of hair that led down, down, down.

Damn it.

Holding his breath, Dare prayed his face didn't reflect the anticipation currently bottled up inside him. He noticed the minor twitch of Noah's fingers as he flipped the button on his jeans loose. Dare matched his movement, unbuttoning his own jeans.

Noah pulled his zipper down; Dare did the same.

When Noah pushed his jeans down his hips a little bit, revealing navy blue boxers, Dare...

Stopped.

Shit. He'd gone commando today because he'd been in such a rush, grabbing underwear hadn't been high on his priority list.

Suddenly this wasn't a fair fight.

"Problem?" Noah goaded.

Dare narrowed his eyes, then pushed his jeans down slightly. "Not at all."

His breath lodged in his throat when Noah's eyes darted down to Dare's waist, heat infusing the chocolate depths. When Noah's eyes widened, Dare paused.

This wasn't a game he was going to win, no matter how much he wanted to, so he decided to save face.

For both of them.

"Wouldn't want to tempt you with something you can't have," Dare grumbled, preparing to pull up his zipper.

Noah didn't flinch. "Not like I haven't seen it before."

Dare cocked his head to the side. "And I'm sure it took you a long damn time to forget about it, too."

"Not that long," Noah returned, but Dare suspected that was a lie.

Or maybe that was just wishful fucking thinking.

"Oh, it's still long," Dare countered. "And thick. Very, very thick."

Noah rolled his eyes.

Dare smirked. "Fine. You think you can handle it?"

Noah's Adam's apple bobbed slowly, his eyes once more sliding down Dare's chest, and he felt the heat like a physical caress.

Figuring what the hell, Dare shoved his jeans down his legs, letting them pool at his ankles. And there he stood, stark naked, except for the denim now trapping his feet and the damn shoes he'd forgotten to take off.

But instead of shoving his own jeans down, Noah grabbed his clothes from the bed and then spun around and went right for the bathroom, sliding the door closed behind him.

And somehow, Dare managed to breathe.

Right before he stumbled and fell flat on his naked ass.

MOTHER OF ALL things holy. What the fuck had made him do that?

Taunting Dare?

Stupidest thing ever.

Unfortunately, Noah hadn't had enough to drink to blame it on the alcohol.

Planting his palms flat on the wall, he stared at the tiled floor and tried to catch his breath.

Pierced nipples. Fucking hell.

He heard a noise from the other room—sounded as though something had crashed—followed by "son of a bitch," and he couldn't help but laugh, picturing Dare on his ass—naked, jeans around his ankles.

And then his breath escaped him again as the image of Dare reappeared, standing gloriously naked, save for the denim shackles on his legs. He couldn't stop thinking about the smooth planes of Dare's sun-bronzed chest … and the sexy pierced nipples … mmm, the ripped abs… Oh, and his cock… The man had been half-hard and damned impressive in that state.

Fuck if that hadn't been the best goddamn sight he'd seen … in a decade and a half.

No question, Dare was the hottest man Noah had ever laid his eyes on. Definitely more impressive at thirty-four than at nineteen, which was saying something. All smooth, bronzed skin, perfectly sculpted muscles, and those sexy-as-hell nipples… Noah would never forget that image. Not if he lived to be two hundred.

Remembering why he'd chickened out and snuck into the bathroom, Noah quickly changed in the tiny, cramped space, then took several slow, deep breaths before stepping out into the cabin to find Dare… Looked as though he'd left.

Slowly inhaling and exhaling, Noah willed his heart rate to slow down as he dropped onto the edge of the bed and stared at the tiny space. He would be spending a week in this cabin with Dare. Seven long, lonely nights.

He honestly couldn't remember the last time he'd spent the night with a man. It had been a long time ago. Hell, he hadn't even been with a man in six months, and even then, it had been an ex-semi-boyfriend whom Noah had heard from. They'd slept together after sharing dinner and a couple of beers, and Noah had been quickly reminded why they'd gone their separate ways in the first place.

They simply didn't mesh.

He hardly remembered that night. Then again, right this second, he couldn't even remember why the hell he and Dare had broken up, and that had been far more impactful than a brief tumble in the sheets.

Oh, yeah. Dare had wanted long-term and Noah had been … stupid.

But none of that mattered.

Right now, he needed to get out of this stuffy little cabin and get some air. Maybe then he'd be able to go to dinner, meet the rest of the people they'd be spending time with over the course of the next week.

After that, perhaps he'd be able to figure out a way to survive the rest of this trip.

Without jumping Dare Davis's bones.

HUDSON BALLARD STOOD at the back of the room, trying to blend in with the wall. It wasn't that he didn't want to be here in a room full of people he didn't know, but he'd learned over the years that people tended to shy away from him when they learned he couldn't speak. Being on the sidelines had simply become natural for him.

"Hey, bro. What's up?"

Fearless

Hudson turned to see his brother, AJ, holding two glasses as he stopped beside him. Hudson graciously took one when AJ passed it his way.

"You good?" AJ asked.

Hudson nodded, sipping his drink as he continued to scan the room, looking for the one man he knew he shouldn't be paying any attention to. Especially since it seemed Teague was doing his best to piss him off by flirting with every damn thing with a dick.

"So, where's this boy toy of yours?" AJ smirked.

Hudson flipped him off. Teague damn sure wasn't his boy toy, and the only reason AJ said that was because Hudson had made the comment that Teague was too damn young for him the last time AJ had brought him up. For some unknown reason, the Pier 70 crew thought Hudson was only thirty-one, and he'd never bothered to correct them. It had made it a little awkward when they had surprised him with a birthday cake with the numbers three and one on it on his last birthday, but he'd suffered through. Apparently someone had read his application wrong because he'd just turned thirty-five, making him ten years older than Teague. Far too old to be entertaining the notion of screwing a twenty-five-year-old kid.

"Okay, fine. My turn." AJ glanced around the room and Hudson followed his gaze. "Who's the blonde? She single?"

Hudson's eyes widened as he stared at his brother, shaking his head when AJ made eye contact.

"What does that mean? She's not single?"

Hudson set his drink on the table and used his hands to explain. *You do not want to mess with Milly.*

"Milly, huh?" AJ's gaze once again slid over to where she stood talking to Gannon and Cam. "Interesting name."

Hudson punched his brother in the arm. *No, not interesting. Nothing about her is interesting. Leave her alone.*

AJ laughed. "Since it seems to me that you're trying to warn me away from her, I'm gonna assume she's single."

Hudson shook his head again. *Not warning you away from her. Her away from you.*

"Oh, come on."

It wasn't that Hudson cared one way or the other if AJ went after Milly—he was a good guy and all—but the last thing Hudson needed was for something to happen to piss off his bosses. He happened to enjoy the fuck out of his job and wasn't interested in looking for another.

He elbowed AJ to get his attention, then signed: *Seriously.*

AJ's smile widened. "I promise, I'll be good." His eyes scanned the room once again. "Plus, it looks to me like you've got someone who could keep you pretty busy if you'd stop pretending you didn't want to bang his brains out."

Once again, Hudson shook his head in disbelief. Sometimes he couldn't believe the shit that came out of his brother's mouth.

But, at the same time, he didn't disprove his brother's theory when his eyes slammed into Teague across the room.

Six

DARE HAD KNOWN he wouldn't last another second in the same cabin with Noah, so he'd changed in record time—thankfully, Cam had insisted that tonight's dinner was casual, so Dare had opted for shorts, a T-shirt, and flip-flops—then went straight for the nearest outdoor bar he could find. Now he was walking the length of the ship, carrying a beer he didn't particularly care for, and trying to get the image of a half-naked Noah out of his head.

He was still tempted to chase down Milly and insist that she change his cabin, or better yet, he would go straight to the check-in desk himself and … what? Show Noah that he was too much of a pussy to stay in the same cabin with him?

Not a fucking chance.

Dare didn't back down from … well, a dare.

His mother must've been high when she'd named him. Wait. She had been.

Never mind.

The more he walked, the better he felt. He could do this. He was fearless, damn it. No mere mortal was going to keep him from having a good time on this trip. Nor was his overtaxed brain. It was time for him to shake it off and get with the program. His best friend was getting married in a few days, and Dare planned to be on his best behavior. In spite of Noah Pearson.

Dare managed to completely clear his head by taking a tour of the ship on his own, walking through the casino, by the pools, past the FlowRider surf simulator (definitely on his to-do list), to the rock wall, beneath the zip line (another must-do), around the sports courts and miniature golf, and finally by the freaking ice skating rink. It didn't take long before he felt more level-headed, realizing there were plenty of things for him to do to keep his mind off of Noah. Plenty.

His only problem now was deciding what to do first.

When it came time for dinner, a festivity that he'd been assured was time for them to relax and unwind, meet the others who'd come for the wedding, he had weaved his way through the ship until he was in the room reserved for tonight's event. For a brief moment, he worried he would be underdressed, but he noticed that most of the people he'd seen earlier had opted for casual attire—very similar to his.

As he wound his way through the room, chatting with a few people he hadn't seen earlier, he made his way over to Roan.

"Didn't get the memo, huh?" Dare nodded toward Roan's buttoned-up attire. He was wearing jeans and a polo, so he wasn't exactly dressed up, but he didn't fit in. Hell, even Cam and Gannon had changed.

"Shut it," Roan groaned, taking a sip of his beer. "You no longer look like you're ready to flee. Feeling better?"

"All good," Dare assured him. It was only a little white lie. "Nothin' to worry about here."

Roan chuckled, apparently seeing through Dare's admission that he would make it through this. Regardless, he would. He had to.

"You get settled in your cabin okay?"

Dare glared at Roan. It was clear he knew that Dare was bunking with Noah.

Asshole.

"So, who is he to you, anyway?"

Dare looked away.

Nope. Not going there. Not tonight. Rather than get into a lengthy conversation with Roan, Dare decided to evade the start of Roan's impending inquisition, excusing himself.

"Whatever," Roan called after him. "It'll be a better trip if you're not so prickly."

Dare flipped him off.

Asshole.

He was *not* prickly, damn it.

He was fun. Interesting. Everyone's friend.

Yet, tonight, he couldn't deny it, he felt a little … okay, yes, prickly.

Shit.

Thankfully, Roan didn't seem intent on trying to get him to talk, and for that, Dare was grateful. Only now, as he stepped into the adjoining room, he noticed people were already seated at round tables, while a buffet was being set up on the far side of the room. As he took it all in, he wasn't sure avoidance was going to be simple from here on out.

"You're sitting over there," Milly informed him, a beaming smile on her face as she pointed in the direction of the table directly to the left of where the grooms-to-be were currently sitting. For casual, this sure seemed a little overdone.

Do not mention the cabin. Do not mention the cabin.

He managed not to mention the cabin or his pain-in-the-ass roommate. Barely. "Thanks."

"Don't thank me yet," she whispered, but turned away before he could ask her what that meant.

He took three steps and answered his own question.

There at the table Milly had directed him to was Noah, sitting to the right of the little white card that had Dare's name on it.

Fucking lovely.

How the hell was he supposed to get out of this?

Remembering his earlier pep talk, Dare squared his shoulders and headed for the table, grateful when he saw Hudson and Teague were also seated there, only they didn't look any happier to be at the same table. Looked as though Milly was playing matchmaker again.

Taking his seat, Dare downed half of his water before Hudson kicked him—hard—under the table.

"Fucking shit," Dare hissed, glaring at Hudson.

Hudson responded by nodding his head toward Noah.

Reaching down, Dare rubbed his shin, continuing to hold Hudson's stare.

"Fine," he muttered, realizing he was being forced to introduce them. Although he still wasn't sure why that was his problem. "Hudson, Teague, this is Milly's stepbrother, Noah Pearson. Noah, this is Hudson Ballard and Teague Carter. They work at the marina, too."

Hudson gave a chin nod in Noah's direction, prompting Dare to explain. "Hudson is mute, but he can hear. He knows ASL, in case…" Dare stopped talking when Noah began signing.

Well, fuck.

He hadn't expected that.

Teague looked as disinterested as ever, his attention on the beer in his hand and the others seated around them. Anything to keep from looking at Hudson, it seemed. Dare briefly wondered where Hudson's brother was.

Fearless

He glanced around, checking out the others, trying to identify them one by one. Anything to keep from joining the conversation at the table. Cam and Gannon were talking to Cam's father, Roan was chatting it up with Cam's sister, Holly. There were others he didn't know, all decked out in their cruise attire now, laughing and joking and having a good time. As he finished his perusal of the room, he noticed Hudson's brother talking to Milly, making her smile brightly.

Interesting.

Dare drained the rest of his water and looked at Hudson, watching his hands.

What the hell?

"No, no way. You are not gonna talk about me behind my back," he told Hudson firmly.

Hudson grinned, then signed: *We're in front of you, so that's crap.*

Noah chuckled.

Hudson signed to Noah: *So, how do you know him?*

Dare groaned.

Noah signed back, which pissed Dare off because he could've easily said the words aloud. Hudson could hear, as he'd explained.

Dare watched Noah's hands intently.

We were friends at one point in our lives.

Friends? That's what they were?

Whatever.

So, did you break up with him or he with you? Hudson's question was followed by a shit-eating grin.

Asshole.

Noah gave a side nod in Dare's direction.

Dare turned and glared at him.

Noah laughed.

Nope. This was not going the way he'd planned. He hadn't been given enough notice to be prepared to have to sit through a meal with Noah.

Then again, nothing in his entire life would've prepared him for seeing Noah again, period.

Nothing.

DINNER WENT MUCH more smoothly than Noah had anticipated it would, especially after he'd realized he was seated at the same table as Dare. Well, technically he was within inches of the man, but he hadn't noticed.

Much.

Okay, so that was a huge fucking lie.

He'd noticed.

In fact, he had taken in every little detail from how good Dare smelled—something musky and potent—to how warm his skin was when Dare's arm had accidentally brushed his at one point.

Luckily for all parties involved—except maybe Teague, who looked as though he wanted the table to open up and swallow him—Hudson had carried the conversation, which had provided some distraction. Because it suited him, Noah had opted to sign his responses, rather than speak them aloud. Mainly because he'd realized early on that the fact that he knew American Sign Language had taken Dare by surprise. Then, it had pleased him when he'd noticed Dare keeping up with the conversation.

"Since when did you learn sign language?" Dare asked when the dinner plates were being cleared away.

"Since when did *you*?" Noah retorted. Dare didn't seem impressed by his counter, so Noah explained. "About ten years ago, we were called out on an out-of-control brush fire that was threatening a nearby neighborhood. When we came upon a house that still had occupants inside, we were advised to urge them to leave due to the danger. The husband and wife were both deaf. Although I managed to communicate by typing the instruction on my phone and having them read it, I figured it would be beneficial—for any future instances—to learn. So I did. Your turn."

Dare nodded toward Hudson. "He's our boat mechanic, and though he can hear me just fine, I wanted to be able to talk to him, not *at* him. So, in order to level the playing field, I decided to learn."

Interesting. The Dare he had known fifteen years ago wouldn't have bothered.

Or—something he didn't want to think too much about—perhaps he would have and Noah simply hadn't known him as well as he'd thought he had.

They announced that dessert was being added to the buffet, but Noah opted to decline, choosing to watch the interactions around him, namely Cam and Gannon, who were seated at the head table directly to the right and in front of him. The two of them looked incredibly happy, surrounded by their family and friends.

Noah couldn't help but be glad he was part of this, even if the situation was far from ideal. The last time he'd been to a wedding was when Milly's father had married his mother. If he was completely honest with himself, he hadn't paid much attention during that stressful period because he hadn't been happy they'd decided to get married in the first place. Even though he didn't have anything against Milly's father, he'd felt as though his mother was letting go of his father forever. It had been a stupid reaction, but one he couldn't change. He had since apologized to them both for it.

There was a tap on Noah's shoulder, and he turned to see Gannon and Milly standing at his side. He instantly glanced back at the table where Gannon had been a minute ago and noticed it was empty.

Weird. He could've sworn he was just watching them.

"You got a minute?" Milly inquired, doing that chin nod thing that signaled she wanted to talk to him away from the table.

"Excuse me," he said, placing his napkin on the table and getting to his feet.

He followed Gannon and Milly out into the hallway, his curiosity growing.

When the two of them stopped and turned toward him, Noah patiently waited for whatever it was they had to say. He noticed Milly's eyes snap over to Gannon, as though she was silently urging him to talk. When he didn't, Milly huffed.

"Gannon wants to ask you something."

Noah shifted his attention to Gannon. "Sure. What's up?"

Fearless

Gannon swallowed hard and it was clear whatever he wanted to ask wasn't easy for him. On top of the nervous tension radiating from him, Noah noticed he was paler than he'd been earlier. Gannon cleared his throat and then wiped his hands on his shorts. Yep, extremely nervous.

"I wanted to know if you'd be one of my groomsmen." Gannon cleared his throat again, locking eyes with Noah. "It's just that I don't have any family ... well, other than Milly, so I don't have anyone to stand up for me besides her. And since Cam has Roan, Dare, Teague, and Hudson, I kinda—"

Noah stopped him mid-ramble. Placing a hand on Gannon's shoulder, he smiled. "Man, I'd be honored. Seriously. And I think it's safe to say that you've got more family than you realize."

For a brief moment, Noah was almost certain he saw a sheen of moisture in Gannon's eyes. But then it was gone as Gannon righted his glasses.

"Thanks. It means a lot to me."

Noah looked over at Milly, who was beaming. He wasn't sure he'd ever seen her smile that big.

He turned back to Gannon. "Welcome to the family."

Before he could turn around and go back into the room, Milly threw her arms around his neck and hugged him tight. "Thank you, thank you, thank you. You don't know how much this means to him. And to me."

Hugging her back, Noah smiled. "It really is an honor, Mill."

With that, Milly released him, then took Gannon's hand and led him back into the room. Noah followed behind them, made his way back to his table, and took his seat next to Dare.

"Everything okay?" Dare whispered, leaning toward him.

"All good."

"Okay, so I hope everyone's having a good time so far." Noah looked up to see Milly standing behind Cam and Gannon, holding a microphone in one hand and her trusty clipboard in the other.

"As you know, this is day one of this seven-night cruise. We've got a lot happening over the next week, the most important, obviously, being these two guys getting hitched."

Applause erupted, causing Milly to pause.

"Yes, I know. We're all waiting for that to happen. But, in the meantime, you get to enjoy your time on the boat."

"It's a ship!" someone yelled from the back of the room.

"What was that?" Milly asked, looking around to find the source of the outburst.

"It's a ship," Teague explained. "You called it a boat. I was just correcting you."

"What's the difference?" Milly asked with a chuckle.

As though it had been pre-planned, several people spoke up in unison. "A ship can carry a boat, but a boat can't carry a ship."

More laughter ensued.

Milly grinned. "Well, there you have it. I've been schooled." She glanced down at her clipboard. "Tomorrow will be the first stop, which will be CocoCay, Bahamas. We'll be there around seven in the morning. Up to you on whether you enjoy the day on the island. I've made sure that each morning you'll have breakfast available to you right here if you want it. The rest of the time, you're on your own, but you know the meals are included, so stuff yourselves stupid."

Noah laughed along with the others.

Milly glanced at her clipboard once more. "Okay. Then on day three—which will be Tuesday—we'll be cruising all day. No stops. Then on Wednesday, we're gonna be in St. Thomas. The ship arrives at eleven in the morning and departs at seven. The rehearsal dinner is scheduled for eight. Please be there. It's important. We don't want any mishaps." She looked down again, and then Milly's smile widened as she lifted her head. "And then on Thursday, we'll be stopping in St. Maarten, which you're welcome to enjoy as long as your butt is back on this"—Milly looked at Teague—"*ship* in time for the wedding. We arrive at eight and depart at five, so that's more than enough time to get your beach on. The wedding is at seven. Like I said, be here on time." She glanced from one person to the next. "Do not make me hunt you down."

More laughter.

"After that, on day six and seven, we'll be cruising the entire time until we return to port on Sunday morning." Milly looked up again. "With that said, I hope you have a blast. This boat is so freaking big you may have to hunt these two down if you want to hang out with them, but they'll be here somewhere. And like I said … Thursday. Wedding. Do not be late." Milly glanced at Gannon. "You want to say anything?"

Gannon shook his head. Noah looked closer and realized he was still extremely pale, and based on his plate, he hadn't eaten anything. Definitely not a good sign.

Cam took the microphone and got to his feet.

"I just want to thank everyone for coming. We want you to enjoy the cruise. It's your vacation as much as it is ours, so don't worry about us. Do your thing, have fun. Like Milly said, we'll be around. Can't promise that we'll emerge from our cabin much"—Cam glanced at Gannon and Noah noticed the blush that tinged Gannon's cheeks—"but we'll definitely be around. Again, thank you all for being here. It means more to us than you know."

There was more applause and Noah joined in. When the noise level settled, he looked around, noticing that Dare had disappeared from the table. He searched the room, finding Dare on the far side talking to someone. A guy. A good-looking guy Noah hadn't been introduced to.

Noah watched the two of them closely, and when Dare leaned in and whispered something in the man's ear, he felt his heart slam into his chest. He swallowed hard and got to his feet.

Although he was having an irrational reaction to what he was seeing, Noah did not want to watch Dare flirt with some guy. If he was going to survive this trip, he needed to remember that Dare was from his past, not his present or his future. So whatever Dare Davis did was of no concern to him.

Didn't mean he was going to sit back and let it play out in front of him.

Seven

REFRAINING FROM GOING after Noah wasn't easy, but Dare managed to keep his feet rooted to the floor as he watched the man dart out of the room as though his ass were on fire. After sneaking over to get dessert, Dare had found himself having a conversation with Hudson's brother, AJ. They'd been talking about how strange it was that Dare had never met the guy, then laughing because they'd witnessed Hudson and Teague glaring at one another, again. Because he'd been so caught up, Dare hadn't seen the reason for Noah's quick exit, but now he had to wonder.

Although he was curious—and yes, maybe a little worried—he fought the urge to chase after him. He told himself not to because he didn't want to arouse suspicion from his friends. Why he'd wanted to go in the first place didn't even matter because he knew he shouldn't. Fifteen years had passed since he'd broken up with Noah. What bothered the guy now was of no concern to him.

Only he did care, damn it.

For whatever stupid reason.

And now, he couldn't fight his curiosity any longer.

"Where're you going?" Milly called out to him when he was inches from the door. "I was serious when I said you better go back to your cabin if you're gonna get naked."

Dare stopped mid-stride, spun around to face Milly, and grinned. "Trust me, I'm not gonna be gettin' my freak on."

"Darn. Someone should." She looked sincerely disappointed.

Dare came to stand directly in front of her, then glanced back through the doorway where Noah had exited a short time ago. Taking a deep breath, he turned back to her. "Is Noah all right?" he asked.

Milly's gaze followed his past the door and into the open area outside the banquet room. "Why? What did he do?"

Dare shrugged. "He bolted earlier. Looked like something was bothering him."

Milly seemed to consider that, but her eyes didn't clear. She still appeared confused.

Appeared Milly didn't know Noah as well as Dare had thought she did. Whether that was a good thing or not was yet to be seen.

"I'm gonna go check on him," Dare told her. It was probably the worst idea he'd had since the night he'd tried to out-drink Hudson. Never mind the fact that Hudson outweighed Dare by probably twenty pounds and Dare had absolutely no tolerance for tequila. Still.

"Let me know." Dare heard the concern in her voice.

"I will. Keep the party alive in here," he told her with a smile, then turned and headed out of the room.

Fearless

It took twenty minutes to find Noah. He wasn't at the casino—though Dare hadn't really expected him to be for some reason. He hadn't been on the basketball court, either. Or at any of the outdoor bars. Nope, after wandering around aimlessly, Dare finally found Noah on the rock wall. Noah had shed his socks and shoes, rolled up the sleeves on his navy blue shirt, and was now halfway up to the top, beside him a couple of kids who were struggling but transfixed by Noah's speed and dexterity.

Dare sweet-talked his way to the front of the line, then strapped into a harness after kicking off his flip-flops. Once he was nice and secure, he started up the wall. It didn't take him long to catch up to Noah, who was nearing the top.

"What's up?" Dare asked casually, stopping beside him.

Noah's head snapped around, but he didn't smile.

"Fancy meeting you here," Dare added.

"What do you want?" Noah repositioned his grip on one of the handholds.

He wanted a lot of things. Like to know why the hell he hadn't been good enough for Noah back then. But he knew that wasn't what Noah meant, so he ignored the question.

Dare glanced up, then dropped his gaze to Noah's face once again. "You up for making this interesting?"

Noah looked up. "What'd you have in mind?"

"Well, first, we start over on the ground. First one to the top…" Hell, he hadn't thought this one all the way through yet. Then it hit him. "Has to buy drinks tonight and gets to decide what we do next."

"We?" Noah sounded skeptical.

"Yeah. You. Me. The mouse in your fucking pocket."

That earned him a smile. "You're on."

"Just remember, I'm not that skinny guy you used to know."

"And you should remember, I'm a firefighter."

Remember? Hell, that was something Dare would never forget. Not in a million years. If he had to guess, he'd be having a few erotic dreams about it in the very near future.

A couple of minutes later, they were back at the bottom, convincing the attendant to let them go once more. Because the kids in line seemed to be getting a little frustrated, Dare turned back to the group.

"Okay, y'all, my buddy here—his name's Noah. You know, like 'No, uh, I can't beat you.' And my name's Dare. You know, like 'I dare you to say I won't beat you.'" Some of the kids moved closer, grins forming. "So here's the deal. Noah thinks he can beat me to the top." Dare shook his head. "It's not true, but he doesn't know that yet. And I need for y'all to root for who you think'll win." Dare stabbed his chest with his thumb, and he noticed Noah was shaking his head. "Wha'd'ya think?"

"I think he'll beat you," a big kid in the front said, his beefy arms crossed over his chest.

"Do you now?" Dare asked. "We'll see. But I need you to get excited." He focused on the other kids. "Can you do that?"

A chorus of agreement exploded in the air and Dare turned to face Noah.

Wiping his hands on his pants, Dare offered Noah a smile, then turned to the wall and placed his hands on the first holds. According to the kid manning the attraction, the front side of the wall was the hardest to scale.

They'd see about that.

Glancing over his shoulder, Dare met the gaze of a little girl. "You say go," he told her.

"Ready," she hollered, her cheeks puffing up. "Get set… Go!"

Fearless

They both started up the wall, hands gripping the holds, bare feet easing into the spaces that would push them higher. Dare set his focus on the wall, refusing to let Noah beat him. He knew better than to underestimate anyone, but he damn sure wasn't in this to lose.

Noah moved quickly, faster than Dare had initially thought he would. The man was all ripped muscle, moving with a speed that shocked even those on the ground, based on the sound of their gasps and excited cheers.

Dare glanced over his shoulder. "I can't hear you!" he told the kids. "Louder. I need some encouragement up here."

The cheers grew louder and a group of them started to chant his name. Dare turned back to see that Noah was several feet ahead of him. He started up again, making sure to keep a firm grip on the faux rocks that had been strategically placed.

But this … it was too easy.

Once Noah was close to the top, Dare figured it was time to focus.

He gave one more look over his shoulder, grinned, and then…

Dare practically flew to the top, leaving Noah staring after him. Rather than ring the bell right off, he waited for Noah to join him. Before Noah's hand could grip the top, Dare rang the bell and the kids started to clap.

Noah met his gaze. Those chocolate-brown eyes held a hint of amusement. "Still just a big kid, aren't you?"

That sucked every ounce of his enjoyment out of the moment, and, mindful of the kids below, Dare resisted the urge to flip Noah off.

But he left him with a few parting words, said low enough that only Noah could hear. "I wasn't a kid then and I damn sure ain't a kid now. Don't blame me if I always knew exactly what I wanted."

With that, he released his grip and propelled down to the ground, pasting on a smile for the excited kids who were now cheering as though he'd done something incredible. He high-fived a few before snatching up his flip-flops and walking away from Noah.

For the second time in his life.

AS SOON AS the words left his mouth, Noah knew he'd fucked up. He hadn't meant them the way they'd come out, which also meant he hadn't meant them the way Dare had taken them, either. Not this time and certainly not the first time years ago.

"I want more than this," Dare clarified. "I'm talking forever."

"Babe, you're just a kid. Forever's a long damn time."

Noah certainly wouldn't win any awards for being a smooth talker, that was for sure.

Yep, he could still hear those words echoing from a long-ago memory. Noah had wanted to take those words back as soon as they'd come out, but it had been too late. He'd sealed the fate of their relationship with those crass words, though he honestly hadn't meant to hurt Dare. He'd just been so young.

And now... Well, Noah had meant them as a joke. He'd been caught up in Dare's excitement, having fun and not thinking about anything other than their competitive spirit. Clearly, Dare hadn't taken it that way.

Fearless

Once down off the rock wall, Noah pulled on his socks and shoes and went in search of Dare. He had no idea how to find one man in the sea of people aboard the ship, but he didn't plan to give up until he did.

An hour later, he found Dare sitting out by the pool, the inky night sky laid out all around them.

"This seat taken?" Noah asked, nodding toward the empty lounge chair beside Dare.

"Yeah, it is."

Knowing Dare was simply being hardheaded, Noah dropped onto the chair and stretched out his legs. "Look, I'm sorry."

"Don't be. I've always known what you thought of me."

"It's not like that," Noah stated, his tone firm.

"No? Coulda fooled me." Dare lifted his beer bottle to his lips but didn't look at Noah. The icy chill from the man's attitude could be felt for miles around. Noah half expected to peer over the edge of the ship to find a glacier sliding by.

Sighing, Noah relaxed against the chair and stared up at the sky. Apologizing to Dare was futile. He knew he could say it a million times over, but if Dare didn't want to hear it, he wouldn't listen.

And it appeared he wasn't listening now.

"You were pretty good on that wall," Noah told him, wondering if changing the subject would help. "And you were good with those kids."

Dare didn't respond.

"Technically, you won. Which means you get to decide what we do next."

"We?" Dare questioned.

"Yeah, you know, you, me, and the mouse in my fucking pocket."

Dare snorted. "You never were very funny."

90

"True," he relented. "But I've always been hot."

Another snort from Dare.

"What do you want to do?" Noah asked.

"Sit here. Where it's quiet."

Noah turned his head and stared at Dare, hoping he would look back at him. It took a few seconds, but finally he did. And for a few seconds after that, Noah couldn't pull his gaze away. Looking at the man brought back so many memories. Some good, some not so good. One thing that was still the same, though, was the way Noah felt when he got lost in those hazel eyes. And he found himself getting lost again.

"Dare…"

Before he could get a sentence out, Dare was sitting up. "I'm gonna call it a night. Big day tomorrow. The kid in me has always wanted to go to the Bahamas."

Noah sighed.

When Dare was on his feet, Noah stared up at him. "I know I fucked up."

Dare turned to look at him, his forehead creased. "Then or now?"

Both. Not that he was going to tell Dare that. Not yet. They still had seven more days on this ship, and he did not want to piss the man off by hashing out something that had happened fifteen years ago. They simply needed to find a way to get along for the next week, and then they'd be home free. Noah could go back to his normal, boring life and Dare could…

Noah didn't even know anything about Dare's life.

"How about a truce," Noah blurted, hopping to his feet. "For the remainder of the trip, we're just two guys sharing a cabin."

Dare studied him, and Noah fought the urge to squirm beneath the scrutiny.

Fearless

When a smile tugged at the corners of Dare's mouth, Noah's breath seized in his lungs. That smile ... it still had the ability to make his insides quiver.

"You really think you can spend seven days with me and not want to jump me?"

That was the Dare that Noah knew. The man he'd fallen in love with all those years ago. "I was thinking the same about you."

Dare's gaze slowly raked over Noah's body, but the words that followed belied the heat in his eyes. "I don't think I'll have a problem."

"Is that a dare?" Noah asked.

"What? You think you can refrain from wanting to run your hands over this?" Dare motioned toward his own body. "I don't think you have it in you."

Noah shrugged. "Do you still snore?"

Dare snorted. "I never did snore. That was you."

"Right. Me."

Dare held out his hand. "Shake on it. Seven days. Roughly one hundred and sixty-eight hours. We're just two guys sharing a cabin. And you're not allowed to touch."

The guy always had been really good at math, although he pretended not to be.

"It sounds to me like you want me to touch." Noah took a step closer, the heat of their bodies colliding between them as their palms clasped.

"Not a chance." Dare's voice wavered slightly.

Noah leaned in, his cheek brushing Dare's as he moved close to his ear. "We'll see about that."

While they were still standing close, Noah shook Dare's hand, sealing the deal.

Why did he get the distinct feeling he was also sealing his fate once again?

Eight

RATHER THAN TEMPT fate, Dare escaped to his cabin, leaving Noah out on the deck. He could still feel the warmth of Noah's breath against his cheek, and his dick twitched to life once again.

The man made his body hum and he didn't like it one damn bit.

Okay, he liked it a little.

A lot.

Yes. A fucking lot.

Not that it mattered.

Despite the fact that he'd managed to call a truce with Noah, Dare had a hard time envisioning them making it through this trip intact. If it weren't for the fact he'd promised to be on his best behavior, he likely would've called Noah to the carpet.

A big kid.

He'd show Noah.

He was not a fucking kid. Not any part of him.

So what if he wanted to have fun. Life was too damn short and full of too much shit to fret over the little things.

A knock sounded on his door and Dare sat there, expecting Noah to come in.

"Noah? Dare? Are you in there?"

That wasn't Noah.

Fearless

Launching himself off the bed, Dare reached for the door and pulled it open, finding Milly standing in the hall, smiling back at him.

She was holding two suit bags.

"Your tuxes for the wedding," she told him, holding them out for him to take. "Figured you could keep them safe in here until then. Is Noah here?"

Dare shook his head as he took the hangers that were hooked over her hand. He hung them on the mirror over the vanity.

"Did you talk to him tonight?" Milly asked when she followed him into the cabin.

"For a minute."

"And?"

"And what?" Dare turned to face her.

Milly's hands went to her hips and she cocked her head to the side. "Sit down."

Dare sat.

"Honest to God, I had no idea that you two knew each other. If I'd known…"

Dare knew that grin. It was one that Gannon feared, and Dare was beginning to understand why.

"If you'd known…?" he prompted.

"I would've asked a million questions."

"Like?"

"Like how the two of you know each other."

"It's a long story." He didn't elaborate, hoping she would let it go.

"It's a long trip," she countered. "And I've got wine."

"I don't drink wine," he told her.

"Well, I can get beer."

Dare shook his head. He didn't need anything clouding his mind more than it already was.

"So, spill it." Milly hopped up onto the twin bed that Noah had taken for himself.

"It was a long time ago," he explained, not wanting to go into it.

"You dated?"

"Yeah." They'd dated.

"For how long?"

"Twenty-five months."

"Wow. That was specific. So, why'd y'all break up?"

Dare shrugged. He seriously had no desire to talk about this with her. Or anyone, for that matter.

"You're the one who got away, aren't you?"

Dare spun around to face her. "What are you talking about?"

Milly smiled. "I always suspected someone had slipped through Noah's fingers at one point."

"Why do you figure that?"

"Because I've tried numerous times to set him up. He insists he's not interested."

"Doesn't mean someone slipped through his fingers." That was absurd.

"No, but the fact he said so does."

Dare didn't know if Milly was baiting him or not, but he refused to play into her hands. He appreciated her good intentions, but the last thing he wanted was to go back in time. He wasn't the same guy he'd been when he and Noah were together. Though he didn't think Noah thought as much.

It was true, though. He wasn't looking for the same things in life anymore. He had a dream job, a small but decent place to live, he saw his grandmother all the time, he'd managed to gain himself a dog, although he'd never wanted a dog, and he wasn't looking for a happily ever after. Very different than nineteen-year-old Dare.

Fearless

And above all else, he didn't want to talk about his past.

Desperate to change the subject, Dare asked, "So how'd your dad meet his mother?"

"Some work function." Milly pushed a strand of hair behind her ear. "Noah's mother works as an administrator for the fire department. My father is an arson investigator."

Well, that made sense, but it didn't explain about Noah's father. "And Noah's dad?"

Milly's eyes softened. "His dad died when he was twenty-three. Car accident. My dad was the first man his mother dated after that, but that wasn't until years later."

Dare hoped he was successful in hiding his surprise. If Noah's father had died when he was twenty-three... That was how old Noah had been when the two of them had broken up.

Suddenly, the door opened and Noah stepped inside, his eyes sliding to Milly, then Dare, then back again.

"Hey," Milly greeted him. "We were just talking about you."

"No, we weren't," Dare blurted, shaking his head adamantly.

He was surprised when Noah smiled. "Talking about how handsome I am?"

Dare narrowed his eyes. "No. As a matter of fact, we were talkin' about how your eyes nearly bugged out of your head when you saw me naked earlier."

"You saw him naked?" Milly exclaimed, clapping her hands like one of those kids back at the rock wall. "Tell me everything."

Noah huffed a laugh. "His nipples are pierced."

Dare felt his face heat.

"I already knew that." She glanced at Noah. "He chooses to walk around shirtless most of the time. But"—her voice lowered as she looked back at him—"is your penis pierced like Cam's?"

Dare tried not to choke, but he couldn't help it. "No needles have ever touched my … err…"

"Damn," Milly huffed, clearly disappointed. "I've been begging Cam to let me see his, but he refuses."

Noah and Dare both laughed. Dare couldn't blame Cam one bit.

"Mark my words," Milly announced, getting to her feet. "One day I will see that man's penis."

"Quote of the day," Noah noted.

"Well, I guess I'll leave you two boys to it. Let you get naked and whatnot. I'll be in my cabin if you need me."

Dare tried to come up with a reason to ask her to stay, but he came up empty. The last thing he needed was Milly trying to pry into their past while Noah was in the cabin with them.

"Oh, and we're having breakfast in the morning. Be there by nine. Dressed," she said with a wink. "Ta-ta for now. Sweet dreams."

"Night," Dare called after her, looking at anything he could to keep from looking at Noah.

And when the door closed behind her, the tiny cabin felt even smaller. If that was even possible.

NOAH WILLINGLY WALKED into burning buildings, but stepping farther into this cabin with Dare was the most difficult thing he'd ever done. Although they'd called a truce, he wasn't sure how to proceed from here. Finding Milly there had been a welcome surprise, but she'd disappeared too quickly. As soon as she'd stepped into the hall, the awkward tension returned.

Dare moved over to his suitcase, unzipped it, and reached inside without looking.

It didn't pass his notice that Dare hadn't bothered to unpack. Whether that was because he wanted to be prepared to flee if necessary or if he was simply the same messy man he'd always been, Noah wasn't sure. It took everything in him not to unpack for him and put Dare's clothes where they belonged.

But that wasn't his place. Plus, he wasn't that obsessive.

Okay, yes, he was. But he was going to refrain.

Maybe.

"I'm gonna shower." Dare retrieved his clothes from his suitcase, then shoved it back in the corner.

Knowing the statement didn't require a comment, Noah kept his mouth shut. And when the door closed behind Dare, he did his best not to think of the man naked in the shower, the hot water sluicing over all of that bronzed skin. Those pierced nipples...

Damn. He should've gotten laid before he'd come on this trip. It probably would've made things a little easier. As it was, his dick was painfully erect, and he had no way of relieving the tension until he managed to get a little privacy.

Figuring the safest thing for him to do was go to sleep, he pulled off his shoes and socks, followed by his jeans and his shirt, then yanked the blankets back on the hard twin bed before climbing in. He didn't bother turning off the light, and once his head hit the pillow, he was too tired to get up again. Figuring Dare would take care of that when he was done with his shower, Noah closed his eyes.

A moment later, he heard the bathroom door slide open, and the scent of soap drifted into the room.

The cabin suddenly smelled like Dare. Musky, sexy. Not much different than what Noah remembered. He had always loved that about Dare. Although Noah was obsessive about most things, Dare was only obsessive about being clean and smelling good. He remembered how Dare used to shower morning and night, no matter what they had done that day.

"You asleep?"

"No," Noah muttered, keeping his eyes closed.

"Too bad."

The light went off and then the bed beside him rustled.

"Too bad, why?"

"Because I would've woken you up with my question."

"And you don't want me to sleep?" Noah asked, smiling to himself.

Same old Dare. Always needling him. Surprisingly, Noah found that he had missed it. A lot more than he was willing to admit.

Dare moved around loudly. "Shh. I'm trying to sleep."

Noah laughed, then turned his head toward the bed Dare was in. The moonlight slipping through the sheer curtain over the window provided enough light for Noah to see by. Dare was nothing more than a lump in the bed, his sleek back the only thing Noah could see. He noticed ink scrolled across Dare's shoulders, but in the darkness, the only word he could make out was regret.

Not for the first time, he wondered if Dare had any, but he wasn't about to ask. Definitely not now. Instead, he released a breath, then closed his eyes again.

"Was it hard?" Dare asked.

"What?" Noah replied, his stomach clenching as he contemplated all the questions Dare might possibly ask.

"Your dick?"

Okay, so that wasn't one of the questions he'd been anticipating.

"When I was in the shower," Dare continued. "Did it make your dick hard? Were you thinking about me all ... wet?"

Yes. "No." He hoped he sounded convincing.

"Liar."

"I'm not lying," Noah insisted.

There was more rustling, and Noah opened his eyes to see Dare lying on his back, hands behind his head, face tilted toward him. "Show me."

"What?" Noah frowned. "You're crazy."

"If you're dick's not hard, prove it."

"Why?" Okay, so *that* wasn't what he'd meant to say.

"Thought so."

"It wasn't hard," Noah lied.

"But it is now?"

"No," he lied again.

He was hard as fucking granite and the more Dare spoke, the worse it got. The sexy rumble of Dare's voice in the dark did something to him.

"But *you* are," Noah countered, continuing to watch Dare.

"Not at all."

Noah knew Dare was lying because he could see the sheet tented at Dare's waist.

Fuck.

This was not a good idea.

He felt like a damn teenager. It reminded him of the time when he was sixteen and he'd had his first serious crush on his best friend, who he had learned months later had been crushing on him, too. Needless to say, they'd had some enjoyable sleepovers from that point forward.

Dare nodded. "Okay, yes. Hard as stone." He held Noah's gaze in the darkened room. "Wanna feel? With your mouth?"

Noah laughed, then rolled over, facing away from Dare. "Go to sleep, Dare."

"Your loss."

It most definitely was.

Nine

Monday, May 30th
Cruise, day two

DARE WOKE UP the following morning with a hard-on that wouldn't quit. The first thing he noticed was the gentle rocking of the ship, along with the eerie silence in the small cabin. Forcing his eyes open, he blinked until he cleared the sleep from them, listening for the sound of Noah snoring—which, yes, he still did, thank you very much.

Looked as though Noah was already gone.

Hmm.

Glancing over at the other bed, Dare found it empty, which only disappointed him a little. Lifting his head from the pillow, he peered around the cabin. Nope. No Noah. He was definitely alone, save for his cock, which had taken on a life of its own.

Sliding his hand beneath the sheet and into his boxers, Dare took his aching dick in hand, stroking slowly as he relaxed once again, staring up at the ceiling. What would Noah say if he could see him now? Would he think Dare was imagining Noah's hand on his dick? Noah's warm, callused hand stroking up and down, slow and easy…

Fuck.

He was not thinking about Noah.

Or Noah's hand.

Or Noah's mouth.

Or…

Dare had to push his boxers down over his hips to give his dick some breathing room. He kept a steady pace, trying to slow his breathing, wanting to savor the moment. These few minutes alone might be all he had for the entire day. If he was expected to deal with Noah for the duration, he had to do something to relieve some of the tension. It didn't seem to matter that his heart was keeping its guard up; Dare's body had other ideas where Noah was concerned.

Closing his eyes, he continued to jack his dick, trying not to think about Noah sleeping in that bed beside him. It hadn't been easy falling asleep last night, but at some point, he must have. Thankfully he hadn't dreamed about setting his apartment on fire simply so he could see a hunky fireman come put it out. In fact, he hadn't dreamed about anything, or if he had, he couldn't remember.

Turning his head, he opened his eyes and stared at Noah's pillow, noticed the slight indent, the way the blankets were neatly turned down. His thoughts drifted back to seeing Noah yesterday, for the first time after fifteen long years. The man looked as good as ever. Same sparkling brown eyes, same thick, dark hair, angled jaw, slightly crooked nose. And the muscles… And his lips… Dare tightened his grip and quickened his pace, allowing the sheet to fall to his thighs.

He fought the urge to groan as he thought about Noah's mouth … how it would feel on his, or better yet, wrapped around his dick.

He groaned.

Fearless

Unable to stop, Dare closed his eyes and imagined Noah sucking him, taking him deep into his beautiful mouth, using his wicked tongue, swallowing him greedily the way he used to. It didn't take long before he was gritting his teeth, the intense sensations pooling low, a subtle electrical charge starting at the base of his spine.

Fuck.

"Noah," he whispered, swallowing hard. "Fuck."

The next thing Dare knew, he was coming hard and fast, splattering his belly and chest, his breath rushing out of his lungs.

Before his muscles relaxed, he heard the door to the bathroom slide open. He reached for the sheet, yanking it over his naked body as he peered down past his feet to see Noah coming out of the bathroom.

Maybe the ship should think about putting one of those occupied signs up. A big, bright, red one. That flashed. And played music. Yep. Music would've been good. So, you know, he would've had a heads-up. And *this* wouldn't have happened.

"Thinking about me this mornin', huh?" Noah asked casually, his gaze slowly traveling over Dare.

Dare frowned. "You? Why would I be thinking about you?"

"You never were a quiet lover," Noah remarked. "Not even when it came to self-love."

Dare smirked. "I'm surprised you didn't watch. You never were one to look away."

Noah matched his grin, then glanced at the clock. "Oh, did I mention? It's eight fifty-five. You've got five minutes to get to breakfast." Noah nodded toward Dare. "And I'm thinkin' you might need a shower."

Dare fought the urge to look at the clock. Instead, he opted for taunting Noah. "I'm sure I could make it if you wanna lick me clean."

The heat in Noah's gaze was unmistakable, but much to Dare's dismay, he didn't have a comeback. Not sexual, anyway.

"I'll save you a seat," Noah noted, glancing back at Dare over his shoulder as he reached for the knob on the door. "But you better hurry."

The instant the door closed, Dare flew out of the bed. He scrambled to find clothes still packed in his suitcase, then glanced at the clock.

"Fucker," he mumbled to himself, taking a deep breath.

It was only eight fifteen.

NOAH STEPPED INTO the hall, then took a moment to lean against the door, trying to calm himself down. The last thing he needed was to run into Milly when he was half out of his mind with lust.

When he closed his eyes, he could still see Dare lying on that bed, stroking himself to completion.

Damn.

Fearless

Turned out that Dare was right about one thing. Noah had been known to watch. Which explained why he hadn't been able to look away when he'd unknowingly opened the bathroom door to witness Dare jacking off on the twin bed, the crisp white sheet pooled over his thighs. Noah had been stunned motionless, unable to swallow or to look away from the impressive sight. He'd been transfixed, watching as Dare's thick cock tunneled in and out of his fist...

For those few minutes, he'd even allowed himself to remember all those times when Dare had jacked off for him, allowing him to watch. And the times when Dare had fucked his ass so perfectly Noah could hardly breathe afterwards.

Noah shifted, trying to readjust his dick, which was straining against the zipper of his cargo shorts and making them uncomfortably tight.

He'd barely managed to close the bathroom door after watching Dare come, Noah's name on his lips. It'd been the most beautiful sight he'd seen in probably fifteen fucking years. More than anything, Noah had wanted to walk right across that room, ignore all those years and the bad memories that separated them, take Dare in hand, and get him hard again just so he could suck him off.

Noah feared this was starting to become a problem.

He was supposed to be here as a favor to Milly.

He was supposed to be here to keep an eye on his stepsister.

He was supposed to be here because her friends were getting hitched.

He was *not* supposed to be lusting after Dare Davis.

Or thinking about how he tasted, how he would feel when Noah slid deep into his body.

But he was.

He so was.

And he didn't know how he was going to make it through the next seven days without jumping Dare. That was the deal. He couldn't. He'd made a pact, agreed he wouldn't, but with temptation like that...

He was only human.

Taking another soothing breath, Noah pushed away from the door and started down the hall. He thrust his hands into his pockets and focused on the thick carpet lining the corridor.

"Morning."

Stopping mid-step, Noah turned to see Milly coming up behind him.

"Morning." He wondered briefly if she'd seen him a minute ago during his attempt to pull himself together.

Her smile was sweet and mischievous, which meant it could go either way. "You look ... like a man who did *not* get laid last night."

Noah shook his head in disbelief.

"So you didn't?" She moved closer. "Or you did? You don't have to give me details. It's still early. You can save those for later. Over drinks."

Noah frowned.

"What?" Milly asked innocently.

"Have you ever heard of this thing called minding your own business?"

Her eyes widened slightly. "No," she said deadpan. "What is it? Should I know about it? Was it a public school thing? It was, wasn't it?"

Noah chuckled, then started walking again, Milly falling into step beside him. Before they made it to the end of the hall, Cam was running toward them from the opposite end, panic etched on his face.

"What's wrong?" Milly asked, all humor in her tone gone.

"Gannon's … well, he's sick." Cam took a breath, his eyes wild. "He's been up most of the night, puking his guts up."

Noah watched the two of them.

"What's wrong with him?" Milly questioned, her hand resting gently on Cam's arm, an obvious attempt to calm him down. "Is it the flu?"

Cam shrugged.

"I'm guessing it's motion sickness," Noah offered.

"Shit. Why didn't I think of that?" Cam asked.

Maybe because the guy had other things on his mind. Noah held Cam's gaze. "Is he wearing a patch?"

Cam's eyebrows furrowed. "No. What type of patch?"

"They make them for motion sickness," Noah explained.

"Shit." Cam shook his head.

"Does he have anything for it?"

"No," Cam said on an exhale. "I didn't even think about it. I can't believe I didn't think about it."

"Relax." Milly's tone was soothing as she squeezed Cam's arm, her eyes landing on Noah's face. "What can we do about it?"

"Let me go down to the clinic," Noah stated. "I'm sure they'll have something he can take while on board the ship."

Cam nodded. "It's bad."

"Well, the good news is that the ship's docking soon. We're at CocoCay for the day," Milly explained. "Maybe if he gets off the boat for a while, he'll feel better."

Footsteps sounded from behind him, but Noah didn't turn to see who it was. He didn't need to when Cam and Milly glanced past him, both looking as though the newcomer would save the day.

"Hey." The familiar voice came from over Noah's left shoulder.

"I'll be back in a few," Noah told Cam just as Dare came to a stop beside him.

Now it was a regular old party in the hallway.

"What's up?" Dare looked between the three of them as he effectively boxed Noah in and kept him from being able to leave.

Noah couldn't help but inhale the delicious scent that accompanied Dare. If the guy expected Noah to keep his hands to himself, he was going to have to do something about that. He couldn't walk around smelling like Armani and expect Noah to be a gentleman. It was too much.

"Gannon's sick," Cam told Dare.

"I'll be back in a minute," Noah repeated, excusing himself.

"Where're you goin'?" Dare asked, placing his hand on Noah's arm.

"He's gonna go get some medicine," Milly explained. "Go with him. And y'all hurry."

Great. Just what Noah needed.

An extra hit of sexy first thing in the damn morning.

Ten

DARE FELL INTO step with Noah, sneaking a quick peek at the guy's delectable ass encased in those shorts. Yum. He shouldn't have been looking, but he couldn't help himself. Admittedly, it had been a long time since Dare had felt any sort of attraction to a guy. At least on this level.

That all-consuming desire to jump on top of the guy, wrestle him right out of his clothes, and lodge himself deep inside his body...

Mmm.

Yeah. Damn long time since that had happened.

"You okay?" Noah asked when they made it down the stairs to the main level of the ship.

Dare looked up at Noah's face, realizing he'd been busted ogling Noah's ass.

Oh, well.

A group of people passed by as Noah leaned in close to Dare's ear. "You're picturing me naked, aren't you?"

Dare choked out a laugh. "Not a chance."

"I look good, don't I?"

Dare frowned at Noah.

"Naked," Noah explained. "I look damn good naked."

A woman passing by watched them intently, her eyes wide as she cast a quick glance over Noah. The appreciative gleam in her gaze said she wasn't going to argue with Noah's assessment of himself.

Sorry, honey, he doesn't swing that way.

Not that Dare cared which team Noah batted for. Dare wasn't interested in Noah. Granted, that didn't explain why he wanted to shoo the woman away.

"I've seen better," Dare lied, smirking at Noah.

"Does it hurt?" Noah lifted one dark brow.

Dare glanced down at himself, not sure what Noah was referring to. He met Noah's gaze with a questioning look.

Noah started down the hall, and Dare followed after him.

"Lying to yourself. Does it hurt?"

Dare shook his head just as they stepped into the clinic. This was the side of Noah he had honestly forgotten about. The guy who teased simply because it was fun. Yep. That guy wasn't all that bad.

He stayed back while Noah went to the counter and talked to a slender woman, whose gaze only briefly left Noah to acknowledge Dare. She smiled at him, then her eyes slipped back to Noah, scanned him briefly as Noah explained to her what he needed. Within minutes, he received a small envelope with what Dare assumed were motion-sickness pills.

When Noah headed for the door, Dare fell into step with him. "What makes you so sure it's motion sickness?"

"Unless the guy is trying to get out of getting married…"

"Not a chance," Dare stated instantly. "Hell, Gannon would've married Cam a million times over by now if Cam would've agreed."

"Well, I figure it's either motion sickness or food poisoning. Since we haven't heard of anyone else getting sick from dinner, it's probably safe to assume this is it."

True. Dare had probably eaten more than anyone in the room last night and he felt fine. But he wasn't done questioning Noah yet.

"And if you're wrong?" Dare countered.

"I'm not."

"How can you be so sure of yourself?"

Dare had to admit, that trait was fucking sexy as hell. He liked the cockiness in Noah's tone when it came to his certainty. Still, he was having fun riling the guy.

Noah tossed a quick glance over his shoulder at Dare. "I'm just that good."

Whatever. "Well, if you're wrong…"

Noah stopped abruptly, causing Dare to slam into him before stumbling to the side. He reached for the wall so he could get his feet under him, at the same time Noah crowded him until he was up against the wall of the corridor leading to the stairs. The movement surprised him, and Dare wasn't able to think when Noah was that close.

Damn, he smelled good. Not of cologne, though. It was a fresh scent. Soap and fabric softener or something. He briefly wondered if Noah still did a load of laundry every single day the way he had when they were younger.

"If I'm wrong"—Noah lowered his voice until the gravelly tone was barely above a whisper, his mouth dangerously close to Dare's ear—"then I'll suck your dick right here in this hallway. How's that for confidence?"

"You're gonna walk all the way back down here to—"

Noah cut him off with a hand over Dare's mouth, their gazes locked. When Noah released him, it took almost more willpower than he had not to grab Noah and…

"If I'm wrong," Noah repeated slowly, "I'll bring you right back down to this hallway, drop to my knees, and take your cock in my mouth."

"Is that a threat?" Dare managed to wheeze through the lump in his throat. Just the thought of Noah on his knees with Dare's cock in his mouth made it damn difficult to breathe.

"It's a promise. And I remember how much you enjoyed my mouth on your dick."

Dare puffed up his chest, forcing Noah back a bit. "I don't remember anything of the sort." It was suddenly the only thing he remembered.

Noah took a step back and smiled. "That lying thing … that's new."

Yeah. It was.

And Dare didn't have any intention of stopping.

Not if he was expected to make it through the next several days in one piece.

IT TOOK TREMENDOUS effort to back away from Dare, but Noah managed.

What he really wanted to do was drop to his knees, free Dare's cock, and deep throat him right there in the hallway. He didn't give a fuck who might see them. Seemed he hadn't calmed down as much as he'd thought since that live porn show he'd witnessed earlier. And the longer he was around Dare, the worse it seemed to get.

He offered a quick wink, trying to play off this little scene as fun and games. Unfortunately, Noah's dick didn't understand the games part. It was ready for the fun, though. More than ready.

Oddly enough, Dare didn't say anything more, so Noah turned back toward the stairs, then led the way up to their floor.

"What cabin are they in?" Noah asked, glancing down the hall.

Dare stepped in front of him, taking the lead. "Don't look at my ass."

Noah instantly glanced down at Dare's ass, nearly slamming into Dare when he stopped. He took a quick step to the side and waited while Dare knocked on the door and was instructed to come in.

"Holy fuck," Dare muttered when they stepped inside. "I end up in a shoe box with The Great Snore-dini and y'all get this? It's bigger than my apartment."

So Dare lived in an apartment. Good to know.

No. Wait. It didn't matter where Dare lived.

Remembering why he was there, Noah sidestepped Dare, holding out the small brown envelope the nurse at the clinic had given him. "The instructions are on the packet. He needs to take one as soon as possible. If he thinks he can keep it down."

Cam nodded, then turned.

There, lying on the bed in the fetal position, was Gannon looking noticeably green.

Yep, definitely motion sickness.

It wasn't necessarily that the ship moved all that much, but for people who were even the slightest bit queasy from movement, it could be a problem.

"He might feel better sitting outside," Noah suggested. "The fresh air'll help."

"We tried that." Cam was shaking his head as he glanced over at Gannon. "Actually made it worse."

"Then keep him in bed until he feels better. Long enough for the pill to start working, at least," Noah instructed.

Cam nodded. "Thanks."

"No problem." Not wanting to overstay his welcome, Noah turned to leave.

"Y'all need anything else?" Dare questioned. "We can grab some foo—"

Noah placed his hand over Dare's mouth once more, feeling his warm breath against his palm. Lowering his voice, he said, "Don't mention food."

Dare met Noah's gaze and nodded.

"Come on. Let's give 'em some space."

Dare frowned, his voice low when he whispered, "How will I know if you were right or not?"

Noah leveled him with a look, then grabbed Dare's thick shoulders and turned him toward the door. "I'm right."

"But how will I know?"

"We'll see y'all in a bit," Noah called out, pushing Dare out into the hall.

Surprisingly, Milly didn't say a word, but Noah had noticed the way she'd watched the two of them the entire time.

"You ready to eat?" Dare questioned once they were in the hall.

Not knowing whether or not that was an innuendo, Noah looked back at Dare.

"Food," Dare clarified. "You know ... sausage."

Noah shook his head, then turned back toward the stairs.

"Oh. We going back to that hallway already?" Dare questioned, his tone innocent, but Noah knew the man was still teasing him.

Fearless

If Dare wasn't careful, Noah would do what he'd been wanting to do since the minute he'd first seen him after all these years. Only, Noah knew if that happened, neither of them would walk off this ship in the same condition they'd boarded it in.

And he hadn't yet figured out how to clear that little obstacle just yet.

So for now, they'd have to settle for food.

MILLY SAT IN the upholstered chair in the corner of Cam and Gannon's cabin, continuing to watch the empty space by the door after Noah and Dare had vacated. She had a million questions running through her head, but she wasn't sure she should give voice to any of them. Never in her wildest dreams would she have thought that Dare and Noah knew each other.

Granted, from her perspective, they sure did make one hot couple.

"Do you know what their history is?" she asked, not directing the question at anyone in particular.

Cam stepped in front of her, blocking her view. She looked up at him, and he nodded toward the sliding doors that led out to their private deck.

Getting to her feet, she cast a quick glance at Gannon, who was still lying on the bed, curled up in a ball. She felt so bad for the guy. He'd been looking forward to this trip for so long and now … what a way to spend the first morning of your wedding vacation.

Once outside, Cam closed the door behind them, then stepped over to the railing and rested his forearms on the bar.

"Has Dare ever mentioned Noah?" Milly asked, clarifying what she meant by history.

"No." Cam shook his head as he peered over at her.

"And you've known him the longest?"

Cam nodded. "I met him when I started working for a small marina back when I was in high school."

"And you've never known him to date Noah?"

Cam shook his head.

"Well, they definitely have history." She tried to imagine them together as teenagers as she stared out at the water. "Dare said they dated for a little over two years, but he wouldn't give me any more details."

Cam didn't respond, but she hadn't expected him to. He wasn't the best person to gossip to. Roan was far better for that sort of thing.

"I think Dare's the one who got away," she told Cam.

"What makes you think that?" There was a hint of interest in Cam's ocean-blue eyes.

"Have you seen the way they look at each other? It's like they're singeing the other's clothes off with their eyes. Heat like that doesn't just happen."

Cam grinned. "I beg to differ. I'm pretty sure I managed to make Gannon's suit smolder that first day y'all showed up at the marina."

Milly laughed. "Probably true. But still. Once you find that sort of thing, you don't let it willingly get away from you."

"Are you speaking from experience?" Cam looked interested now.

"Nope. Not me." That was the truth. Milly hadn't had a serious relationship in her life. Mainly because she tended to go for losers. It wasn't a conscious decision; it simply happened. "And this isn't about me. It's about them. Plus, it's not just heat between those two, although it seems that's what they're focused on right now."

"Probably so they don't have to deal with the issues," Cam noted.

"Men." *Why were they so dense?* "I want to know what happened."

"No, you probably don't."

"I do," she mused, letting her mind wander. What if the universe had brought them together on this boat for a reason? Could this be their second chance? Second chance romance ... she liked the sound of that.

"What do we do if Gannon doesn't get better?" Cam asked, changing the subject.

"He'll get better," she told him, patting his arm. "The guy won't miss his wedding for anything. Even if it means he carries a bucket up there with him."

Cam cringed and Milly laughed.

"I hope this works."

It would. It had to. They had a wedding only four days away, and Milly hadn't been joking when she'd said Gannon would be there. She knew him. He wouldn't miss marrying Cam for the world.

"So ... what do we do now?" Cam asked, turning around and leaning back against the rail. "While we wait to see if it works?"

Milly chuckled. "Well, you could always show me your penis."

Cam choked and Milly had to pat him on his back.

She understood her request probably made him uncomfortable, but if Cam didn't show her his, she might never get to see one up close.

One day she *would* see this man's pierced penis.

Of that, she had no doubt.

Eleven

DARE SENT UP a silent thank you to the water gods that breakfast had been uneventful, unlike the rest of his morning. They'd been herded through a buffet line in a room that had been reserved for the wedding party. Not everyone had shown up for the morning festivities, some probably sleeping in, others doing something other than overindulging on soggy eggs and greasy bacon.

Dare didn't discriminate when it came to food. Soggy and greasy were adjectives his stomach jumped up and down for. He ate like he wouldn't get the chance to again. Probably more so because he was doing his damnedest to ignore his temporary roommate than anything else.

For some reason, he was hyperaware of Noah. To the point of distraction. And that was saying something considering the crazy morning they'd had already.

Between Noah catching him with his dick in his hand, Gannon being seasick, Hudson and Teague arguing—silently, and about what, Dare didn't know—and Dare unable to stop thinking about Noah giving him a blow job, he was mentally exhausted.

And the day hadn't even really begun yet.

At least he was full.

"Have you seen Roan today?" Dare asked as he picked up his glass of orange juice.

"I'm pretty sure I've been with you the whole time," Noah answered around a mouthful of eggs.

Right.

Dare took a drink, watching Noah.

"Why?" Noah asked. "Need him for something?"

"Nope. Just curious." And doing his best to find some neutral ground. Something to keep his mind from wandering to thoughts of Noah sucking him off in the hallway. It wasn't easy. It was as though his dick was an antenna and the only station it was tuned to was the Noah blow job channel.

A few minutes later, Noah wiped his mouth and pushed back his chair. He got to his feet without saying a word, and for whatever reason, Dare got up and followed him.

"So, what's on the agenda for today?"

"I'm gonna go check on Gannon," Noah said as they headed out of the banquet room.

"I'll come," Dare told him. "After all, if you're wrong…"

God, he hoped Noah was wrong, because he seriously was beginning to anticipate those lips wrapped tightly around his dick.

Noah chuckled but didn't say anything.

It wasn't easy for Dare to keep quiet—it wasn't in his nature—but he managed to remain silent for most of the way to their floor. All he had to do was think about what would happen if Noah was wrong. Would he really go back to that hallway, drop to his—

Dare slammed right into Noah's back when Noah came to an abrupt halt. He looked up to see they had arrived at Cam and Gannon's cabin. Apparently he'd been much deeper into that fantasy than he'd realized.

Noah slowly pivoted around to face him. And because they were both six foot even, they were nose to nose, eye to eye, swapping air. Dare swallowed hard, suddenly overwhelmed with the urge to kiss this man.

"Stop looking at me like that," Noah whispered.

"Like what?" Dare asked just as softly.

"Like I'm chocolate cake."

"I don't like chocolate cake," Dare told him. It was true. He didn't.

"Liar. Everyone likes chocolate cake."

Dare gave an almost indiscernible shake of his head. "I like cheesecake," he explained, keeping his voice low, never breaking eye contact.

Noah's smile was slow and bright, which didn't ease any of the sexual tension that stretched between them.

Figuring he would go for broke, Dare added, "With *strawberry* sauce."

Noah's gaze dropped to Dare's lips, and that band of awareness tightened around Dare's chest, making it impossible to breathe.

Noah was going to kiss him.

No, wait, he was going to kiss Noah.

Stop the train. Someone was about to get off, because *no one* was going to be kissing *anyone*. Dare didn't even *like* Noah.

What the hell was he thinking?

Still, he didn't back away, trapped in Noah's intense gaze.

Suddenly, the door to Cam's cabin opened, and surprised, Dare stumbled backward, catching himself with a hand on the opposite wall.

"What's up?" Roan asked cheerfully, standing in the doorway, a devil-may-care grin on his face.

The guy had obviously planned his little interruption and seemed rather amused by his actions.

"Hey, Roan. Have you met Milly's stepbrother yet?" Dare asked, not looking at Noah or Roan as he eased around them and into the cabin. He called back over his shoulder, "Noah, that's Roan. Roan, that's Noah. Have fun, y'all."

Fuck, that was close. Two seconds more and Dare would've had to turn Noah down and make him feel bad for wanting to kiss him.

Okay, so the lying thing *was* getting a little out of hand.

NOAH WASN'T SURE what had just happened, but he was thankful for the interruption.

Or maybe he wasn't. He'd need a minute to think about that.

Right now, though, he found himself nodding at Roan, though an official introduction had already been made by Milly yesterday when he'd boarded the ship.

"Good to see you again." Roan's smile was mischievous as he stepped back and allowed Noah to enter the room.

"How's Gannon doing?" Noah glanced around the cabin, looking for the patient.

"Much better." Roan nodded toward the balcony door. "He's out on the deck, getting some fresh air. I think your miracle pills worked."

"The nurse said he'd need to take them every day."

"I don't think that'll be a problem. Guy's finally got some color back." Roan chuckled. "A color other than green."

That was good to hear. It would really suck if Gannon was down for the count and unable to go through with the wedding. Then again, Milly had said he would do whatever it took to marry Cam.

"Where's Milly?" Noah asked as they headed toward the door to the private deck. Noah could see Dare outside, already chatting it up with Cam and Gannon.

"She went to the spa. Something about a massage, then getting her hair and nails done."

"But the wedding's not for three more days." Why in the world would she be getting her hair done?

"Hey, I don't question the weird shit women do. I'm just thankful I don't have to live with one."

Okay, so Roan had a good point.

The warm ocean breeze drifted into the room when Roan opened the door, the sound of voices tumbling in along with it. Noah diligently followed him out onto the deck.

"So, what's the plan for the day?" Dare was asking Cam, his full attention on his friend.

Noah found it amusing that Dare didn't even look his way. After what had transpired between them in the hallway, it was telling. Dare had been a hairsbreadth away from kissing him, Noah knew it. Granted, he'd been hovering on the brink, as well.

It was probably for the best that Roan had interrupted, and there was no doubt in Noah's mind that Roan had timed that well. He'd known they were out there. Had Dare's friend waited a fraction of a second longer, there was no telling what would've happened.

Noah wouldn't have resisted Dare. He wasn't even sure he could.

Fearless

It was one of those inexplicable phenomenons. He was attracted to Dare, they shared a history, there had been a significant amount of emotional pain at one point in their lives, but right this minute, none of that seemed to matter. At least not to Noah. He didn't know why, either, because yes, there were still some unresolved issues between them, but surely those had expired by now. Wasn't there a statute of limitations on that shit? Like an expiration date?

Was it possible for them to start over?

"I vote for getting off the ship," Gannon announced.

"I'm up for anything," Cam agreed.

"A few hours on the beach, some Jet Skis, maybe a little snorkeling," Dare added, still not looking at Noah. "Sounds like a damn good plan to me."

"I think I'll forego the water," Gannon added, his nostrils flaring. "But y'all have fun."

"I've got some things to help Milly with," Roan told them. "I'll probably stay on the ship, maybe hang with Hudson or Teague."

Noah didn't figure it was his place to make a suggestion, so he kept his mouth shut.

Until all eyes turned to him.

That was when he looked directly at Dare.

"I'm up for some time in the water," he told them, pulling his eyes from Dare's face to look at the others.

"Then it's settled." Gannon got to his feet, a little unsteady. He was still slow-moving, but Noah figured the guy was dehydrated. "Dare, Noah, and Cam can go snorkeling while I sit on the beach and pray to the sand gods."

"I'll hang with you," Cam told Gannon.

Gannon looked at Roan. "You sure you don't wanna come?"

Yes, please come. Please don't let me and Dare spend the freaking day together. Alone.

"I'm good," Roan told him.

Shit.

Noah noticed that Roan was looking between him and Dare. He wasn't sure what was going through the guy's mind, and he definitely wasn't going to ask.

Hell, as it was, Noah wasn't sure what to think of all this.

But he knew one thing for certain…

He hadn't anticipated spending the day alone with Dare. And he only hoped they both made it back to the ship without breaking their pact.

Or wait.

Maybe he hoped they made it back to the ship *after* they'd broken it.

Either way.

Twelve

AS IT TURNED out, those religious zealots were right. Hell was hot.

What they hadn't mentioned was that hell consisted of warm breezes, white sandy beaches, beautiful, clear blue waters … and a fireman with no shirt.

Apparently, Dare hadn't atoned for his sins, because he'd somehow ended up there.

For the past two hours, he had damn near bitten his bottom lip clear off his face as he'd tried his damnedest to ignore Noah in those black-and-white shorts, with the wide expanse of muscles in his phe-*fucking*-nomenal upper body on full display.

Back when they'd been together, Noah had been slim, a few muscles here and there. *Nothing* like the beefy guy he was now with his thick biceps, washboard abs and well-defined chest, solid thighs and tight fucking ass.

Christ. The guy probably spent hours a day in the gym.

Or he ate his spinach.

Something.

This wasn't what Dare had thought would happen on this trip. He'd expected to hop on a ship, have a few drinks, maybe drop a few dollars at the craps table, have some laughs with his friends, watch his pals get married, and sleep a little more than usual.

Not the case.

Instead, gambling and sleep were the absolute last things he was thinking about. In fact, his big head was getting very little input in at all. Everything was being filtered through the little man in his shorts.

"You good?" Noah questioned, pulling off his mask as they trekked back up onto the sand.

"Perfect. You?" The lying thing was getting easier.

"That was fun."

Fun. Yes. Dragging around a granite club in your shorts was fun.

Oh, wait. That was just Dare. He was the one who'd been sporting the hard-on for the past couple of hours, not Noah.

Dare sighed, dropping onto the sand and flopping onto his back, allowing the brilliant sun overhead to heat his skin. He loved it here. The scenery—not including the fireman—was to die for.

Noah eased down beside him, leaning back on his forearms and looking out at the water.

Dare did his best not to watch as Noah's abs contracted.

"So, how long have you worked at the marina?" Noah asked, his tone curious.

"I'm a partial owner." He didn't know why, but he felt the need to clarify that.

"Okay." Noah frowned. "How long have you *owned* the marina?"

"A while," he replied.

"I remember you'd mentioned working at a marina when we were together. Summer help, I think. The same one?"

Reluctantly, Dare offered the information Noah was seeking. "No, different one. I met Cam…" Dare was going to say shortly after they'd broken up, but decided not to. "We've been friends for a while. I worked at a marina on Inks Lake after…" Again, Dare didn't mention their breakup. "Anyway, Cam started working there right before he graduated from high school. When Cam decided to open a marina of his own a few years later, I joined in. Pier 70 has been open for a decade."

"You like it?"

"Best fucking job in the world." And that was the truth. Dare wouldn't trade it for anything. He lived and breathed for that place. It was where he felt at home.

"I know the feeling."

Dare glanced over at Noah. "So this firefighter gig… It finally worked out for you, huh?"

"Yep."

Dare remembered Noah had wanted to be a firefighter when they'd been together. He had just started looking into it right before they'd split. Noah's dad was a firefighter, something Noah had admired in the man. He'd been hopeful to one day follow in his father's footsteps.

Funny how Dare couldn't remember what he'd had for dinner last week, but he could remember fifteen years ago like it was yesterday. Fuck, he could still remember the day he'd met Noah. They'd been at a party for a guy who'd ended up being a mutual friend. Dare had been just as taken by Noah then as he was now, so he'd started chatting him up. They had laughed, they had danced… And the rest was history.

Then twenty-five months later, life as he'd known it had ceased to exist, and he hadn't been the same since.

"I bet your dad was proud," Dare mentioned, shielding his eyes from the sun as he stared out at the water.

Noah didn't respond, causing Dare to peer over at him again. When it was clear he wasn't going to say anything, Dare sighed. He remembered Milly's comment about Noah's dad dying. Had to have been roughly around the time when they'd broken up since Noah would've been twenty-four that August.

Not that Dare had kept track of that or anything.

Based on his lack of response, Noah wasn't going to share that piece of himself with Dare. And that told him all that he needed to know about where he stood with Noah. Even after all these years.

Wanting to change the subject, he asked, "Think we should head back to the ship? It's gonna take some time for me to get the sand outta my shor—"

Before the sentence was finished, Dare found himself crushed between Noah's hard body and the sand, the man's face blocking the sun. He didn't even have a chance to ask *what the hell* before Noah's warm, smooth lips were on his.

Fucking hell.

Dare knew he should push Noah away, tell him that he was years too late for this, but holy mother nature and all things water related... He couldn't bring himself to do it. Wrapping his arms around Noah's neck, Dare thrust his fingers in Noah's wet hair, holding him as though, any second, he would disappear. He met Noah's tongue with his own, no hesitancy whatsoever.

"Fuck, Dare," Noah whispered, his fingers twining in Dare's hair, tugging tightly. "I... Aww, hell."

Noah's words were cut off when their tongues collided once again. Dare tilted his head, getting a better angle as he kissed Noah for all he was worth. This man undid him in ways he'd never thought he'd experience again. He ached for him, and nothing—not even blessed air—was better than the feel of Noah's mouth on his.

When Noah finally pulled back, putting a breath of space between them, Dare squinted up at him.

"You know, it's probably a crime for two men to kiss on this beach," Noah mumbled softly, his eyes never leaving Dare's.

"Probably," Dare agreed.

Honestly, he didn't really give a fuck.

About anything.

Wasn't sure if he ever would again.

NOAH HAD NO clue why he'd done it, but one instant, he was reclining on the beach, watching Dare, the next, he was hovering over him, kissing him with years' worth of pent-up passion, attempting to make up for the fifteen since the last time he'd kissed the man.

And now, although he'd managed to wrangle a fraction of his self-control, he didn't really want to stop. But he was serious about this possibly being illegal. Though they'd legalized marriage in the States, that didn't mean it was legal for two men to make out on a beach in the Bahamas. Hell, it very well could be, but he really didn't know. Last thing he wanted was a confrontation with anyone about it.

Not to mention, a little privacy would be nice.

As he stared down at Dare, he watched the storm clouds fog his usually clear hazel eyes. Whatever moment they'd shared was gone, and Noah was losing Dare to the past once more.

When Dare pushed at his chest, Noah relented, sitting up and allowing Dare to get to his feet. With a sigh, Noah stood, brushed the sand off his legs as best he could, and then started after Dare as he headed back toward the ship.

Yep. Moment definitely gone.

As he followed, he tried to think of something to say.

I'm sorry for trying to inhale you.

Was that kiss as good for you as it was for me?

When we get back to the room, can I help you get the sand out of your shorts?

None of those were appropriate questions, and based on the rigidness of Dare's spine, he wouldn't find the humor in any of them, so Noah kept his mouth shut. Putting one foot in front of the other wasn't easy when he was preoccupied with admiring Dare. His eyes were drawn to his beautifully sculpted physique—that perfect ass, the narrow waist, wide upper body—as well as the script inked on his shoulder.

We only regret the chances we didn't take.

Perhaps it was a little presumptuous, but Noah had to wonder if that had something to do with him. Did Dare regret walking away from him? Had he thought about him since then?

Noah damn sure regretted letting Dare walk away and not only because he was in the position he was in at the moment. He'd thought about the man plenty in the years that had separated them. Granted, he'd never thought they'd be face-to-face again, and he damn sure hadn't anticipated kissing Dare.

But he had. And now he wasn't sure he would be able to walk away without getting some sort of closure.

Fearless

Before he knew it, they were back on the ship and walking into their cabin. Noah narrowly missed getting hit in the face with the door when Dare released it, the damn thing swinging closed.

He didn't get a chance to say anything before Dare had stormed into the bathroom and slid the door shut, effectively putting an end to a damn near perfect morning.

Right up to the point when Noah had fucked it all up.

Not that this was the first time. Noah had a track record of screwing shit up where Dare was concerned. Back when they'd been together, Dare had been the attentive one, always ensuring Noah was taken care of. There had never been any doubt in Noah's mind that Dare had loved him back then. And in the years since, Noah had always compared every man he'd met, every potential relationship he could've had, with that one. No one had ever lived up to Noah's expectations. No one but Dare.

And now here they were again, fifteen years later. The sexual tension was a living, breathing thing. Something Noah couldn't ignore no matter how hard he tried.

For some reason, he had thought they were on the same page, which was why Noah had kissed Dare.

He peered up at the closed bathroom door.

Apparently he'd jumped to conclusions where Dare was concerned. The wrong conclusion.

Taking a deep breath, he relaxed his shoulders. He had to fix this. He had to find a way to apologize.

Not wanting to wait, Noah took a step toward the bathroom. He stopped before his hand was on the door. He had two choices. He could pursue this and risk being rejected by Dare, which would hurt. Or he could ignore the attraction and let Dare slip through his fingers once again.

Having spent the last fifteen years wishing there had been a different outcome where he and Dare were concerned, Noah knew there was only one right answer.

Thirteen

THE INSTANT HE had the bathroom door closed, Dare flipped on the water, barely resisting the urge to put his fist through the wall. The emotions that churned inside him were so damn powerful they stole his breath.

Anger mixed with need, hate mixed with love, fear mixed with hope... It consumed him in ways he'd never wanted to experience again. It was because of Noah and the hell he'd endured after their breakup that Dare hadn't let himself feel this way for anyone since. Only Noah. Back then.

Not one single man had held a candle to Noah in the years since, and Dare hated the idea that no other man ever would, but he was beginning to think that might be the case.

Noah had fucking kissed him.

And it had been good.

So good.

Like, cheesecake good.

Sighing, Dare pushed his shorts down and left them on the floor while he allowed the water to wash the sand from his body. He didn't reach for the soap, needing a few minutes to get his bearings. Shit, he was surprised that they'd made it back to the ship. His brain was overrun by thoughts of Noah, memories bombarding him. From back then as well as now.

All the time they'd spent together, all the years they'd spent apart. How much he had loved this man, how much he had hated him in equal measure.

Okay, that wasn't true. Dare had never hated Noah. He had wanted to, but no matter how hard he'd tried, he'd never gotten to that point.

"Son of a bitch," he groaned, planting his hands on the wall and leaning over, attempting to catch his breath. If he didn't know better, he would think he was having a panic attack.

But that couldn't be the case.

He was stronger than this. The emotions didn't own him; the feelings didn't control him.

Not anymore.

The sound of the door sliding open had his body tensing, but he fought the urge to turn around. He couldn't face Noah right now.

"What do you want?" he grumbled.

The door slid closed again and he was grateful that Noah had opted to give him—

"Fuck." He moaned when Noah's strong arms wrapped around his body, hugging him from behind.

Dare could feel the heat of Noah's naked body at his back, the smooth skin of his chest, the hard ridge of his dick…

Memories assaulted him. Not once in all the years since Dare had walked away from Noah had he ever felt this overwhelming intensity the way he did in Noah's arms. It was hard to explain what it felt like. Sort of like those first moments when a roller coaster crested the first big hill. There was a nervous flutter in his stomach, and he felt as though his lungs weren't getting enough oxygen.

And he liked that feeling.

Which was stupid, because never once in the fifteen years since he'd walked away had anyone hurt him the way Noah had. Then again, Dare had never loved anyone the way he'd loved Noah, either.

For some reason, Noah had the power to shatter him, and he didn't fucking like *that* feeling one bit.

"We can't do this." Dare kept his tone firm, even though there wasn't much conviction behind the words.

"We aren't doing anything," Noah whispered, his voice barely heard over the sound of the water.

No? Sure didn't feel that way. Dare sighed. "I think it's safe to say that two naked men in the shower together doesn't qualify as *not* doing anything."

Noah chuckled. "Said no straight man ever."

Okay, fine. He had him there.

Although his body was rioting, his dick hard as stone, Dare managed to remain where he was, his hands on the wall, facing away from Noah.

"Why'd you kiss me?" As soon as the words left his mouth, Dare hated himself for asking the question.

Noah didn't respond immediately, but he didn't pull away, either. Dare could feel Noah's breath against his back, the warmth of his body practically wrapped around him. He hated the feeling almost as much as he loved it.

There was a deep sigh, followed by, "You're too much temptation for me."

The honesty in those words surprised Dare, but the response didn't. Back when they'd been together, the sex had been phenomenal. Day and night, they could fuck each other into oblivion, never getting enough. But looking back, Dare knew that was all it had been between them. At least for Noah.

"I'm not that same guy anymore," Dare said, putting words to his thoughts.

"I'm not, either."

Noah's lips slid over his shoulder blade and Dare closed his eyes. As much as he wanted this, to spend a few minutes losing himself in this man's arms, he couldn't do it. He couldn't walk away again. It had damn near killed him the first time, and he wasn't about to spend the next fifteen years trying to forget the only man he'd ever loved.

"Don't do this, Noah," Dare finally said, forcing the words to be hard.

Those strong arms released him and still Dare didn't turn around. Something squeezed in his chest, a memory of how easy it had been for Noah to let go when Dare had spent years trying to get over the man.

Without another word, Noah left the small bathroom stall, leaving Dare there to try to collect himself. It wasn't easy, but he'd been through worse.

Funny how his best and worst moments all centered around the same man.

Then again, there really wasn't anything funny about it at all.

ALTHOUGH IT WASN'T easy, Noah forced himself to walk away from Dare. He dried himself off, grabbed a pair of shorts and a T-shirt, and left the cabin while the shower was still running. Giving Dare some space seemed like the only logical thing to do.

What the fuck had he been thinking?

Fearless

Whatever it was, Noah knew he damn sure hadn't been using his big head when he'd made the decision to kiss Dare. Or to join Dare in the shower. As for the latter, he had desperately wanted to fix the damage he'd done. Instead, he'd only made it worse.

He made it to one of the outdoor bars and ordered a beer, not wanting to get blitzed but hoping for something to relieve some of his tension. With bottle in hand, he wound his way through the crowded pool area and found an empty lounge chair at the back, shielded by a big blue awning.

He didn't know how much time passed as he sat there and watched the people around him. Happy families, loving couples, excited children, even groups of friends, all there enjoying themselves. Part of him was envious of what these people had. They had each other.

Unlike them, Noah had spent the better part of the last fifteen years alone, by his own choice. After Dare had left, after his father had died, Noah had cut himself off from everyone. He'd immediately applied for the fire academy, and when he was accepted, he hadn't looked back.

All of his time and energy had been focused on his career. Then the roofing opportunity had come along, and he'd found a way to spend nearly every waking moment working. Until now, it had been enough. Or maybe it hadn't and he'd merely been fooling himself.

"What're you doing out here?"

Noah squinted over his shoulder only to find his stepsister standing beside him. She was wearing a bikini and a sarong, her blonde hair pulled into some fancy updo, perfectly styled. She was all dolled up and ready for...

What the hell was she all dolled up for? The wedding wasn't for another few days. Minus the dress, she looked ready to walk down the aisle herself.

He remembered she'd asked a question. "Same thing you are." Sounded good, although he seriously doubted that was the case. Milly probably wasn't running away from a naked man from her past.

"I doubt that," she said, chuckling as she took a seat beside him.

Okay, maybe she could read his mind.

Curious, he glanced her way. "Why are *you* here?"

"Because I'm driving everyone crazy."

"But that's your job," he teased.

"I guess. Coordinating the wedding isn't all that easy."

Noah grinned at Milly, taking a long pull on his beer. "I wasn't talking about that. I was referring to you being Milly."

"Ha ha. Funny." Milly glanced over at him. "So, how was the beach excursion?"

Noah frowned, turning his attention back to the people. "I fucked it up."

"How'd you manage that?"

Dropping his head back, Noah closed his eyes. "I kissed Dare."

"I knew it! I knew he was the one who got away."

Well, that was one way to put it, though that sounded far more romantic than it actually was.

"Spill, big brother. I want to know everything."

"Trust me, you don't." She really didn't, he could assure her of that.

"You loved him, didn't you?"

Although her tone was still curious, he could sense the sympathy there, as well. Perhaps that was how he found himself spilling his guts.

"We dated a long time ago. Fifteen years ago. Dare was just a kid at the time, but things had gotten somewhat serious, I guess."

139

"You're older than him?"

Noah nodded. "By a few years, yeah."

"What do you mean by serious? As in, you loved him?"

He nodded again.

"How long were y'all together?"

"A little over two years."

"So why'd y'all break up?"

I was stupid. He managed to keep that to himself. "Dare was looking for something serious; I wasn't."

"But you said you loved him. What could've possibly been more serious than that?"

Noah turned his head to find Milly watching him, her expression wrought with disbelief.

"He wanted to take things to the next level. Move in together. It wasn't the right time."

"You weren't ready for that?"

"Oh, I was ready," he blurted.

"So what was the holdup?"

"Dare was only nineteen. He was too damn young to settle down with someone."

"I'm confused. I thought you said he wanted to take things to the next level?"

"He did."

"So why would he think he was too young?"

"He didn't." And that was the problem.

Milly cleared her throat. "So *you* thought he was too young? Did you tell him that?"

Oh, yeah. He'd told him, all right. He took a sip from his beer as he nodded.

"Did Dare agree?"

Of course not. "No."

Milly snorted. "I'm usually pretty adept at keeping up with conversations, but I'll admit, I don't have a freaking clue where you're going with this. Let me see if I've got this straight." Milly held up a hand and started ticking things off on her perfectly manicured fingers. "Dare was nineteen. He wanted to move in with you. You loved him, and it sounds like he loved you. But you thought he was too young."

"That's the gist of it."

"How old were you?"

"Twenty-three."

"Oh, well there you go. You were a man of the world by then. I can clearly see why you got to tell him he was too young."

Noah narrowed his eyes at Milly, fully expecting to see the sarcasm dripping off her lips.

Her words made him defensive. "You know Dare. He's not the epitome of maturity, even now."

Milly's golden eyebrows angled down. "Not sure I follow. I *do* know Dare. Maybe not as well as you did back then, but the guy I know is pretty damned mature."

Was she serious? Were they talking about the same person? Noah shook his head, disagreeing with her. "He's always making jokes and never takes anything seriously."

Milly nodded briefly, seemingly understanding his point of view, and Noah let out a sigh of relief, grateful that she understood.

That was until she opened her mouth.

"Looks to me like you mistook his fun-loving side for immaturity, because the guy I know runs a marina with three of his closest friends. He goes to work every single day, takes care of business. No matter what. He's got a grandmother he financially supports, not to mention visits at least twice a week, every week. And don't get me started on Lulu."

"Who's Lulu?"

Fearless

"The marina dog," she explained. "Dare refuses to leave Lulu at the marina overnight by herself, although Cam and Roan both live in apartments above the place, so he takes her home and pays a ridiculous amount to his landlord just to keep her there overnight. Sure, he's fun to be around, and he always keeps everyone laughing, but I damn sure don't find fault in that."

Okay, not how he'd pictured this playing out at all. For once, he had hoped someone would be on his side. Then again, after all that, *he* wasn't even on his side.

After sucking down more of his beer, Noah dropped his head back and stared up at the blue awning. "I fucked up, Mill. I fucked up then and I fucked up now."

"How did it end?" she asked, her tone softer than moments before.

He knew she wasn't talking about today. "He left in the middle of the night. Packed what few things he'd had at my place, and I never saw him again."

"You didn't go after him?"

Noah shook his head. He'd wanted to, but he never had. In his defense, he had a damn good reason for that.

"Well, you're an idiot."

His head snapped around, his gaze slamming into Milly's. He was just about to tell her exactly what he thought when she held up her hand and smiled.

"And he's an idiot. And anyone who looks at the two of you would be an idiot if they didn't see just how much you still love each other."

It was his turn to snort. "It's been fifteen years, Mill. I'm thinking love's no longer the problem."

"No?" Milly leaned forward. "So you're telling me you don't love him?"

"I didn't say that, but I'm not admitting it, either." He ran his hand through his hair. "Fuck. I came face-to-face with him less than twenty-four hours ago, after fifteen fucking years. I'm not sure I understand how I'm even having this conversation."

"Sometimes time doesn't matter. When you really, truly love someone, I don't think that ever dies. No matter how much time you spend apart."

Noah shook his head, not wanting to agree.

But still, he couldn't deny it, either, because, unfortunately, Milly had nailed it.

Fourteen

BEFORE GETTING DRESSED and resigning himself to finding something to eat, Dare had spent the last couple of hours alone, lying on his bed in his cabin, staring at the ceiling, and trying to figure out how things had gone so wrong so quickly. One minute he and Noah were making a pact that they would survive the trip without jumping one another, and the next minute Noah was kissing him.

Worst part, Dare wanted Noah to kiss him again.

And again. And…

Damn it. It was all he could fucking think about.

Except hooking up wouldn't be good for either of them, because once they left this ship, it wasn't like Dare would see Noah again. They'd built lives for themselves, and although Dare didn't know much about Noah, other than he'd become a firefighter, he had to assume that Noah had a full life—one that didn't include Dare in it. And based on the way Noah had dodged his question earlier, Noah had no intention of allowing Dare to be part of it, either.

Not that he wanted to be.

Damn, and there he went lying again.

When his stomach growled for the twentieth time, he managed to push himself up off the bed, pull a pair of shorts and a T-shirt out of his suitcase, and get dressed. Rather than mess with his hair, he grabbed his Dallas Cowboys ball cap and pulled it on before slipping his feet into his flip-flops.

He made his way down to the main level, intending to find food. As he walked toward the food court, he stumbled upon Noah, who seemed to be doing the same thing, searching for dinner. He was about to pretend he hadn't noticed the man when Noah glanced over, their eyes locking. Before he could hightail it out of there, Noah headed his way.

The awkward tension that had been absent for much of the day when they'd been at the beach had returned in full force. Dare had a hard time looking Noah in the eye, much less finding something to say that would make this day better.

"I'm sorry."

Confused, Dare focused on Noah's face. "For what?"

"For kissing you."

Dare shrugged as though it didn't matter. "Happens all the time."

Noah laughed and a little of the tension eased from Dare's shoulders.

"Does it?"

Dare nodded. "Yep. Hot guys find me irresistible. They're always kissing me."

"Good to know." Noah's smile brightened. "That you find me hot."

Of course he would fixate on that part.

Dare didn't respond.

Noah glanced over his shoulder at the food court. "You hungry?"

His stomach growled loudly, answering for him.

Noah's lips curled up. "Want to have dinner with me? I promise not to trip and let my lips fall into yours."

Dare cocked his head to the side, pretending to be considering this. "And what about the naked shower thing? How do you propose we keep that from happening again?" Part of him wished it would happen again.

"I'll work on that and get back to you."

"Fine. Then I'll have dinner with you. Maybe we can come up with a plan." Dare didn't add *one way or the other*, which was what he was thinking.

They grabbed burgers and fries, then found a seat at an empty table for two.

"I see you still take in food like you did years ago." Noah tilted his head at Dare, nodding toward the now nearly empty tray.

"I'm a growing boy." It was a damn good thing he had a fast metabolism. "I stay pretty active at work."

"What is it that you do at the marina?" Noah sounded genuinely curious.

"We take clients out on boats if they need a guide for the day. I do some teaching of how to drive the Jet Skis. I've also been designated as the one to help out when kids want to learn how to ride them. Seems I've got a knack for it or something." Or so Cam and Roan always told him. Dare believed it was due to the fact that the two of them were scared of the shorter humans, but whatever. He enjoyed it.

"Sounds like fun."

Dare looked at Noah, trying to see if he was making fun of him. He saw only admiration staring back at him, which made him feel good. "I love it. Never thought I'd have a job spending my day on the water, having fun. I wouldn't trade it."

"Can't say I blame you."

"What about you? The firefighter thing... It as interesting as it is on television?"

Noah grinned after wiping his mouth with a napkin. "It can be. Then again, on TV, they condense the most exciting events down to one hour a week. Not nearly as eventful in a twenty-four-hour period, but it has its moments."

"When do you work?" Dare grabbed his drink and downed the rest of it.

"Twenty-four on, forty-eight off." Noah pushed his tray away, signaling he was finished. "I've also got a roofing business that keeps me busy in the meantime. But I don't let that get in the way of the station."

"Roofing?" Noah didn't look like a man who did a lot of manual labor, but maybe that explained the incredible physique.

Placing his elbows on the table, Noah picked up his drink. "At first, it was a way to supplement my income. When that was no longer necessary, I kept it up as a way to fill my time."

Dare continued to watch Noah. That was interesting information. Sounded as though Noah had his hands full. Glancing around, he realized the place was still busy. "You wanna head outside? Maybe get a beer or something?"

Noah grabbed his tray and stood. "I'd like that, but I'm thinking less beer, more margaritas."

"You had me at margaritas."

Dare didn't want to get his hopes up, but he saw the night taking a much better turn than the day had. Provided he could continue to remind himself that Noah was off-limits, he figured they'd do just fine.

Then again, Dare never had been one to read the warning signs, much less heed them. If the sign said don't feed the bears, Dare was the first one looking for steak.

Fearless

NOAH WASN'T SURE how he'd managed to salvage the day after all the shit that had happened, but he wasn't complaining. In fact, he was now sitting on a lounge chair beneath the stars, drinking a margarita, and enjoying the time with Dare only a foot or so away from him.

It'd been pure luck that he'd run into Dare when searching for food. As it was, Noah had been thinking about going up to the cabin to invite Dare to dinner. Anything to try and salvage what few gains they'd made before Noah had gone and fucked it up.

Looked as though the planets were aligned in his favor.

He could only hope they remained that way for the rest of the trip, because heaven knew he'd fuck shit up faster than anything if given the opportunity. And he damn sure didn't want to fuck things up with Dare. Not again, anyway.

"You ever been on a cruise before?" Dare asked.

"First time. You?"

"Not like this. I took a cruise about five years ago on a much smaller ship. Not nearly the amenities."

"Who'd you go with?" Noah wasn't sure he wanted to know, but he had to ask.

"Cam and Roan. We spend so much time on the water, and none of us had done it, so we figured what the hell. We had a good time."

Noah hoped that this trip surpassed that one in terms of fun had by all. He didn't know why he wanted to make memories with Dare again; he just did.

Ever since he'd had the conversation with Milly, he'd thought about how he had acted toward Dare since his arrival on the ship. They did have history. A very emotional time for both of them, and though they'd gotten this far without the other, he wasn't sure he wanted to keep moving forward without Dare in his life. Even if they could only be friends.

To test his friendship theory, Noah figured he'd go for a personal question. "Tell me about the last date you went on."

Dare rolled his head to the side, pinning Noah with a questioning gaze.

"Oh, come on," he urged. "Two friends, drinking margaritas, talking about the good times, right?"

Dare turned back away, sipped his margarita, then sighed. For a brief second, Noah didn't think he was going to answer.

"It's been a while. And I'm not sure it qualified as a good time."

"How long's a while?" Noah kept his attention on Dare.

"Eight months."

Holy shit. Noah wasn't quite as nervous as he had been.

"You take him out? Or he take you out?"

"He asked me." Dare made eye contact again. "For the record, it might sound strange, but I haven't really dated in years. I've had a few one-night stands here and there, but even those are few and far between."

Noah had a million questions he wanted to ask—the foremost being *how few* and *how far between?*—but he banked them for later. He settled with keeping on the original topic. "Where'd y'all go?"

"He took me to dinner." Dare looked away again. "Actually, I met him at the restaurant because I didn't want him to know where I lived. Privacy and all that. I met him when I went to a bar with Teague one night." Dare took another sip of his drink. "Of all the places the guy could've picked, he wanted to go to Denny's."

Noah frowned, trying to process what Dare had just told him. Then he couldn't help it, he cracked up laughing, nearly spilling his drink all over himself as he folded over. "Denny's? Really? When is that appropriate for a first date?"

"When is it appropriate for *any* date?"

"Okay, true." Noah tried to calm down. "Did he say *why* he chose Denny's?"

Dare chuckled before he responded. "Apparently he had an affinity for their omelets. Needless to say, we didn't go out again." Dare met his gaze. "What about you? Tell me about your last date."

"I guess it wasn't really a date. I met an ex-boyfriend at a bar for drinks."

"When was this?"

Noah liked the fact that Dare was fishing for details. "Six months ago."

"That's the last date you went on?"

"It is." Noah drained the rest of his drink. "Let's just say I don't have a good track record in the dating department."

"I feel your pain." Dare stared up at the sky while Noah watched him. "Dating leads to relationships, and I don't do relationships."

"At all?" Noah wondered when the last time was that Dare had had a serious, long-term boyfriend.

"At all."

"When was the last?"

Dare sighed again, then turned his head and held Noah's stare. "You."

God, please forgive him, but although that news was sad, it also made Noah want to fist-bump the air. He settled for responding instead. "Don't feel bad. My last relationship was five years ago. It lasted two months. That's the only other real relationship I've had since … you."

"Boy, we're just a couple of real winners, aren't we?"

"I'll drink to that."

Dare grinned, holding up his empty glass. "Well, you're gonna have to go get us more drinks if that's the case. But nice of you to offer."

Noah laughed, thankful they'd made it through that conversation relatively easily. And for that, he didn't have a problem getting more drinks.

Fifteen

Tuesday, May 31ˢᵗ
Cruise, day three

THE FOLLOWING MORNING, when the sun came shining through the window into their cabin, Dare covered his head with a pillow and groaned. He heard Noah roll over, and he peeked out to see him doing the same.

"Remind me never to let you talk me into Fireball shots again. Seriously."

Noah's words were muffled by his pillow when he said, "I don't think that was my idea."

"Sure it was." It really wasn't. Dare had brought it up, but he enjoyed pointing fingers at Noah. Made things more interesting.

"Good thing my stomach's lined with lead."

"What about your brain?" Dare had a pounding headache right behind his eyes, and he needed water.

"I could use some aspirin."

"Who's going to get it?" Dare was hoping Noah would offer.

"In my case in the bathroom."

Well, that made things a hell of a lot easier. "What about water?"

"Sorry, didn't pack that with me." Noah chuckled.

"What about food?"

"You're always hungry, aren't you?"

Dare lifted from the pillow and glanced over at Noah. "Always."

"Good to know."

Neither of them moved, and they must've fallen back asleep because the next time Dare awoke, Noah was in the shower. He recalled the last time Noah had emerged from the shower when he'd been jacking off. Figured he probably shouldn't get himself in that predicament again. Considering his dick was only half-interested in waking up for the day, it wasn't that big of a deal.

"You're awake."

Dare glanced over at the bathroom door to see Noah emerging. His hair was wet, and he was wearing what appeared to be swim shorts. Not that Dare noticed the shorts all that much when there was so much naked torso going on. He hoped he wasn't drooling. "Maybe."

"Thought I'd run down and grab some food. Bring it back up."

"You should probably know, I'm a whore for food." Realizing what he was saying as the words were coming out of his mouth, Dare flopped back on the bed and sighed. "Didn't mean it like that."

Noah chuckled. "Take a shower while I'm gone. You'll feel better. There are no stops today, so I figured we'd check out some of the things to do on this thing."

Dare liked the fact that Noah was including him in his plans. He wasn't sure what to think about it yet, but he couldn't deny that he looked forward to spending the day with Noah.

Or he would, once his fucking head stopped pounding.

"I'll be back in a minute."

Dare nodded, watching as Noah headed for the door.

When the door shut behind Noah, he managed to force his lazy ass out of the bed and stumbled to the bathroom. Maybe a shower would make him feel more human. If not, he could always take another nap.

Except he didn't want to take a nap. He wanted to wash the hangover away, then move on to the important stuff. Like getting out of this cabin and enjoying some time on the ship. Up to this point, the trip had been touch and go. Since last night when he'd had dinner with Noah, Dare had decided he would let things work themselves out. He had absolutely no expectations.

Turning on the water, he shed his boxers and stood beneath the spray. It wasn't warm, but it wasn't cold, so he gave it a second. While he stood there, eyes closed, he thought about Noah. They'd shared some laughs last night, and it had felt like old times. Not once had he thought back to what had happened between them, and it had helped him to relax. The margaritas hadn't hurt, either. Nor had the Fireball shots.

Then again, the alcohol had dulled a lot of his senses, including how he felt about Noah.

The truth was, Dare still had feelings for the man. Those feelings were causing problems because he couldn't seem to get past them. It didn't help that he and Noah got along so well. They'd always had an easiness between them that Dare didn't feel around most people.

Reaching for the shampoo, Dare washed his hair, then grabbed the bar of soap. The heat from the water was doing wonders for his headache, so he took his time lathering up. The next thing he knew, he was stroking his dick, imagining Noah in the shower with him. Had Noah done that a few minutes ago? Had Noah jacked off to thoughts of him?

He hoped he had. He wasn't sure why, he just did.

His dick swelled in his hand as he jerked himself harder, faster. There was no way he'd make it through the day unless he took care of business now. The mere sight of Noah without a shirt had sent his hormones rioting. Without some form of release, Dare knew he couldn't be held responsible for his actions. Not where Noah was concerned.

He leaned back against the wall, spreading his legs wide. Reaching down with his other hand, he fondled his balls while continuing to jack his dick roughly. With his eyes closed, he could almost imagine Noah stroking him. As his release barreled down on him, Dare held his breath and let the climax rip through him while he gave in to his imagination, picturing Noah right there with him, mouth open while Dare came on his tongue.

"Fuck." His dick jerked again.

He knew he couldn't give in and be with Noah, but he was beginning to think it was inevitable.

And he wasn't sure how he felt about that yet.

Or, more importantly, how he was going to avoid it.

BEFORE HEADING DOWN to the main floor, Noah stopped at Milly's cabin to check on her. He hadn't seen her since yesterday when they'd had their chat by the pool. Since his cell phone didn't work on the ship, he had tucked it into his suitcase, not bothering to check it. Considering he'd promised to keep an eye on her, he figured he should at least attempt to do so.

Fearless

Noah knocked on her door, but no one answered. It was only nine, and though he'd never known Milly to be a morning person, he figured she could've been downstairs already. As he turned to go, he heard the sound of the lock disengage, and he pivoted back around to see Milly peeking out through a small crack in the door. She definitely hadn't been awake.

He took in what little of her he could see. Her fancy hair from yesterday was long gone. She had definite bedhead as well as dark rings from her mascara around her eyes.

"Good morning," he greeted, smiling.

Milly's smile widened. "I hope you're here to bring me breakfast."

"I can. I was just going down to get something for Dare." Hmm. That sounded far more intimate than he'd meant it to.

Apparently his stepsister agreed. Her eyebrows lifted and she pulled the door open a little more. She appeared to be hugging a sheet against her chest. It was almost as though she was hiding something in her cabin.

Wait…

Noah leaned forward and lowered his voice. "Is someone in there with you?"

He could see the smile reach her eyes. "Maybe."

"Do I even want to know?"

"Probably not."

"Do you want me to bring you breakfast? For two?"

Milly glanced over her shoulder, then back at him. "No, I think we're good. Thanks, though."

"I would say be good, but I think that's no longer an option."

Milly chuckled. "I'd have to agree with you." She paused, her eyes twinkling with mischief. "Oh, and for the record, I no longer need to see Cam's pierced penis. I now have a firsthand experience under my belt."

Good Lord. He could've gone his whole life without knowing that.

Shaking his head, Noah left her to get back to whatever it was she'd been doing. Or rather, whoever it was she'd been doing. And she was right, he really didn't want to know.

Twenty minutes later, Noah returned to the cabin to find Dare semi-dressed and sprawled out on the bed on his stomach looking at the book that detailed all the amenities aboard the ship.

"Did you know we can get our teeth whitened, our faces injected with poison, *and* a haircut, without ever leaving the ship?"

No, he had not known that. Not sure he'd needed to, either. While Dare flipped the page in the book, Noah set the bag of food down beside him. Without getting up, Dare managed to retrieve one of the sausage biscuits from inside and unwrapped it, still staring at the book on the bed.

"Or we could learn how to fold napkins, take dance classes, and even learn a language." Dare looked up. "Who comes up with this shit?"

Noah shrugged. "I've always dreamed about folding napkins."

Dare narrowed his eyes, his mouth full of biscuit. "Really?"

Laughing, he shook his head. "I was thinking we could do the zip line and the surf simulator. But, you know, if the napkin folding has always been *your* dream…"

Dare stuffed the rest of his sandwich in his mouth and sat up. He chewed quickly, then uncapped the bottle of water Noah had brought for him and drank half.

Noah's gaze traveled the length of Dare's long neck, watching as he swallowed. Somehow Dare even made drinking water sexy.

"Nah. I'm good with those." Dare glanced back at the book, turned the page. "However, a massage doesn't sound all that bad."

It really didn't.

"We've still got a few more days on the ship." Noah wasn't sure when he'd started thinking of this as their vacation, but he did. He found himself planning out things they could do already, and he knew he had to rein it in.

"True." Dare got to his feet and grabbed a T-shirt. "But simulated surfing and zip-lining it is." Dare pulled his shirt over his head, cutting off the delicious view Noah had had. Dare met his gaze. "Wanna make this interesting?"

Noah's dick twitched at the idea. It was a good thing he'd spent ten minutes with his hand already that morning or he might've been in a world of hurt. "What did you have in mind?"

Dare shrugged, then grabbed the water bottle as he pushed his feet into his flip-flops. "Not sure yet. Let me think on that."

Noah had a few things in mind, but he decided against sharing them. No sense in getting himself in more trouble than he already was.

BEFORE HUDSON HAD opened his eyes this morning, he'd known something had happened last night. Something that would change the course of this trip. Something that could ultimately affect him for days, even months to come.

He'd woken up alone.

Granted, that wasn't the problem. He'd woken up alone every day for the past couple of years without issue. He chose not to have overnight guests because he didn't particularly care to put himself in that position. But it wasn't the lack of a man in *his* bed that was the issue.

It was the lack of a man in the *other* bed.

The problem was the fact that AJ was supposed to be in the same cabin as him, yet he hadn't slept in the other bed last night, and that could only mean...

Hudson didn't know what it meant, but he had a pretty damn good idea.

Since AJ was a big boy and he could take care of himself, Hudson wasn't worried about him. However, he was worried about the messes that AJ seemed to get himself into. Since he'd had his eye on Milly from the moment he'd seen her, Hudson had to assume that he'd spent the night with her. Last night, when they'd all been at the adult pool, he had personally witnessed AJ and Milly getting a little cozy. It only made sense that they would've spent more time together, which had probably led to...

Nope. Not interested in thinking about that.

Unfortunately, there was nothing he could do about it, either. He didn't have cell service out here on the ocean because he hadn't seen the need to pay for Wi-Fi on the ship, so he couldn't text AJ without costing himself a fortune. Since the predicament wasn't that big of a deal—although it was a big fucking deal—he decided to let it go.

Fearless

After taking a shower, he made his way down to the restaurant for breakfast. Rather than sit at a table by himself, he opted to get his food to go, then took it out onto the deck to get a little sun.

That was the second mistake of the day, the first having been waking up.

While he sat off the beaten path, he caught sight of Teague talking to two attractive guys who looked to be roughly Teague's age. Teague was intimately close to both of them, sharing a lounge chair, and they were laughing at whatever Teague was talking about.

Hudson remembered the off-handed remarks Teague had made in the past. The ones that referenced his desires to be with more than one man at the same time because one would never be enough for him. Every time Hudson heard that, he wanted to pin Teague to the wall and show him just how damn good the *right* man could be. Fuck that three-way bullshit.

For some strange reason, seeing Teague get all cozy with the two guys pissed Hudson off. Or maybe it didn't. Perhaps that was jealousy rearing its ugly head.

Either way, his appetite dissolved entirely, and rather than torture himself unnecessarily, he got to his feet, tossed his food in the trash, and decided to go burn off some energy at the gym.

He had to briefly wonder if he was the only one who wished this trip was over.

Sixteen

"YOU KINDA SUCK at that." Dare laughed when Noah emerged from the surf simulator. He'd lasted all of two seconds before he'd wiped out. It had been beautiful.

And fucking hilarious.

"Yeah, thanks." Noah was still spurting water.

"No problem. Wanna go again?"

"I'm not out of the game yet. That was a practice run." Noah stood up straight, a challenge in his eyes. "Did you still want to make a wager?"

Based on Noah's first performance, Dare knew he'd win, so whatever he came up with needed to be in his favor.

However, he wasn't sure what to wager. His mind, of course, went to sex. Namely blow jobs in the hallway, but he knew that wasn't an option. He needed to keep his distance from Noah, although the man was making it damned difficult. He liked the idea of establishing a friendship with Noah, and that meant sex was off the table.

"Loser buys lunch."

Noah laughed. "Lunch is free on the ship."

Right. "Loser buys drinks."

"Drinks are billed to the room." Noah narrowed his gaze, then grinned. "We *share* a room. A room that's billed to Gannon, at that."

"True." But that was beside the point. "Are you worried you'll lose?"

Noah cocked his head to the side. "Come on, pretty boy. Let's get this over with."

"Why does everyone insist on calling me pretty? I'm not pretty. Not by a long shot." Dare continued walking with Noah as they worked their way back to the line of people waiting to jump into the giant wave machine. "I'm handsome. Gorgeous, even. Not. Fucking. Pretty."

Noah snorted.

A couple of girls in front of them turned back and smiled, giggling as they did.

"Do you think so?" he asked them. "He called me pretty. Am I pretty?"

Noah placed his hand on Dare's arm, the heat immediately sinking into his skin and making his dick twitch in his shorts.

"Maybe a little," the blonde chick said.

The brunette beside her nodded.

"Whatever. Sexy, yes. Definitely not pretty." He pretended to grumble as he looked to his left to see Noah staring back at him, laughing. "Quit that shit. I'm not pretty."

"Not when you get all sassy, no."

"*Sassy?*" Dare turned to face Noah completely, causing Noah's hand to fall from his arm. "You did *not* call me sassy."

"I kinda did."

Dare heard the women giggling, but he didn't look away from Noah. Instead, he leaned forward and pressed his lips close to Noah's ear. "I'll show you sassy."

When he pulled back, Dare saw the girls still staring at them. He wasn't sure what they were looking at or why their eyes were so bright.

The brunette answered that question when she opened her mouth. "Why is it that the hot ones are always gay?"

"I know, right?" The blonde frowned.

Dare smiled, his attention still rooted on Noah. "See, she called me hot. Not pretty."

"How do you know she wasn't talking about me?" Noah countered.

"Because you're…"

Noah's eyebrows lifted. "I'm what?"

"Okay, fine. You're hot. Whatever."

Dare turned back to the line and moved forward when the girls did. For the next few minutes, they waited there patiently, watching as person after person wiped out in the water, a few hanging for quite some time beforehand. When it was finally Dare's turn again, he decided to up the ante. Before he took the board from the attendant, he glanced back at Noah.

Keeping his voice low so that the kids in line couldn't hear him, Dare kept his eyes locked with Noah's as he said, "Let's make a day of it. Loser gives the winner a blow job."

With that, he spun back around, ready to take his turn.

HOLY FUCK.

Did he have water in his ears?

Noah absently put a finger in to see if his ear was clogged. Nope.

Fearless

He stood motionless, his brain processing what Dare had said before he'd walked away. *Loser gives the winner a blow job.*

Great.

Now how the fuck was he going to get out of this one?

Not that he really wanted to. The mere thought of Dare Davis and a blow job—giver or receiver, it didn't much matter—was enough to make his dick stand up and take notice. He immediately thought about algebra equations. This was not the place for his dick to decide to get excited. There were kids around, for fuck's sake.

He turned his attention to Dare and frowned.

The question he wanted to ask himself was, did he want to win or lose? As far as he was concerned, this was a win-win situation. For him, anyway.

Except it wasn't. They weren't supposed to be flirting, let alone offering blow jobs. But he'd heard Dare loud and clear.

Trying to keep his mind out of the gutter, Noah focused on watching Dare, who was now in the water, easily maneuvering that board. He wasn't the only one who was impressed by Dare's skill. As he looked around, he noticed a lot of eyes were on Dare.

The guy didn't have a problem getting to his feet, when most people had a hard time holding on to the damn thing, much less moving on it. Since this was their second time, he figured Dare had probably gotten the hang of it. Then again, he'd seemed to have mastered it the last time, which was telling.

Noah, on the other hand, was about as uncoordinated in the water as they came. Unless it was coming out of a fire hose, he didn't spend much time around water. He might've been water-skiing once in his life. Maybe twice. He was good at a lot of things, but surfing … not so much.

Still, he wanted to win this bet for no other reason than the fact that he would have a say in what happened between them. He'd learned his lesson yesterday when he'd kissed Dare.

From that moment on, Noah hadn't been able to stop thinking about the man. It was obvious that Dare was simply being the carefree, fun-loving guy he was known to be. Only this was a bet that could drastically change things between them. Noah had to wonder if Dare realized that or if he'd simply spouted the first thing that came to mind.

Who knew when it came to Dare.

What Noah did know was that he was enjoying the easy friendship they were establishing. He liked hanging out and letting loose for a little while. He didn't take the opportunity much, because he'd decided long ago that work was more important. He hung out with a couple of the firefighters from time to time, but he didn't have any close friends. Not like Dare did.

Noah smiled. For a few days, he could be carefree and enjoy this time with these people. That was the reason they were there. And right now, nothing was important except spending a few relaxing hours outside under the sun with the guy who made him smile.

Speaking of smile…

Noah cracked up laughing when Dare stepped wrong and ended up being shot backward by the water. The crowd applauded while Noah tried to contain himself. There was no way he was going to win this, but he knew he had to put forth the effort.

If he was going to go down in flames, he was going to enjoy the fuck out of it.

Seventeen

BY THE TIME the sun was down and night had fallen, Dare wasn't sure who the real winner from the day was. In fact, it very well could've been a tie.

Sixty-nine, anyone?

Sure, he'd slaughtered Noah when it came to anything in the water, although the best part had been when the pressure from the water had damn near taken Noah's shorts right off with all eyes on him. Dare had to admit, the guy had been pretty damn quick when it came to keeping his unmentionables unmentioned. They'd all gotten a quick shot of a full moon, but nothing more.

So in order to make it fair, they had ventured on to other things. Like ice skating. For the record, that shit was not cool. Dare wasn't a fan of gliding around on the ice and trying not to land on his ass. He'd failed miserably. Several times. On the other hand, Noah had looked like a freaking hockey player out there with all his fancy moves.

But Dare had survived.

They'd done the zip line, but there really wasn't anything competitive about that. They'd learned that they both enjoyed it, neither of them affected by heights. When they'd been there, they had stumbled upon Cam and Gannon. Gannon had nixed the idea, but Cam had given it a go.

It'd been the same with miniature golf. If anything, Noah might've beaten him by a couple of strokes *(ha ha … strokes)*, but that was all. They would have to tally it up to figure out who'd won. Dare really wasn't sure.

Now that they had showered (separately, thank you very much) and had dinner, they were heading out to the deck where a movie was playing on a giant screen.

Definitely not a bad way to spend a Tuesday.

Granted, Dare was pretty sure they were both avoiding the giant elephant on the ship. The one that started with *blow* and ended with *job*. The stupid wager Dare had made on a whim. Neither of them had talked about it all day, but it had lingered in the back of Dare's mind for hours. Hell, he was still thinking about it.

As he drank a beer and relaxed in the chair sitting next to Noah, he tried *not* to think about it. When his arm brushed Noah's, the electrical current that ignited reminded him of it. Then again, every time his lips touched the rim of his beer bottle, he was reminded of it. Also when the wind blew.

Yep, he had a one-track mind, all right.

He cast a sideways glance at Noah and wondered if he was also thinking about it.

Not that he was going to ask.

Dare was half-tempted to pretend it'd never happened. His dick wasn't on board with that idea, but it seemed the lesser of two evils. What if they did give in to this unruly attraction? What kind of damage would it do? If any?

He knew he didn't have a problem with a casual sexual encounter. He'd had plenty over the years. Not once had he allowed it to affect him emotionally. That was what he'd learned to do. Keep a distance. Make it easy and fun. Nothing more.

Surely he was capable of keeping that up with Noah.

He glanced at Noah again.

Or maybe not.

NOAH HAD DECIDED halfway through the day to pretend that Dare hadn't wagered a blow job. He'd also decided to pretend he hadn't almost lost his shorts during his second attempt on the wave machine.

Okay, he'd *tried* to pretend. On both counts.

Surprisingly, pretending the second hadn't happened was a hell of a lot easier than the first.

Didn't mean he hadn't busted his ass in an attempt to beat the man, but still. It had been a silly, spur-of-the-moment suggestion that was better left several hours behind them. Except he was having a damn hard time not thinking about it.

Every time he did, he peered over at Dare only to find Dare staring at the screen. Clearly he wasn't having a hard time battling the urge.

"What is this shit?" Dare whispered, pointing toward the screen with his beer bottle.

Okay, maybe he was.

Noah shrugged. "No idea. Thought maybe you knew."

"Nope. Completely lost."

"You wanna keep watching it?" Noah didn't care what they did as long as they didn't go back to their cabin. He would prefer to spend the rest of the night walking around the ship than going back to the cabin, where temptation would turn into a tangible thing.

"I'm good." Dare sighed. "Good to chill for a while."

Dare's arm brushed against Noah's again, and he was tempted to hold Dare's hand. When was the last time he'd held someone's hand? Years, for sure.

Lifting his beer to his lips, Noah managed to refrain. Until the next time that it happened. He wasn't sure what spurred him to do it, but he was close enough that he could simply rest his hand over Dare's. When he felt Dare's eyes on him, he cast a sideways glance, waiting for Dare to pull away.

He didn't.

In fact, Dare flipped his hand over and linked their fingers. The churn of excitement filled his chest. He felt like a teenage boy experiencing this for the very first time. The emotion bubbled up inside him, but he managed to hold it in, forcing his attention on the screen. He wouldn't have been able to say what the movie was even about, because the only thing he could focus on was their clasped hands.

In a weird way, this was so much better than a blow job.

Okay, in an entirely different way, but it was.

Dare leaned over. "This isn't weird, is it?" There was a hint of wonder in Dare's tone, as though he couldn't believe it.

"No. It's not." It was comforting, actually.

"So who taught you to ice-skate?" Dare asked.

"No one." Noah had never been taught; he simply had a pretty good sense of balance.

"Do you like hockey?"

Noah shifted his attention from the movie to Dare, twisting slightly in his chair to see him better. "Yeah. Why?"

Dare shrugged. "That's what you reminded me of. A hockey player."

"What about you? You like hockey?"

"Love it. Gannon happens to be friends with the guy who owns the Austin Arrows. Got us season tickets last year."

Fearless

"No shit?" Noah didn't bother to mention that the Austin Arrows had had their shittiest year since the inception of the team. Probably no need to point that out.

"Maybe when the season starts again, we can go to a game."

Noah nodded. He would like that. A lot.

And in the meantime, he wanted to spend the rest of the night right here.

Beside Dare.

Not moving.

MILLY SAT BESIDE AJ while they watched a movie outside under the stars. About fifteen feet in front of her, she noticed Dare and Noah were doing the same. At first she was surprised to see them there, had even been tempted to go join them, but she'd decided against it when she'd seen Noah take Dare's hand.

Although she had stuck her nose where it didn't belong when it came to Gannon and Cam, Milly knew she couldn't do the same with these two. Then again, based on how cozy they were, she probably didn't need to. Her talk with Noah yesterday had been enlightening—probably for him as much as for her. No doubt in her mind, the man had feelings for Dare.

For a brief moment, she wondered what that felt like. To be reunited with someone from your past, someone who'd left such a huge mark on your life…

She dared a glance at AJ and smiled to herself.

Last night, they'd had a few too many drinks and things had happened. This morning, when she'd awoken to find him still in her bed, she'd been a little surprised. But it had been a good surprise.

Granted, she absolutely did not see this going anywhere at all, despite how much she had enjoyed his pierced penis. But it hadn't all been about mind-blowing orgasms. They'd had plenty to talk about, because oddly they had a lot in common, but Milly continued to keep her heart guarded. She knew there was no long term where AJ was concerned. He was a good guy, a gentleman. He had a full-time job, a house, and from their conversations, he had aspirations.

Those were qualities that men who were looking for long term with her tended to lack, and she'd learned to deal with that over the years. In essence, AJ was too much of a grown-up for her, and there was no reason she was going to get her hopes up.

So, she'd passively suggested they enjoy their time together while they were on the ship, making light of any kind of future. For a brief instant, she'd thought she'd seen a little regret in AJ's eyes, but she didn't know him well enough to be sure.

Not that it mattered. Her focus wasn't on herself and she didn't plan for it to be. They had two more days before Gannon and Cam tied the knot, and truth be told, she simply wanted to get to that day. She wanted to watch her best friend marry the love of his life. It made her heart swell to think of the love those two men shared for one another.

She peeked over at AJ once more.

Maybe one day she would be lucky enough to find that.

But she definitely wasn't holding her breath.

Eighteen

Wednesday, June 1ˢᵗ
Cruise, day four

DARE WASN'T SURE which way was up.

Not literally, of course. He could see the ceiling from where he lay on the twin bed, so it was rather obvious. However, the overabundance of emotions churning through him was throwing him off his game.

They were on day four of the trip, the boat currently docked in St. Thomas. Dare had already spent a few hours at the beach with Noah before returning to the ship, only at that point, things had gone a little sideways. Once on board, he and Noah had gone their separate ways. And now Dare was alone, passing the time before he had to be at the rehearsal dinner. While he wondered if Noah would make an appearance, he continued to reflect on all that had happened.

Technically, nothing had happened yet. Not between him and Noah.

Well, nothing more than the smoking-hot kiss they'd shared on the beach a couple of days ago and the few minutes they'd spent naked in the shower together. The latter was far more innocent than even his memories wanted to portray.

And last night…

Perhaps that was the strangest of all. They'd spent a couple of hours on the deck, holding hands and watching some crappy movie before returning to the cabin. As though nothing had happened between them, they had crawled into separate beds and fallen asleep almost immediately. Granted, Dare had then dreamed about sucking a certain hot firefighter's dick, but it hadn't come to fruition.

He was beginning to think that it wouldn't, which confused him.

No doubt in his mind that the blow job wager was what had thrown things off course, though. Ever since last night, Dare had felt the tension increase between them. Something was going on, something more than he had anticipated, but it was clear neither of them knew how to address the situation.

Part of him had expected Noah to be a little more receptive, possibly a little more aggressive even.

But no.

It was as though the bet had never taken place. Then again, that was probably a good thing, considering.

Not that he should be thinking of any of that. He should've been getting ready for the rehearsal dinner so that he could spend the next couple of hours with his buddies, gearing up for tomorrow. D-day. Yep, Cam and Gannon would be tying the knot, and here Dare was thinking about all the things he wanted to do to Noah. Clearly he'd lost sight of his priorities somewhere along the way.

Probably had started the first time Noah had taken his shirt off.

Or maybe even the first time he'd laid eyes on Milly's stepbrother at the beginning of the trip. Ever since then, he'd been unhinged.

Fearless

Dare sat up on the bed and tried to relax his shoulders. He needed to get his head on straight. As it was, Noah had been avoiding him for most of the day, claiming he needed to spend some time with Milly, to help with the wedding, or so he had said. Since Roan was helping her with everything she needed help with, he knew it was a way for Noah to put some distance between them.

Again, probably not a bad thing.

Pushing off the bed, he opted to take a shower and get ready. There were still a couple of hours before the dinner, but he couldn't sit in the cabin any longer. Since he hadn't seen Noah in a couple of hours, Dare figured he'd be back at some point to get ready, and for some reason, he didn't want to be there when that time came.

Two hours later, Dare managed to make his way to the banquet room where the rehearsal dinner was being held. After showering and getting dressed in a pair of jeans and a navy-blue polo, he'd reluctantly resigned himself to not seeing Noah before dinner, so he'd gone down to the main deck and had a beer, sitting alone at one of the bars and watching people enjoying themselves.

He had run into Hudson at one point, and they'd talked about what the night would entail. Since Dare had never actually been to a wedding, he'd mistakenly thought they were going to do a walk through—hence the word *rehearsal*—but felt immensely better when Hudson had informed him (after silently laughing his ass off) that wasn't the case. According to the man, Milly had everything under control, and she'd taken to working directly with the wedding coordinator, so tonight would only consist of a few reminders of where they needed to be tomorrow night and when.

Everything—at least in theory—seemed to be right on track.

Everything except for the fact that Noah Pearson was avoiding him, and Dare didn't understand why.

Did the guy think Dare was going to attack his dick with his mouth?

Okay, maybe he'd thought about it once.

Twice.

Whatever.

FROM THE MOMENT Noah had walked into their cabin last night until the second he'd managed to escape this morning, he had thought of nothing more than helping Dare out of his clothes and devouring him.

He hadn't, though.

He had spent a terribly long time thinking about it, however. Especially when they'd gone down to the beach and spent time in the water. During those two torturous hours, Noah had learned that he had very little patience when it came to Dare. And he'd come up with only one way to prevent the inevitable.

Instead of facing the music, he had bolted. Quickly. And for a long period of time, using Milly as an excuse.

Granted, that probably wasn't the most adult way to handle the situation.

If he had to do it all over again, he would. Which kind of sucked.

Fearless

Now that he'd managed to shower, shave, and dress, he felt somewhat more put together. He also hadn't seen Dare in hours, so that helped, too. Not that he didn't want to see Dare. Quite the opposite, actually, but he was trying to do this the right way. In only a few short days, they'd managed to rekindle the friendship they'd once had, and Noah didn't want to do anything to ruin that.

Sex would ruin that, of that he was certain.

Which was why he was hiding from Dare.

Now, as he waited in the hall outside of Milly's cabin, Noah glanced at his watch. They still had roughly half an hour before dinner. However, he'd been sure his stepsister had insisted they get down there a little early. He wondered how long it took women to really get ready for something like this. For him, it required a razor, a shower, and the clothes he had already planned to wear. Ten minutes, maybe fifteen, tops. Apparently, women required a *lot* longer.

He knocked on her door again.

"Hold on!" Milly called out a second before she turned the knob and pulled open the door.

Pushing it in farther, he peeked inside to ensure she was decent. He found Milly staring into the mirror, putting her earrings in.

"Sorry. I'm hurrying."

"I'm not the one on a deadline," he told her.

"I know. I know. Gannon's always getting on me about these things." Milly smiled as she ran her hand over her dress. "It's a wonder I get to work every day on time."

"You've still got time." He didn't know what she planned to do before the meal was served, though.

"Nope. I'm ready. This is as good as it gets."

"Well, if it's any consolation, you look beautiful."

She seemed to release a breath when he said that.

"Thank you."

The next thing Noah knew, they were stepping out into the hall, Milly on his arm.

She smiled up at him. "You feeling any better?"

As he led her down the hall toward the elevator, he glanced over at her. "Much." It wasn't a complete lie, but it wasn't the truth, either.

"Just relax. Things will happen as they're meant to happen."

Noah nodded. He'd broken down and shared some of his fears with Milly when he'd been talking to her over lunch earlier that day. He hadn't planned for all those feelings to come gushing out of his mouth, but once they were out there, he'd felt a little better. Then again, Milly had already suspected something was going on between them since she had evidently seen them holding hands last night.

Holding hands was only the tip of the iceberg when it came to things Noah wanted to do to Dare, but it seemed that simple, intimate gesture had totally thrown him for a loop. He wasn't even sure which way was up anymore, and quite frankly, it scared him.

Once downstairs, Noah navigated the busy main floor until they made it to the corridor that led to the banquet room. He offered Milly another quick smile as she released his arm.

"Good luck," she whispered.

"Thanks." He'd definitely need it.

As he walked farther into the banquet room, his eyes immediately zeroed in on the sexy man currently having a conversation with Hudson and Teague at the same table they'd shared the first night on the ship. Looked as though Noah would be sharing dinner with Dare again. He hoped that was a good thing.

After wiping his sweaty palms on his slacks, Noah made his way over to the table, smiling down at Dare as he took the seat beside him.

"Hey." Dare's greeting held a hint of confusion, but Noah didn't detect any animosity.

"Hey," Noah replied, leaning over and brushing his arm against Dare's. He wanted him to know that things were cool between them, even if they weren't. Not completely, anyway.

He wasn't sure what, if anything, was going through Dare's mind, but Noah was having a hell of a time trying to keep things in perspective, trying to remember what was off-limits to him. He wanted Dare, and he was fairly certain Dare wanted him, only Noah knew that moving forward wasn't the way this was supposed to happen. He needed to remember that their chance at love was in the past, not the future.

This was about friendship, and Dare didn't need Noah thinking otherwise and screwing up a good thing. Sure as shit, Noah knew if he accepted his feelings for Dare at this point, he would be doing just that.

Hopefully he could pretend long enough to make it through a meal together.

An hour later, after dinner had been served and devoured, and as dessert was being brought out, Noah felt more relaxed. He'd spent the majority of dinner being regaled with humorous stories of life with Dare. To his surprise, Hudson had been a fountain of information, continuously telling one story after another about life at the marina.

Dare had argued a time or two, insisting that Hudson had the story all wrong, keeping everyone at the table laughing along with him. It had been nice, to say the least, and again, Noah found himself enjoying a moment with Dare that he didn't want to end.

The clink of metal against glass sounded, and Noah's attention was drawn to Cam's father, Michael Strickland, an older man with a thick white mustache, whom Noah had been introduced to on the first day, sitting at the table with Cam and Gannon.

"First, I want to thank you all for coming. I hope you've had a chance to enjoy the cruise so far," Michael said to the group as he got to his feet. "It's quite an honor to have y'all here to celebrate my son's upcoming nuptials. It's a little hard to believe that the day has finally come. We've spent the past year waiting for this moment to get here." The man looked at Cam directly, then over to Gannon before turning back to the group.

"A father has one goal in his life and that is to set a good example for his children. To raise them right, teach them to embrace what life throws at them, and to overcome the obstacles put in their path. I would like to think that I did a good job of that." Mr. Strickland smiled, then took a sip of water. "I don't think I can truly express how proud I am of these two men. Though I know their relationship hasn't been easy"—Mr. Strickland peered around the room—"but what relationship is, right?"

Cordial laughter ensued.

"Despite the obstacles they've had to overcome, these two have forged ahead, walking side by side, hand in hand, to do it together. And this time tomorrow, I'll be welcoming another son-in-law into my family."

Cam's father took a moment, apparently choked up, but he forced a smile. "I wish Cam's mother could be here with us. She would be so proud, just as I am. But I know she's watching from above, making sure that these two remarkable men will have the perfect day."

Fearless

For a second, Noah felt his chest tighten as he thought about his own father, the hole that had been created in his life when he had tragically died. A car accident had stolen his father from him, leaving a void even bigger than the one he'd been dealing with at the time.

"I want to propose a toast," Michael continued, glancing over at Cam and Gannon once more. "To a lifetime of happiness. Together."

A chorus of "cheers" sounded, glasses clinking together, and Noah joined in, not thinking when he clinked his glass against Dare's, their eyes meeting momentarily.

For a brief second, he allowed himself to travel down the *what-if* road.

What if he and Dare had stayed together?
What if he and Dare had gotten married?
What if...

"Are you okay?" Dare asked, his voice soft, but loud enough to interrupt Noah's thoughts.

Noah nodded, clearing his throat. "I'm good."

Thankfully, Gannon saved the day when he got to his feet, smiling at everyone.

"I have to say, I never thought I'd see this day." Several people laughed, and Noah noticed Gannon was still a little pale, but far better than he'd been on the first day. "First of all, I'm on a cruise, and I can honestly tell you that if it weren't for the fact that this man means more to me than dry land, I probably wouldn't be here." More laughter. "But I am, and because he's by my side, I know that I can overcome my fears, of which I have many. So, I want to thank each and every one of you for coming, because tomorrow will, no doubt, be the best day of my entire life, when I finally get to call this man my husband."

Applause erupted and then conversation picked back up.

Only then did Noah excuse himself, suddenly in desperate need of air.

Nineteen

OKAY, DARE HAD to admit that Noah's vanishing act was getting a little tiring. He wasn't sure what had caused Noah to run out of the room, but sure as shit, he'd taken off like his ass was on fire.

As he drank his beer, he noticed Hudson was looking at him, a question on his face.

Dare shrugged. He didn't know what Noah was up to, didn't know what had caused him to jet, and he didn't know whether or not he should go after him.

Things were getting way too real between them. To the point that Dare wasn't sure digging into Noah's personal feelings was a good thing right now. As it was, he felt a little abandoned due to Noah's disappearance earlier in the day and now...

He didn't know what to think.

Hudson signed: *You want me to go check on him?*

Dare shook his head. No, if anyone had to check on Noah, it needed to be him. Mostly because Dare didn't want it to be anyone besides him.

After downing the rest of his beer, he excused himself from the table and headed in the direction Noah had gone.

For the second time during the trip so far, Dare spent nearly half an hour searching for Noah. Unlike last time, though, he didn't find Noah on the rock wall attempting to burn off his frustration. This time he found him leaning on the rail overlooking the dark ocean. He paused, wanting to take in the sight of him before he approached. The man still managed to make his heart skip a beat even though he knew that wasn't necessarily a good thing.

Taking a deep breath, Dare made his way over to Noah, rested his arms on the rail beside him, and mirrored his stance.

"You okay?" He glanced over briefly.

Noah nodded.

"You sure?"

More silence, this time without the nod.

Dare turned around and leaned back against the rail. "Talk to me, Noah. What's going on?"

Noah looked over but didn't answer. Dare knew there was something on his mind, he could tell by the pained expression on his face, but he didn't know what. He tried to replay what had been said right before Noah had dashed out of the room, but he couldn't recall.

"Is it me?" He hated the insecurity in his tone, but he couldn't help but ask.

Noah met his gaze briefly. "Maybe a little."

Okay, that hurt.

"But not in a bad way." Noah's smile was sad.

"Then in *what* way?"

Dare watched as Noah's attention returned to the water.

"I was just thinking about my father."

A sudden sadness settled in Dare's gut. He hadn't yet heard the specifics on what had happened to Noah's father, but he knew he'd died sometime within the few months after they'd broken up. He wanted Noah to open up to him, to share what had happened, but he refused to force him. Up to this point, although the sexual tension was like a rubber band stretched to the max, the emotional connection between them was lacking. Noah hadn't yet let Dare in and he was beginning to think he wouldn't.

Figuring it wouldn't hurt to spur the conversation, Dare decided to admit what he knew. "Milly told me your father died when you were twenty-three."

Noah nodded, then cast a sideways glance at Dare. A strange sense of foreboding washed over him, and he suddenly didn't want to know any more.

"If I'd known, I would've been there for you." No way would he have wanted Noah to go through that alone. "How did he die?"

"Car wreck."

"I'm so sorry. When did it happen?"

Noah's expression hardened. "My father died the day after you left. That night, actually."

Oh, fuck.

Noah stood up straight, his hands tightly gripping the railing. "In fact, my father died coming to see me because I was so fucked up from you walking away, he was worried about me."

Oh, fuck suddenly didn't begin to describe the horrible sensation consuming him. If what Noah was telling him was true—and Dare couldn't think of any reason for Noah to lie about this—then that meant...

"Oh, my God." He could hardly breathe. His chest felt as though there were a ten-ton weight sitting on it.

He was responsible for Noah's father's death. It was *his* fault.

Dare swallowed hard.

And that...

No matter how much he wished it weren't true, that meant no matter what had transpired between them these last few days, Noah would never be able to forgive him.

And Dare couldn't blame him.

NOAH COULDN'T REMEMBER the last time he'd talked about his father with anyone. Even his mother had given up trying years ago. The guilt he lived with made it damn near impossible to discuss, but what he told Dare was the truth. His father had been on his way to Noah's apartment the night after Dare had left, but he'd never made it there.

"God, Noah, I'm so sorry."

The familiar anger he felt when he thought about his father's death, about the cruel way the universe had taken the most important man in his life from him choked him. For the longest time, he had pushed aside the guilt and blamed Dare for everything. If Dare hadn't left, Noah's father would probably be alive today. If Noah hadn't called his father that night, completely devastated because he'd lost the man he loved, his father would probably be alive today.

Even after years of therapy—something his mother had insisted on after he'd fallen into a deep depression—it was sometimes hard to remember that it wasn't his fault. It wasn't Dare's fault, either.

"I really don't want to talk about this," Noah finally said, his fingers cramping as he gripped the railing.

"Of course you don't."

Noah's head snapped to the side as he stared at Dare. The comment was said with malice, not sympathy as he'd expected. "What the fuck does that mean?"

"It means you're not willing to open up to me." Dare stood up straight, his hands balled into fists, his anger evident on his face. "It's no different now than it was back then."

"Fuck you, Dare." Noah didn't know what to say to that. He hadn't expected Dare to turn this into an argument, but he should've known better. "And you're not much different, either, are you? Picking a fight when this isn't even about you."

Dare nodded, but Noah wasn't sure why.

"I'm sorry about your father. I didn't know. Had you bothered to reach out to me, I would've been there for you."

Noah's anger intensified. "If you hadn't walked out on me, it wouldn't have happened."

Shit. He hadn't meant to say that.

The way Dare stepped back as though he'd been slapped was proof that Noah's words were harsher than he'd intended.

"I get it. It's my fault." It wasn't a question. "That's clear."

"It's *not* your fault," Noah blurted, needing Dare to know he really didn't blame him, no matter what the hell he was saying. He had, sure. At one point. For a really long time, actually, but not anymore.

"Oh, but it is. I can see it in your face. If I hadn't left, your father would still be alive today." Dare turned as though he was going to walk away, but he stopped and turned back. "There are a lot of things in my life that I regret, but walking away from you has always been the biggest. But this explains a lot. And I'm sorry, Noah. I'm truly fucking sorry."

Dare turned and walked away, taking another piece of Noah's heart with him. He hated to let him go, but he didn't know what to say, didn't know if there was anything to say that would salvage this.

The memories of that horrific night swamped him.

"Noah, talk to me."

"I don't feel like talking, Dad." He didn't feel like doing anything. Well, nothing except drowning his sorrow in the bottle of whiskey he'd been chugging for the past few hours.

"Talk to me, son."

"Nothin' to talk about." His words were coming out through numb lips. *"Dare's gone. It's over."*

"When did he leave?"

"Last night sometime." Noah wasn't sure exactly when. He only knew they'd gone to bed together and he'd woken up alone.

"Have you called him?"

Noah took a swig from the bottle. *"Nope. Not goin' to either. Fuck him."*

"Noah."

"What? It's cool, Dad. I've got my whiskey; I don't need anything more."

"Why don't I come get you and you can stay the night here with your mom and me?"

Even intoxicated, Noah could hear the concern in his father's tone. *"I'm not leaving my apartment. I'm gonna sit right here and drink myself stupid."*

"Noah…" His father sighed. *"Then I'll come stay with you. I'll sleep on the couch tonight."*

For some reason, that small offer made tears form in Noah's eyes. He'd fought the urge to cry since the moment he'd woken up to find Dare and the few things he'd had at the apartment gone. His toothbrush, his razor, the few pairs of boxers Noah had washed and left on top of the dryer ... all of it gone.

A sob tore free from his chest and Noah put the bottle on the table. "He's gone, Dad. He left me."

The dam broke and the tears came flooding out of him.

"I'll be there in a few minutes, Noah. Stay right there, son."

Noah hung up the phone and let it drop to the cushion as he folded in on himself and let the tears fall. He hated to admit it, but he needed his father right then. He needed someone to console him, to assure him that his heart wasn't going to come out of his chest, because the pain was unbearable.

The next thing Noah knew, he was waking up in the same spot he'd obviously cried himself to sleep in. He heard the phone ringing, but didn't know where it was coming from. Forcing himself to sit, he dug around in the cushions until he found the handset.

"Dad? What time is it? I thought you were coming over."

"Noah."

The fuzz from the alcohol and sleep disappeared instantly when he heard the anguish in his mother's voice.

"What's wrong, Mom?"

"Oh, God, Noah. It's your father..." She choked on the words. "He's ... dead."

And just like that, his entire world had started spinning out of control. From that phone call, Noah had developed an anger so deep, so immense, he hadn't been sure he would ever be able to lay eyes on Dare again. It didn't matter that Dare wasn't at fault. The man they assumed had fallen asleep at the wheel and had been driving on the wrong side of the road—hitting his father head on and killing them both instantly—was responsible.

And it sucked because they didn't even have complete closure on that. The autopsy proved the man who had hit his father hadn't been drinking, and the only information they had was from the man's wife, who said he'd been driving back from a business trip. It had been a tragedy, on both sides, and, yes, ultimately the man who had been too tired to drive was responsible.

But it had been so much easier to blame Dare.

Truth was, from the minute he'd laid eyes on Dare a few days ago, he had intended to never share that little detail with him. He didn't blame Dare. He didn't blame himself, either.

Not anymore.

His chest ached and it was hard to breathe. Here he'd been thinking about the what-ifs ... about what their life could've been like. Although nothing would ever bring Noah's father back, he had been given a second chance with Dare. *They'd* been given a second chance.

But just like the first time, Noah had gone and fucked it up.

Twenty

UNABLE TO GO back to the cabin and be alone, Dare went to find Roan. He needed someone to talk to. He would've preferred to chat with Cam because the two of them were closer, but he wasn't about to drop his problems on a man who was getting married tomorrow. And Roan had offered.

After knocking on Roan's door, Dare realized he wasn't there, so he headed back down to the main floor. Figuring he could take half an hour to seek him out before he gave up, Dare started walking.

He was at the twenty-minute mark when he found Roan with Teague in the casino.

"Hey, man. What's up?" Roan peered up at him from his seat at the blackjack table. "Oh, shit."

Dare didn't even have to answer before Roan was gearing up to quit the game. He hated that he'd interrupted, but at the moment, he really needed Roan.

"You cool?" Teague questioned from his seat beside Roan.

Dare nodded. He doubted it seemed sincere.

"I'm out, too." Teague got to his feet and took his chips after passing over a tip for the dealer. "Come on, bro. Let's go get a drink."

Unable to refuse the company, Dare followed Roan and Teague. They stopped at one of the bars, ordered shots of whiskey, then found a table nearby. There was music playing from the speakers in the ceiling, but it wasn't too loud to hear himself talk, but loud enough to help ease the thoughts from his mind, so Dare managed to relax.

"What's up, man?" Roan leaned on his elbows, watching Dare closely.

Dare wasn't sure how to share the details, but he figured he had to get them out there. Rather than dropping hints, he went ahead and told them about the conversation he'd had with Noah a little while ago.

"Fuck. That's rough." Teague was watching him closely, a frown on his face. "But man, you have to know it wasn't your fault. You said Noah even said so."

Dare grimaced. "How do you figure that? If I hadn't walked out on him…"

"The same can be said for Noah," Roan stated.

"How so?" Dare wasn't buying it.

"If Noah had accepted where the relationship was going, you wouldn't have left."

"I should've stayed. I should've tried to work it out. If I hadn't been so selfish that night…"

"That's bullshit, Dare," Roan bit out. "Don't you dare go taking that guilt on. How did he die?"

"Car wreck." Dare didn't know any of the details. He hadn't gotten that far into the conversation with Noah.

"Regardless, it doesn't matter. You're not at fault," Teague offered before downing another shot.

"I don't know how Noah doesn't hate me," Dare mused aloud. And he really didn't.

"Because he loves you, man." The way Roan said it sounded so matter-of-fact.

Dare snorted. "Not even close."

"I saw the two of you together." Roan leaned back in his chair. "Y'all looked pretty fucking cozy to me."

Teague lifted an eyebrow, as though encouraging Roan to explain.

"They were watching that movie last night. Holding hands and everything."

Roan was right, they had been. And that short span of time seemed like a lifetime ago. Especially since Noah had spent the majority of today ignoring him.

"That's the reason you shouldn't do relationships," Teague offered. "One minute you're pissing rainbows, and the next your world's upside down and sideways."

Pissing rainbows, huh? Dare hadn't heard that one before. Then again, Teague always came up with some off-handed shit.

"Love's not all bad," Roan grumbled.

Dare laughed. The way he said it was quite the opposite of the words.

Teague grabbed another shot glass and held it while he spoke. "Regardless, this guy shows up out of the blue after, what ... fifteen years? That's gotta be somethin'. Seriously. Maybe you're one of those who believes in fate and shit. Maybe this is your destiny."

Dare stared at Teague, dumbfounded.

Roan spoke up. "Dude, you should probably lay off the whiskey."

"What? I'm serious." Teague looked at Dare again. "Did you know he was Milly's stepbrother?"

"No."

"Did he know about you?"

"No."

"Yet somehow y'all are back together again."

"We're not together." Dare felt the need to clarify that. "Not even a little bit."

Okay, maybe a little bit.

Or rather they had been before Noah had dropped that little bomb on him a while ago.

Now Dare didn't even know what he wanted.

Roan leaned forward. "Give it a chance. That's all I can tell you. You never know what might happen."

Dare smirked. "I hope you know I'm gonna use that on you one day."

Roan shook his head. "You won't have to. Love damn sure ain't my thing."

"I'm right there with you," Teague chimed in. "Right there with you. Now who's gettin' the next round?"

NOAH WASN'T SURE how long he'd been standing in the same spot his feet had rooted to since before Dare had left, but he figured it had to have been a while since the main deck was clearing out. He knew he should've gone up to his cabin and gone to bed because they had a big day tomorrow. Not only was it the last stop on the cruise before they headed back to Florida, but Cam and Gannon were also getting married.

Yet the idea of spending the night in the same cabin with Dare was disconcerting. Only because he hated how things had been left between them. He honestly didn't blame Dare for what had happened, but he doubted Dare would believe that, no matter how many times he tried to explain it.

"What're you doing out here so late?"

Noah turned to see Gannon stepping up beside him. "I think I could ask you the same question."

"Can't sleep."

"Nervous?"

Gannon shook his head. "Excited. I think I'm driving Cam crazy."

Noah chuckled. "I can see that happening. No more motion sickness?"

"Only a little, but not nearly like it was on that first day."

Noah noticed Gannon was still a little pale. "Good to hear."

Gannon leaned his forearms on the rail. "What about you? Why're you out here?" Gannon glanced around him. "Where's Dare?"

Not wanting to get into the details of their falling-out because tomorrow was Gannon's wedding day and the guy didn't need anything else to worry about, he opted for a question of his own. "How did you know Cam was the one for you?"

Gannon smiled. "I think I knew it the first time I looked at him."

"Really?"

"God, no." Gannon laughed. "He was hot, sure. But we had quite a few ups and downs in the beginning. Things he needed to overcome, things I had to address."

"So you had to work at it?"

Gannon put one foot on the bottom rail and pivoted so that he was facing Noah. "Of course we did. It's what you do in a relationship."

Silence lingered between them while Noah tried to come up with something to say.

"This about Dare?"

Noah sighed, then nodded.

"Milly told me about you and him. Anything you want to talk about?"

There were a lot of things he wanted to talk about, but Noah knew Gannon was not the man he should've been talking to. He needed to have this conversation with Dare; he just didn't know how to make that happen. Not without fucking things up again, anyway.

Noah opted for simple. "We've got history. At one point in my life, I was in love with him."

"But you're not now?" Gannon's tone held a hint of skepticism.

This time, Noah decided to tell the truth. "I'm pretty sure I'm still in love with him. And that's not the issue."

"Then what is?"

"I don't know how to make this work."

"Have you told him?"

Noah shook his head. "Dare is not ready for that. We've only been back in each other's lives for a couple of days."

"Yet you can admit that you're still in love with him." It wasn't a question, so Noah waited to see where Gannon was going with this. "What makes you think he doesn't know how he feels about you?"

He didn't know for sure how Dare felt and he was scared to ask him.

"The only advice I have for you is to tell him how you feel. Maybe he doesn't feel the same, but you won't know until you talk about it."

"And if he doesn't?" Noah knew Gannon couldn't answer that, but he asked anyway.

"If he doesn't, then you've got closure and you can move on."

Unfortunately, that was true.

Gannon stood up straight. "Well, I've got to get back to Cam. I'm sure he's missing me by now." Gannon chuckled. "I haven't given him a hard time in about an hour. I'm sure he's waiting for it."

Noah smiled. "Looking forward to tomorrow."

"You and me both." Gannon's smile widened. "Oh, and thanks again for agreeing to be a groomsman. It means a lot."

"You're family. I'm happy to do it."

Noah leaned on the rail once again when Gannon left. He stared out into the darkness. He didn't know how things would work with him and Dare, but he knew Gannon was right about one thing. He had to get closure.

He just didn't like how final that sounded.

Twenty-One

Thursday, June 2nd
Cruise, day five

DARE WOKE UP to the sun shining in through the window and the cabin empty. He knew Noah had returned at some point last night, but neither of them had said anything. When Dare had woken up that morning, Noah hadn't been there. After Dare had spent a couple of hours on the beach— wanting to be able to say he'd been to St. Maarten—then come back to the cabin for a nap, he hadn't seen Noah anywhere. And now, only an hour and a half out from the wedding, he didn't think Noah was going to make an appearance.

It seemed Noah was still having issues with him and he needed some space.

After finding out about Noah's father and how his own actions had caused the man's death, Dare couldn't blame him. Not one bit.

Oh, it hurt like a motherfucker to know he'd been the one to cause Noah's father's death. Even though everyone— including Noah—was trying to tell him otherwise, he wasn't buying it. Had he not chosen that day to walk away from Noah, his father wouldn't have needed to come over to console him; therefore, he would probably be alive today.

Fearless

Simple equation, no matter how you looked at it. And no amount of apologizing would ever be able to make up for that.

Which was why Dare was prepping himself to spend the rest of the trip away from Noah. As far as he was concerned, they'd said all they needed to say to one another. It might've been fifteen years too late, but Dare was finally able to move on knowing that he'd tied up those loose ends that had been left blowing in the wind all those years ago.

After spending the better part of the hour before the wedding trying to forget Noah, somehow, Dare managed to finally push the thoughts back, pull on the monkey suit, and make his way to the location Milly had instructed him to be at, getting there a few minutes early.

"You made it on time," Milly greeted with a huge grin.

"I know you didn't doubt me," he teased, smiling for the first time in hours.

"Of course not. That's why I had it on a ship. I knew you wouldn't have far to go."

"So you're saying this was all for me, huh?"

Her eyes glittered with mischief. "Absolutely."

Dare chuckled. "That doesn't surprise me."

"Come on, I'll take you to Cam."

Dare followed Milly as she led him to a small room where Cam, Gannon, and the others were gathered. There were a handful of people already there—Roan, Mr. Strickland, Hudson, and Teague—all laughing and joking and apparently keeping the grooms at ease. But there was one person noticeably absent, but likely the only person who noticed was him.

Forget Noah for a little while.

In his attempt to forget the hot firefighter, Dare got caught up in the excitement. It wasn't difficult since his closest friend was finally tying the knot, and based on the wide grin on Cam's face, today was likely the best day of his life. There was a tiny part of him that was envious.

"Did you ever really think you'd be here?" Roan asked Cam and Gannon.

"On a boat, no," Gannon admitted, laughing. "But if you're referring to here, as in getting ready to marry this man..." Gannon's gaze slid to Cam. "I knew it the second I saw him."

Cam laughed. "Liar."

"Okay, maybe after the third or fourth time I saw him," Gannon joked.

Thanks to the teasing and the laughter, Dare managed to forget the events of the last twenty-four hours right up until the moment Noah walked into the room.

"Hey, man. Glad you're here," Gannon greeted Noah, slapping him on the back and shaking his hand.

"I should be saying that to you," Noah replied. "Looks like your nerves, as well as your stomach, are settled."

"I feel fantastic," Gannon confirmed. "Thank you, by the way. Those pills worked like magic. I don't think I'd be here without them."

Dare hardly noticed the fact that Gannon wasn't pale anymore, but that was because Dare found himself only a few feet away from the most incredibly attractive man wearing a tux and looking like a million dollars.

Fuck. No man had ever looked that good in a tux. Ever.

As he ogled Noah, his mouth dried up instantly.

"Hey," Noah greeted, making his way over to him after shaking hands with Cam and the others.

"Hey," Dare managed to say, still eyeing Noah.

"Dare and Noah!" Milly called from the doorway. "Y'all are up first."

Right. Wedding.

This shit was about to go down.

"You ready for this?" Noah asked quietly.

"Just another day for me," he said, doing his best to pay attention to Milly and not turn his attention back to Noah.

"You two are going to walk down the aisle and then split. Noah, you're on the left, which is Gannon's side. Dare, you're on the right. Questions?"

Dare shook his head and allowed Milly to lead them down the hallway, then over to an open area that led out onto the ship's deck.

Even with the music that was playing and all the people chattering as he and Noah began walking down the short aisle to where the man in the suit resided beneath an altar decorated with flowers, Dare only heard the pounding of his own heart. At one point in his life, he could've imagined this being his and Noah's wedding day.

But it wasn't. And it never would be.

That was something he would need to remind himself for the next couple of hours.

NOAH ONLY HOPED that he didn't look as awkward as he felt. This whole wedding thing was so far out of his element, but he did what came natural, walking beside Dare—who was definitely pretending Noah wasn't there—down to the front and then veering to the left as Milly had instructed.

It was a wonder he'd even caught that part. From the moment he'd laid eyes on Dare wearing that tuxedo … everything else had faded into the background. He'd never seen the man dress up before, and holy shit, he was a sight.

Even now, as Noah stood at the front while Hudson and Teague walked down the aisle, the only thing he could focus on was Dare. He knew before the night was over that he had to apologize to Dare. For what he'd said last night, for what had transpired between them fifteen years ago, for all of it. One way or another, they had to put the past to rest so they could get on with their lives. Even if it meant that once he stepped off this ship, he would never see Dare again.

Something he hoped wasn't the case.

Noah stepped back when Hudson joined him—apparently standing up for Gannon in order to make things even. He forced his attention to the aisle in time to see Roan and Milly coming down. She was smiling so brightly, almost as though today were her wedding day.

Once the best man and maid of honor were in place, the music changed, and all heads turned toward the doors leading out to the deck. Cam's father stepped out, then Cam, and then Gannon. Mr. Strickland led them to the front, then hugged them both before taking his seat.

The drone of conversation quieted, the music faded, and the only sound was the sea waves far down below against the ship.

The officiant cleared his throat and began, "Dearly beloved, we are gathered here today to unite these two men in the bond of marriage, and to celebrate this sacred union.

Fearless

"Marriage is a universal bond that is recognized and honored even when the forms and traditions may differ from person to person. Marriage is an essential building block of society. No person should attend a wedding without giving thanks for its institution. It is thus with great joy and hope that we come together to witness Cam Strickland and Gannon Burgess join in wedlock."

Though the words trickled through his brain, Noah found himself staring at Dare, unable to look away when their eyes met.

"On this day, these two men will bring all that they have to offer one another. Their hope, their love, even their fears. For the commitment of marriage demands no less. They bring their dreams and accomplishments, as well as their worries and failures. They offer each other their virtues and vices, their fortunes and wants, and their well-being and their neediness. Whatever time brings their way, they shall remain united. For the covenant they make today will bind them together until parted by death.

"On this journey it is love that will make each step easier. Love sweetens shared dreams and comforts the fearful. Love is accomplished in seeing the good and overlooking the bad. In hard times, love brings hope. Love is at the very center of a meaningful life. It is the presence of love that, here today, pervades and enriches this service of celebration and commitment, and we hope will continue throughout their marriage.

"Marriage is different than any other relationship. It celebrates intimacy, and it ties an eternal knot. It is the most significant contract a person will make in their lifetime. It touches the heart more deeply than any other action two people can take. It strengthens the bond in ways too numerous to list."

The officiant paused and looked between Cam and Gannon. "You are about to assume this relationship. You will pledge to each other your love and devotion."

Cam and Gannon both nodded, and Noah noticed that they were looking at only each other. From where he stood, he couldn't see Gannon's face, but he could imagine the love that shone there. And all eyes were on them.

"Cam and Gannon have found that their love for one another is so deep that they wish to commit themselves to each other in marriage. The contract of marriage is one not to be entered into lightly, but thoughtfully and with a deep realization of the obligations and responsibilities it entails. Please remember that love, loyalty, and understanding are the foundation of a happy home. No human ties are more important or more tender."

Noah ignored the pang in his chest, the ache that he realized had started that morning so long ago when he'd woken up to find Dare gone. He had been in love with Dare then; he had been able to envision a life where the two of them would've been together forever. Only he'd fucked that up by thinking he knew what was best for them both.

"Please face one another," the officiant instructed. "Cam, will you take Gannon to be your husband, to live together as best friend, lover, and soul mate? Will you love him as a person, respect him as an equal, sharing joy as well as sorrow, triumph as well as defeat? And keep him beside you for as long as you both shall live?"

Cam smiled. "I do."

"Gannon, will you take Cam to be your husband, to live together as best friend, lover, and soul mate? Will you love him as a person, respect him as an equal, sharing joy as well as sorrow, triumph as well as defeat? And keep him beside you for as long as you both shall live?"

"I do," Gannon said, his words choppy with emotion.

"Do you have the rings?"

Noah watched as Milly and Roan produced the rings, handing them over to Cam and Gannon before the two men faced one another again.

"These rings mark the beginning of a long journey filled with wonder, surprises, laughter, tears, celebration, grief, and joy. May these rings glow in reflection of the warmth and love which flow through the wearers today."

The officiant turned to Cam. "Repeat after me: I give you this ring as a symbol of the love I have for you. Wear it now as a sign of the love we share together."

Cam repeated the words, his eyes never leaving Gannon's face as he placed the ring on his finger.

The officiant then turned to Gannon. "Repeat after me: I give you this ring as a symbol of the love I have for you. Wear it now as a sign of the love we share together."

Noah watched Cam's face, saw the tears that came to his eyes when Gannon managed to choke out the words—reflecting the emotion shared between them. The deep connection between them was clear for everyone to see. It was evident that these two men loved one another and this day … their wedding day … it would bind them together for eternity. Although Noah suspected the ceremony wasn't even necessary because their bond had already been established.

The officiant spoke again, "Being one unbroken circle, your rings symbolize unending love. May these be a constant reminder of this moment when you have pledged your everlasting love to one another. We have heard your vows and your promise of faithful love. May joy be with you from this day forward. I, by virtue of the authority vested in me, declare you to be wed, according to the ordinance of the law.

"You may kiss."

Laughter erupted when Gannon pulled Cam to him, then tilted him back, their mouths never separating.

And it was in that moment that Noah realized, the only chance he'd ever had at what these two men had was standing directly across from him. Not once in his life since had he ever felt anything remotely close to what he felt for Dare.

Now he had to figure out a way to get that back.

While there was still time.

Twenty-Two

ABOUT A MINUTE into the officiant's speech, Dare realized that he'd spent the better part of the day wallowing in self-pity. This trip wasn't about him. It wasn't about Noah. It wasn't about their past or the heartache that came along with it.

This was about celebrating Cam and Gannon and the love they'd found.

And that meant it was time to get back to being the guy who loved a good party and not the guy who couldn't seem to shake off his past. Considering they had opened the doors to the reception room and were gearing up to move everyone inside, Dare knew now was the time to implement that. This was a celebration of love, not a freaking funeral.

Because of that, he made a beeline through the doors while the guests crowded Cam and Gannon, offering their congratulations with hugs.

"Jack and Coke, please," Dare told the bartender as he stepped up to the bar in the reception room.

"Make that two."

Taking a deep breath, Dare turned to face Noah. Before he could say what was on his mind, Noah put his hand up.

"I'm sorry," Noah said softly. "For everything. If it's all right with you, I'd like to start over. As friends."

Well. That was not what he'd been expecting to hear.

He could feel Noah's intense gaze watching him while he pondered what to say.

The bartender returned with their drinks, and Dare took a moment to take a sip, trying to gather his thoughts. Did he want to start over? Or did he want to put the past behind him?

The second option seemed a whole lot easier than the first, but Dare knew he wasn't ready to let go of Noah for the second time, even if it was the best thing for both of them.

He found himself nodding his head. "Okay."

"Okay what?" Noah looked confused.

"We'll start over." Maybe they couldn't get over the past enough to love each other again, but Noah was right. They could be friends.

"Like, from the beginning?" Noah smirked.

Dare couldn't hide his smile. "Who are you again?"

And for a brief moment, Dare imagined himself actually meeting Noah for the first time. It would've been much like it had been that fateful day so long ago. He'd been captivated by Noah very much as he was now. By how obscenely attractive he was, by how beautiful his smile was. Even by that lopsided smirk that promised things Dare wasn't even sure he was ready for now.

Two hours later, after he'd knocked several drinks back, after everyone had settled in, after Dare and Noah had found a table near the dance floor, after Roan and Milly had made everyone laugh with their toasts, and after Gannon and Cam had cut the cake and then finally had their first dance as a married couple, Dare was feeling a little more at ease. It likely had something to do with the whiskey, but he wanted to believe it was because he'd reset his mind and knew what was important tonight.

Fearless

"Excuse me for a minute," Noah said, smiling over at him before getting up and venturing toward the DJ.

Dare couldn't help but watch, wondering what Noah was up to. He went right up to the man who was managing the music and whispered something to him. The guy smiled back and nodded.

Of course, now Dare was curious as to what Noah had requested, but he did his best to pretend otherwise.

A few minutes later, his curiosity was sated and a laugh bubbled up from within.

"You have got to be kidding," Dare said aloud, laughing.

"The Humpty Dance" by Digital Underground came on, and Noah took off his jacket, laying it on a table and moving to the center of the room. Noah used to dance to this all the time, miming the words. Back in the 90s, it'd been amusing, now … it was hysterical.

Still, Noah looked so damn good doing it.

Knowing he couldn't let Noah outshine him tonight, Dare tossed back the rest of his drink, then headed to the DJ with his own request.

A minute later, when Noah's song was over, the room went silent and people were watching them closely as Dare moved to the center of the dance floor, his eyes locked on Noah as he did. He'd long ago shed his jacket, so he rolled up his sleeves while the DJ queued the music.

The minute the song began, Noah started laughing, and Dare lifted his imaginary microphone to his mouth, grinning. This brought back so many memories of good times. Fun times. No real cares in the world, only fun. A time Dare missed more than he would willingly admit.

For the next four minutes and forty-four seconds, he lip-synced the words to "The Real Slim Shady" by Eminem, every word memorized from spending so much time doing this exact thing a million times before.

When the song went off, Dare couldn't contain his laughter as he realized others had joined them on the dance floor, getting their Slim Shady on.

Then the music stopped and...

Dare spun around and saw Milly smiling from beside the DJ when "Tipsy" by J-Kwon came on.

Kind of fitting, actually.

NOAH HADN'T HAD that much fun in ... forever.

He vividly remembered all the times he and Dare had spent dancing, lip-syncing, laughing at the craziness of it all. Those had been good times. A large majority of the guests, both old and young, took to the dance floor to shake their thing while Milly's selection played. Noah danced, never taking his eyes off Dare as he did. The man still had it going on, still knew exactly how to move his body to make Noah's mouth water.

And now, as the music took on a slower pace, he wasn't ready for it to be over. As "You and Me" by Lifehouse began, Noah knew it was now or never. As Dare started to move past him, Noah reached out, letting his hand slide down Dare's arm before taking his hand.

"Dance with me," he whispered, locking gazes with him.

He got the impression Dare was planning to turn him down, and he geared up for the rejection. His heart soared when Dare reluctantly nodded and moved closer. Their bodies came together just as they had in the past. It was intimate and sweet, and Noah wasn't sure how he was going to catch his breath when this was all over.

As he held Dare close, losing himself in the man and the music for a little while, he couldn't block the mental images from their past. Dare's warm smile, his laughter. All the good times and even the bad... He would never forget those two years, no matter how many had passed since.

God, he missed this man, more than he'd even realized.

Noah wanted to spend the rest of the night right here, in Dare's arms, close enough to hear him breathe, close enough to feel the warmth of his breath on his neck. Their cheeks touched, and Noah leaned in a little more than he probably should have, but he couldn't resist. So many emotions flooded him. Emotions he'd kept locked away for so long. Emotions that only Dare Davis could evoke in him.

Noah realized as they slowly moved across the dance floor, a few other couples swaying around them, that this was where he was meant to be. This was what had been missing from his life for so long. All of the days and nights he'd buried himself in work, ignoring everything else was because of this ... because he'd *lost* this.

The song ended far too quickly, and Dare instantly moved away, not meeting his eyes.

"Dare. Please don't..." Noah sighed. "Go."

Noah watched as Dare headed over to Cam and Gannon, shaking their hands, hugging them, then nodding what looked to be a good-night. He continued to stare after him when Dare disappeared out the doors onto the deck where the ceremony had been performed only a couple of hours ago. He caught sight of Milly standing on the edge of the dance floor, her smile sad as she watched him. Her head tilted, directing him in the direction Dare had gone. For a moment, he contemplated going back to his cabin, taking a shower, and going to bed. It was the coward's way out, but he figured it was the safest option. For him and for Dare.

If he did that, Dare would be safe, and Noah's heart would be safe, as well.

But he wasn't sure safe was the right answer right now. Safe was easy. Safe was ... boring.

He no longer wanted safe or boring... Noah wanted Dare. He wanted freedom and laughter, happiness and love. He wanted to be fearless again. He wanted everything he'd given up all those years ago.

And though he knew it wasn't going to be easy, he knew he had to try.

Somehow he got his feet to move, to carry him past the people chatting and celebrating. They carried him all the way out onto the deck, beneath the inky black sky dotted with sparkles high above them.

There were a few people outside, talking softly while they peered out at the water surrounding them. Noah searched the faces for Dare, and when he found him, he stopped walking because he noticed Dare wasn't alone. He was talking to Roan, who was nodding at him. Noah watched as Roan reached in his pocket, pulled something out, and handed it to Dare.

That was when Noah realized Roan had handed Dare his cabin key.

And the bubble of hope that had swelled in his chest deflated, making him feel … the same way he'd felt the first time he'd lost Dare.

"You just gonna stand there?"

Noah hadn't even realized Milly was standing beside him until he heard her voice.

"I am, yes," he said softly, his eyes never leaving Dare.

"So what? You're gonna let him walk out of your life twice?"

"He doesn't want me, Milly. That's clear."

"Oh, wah," she said snidely. "Cry me a river, Noah. How'd you get this far in life if you let everything slip through your fingers?"

He stared at his stepsister in disbelief. Was she really giving him a hard time about this?

Her eyes were soft when she peered at him. "You want Dare? You go after him. Refuse to let him out of that cabin until y'all hash this out. You let him walk away the first time and you hate yourself for it."

He'd never said that, but she was right.

"How do you think you'll feel if you let him do it again?"

Noah shifted his gaze back to Dare. He was still talking to Roan, which meant he had a little time to head him off at the pass. If that was what he was going to do.

Milly was right. He'd let Dare slip away once before. Did he really want that to happen again? Could he live with himself if he did?

Twenty-Three

DARE WAS RUNNING.

Not *literally* running, but he was definitely attempting to get far away from Noah as fast as he could.

And it was all because of that stupid dance.

The one that had left him feeling hollow and hopeful at the same time. He wasn't sure how he'd managed to get through those few minutes without losing it. For that short span of time on the dance floor, he'd been transported back to a different time. Back to the old Dare, the old Noah, the couple they'd once been. Holding Noah, breathing him in… It had brought back too many memories, too much pain. More than he wanted, for sure.

For the first year or two after they'd split, Dare had thought about Noah constantly. Dreamed about him. Day and night, night and day. It didn't matter when, Noah had always been on his mind. As the years had gone by, his memories had grown fuzzy and the ache in his chest had lessened. It had taken a long damn time to get over him, and tonight, as they'd danced, as he'd felt Noah's strong arms around him, Dare wasn't even sure he'd ever stopped loving him.

Fearless

And he hated himself for that. Hated himself because Noah had let him walk away, never attempting to come after him. All this time, he'd thought it had been proof of how little he'd meant to Noah, and that had hurt twice as much as walking away had. Only Noah hadn't come after him for other reasons. For reasons Noah would never be able to fully forgive Dare for no matter what he said.

So, when Noah had called after him, Dare had ignored him, unable to look back for fear he wouldn't be able to walk away. And he had to walk away.

Running into Roan had been pure luck, and when he'd asked his friend if he could bunk in his cabin for the remainder of the trip, Roan had said yes. Albeit reluctantly. Evidently Roan had noticed that Dare was running from something, too.

Apparently he was good at it.

Now, as Dare walked up to his cabin to get his things, he felt a band constricting around his chest. Seeing Noah again was really beginning to fuck with his head.

After unlocking the door, he took a deep breath and pushed it open. He could do this. He could get his things, hide out in Roan's cabin for a couple of days, and by the time they hit Florida, he'd have Noah out of his system once again.

That was the plan, anyway.

The light was off when he stepped inside, so he flipped it on, nearly jumping out of his skin when he saw Noah sitting on the edge of the mattress.

"What are you doing here?" He could hardly hear his own voice over the sound of his heart pounding in his chest.

Noah's gaze dropped down to Dare's hand, and he knew that Noah was on to him. He met Dare's gaze again. "Waiting for you."

"I … uh… I just came to get my stuff."

Luckily he hadn't unpacked, which would make this a whole lot easier. Before he could get to his suitcase, Noah was on his feet, blocking his path.

Or not.

Dare met Noah's gaze head on. He looked worried, but there was a hint of determination in his dark eyes. That band constricted once more, making it difficult to breathe. "Please don't do this."

"I have to," Noah said, his tone soft.

"Why?"

"Because I didn't do it the first time. Had I known then what you were planning that night, I never would've gone to sleep."

Noah talked about fifteen years ago like it was yesterday. But it wasn't. And Dare wasn't that same guy, and he needed to remember the pain that Noah had caused him.

Dare swallowed hard as he studied Noah's face. "You never came after me," he whispered, hating the hurt that slipped out.

"You're right, I didn't. I should have. Everything would be different if I'd come after you that next morning when I realized you weren't there." Noah swallowed hard. "But I didn't. And that's on me."

Dare had expected Noah to make excuses, but he wasn't. He was doing the opposite and claiming it was all his fault, which also wasn't true. Dare wasn't sure what to think about that. Worse, he couldn't even get angry, couldn't tell Noah off the way he'd imagined so many times because he had nothing to argue with.

"Don't go, Dare," Noah whispered, his hand reaching for Dare's.

Emotion clogged his throat as the warmth of Noah's touch seared him. He didn't want to go, but if he didn't, he knew what would happen. And in two short days, this trip would be over, and Dare wasn't sure he could survive another broken heart. Because there was no doubt in his mind that his heart would break if he allowed himself to get close to Noah again.

"I can't do this," Dare said, clearing his throat. "I can't pretend nothing happened between us."

"I can't, either."

"I..." God, he wasn't sure he could spit the words out. Taking a deep breath, he continued, "I don't want to just be your friend." He wanted so much more.

"Me, either."

Dare shook his head. "But I also can't have a fling with you and then walk away."

"No one's asking you to."

Dare straightened, doing his best not to look at the beds beckoning them. "No? Then what are you suggesting?"

Noah's gaze dropped and he shrugged. "I don't know, Dare. I just know that I don't want to spend the next two days with you avoiding me. I'd rather ... spend those two days *with* you."

Fuck.

Dare had no recourse. He couldn't yell, he couldn't be mad ... and he didn't think he could walk away. Not from this. Not from Noah when he was laying it out there.

They'd spent the past four days on the same ship, sharing the same cabin, reliving the same memories, and now there was an opportunity to ... what? He wasn't sure what would happen, but Noah was right. Spending the next two days avoiding him would be hell. Especially when he wanted to spend the next two days with him.

And possibly the days after that.

IT HAD BEEN a close call getting up to the cabin before Dare. Especially since Noah'd had to stop and congratulate the grooms, then slip out before Dare. Somehow Noah had managed, and during the short trek back, he had thought about all the things he'd wanted to say to Dare, all the questions he'd had over the years. His mind was still going a million miles a minute, but he hadn't yet come up with a solid plan.

When Noah had been sitting on the bed in the dark waiting for Dare to arrive, he hadn't been sure what he was going to say then, either, but he knew he had to tell the truth. And the truth was, he didn't know what tomorrow would bring, but he knew if he let this opportunity slip through his hands—the same way he'd let Dare slip through his hands fifteen years ago—he would hate himself.

Didn't mean if Dare turned him down he wouldn't hate himself, too. Rejection was a bitch, and Dare had been the one to teach him that. Back when Noah had woken up to find Dare gone, he'd felt the sting of it for the first time. He'd promised himself he would never let himself endure that again. Until now, he'd been successful. So as he watched Dare's face, waiting for that moment when he pushed him away, Noah held his breath.

He noticed when Dare's gaze slid to the beds again.

"I'm not sleeping with you," Dare muttered.

Noah grinned. "I wasn't planning to sleep with you." It was difficult, but he managed not to laugh. Dare was so fucking adorable, especially when it was obvious he wanted something he was denying himself.

"Whatever. You know you can't resist this," Dare said, glancing down at himself. "You've already proven that."

Noah sobered as he glanced at Dare's mouth. Dare was right about one thing, he couldn't resist, and he no longer planned to. Perhaps Dare would shove him away, but he couldn't hold back even one second longer.

Taking one step forward, he fought the smile when Dare took one step back. They did that same dance until Dare was up against the wall, their eyes locked.

Noah moved closer, pressing against Dare. He cupped Dare's face, the stubble sensually scraping against his palm as he swallowed hard.

"You're gonna kiss me, aren't you?" Dare asked, his voice low.

Noah nodded. "Yeah. I am."

His eyes darted from Dare's eyes to his lips. He had to kiss this man again, needed to feel his lips, his tongue, his hands. But he was scared. Nervous. Noah didn't want to fuck this up.

Pressing his forehead to Dare's, he contemplated what they were doing. He could feel Dare's warm breath against his lips, and he knew Dare was as worked up as he was. They both wanted this, no matter what their words said. It simply wasn't that easy.

Before he mustered the courage to make his move, Dare stunned him, gripping Noah's shirt in both fists, crushing their mouths together as Dare flipped their positions and Noah was the one against the wall. As much as Noah wanted to own this kiss, this was all Dare, and he found himself completely helpless to the onslaught.

They were a jumble of fumbling hands as they grabbed one another, holding, caressing, their lips melding together, tongues sliding effortlessly. Noah's dick was rock hard, his body desperate and aching as he gripped Dare's hips, jerking him forward until their lower bodies were doing a slow, sensual grind that mirrored their mouths.

"Damn you," Dare muttered, his breath warm against Noah's mouth seconds before his lips were crushed against his again.

Noah didn't even care about air as he inhaled Dare, loving the aggression he could feel in Dare's strong hands as he held Noah's head still, owning him with his mouth.

Fuck. This was better than he'd imagined. So much better, and he knew if he didn't stop it now, they would be naked on one of those beds within the next minute. Maybe two. As much as he wanted to feel Dare, skin to skin, he knew now wasn't the time. There was too much emotion, and the last thing Noah wanted was to wake up to find Dare gone in the morning.

Sliding his hands up, Noah gripped Dare's head, forcing their mouths apart. They were both panting, sucking in air, desperate for … more.

"Slow," Noah said as he dragged oxygen into his lungs. "Gotta take this slow."

"You always were the bossy one," Dare replied, leaning forward and pressing his forehead to Noah's.

Noah chuckled, releasing Dare's head and hugging him tightly. "You do that to me," he admitted. "You make me crazy."

Dare pulled back and frowned.

"In a good way," Noah clarified.

Fearless

They remained like that for a few minutes, staring at one another as the frenzied moment dissipated. There was still a hum beneath his skin, but Noah managed to ignore it. Mostly. He truly wasn't looking to rush this with Dare. He'd already fucked up once on this trip; he had no desire to do that again.

"What do we do now?" Dare looked as puzzled as Noah felt.

When Dare's thumb glided over Noah's bottom lip, he closed his eyes, his cock throbbing. He was so fucking hard it hurt.

"I don't know." He really didn't.

"You hungry?"

Opening his eyes, he looked at Dare, trying to see if that was a double entendre or not. Based on the feral look in Dare's eyes, it was possible he was taunting him, but he wasn't sure.

Dare chuckled. "For food. Not for me. I think it's pretty damn clear you want me."

Noah let his head fall back against the wall. He held Dare's stare. "I want you more than you know. But that's not what this is about."

"No?" Dare didn't look convinced.

"No." Noah reached for Dare's hands, linking their fingers together as he lifted them to his chest. "Not yet."

Making love to this man would require too much, and he couldn't handle it right now. The emotion would likely drag him under, and he needed to be ready. He wasn't ready. Yet.

Dare cocked an eyebrow, and when that sinful smirk tilted the very edges of his mouth, Noah realized he was in for it. "Wanna wager how long it'll take before you attack me again?"

Just like that, the easiness they'd known together sucked some of the tension out of the room, allowing Noah to breathe a little more. And because this was Dare, Noah couldn't refrain. "I think the better bet is who's gonna be able to refrain longer."

Dare nodded as though he was considering that. "You're on."

Those two words had Noah's dick pulsing again, and he didn't need to be a gambling man to know he was going to lose this hand. But at least he could put forth a little effort.

Maybe.

Twenty-Four

GETTING OUT OF that cabin was the only option Dare had. That or he was going to strip Noah naked and ride him until the sun came up. Or vice versa. He didn't really care which. Okay, yes, he did, but now was not the time for that. He needed to gather his thoughts.

Plus, he needed to return Roan's key and let him know that he wouldn't need a place to crash after all.

Then he needed to find food.

God, he was starving. He hadn't eaten much at the reception because he'd been too nervous. But even if he had, he would still be hungry. That was how he rolled.

By the time they emerged from their cabin, it seemed most of the other cruise-goers had called it a night. The halls were deserted, as was the main deck, where they ended up after making a quick pass through the casino and then deciding against any more gambling for the evening. As it was, the wager between them was steep enough. Dare knew he didn't have anything else to bet.

So he settled for pizza and soda, which they devoured outside.

For the next hour, they walked around, close but not too close. When he yawned for the third time, Noah suggested they head back, and Dare reluctantly agreed.

He was edgy, he couldn't deny that. Although they were alone out here—for the most part—being alone in their cabin was decidedly different. No one could happen upon them in there, which meant their clothes could fall off. And then he could... What if he tripped and his dick slipped right into Noah's mouth? That could be awkward.

Well, the last part wasn't too bad of an idea, provided it didn't result in any damage to his dick.

However, that wasn't going to happen tonight. Not on purpose and not by accident.

Once back in the cabin, Noah excused himself to take a shower, and Dare managed to pull off the rest of the monkey suit he was still wearing, keeping on his boxers before flipping off the light and climbing into bed. Although he was exhausted, he knew he wouldn't be able to sleep. At least not until Noah emerged from the bathroom. Which he finally did.

"You still awake?" Noah called out softly as he was climbing into the opposite bed.

"Yeah." Dare stared up at the ceiling in the dark, doing his best not to look at Noah. "Still awake."

"You okay?"

Dare could hear the concern in Noah's tone. It had been a long day. Top it off with the emotions that had wreaked havoc on him and he knew he should've been asleep by now.

"I'm good."

"Get some sleep," Noah told him. "We've only got two more full days on this ship, so we'll have to make the most of them."

Dare didn't respond, but he didn't close his eyes, either. He glanced over at Noah, noticing he had turned away from him.

Fearless

He tried to relax, but it was useless. Every muscle was tense, his cock was still throbbing, his balls aching, his body humming. Knowing he shouldn't act on his urges, Dare managed to stay in the bed for a whole ten minutes before finally kicking off the sheet and getting to his feet. When Noah didn't move, he figured he was asleep, but he joined him on the the tiny bed that was hardly big enough for one person, let alone two. That didn't stop him from slipping beneath the sheet and spooning up against him.

Noah instantly leaned into him, pressing his back to Dare's chest. For a brief moment, his breath was lodged in his lungs.

So many memories…

Dare slowly slid his hand up Noah's thigh to his hip. He gently dug his fingertips into Noah's flesh, stopping himself from doing anything more. It was enough to feel Noah's skin, the warmth of his body against his. His cock thought this was going to be a party and it got excited, but Dare ignored it. Or tried to.

Noah rasped his name when Dare pressed his lips to Noah's shoulder, getting closer. When Noah took Dare's hand from his hip, pulling it around him and holding it close to his chest, Dare released his breath. Emotion was hot and fierce inside him as his body recalled so many nights like this.

In an effort to relax, Dare slid his arm beneath Noah's head and inched closer until they were touching everywhere. He twined his fingers with Noah's, his hand still clutched to Noah's chest, and he held him. They remained in that position for several minutes, neither of them moving. The sound of their labored breaths filled the room. Strange how simply being this close could cause his pulse to race as though he'd run a marathon.

Noah's hand squeezed his, but again, neither of them moved. Dare wondered if Noah was as scared as he was. The next step for them could result in never-ending heartache. It had taken Dare long enough to get over Noah the first time; he wasn't sure he could do it again.

Yet he knew right then that there was no turning back. Regardless of the consequences.

IT TOOK A little while, but Dare's labored breaths finally evened out, and Noah suspected he had fallen asleep, which was a good thing. Although he would've given anything to roll Dare beneath him and spend the rest of the night lodged inside the man's sinful body, Noah knew that wasn't the best thing for them. Not tonight, anyway.

And this was good.

Better than good, actually.

Having Dare's arms around him was better than breathing.

Noah expected sleep would eventually come, but until then, he simply lay there, enjoying the warmth of Dare's body against his. It offered a comfort he hadn't had in quite some time. Possibly not since Dare. And while he fought the memories of that long-ago time, Noah promised himself that they would take this slow. Granted, slow was relative, but still. After all, they'd been down this road before.

"Why don't I move in here?"

Noah wasn't sure he'd heard Dare correctly; only the last few words registering as he fought from drifting off in Dare's arms.

Move in here?

Fearless

Was that what Dare had said? Had he heard him right? Or was he dreaming?

His body stilled as his brain tried to come back online. Dare's next words told him he wasn't dreaming and he had successfully fucked this up once again.

"Never mind. I'm still high from the sex."

"Probably." Not sure what to make of Dare's statement, Noah joked it off. "Makes you think crazy shit, huh?"

Okay, definitely not what he should've said. Dare went eerily still behind him, his hand no longer lingering on Noah's stomach. What should've been a nice, relaxing night at home had just taken an awkward turn, and Noah knew right where it was headed.

"Where do you see this going?"

Yep, another argument was coming.

Noah wished he could go back to sleeping, not wanting to hash this out with Dare right now. As it was, he'd been thinking the same thing himself. They practically lived together already because Dare spent so much time there, but Noah wasn't ready to move to the next level yet. Not until he knew Dare was ready. But Dare was only nineteen, far too young to be committing to one person for the rest of his life.

Unfortunately, it wasn't going to go away unless he talked about it. "See what going?"

"Us. I know it's not just the sex that's so great between us."

"But the sex is pretty fucking good, huh?" And it was good. So fucking good.

"Do you love me?"

Noah shifted so he could look at Dare over his shoulder. The question pissed him off. "Of course I do. I've told you that."

"Then what's the problem?"

He needed to see Dare's face, so he eased onto his back when Dare shifted. "You're only nineteen, Dare."

"Ah, good. Glad we're both aware of that. I thought for a second you forgot."

Shit. He hadn't meant it like that. "Dare..."

"No. I don't need you to remind me that I'm nineteen and that you're twenty-three. When you had your dick in my ass, or mine in yours, our ages didn't seem to be an issue."

Jesus Christ. Why did they have to keep doing this? "They're not an issue. The age difference isn't the problem."

And it really wasn't.

"Then what is?"

Okay, enough of the bullshit. He needed to face this head on. He pulled away from Dare and sat up, thrusting his hands in his hair as he tried to formulate his argument.

Dare got to his feet and started pacing the floor. "Are you seeing someone else?"

Noah couldn't believe his ears. Sometimes Dare's insecurity shocked the shit out of him. Like right now. "No, I'm not fucking seeing anyone else. Goddammit, Dare, why the fuck would you ask me something like that?"

"It's the only logical answer I can come up with. You don't want me to move in here, yet you can't give me a reason. Maybe there is someone else."

Noah got to his feet, trying to eliminate the physical space between them.

It wasn't that Noah didn't want him there. He simply wasn't ready for more yet. The keyword being yet. He would be eventually, but he needed time. "No. There's no one else. I love you. Only you. I thought I'd made that pretty damn clear."

Dare didn't respond.

Fearless

"Look…" Noah cupped Dare's cheek, needing his full attention. "Things are good between us. I don't see any reason we should rush it."

"Rush it? We've been together for two fucking years."

Again, probably not the right thing to say, but now that it was out there, Noah needed to clarify. "I know. And you're only nineteen."

"Why do you always say that? It's always about my age, but I don't fucking understand. If I were twenty, would that change things? 'Cause in a few months, that'll be the case. What excuse will you use then?"

Excuse? It wasn't a fucking excuse. "You're too damn young to think about settling down with anyone."

"No! You don't get to do that. You don't get to blame this on me. No one gets to tell me what I am and am not ready for. I get to do that. And honestly, I want more than this. I'm talking forever."

Noah clenched his teeth together. "Babe, you're just a kid. Forever's a long damn time."

Okay, and now he felt like an asshole. He hadn't meant it the way it sounded. But he had meant it. Dare was too young to be thinking about long term.

"Dare… Come on. I don't wanna fight with you."

"You're right."

Noah pulled Dare into his arms, wanting to comfort him. There was no reason they needed to go into this right now. Things were good between them. They had all the time in the world. He didn't understand why Dare was so insistent that they take the next step.

When Dare didn't say anything more, Noah jumped at the opportunity to put this behind them. Pulling back, he looked at Dare. "You ready for bed?"

"Yeah, sure."

"Good. I'm exhausted. Come on. I wanna hold you."

That had been the last time Noah had held Dare in his arms.

Until right now.

Even though Dare had broken his heart, Noah realized he had never gotten completely over him. And here they were.

The true test would come once they were off this ship and the real world had embraced them once again. Fifteen years was a long time. So many things had happened during that time, and they needed to get to know each other again before they moved too fast.

The physical aspect was the least of Noah's worries. It was clear they were both hot for one another. Then again, that had never been a problem. The big question was whether or not they could make this work.

Unlike back then, they weren't too young, they weren't too naïve, they weren't too immature for what would transpire between them. That meant it was up to them to do this right.

So, as Noah drifted off in Dare's arms, he made a silent promise that he would focus on doing this the right way. They would take their time and see where this led them.

Finding love once in a lifetime was a blessing. Finding that same love twice … that was rare.

Fearless

HUDSON KNEW HE should've gone back to his cabin hours ago, but he hadn't managed to get his ass out of his chair. The wedding reception had long ago died out, the grooms had disappeared, most of the other guests had made their way back to their cabins for the night. In fact, the only people left were Hudson, Teague, AJ, and Milly. Even the bartender had bailed.

He should've done the same, but no. He was still here, waiting. For what, he wasn't sure. It wasn't because his brother was in the process of flirting with Milly, either—they were adults; they would do what they wanted to do—though he was keeping a close eye on those two.

No, his concern lay first and foremost with the drunk kid who refused to give up for the night even though the bar was officially closed. Not that Teague was necessarily a kid, but he was acting like one right now, cursing beneath his breath as he fought to sit in his chair while holding on to his empty glass. Hudson had no idea how much he'd drunk tonight, but if his inability to remain upright was any indicator, it was too damn much.

Teague turned in his chair, then stood on unsteady legs.

This should get interesting.

When Teague stumbled and caught himself on a chair, Hudson internally sighed and got to his feet. He approached Teague slowly, waiting for him to acknowledge him. When he did, it was with a frown.

Although he doubted Teague would understand him, Hudson signed: *You need to get to your cabin.*

"Thanks for the bit of advice, Dad," Teague replied belligerently.

Good thing was Teague did understand him. Bad thing was that Hudson was going to have hell getting Teague where he needed to be. It was clear he wouldn't be getting there on his own.

Before he could sign anything more, Teague tripped and practically landed in Hudson's arms. He helped the kid back to his feet, put his arm around his back, and then guided him toward the door. Apparently, he was going to have to do this the hard way.

"Why the fuck do you have to smell so good?" Teague mumbled as Hudson led him toward the elevator. "And why the hell aren't you with your boyfriend?"

Since AJ was his *brother*—not his boyfriend— Hudson didn't even consider answering. If the kid hadn't noticed AJ flirting with Milly, that wasn't his problem. Plus, his hands were tied up at the moment, so he couldn't respond.

It took ten minutes to get Teague up to his cabin, and that was *after* they went to the wrong floor. Twice. In Teague's inebriated state, he had transposed the numbers, but they finally made it. Hopefully.

Hudson signed for Teague to hand over the key card when they reached the door that was supposedly the right one. Teague didn't seem to understand. That or he was purposely being an asshole. With Teague, it could go either way.

"Fuck. Why's the room spinning so damn much?" Teague grumbled, reaching out and grabbing for the wall.

Hudson got his arm around him again, forced his hand into Teague's pocket, and finally recovered the key.

"I didn't say you could touch me," Teague mouthed, his words slurred.

Good thing Hudson hadn't asked.

With one arm around Teague, Hudson managed to unlock the door, push it open with his foot, and then use Teague's body to prop it open while he helped him inside.

"I knew one day I'd get you to my room. Didn't think it'd be so soon."

Hudson had to assume Teague was talking to him since there was no one else around, but he didn't put too much stock in what the kid had to say. He was beyond drunk.

Since he couldn't speak, he couldn't give Teague instruction, so he had to help things along by guiding him toward the bed. When Teague looked up at him, Hudson nodded toward the bed, hoping to get his point across.

Teague's eyes slid down to Hudson's mouth, and he wished he could've groaned to show Teague that this really wasn't a good idea. Unfortunately, no sound would come out, and he was still trying to use one arm to get Teague to the bed. Releasing him would've caused Teague to fall onto the floor, which, now that he thought about it, probably wasn't the worst idea he'd ever had.

"Fuck, I've wanted to kiss you for so goddamn long," Teague said softly, his hand coming up to touch Hudson's mouth.

His brain instructed his head to turn, to dodge the hand, but for some reason, Hudson wasn't listening to his brain. Part of him was caught up in Teague's brilliant blue gaze. His eyes were glassy, but there was so much heat there it was hard to look away.

"Sometimes I wish I could hate you as much as I pretend to."

The words coming out of Teague's mouth stunned him. Their relationship—which consisted of working alongside one another from time to time—was volatile at best. Teague didn't seem to have an issue with anyone at the marina except for Hudson, and he didn't know why that was. Aside from the fact that he'd seen that same heated look in Teague's eyes before, and Hudson had always masked his own physical reaction to the kid, he couldn't think of any other reason Teague would hate him so much.

Now it looked as though he was only pretending.

Hudson wasn't sure what to do with that information.

Knowing this was going to go the wrong direction if he didn't get out of that cabin, Hudson used his bigger body to urge Teague back, closer to the mattress. Before he could force him down, Teague's hand slid behind his neck and he jerked Hudson closer, their lips coming together.

He fought the urge for a moment, but his underlying desire for Teague took over, and as soon as Teague's tongue was in his mouth, Hudson was kissing him back. Rather than let Teague control it, he took over, jerking Teague against him and holding him in place with one arm wrapped around him, and using his free hand to hold Teague's jaw where he wanted him.

The kiss was brutal and incredible, but it didn't take long for Hudson to remember that Teague was intoxicated, and if they were lucky, he wouldn't remember this in the morning. He finally managed to pull back, and when he did, he forced Teague onto the bed, thrusting his hand through his hair as he turned toward the door.

"Where're you goin'?" Teague called out.

Hudson could do nothing more than shake his head as he got out of there as fast as he fucking could. Too bad he wasn't intoxicated, too, because there was no way in hell he was going to forget that kiss.

Fearless

Not for a long fucking time.

Twenty-Five

Friday, June 3rd
Cruise, day six

DARE WOKE BEFORE the sun was completely up. Seemed his little head had been doing wicked things while his big head had been attempting to recuperate. Looked like his little head was far more determined.

He reached down and absently rubbed his cock, realizing what the attraction was. He was still in Noah's bed. Seemed his dick was like a lightning rod. And the man beside him was the electricity.

"Morning." The roughness of Noah's voice had him lifting his eyes.

Dare opened his eyes to find that Noah was lying on his side, facing him, which put them eye to eye. Smiling, Dare met Noah's sleepy gaze. "I didn't know you were awake."

"Something kept stabbing me in the ass. Made it nearly impossible to sleep."

Dare rolled onto his back, his riotous cock tenting his boxers and the sheet. "Sorry."

"Don't be sorry." Noah's hand slid to Dare's thigh, making him suck in a breath. Because the bed was so small, Noah moved closer.

He turned his head and met Noah's gaze. "I hope you know what you're doing." The words were a raspy whisper, but he attempted to inject a warning in there.

"I've had a little practice," Noah answered, laughing.

That wasn't what Dare meant, but he suspected Noah knew that.

He continued to watch Noah's face as the warm hand on his leg hesitantly moved higher, sliding beneath his boxers, grazing his balls lightly before warm fingers wrapped around his dick.

"Fuck." He closed his eyes when Noah began stroking him. There was no urgency in the movement, a simple, leisurely stroke up and down, up and down. "Noah…"

"Say my name again." Noah's words were said softly against his ear as Noah shifted closer, his thigh resting over Dare's. "I love hearing you say my name."

"Noah…" He would say it a million times if Noah would just keep doing that.

"Move the sheet."

Dare pushed the sheet down as he was instructed.

"Take the boxers off."

He didn't hesitate then, either. While he worked them down his hips, then kicked them somewhere across the room, his attention was riveted on the hand curled around his throbbing cock. Noah's thumb grazed the swollen head, swiping the bead of pre-come that had formed.

Noah kissed Dare's shoulder as he jacked Dare's dick gently, steadily. It wasn't enough, but at the same time, Dare feared it was too much.

"I want to take you in my mouth," Noah whispered.

Dare groaned, still watching the erotic movement of Noah's hand.

"I want to wrap my lips right here"—Noah circled his fingers just beneath the head—"and suck you into my mouth."

He wasn't sure he was going to last that long.

Noah's hand trailed lower, cupping his balls. Dare spread his legs, hooking one foot on the edge of the mattress, the other sliding between Noah's legs so he could lift his hips, silently urging Noah lower. He wasn't disappointed when Noah grazed his taint, then continued lower until he rimmed his asshole with his fingertip.

Oh, hell.

"Then I want to put my tongue here." Noah pressed against his sphincter, making him moan.

Dare was going to lose it.

"I want to drive you crazy, make you beg me to fuck you."

Oh, he would beg, all right. Shit, he might start begging now. He bit his lip to keep from doing so.

Noah's hand circled his dick once more.

"Mouth…" Dare barely whispered the word.

"What was that?" Noah kissed his shoulder again.

"Put your mouth on me. Please… Fuck… Noah… *Please* put your mouth on me." Yep, definitely begging.

Noah repositioned himself, trailing his lips down Dare's stomach as he knelt between Dare's thighs. Never once did Dare look away, awed by the sight of the gorgeous naked man between his legs. So beautiful, so perfect.

When Noah's mouth grazed the underside of his cock, Dare reached for him, cupping the back of his head firmly but gently. He wasn't guiding Noah; he didn't need to. He simply needed the connection. Twining his fingers in Noah's dark hair, he watched when Noah's tongue glided up the length of him, circled the head before he opened his mouth, and took Dare's dick inside.

"Oh … fucking … fuck." His brain was obliterated by pleasure, sparks shot straight down his spine, the hair on his arms stood on end as the most incredible feeling overwhelmed him. "Noah… God, yes … suck me. Oh…"

Dare's back bowed, his abs contracted as he attempted to thrust into Noah's mouth. Noah was having none of that, though, controlling Dare's pleasure in a way no other man ever could. That had always been one thing he loved about Noah. They were so much alike in the sense that they were both switches, both controlling, yet they both needed to be dominated at times. It was Dare's turn to be the submissive one now.

Dare closed his eyes, growling as the warm suction drove him wild.

Noah's mouth disappeared momentarily. "Open your eyes. Watch me, Dare. Watch every thing I do to you."

He popped open one eye, then the other. He wasn't sure he could watch without blowing his load, but he was going to make a concerted effort.

WHEN NOAH HAD woken up a short time ago, he hadn't anticipated this happening. But now that it was, he wasn't sure he'd be able to stop until he got his fill of Dare. And that likely wouldn't be today.

This was just the beginning.

He loved the way Dare groaned when Noah wrapped his lips around the swollen head of his cock and sucked him. Dare's dick was thick and long, which made the task of taking all of him in his mouth nearly impossible, but he enjoyed trying. Noah loved the way Dare held his head but never attempted to control him. He loved the way Dare's eyes dilated as he watched what Noah was doing to him.

Hell, he loved everything about this moment.

Noah wanted to spend the rest of the day driving this man wild, because he was just so fucking beautiful when he came undone.

"Noah… Please…"

He freed Dare's dick from his mouth, then took him in hand as he sat back on his haunches, stroking him slowly. "Please what?"

"Please… Anything… Everything… Fuck."

Dare's hips were thrusting upward, driving his dick into Noah's hand. His nipples were hard, the piercings catching the light and drawing Noah's attention.

If Dare was anything like he'd been before, he wouldn't want to come too quickly, which was why Noah released his cock with one last stroke, then crawled up Dare's body, stopping to tease his piercings with his teeth. Dare's hand returned to his hair, holding his head as he ground their lower bodies together. The fingers twined in his hair tightened, sending shards of pleasure-pain straight to his cock.

"Want you in my mouth…"

Who was Noah to argue with that? He worked his way up until he was straddling Dare's chest, feeding his cock into his mouth while he reached down and brushed Dare's hair back off his forehead. In this position, Noah got to control the pace and that was the best thing for now. If he let Dare loose, there was no way Noah would last.

239

Placing one hand on the wall, Noah lifted up so that he could press his hips forward, driving his dick into Dare's luscious mouth, slowly, inch by inch. "Love fucking your mouth... So damn good. That's it, Dare... Suck me."

Dare was by far the most attentive lover Noah had ever known. Even at nineteen, Dare hadn't been a one-inning player, he'd been ready to play through. He was never satisfied with simply fucking, either. It was all about the foreplay. Any other time, that would've been fantastic, except Noah was ready to blow, and the soft, warm friction of Dare's mouth was pushing him closer and closer to the edge.

Noah gripped Dare's jaw and pulled his dick from between his lips. "Not ready to come."

"Good, 'cause I'm not finished with you yet."

That made two of them.

In true Dare fashion, Noah found himself flipped backward, landing on the bed with a thud as Dare came down over him. The guy was far more agile than he appeared. And stronger, given the fact that Noah probably outweighed him by a good twenty pounds.

Noah stared up at him, waiting to see what Dare would do next. When Dare's solid body came to rest on his, Noah wrapped his arms around him.

He realized Dare was staring at his mouth, so Noah made his move, pulling Dare closer and rising to meet his lips. He pushed his tongue into Dare's mouth, but that lasted all of three seconds before Dare pulled back.

"No fair."

Noah frowned, confused.

"You got to brush your teeth this morning."

That made him laugh. Leave it to Dare to bring that up now.

"And?"

Dare was still for a moment, staring down at him, but rather than kiss him again, the man hopped off the bed and strutted over to the bathroom while Noah tilted his head back and watched him upside down.

He sighed as he resigned himself to waiting.

The door closed. The toilet flushed. The water came on in the sink, and a minute later, it went off.

Noah tilted his head back again and watched as Dare returned, only this time he went to his suitcase.

"By the way, pissing with a hard-on isn't all that easy."

Noah chuckled. It did make aiming rather difficult.

"What are you doing?" Knowing Dare, the guy was going to take a shower, too.

He watched as Dare rummaged around in his suitcase, searching by feel only. When he stood back up, he had produced condoms and a small tube of lubricant.

Noah wasn't sure how he felt about that. Dare had packed that stuff for this trip, which meant he'd obviously been prepared for…

"I haven't had sex in nearly a year. Well…" Dare glanced at the condom, then back to Noah. "My hand doesn't count."

Noah's eyes widened at Dare's admission. "A year?"

Dare nodded. "Doesn't mean I'm not prepared for anything."

Knowing Dare hadn't been with anyone in a year… Noah wasn't even sure what to think about that.

Twenty-Six

DARE WASN'T SURE why he'd admitted that to Noah. It wasn't like he'd asked or anything. But the way Noah had been looking at him when he'd produced the condoms had made him want to explain. He was always prepared because one never knew what might happen.

And to think, he wasn't even a Boy Scout and he knew that rule.

But he honestly hadn't expected to use them.

Thankfully, Noah hadn't moved from where he was, so after tossing the condoms and the lube onto the mattress beside him, Dare returned to his previous position, directly over Noah. Now that he had minty fresh breath (hey, a guy had to pay attention to the important things), he could get back to what he'd been doing.

Noah.

As he crawled over the sexy, naked guy on the bed, he smiled. "I see someone was waiting for me." He reached down and stroked Noah's cock, fisting it slowly.

In turn, Noah tweaked Dare's nipple piercings, making him hiss.

"That hurt?"

"Only in a very, *very* good way."

"Good to know."

"Now where were we?" Dare leaned down and brushed his lips over Noah's once more.

Within seconds, their brief interruption was completely forgotten, and Dare was once again lost in Noah's kiss. The way his mouth moved against his, his tongue skillfully controlling Dare's... Yeah, he could get used to this.

Although he enjoyed the foreplay, there was only so much he could take before the chance of him blowing before he was ready became a real possibility. He was closing in on that moment now. Just from Noah's kiss.

Dare wanted ... no, he *needed* to feel Noah inside him, and he didn't want to wait any longer.

Blindly searching the bed beside them, Dare located one of the condoms without ever breaking the kiss. It wasn't easy, but he managed to open it and roll it over Noah's thick cock, then lubed him up, still hovering over him.

Using his own legs to force Noah's legs down, Dare straddled his hips, their mouths still fused, feasting on one another as the cabin warmed from the heat generating between them.

"Inside me, Noah. Need to feel you ... inside me."

Noah reached around him and worked his cock against Dare's ass. He probably could've used more lube, but he didn't want to stop to get it.

"You sure about this?" Noah's mouth traveled over his jaw, his teeth nipping, while Dare forced his hips down, taking Noah inside.

"God, yes." The pain was intense, his body requiring a few seconds to acclimate to the intrusion. The muscles stretched and burned as Noah's cock worked him open.

Noah's hands gripped his hips and stilled him when he attempted to take him deeper.

"Slow," Noah whispered. "Not in a hurry."

Maybe Noah wasn't, but Dare was. He was eager to feel him all the way inside him. If it were up to Dare, Noah would be pounding him by now, except that clearly wasn't on Noah's agenda, which meant Dare had to adjust to Noah's pace.

Not an easy task, that was for sure.

"Ride me," Noah instructed softly.

Dare managed to lift his upper body, planting his hands on each side of Noah's head as he rocked forward and back. Noah still controlled the pace with his hands on Dare's hips, but this was better. Easier.

So fucking good.

It was difficult to look at Noah; so many emotions swamped him. He'd never thought in a million years that they would see each other again, much less be making love again.

There was a pang in his chest that stole his breath. This wasn't making love. This was fucking. It couldn't be love, because Dare had no intention of going back there again. No matter what he was willing to risk, no matter how much he wanted Noah, how desperate he was for more of this, he refused to fall in love with him again.

Sex. Sure. The rest… Nope, not happening.

But he didn't need to worry about that now because this was what he wanted.

"Beautiful," Noah breathed roughly, pulling Dare back to the present.

Dare lifted his gaze to meet Noah's eyes, watching him while Noah fucked him slow and easy. It was a sensual thrust and retreat that felt so fucking good Dare never wanted it to end. When Noah reached between them and stroked Dare's cock, he sucked in air, holding it in his chest as pleasure slammed into him.

"Need more…" Dare leaned down and brushed his lips against Noah's. "Fuck me harder, Noah. Harder."

"On your back," Noah insisted.

Dare thrust back again, then smiled. Didn't need to tell him twice.

NOAH WASN'T SURE why he hadn't thought to push the beds together while Dare had been in the bathroom. It would've made this a hell of a lot easier.

Despite how small the bed was, Noah managed to get Dare on his back, then guided his cock right back into Dare's tight ass before practically folding Dare in half. Dare had asked for harder, and Noah couldn't hold back any longer.

It might not have been a year since Noah had last had sex, but it had been pretty damn close. It'd been even longer since he'd felt something as incredible as this. He knew it had more to do with the connection he had with Dare than anything else, but still. This was fucking heaven.

While he pressed his hands against the backs of Dare's thighs, Noah began fucking him. Slowly at first, then faster, harder, deeper. He watched as his cock penetrated Dare over and over, the sensations so intense his mind went blank for a little while as he took his pleasure from Dare's body. He could hear Dare's moans and his pleas for harder and faster. Noah even managed to give Dare what he asked for, but he was so lost in the moment it was a wonder he held on for as long as he did.

His balls drew up close to his body. The electrical current started in his fingertips and shot all the way down to his toes without warning. "Gonna ... come."

"Come for me, Noah," Dare growled.

That sexy rumble and the way Dare's ass hugged his dick sent him over the edge. He fought for air as his dick erupted, pulsing inside Dare's body.

It took a minute to catch his breath, and when he finally managed, he realized Dare was holding him, his big, warm hands caressing Noah's back. He felt safe like this. As though nothing else in the world mattered.

Dare's hand slid down to Noah's ass and he squeezed. "My turn."

Noah chuckled, getting to his feet and tossing the spent condom in the bathroom trash before returning to find Dare suited up already.

"Bed." The sharp bark of Dare's voice made his dick jump. He doubted he could get hard again so quickly, but stranger things had happened. Considering he was about to get fucked by Dare, it was highly possible.

"Where do you want me?" He met Dare's gaze as he challenged him.

"On your knees. Chest on the bed."

Without complaint, Noah crawled onto the small bed, keeping his ass in the air. Dare stopped him from moving too far, then jerked him back so that he was practically hanging off the end of the bed.

Fully expecting Dare to impale him, Noah nearly came up off the mattress when he felt the warmth of Dare's tongue against his sensitive flesh.

"Oh, fuck." He hadn't expected Dare to rim his ass so exquisitely. His dick returned to half-mast almost immediately. Using his hand, he worked his shaft, enjoying the warring sensation of his hand on his dick and the tongue fucking he was receiving from Dare. "Fuck, that feels good. Too good."

Dare spread Noah's ass cheeks and tongue-fucked him harder, making brilliant flashes of light pulse behind his closed eyelids. He never wanted him to stop. When Dare's mouth traveled up the center of his back, Noah prepared himself for Dare's cock to spear him, but it didn't come.

"Relax, Noah. I'm not in a hurry."

He laughed because that sure hadn't been the case a little while ago. Then again, he knew Dare enjoyed the teasing because, when he finally did come, it would be explosive. Noah moaned softly when Dare worked one lubed finger into his ass, then a second. He rocked back against Dare's hand as those fingers brushed his prostate, making his body hum to life again.

"Dare…" Noah gripped the comforter with one hand, spreading his legs farther apart so Dare would fuck him deeper. "Don't stop. Feels so good." Better than good, actually.

"You ready for me yet?"

Noah nodded his affirmation but realized Dare couldn't see his head. "God, yes. Fuck me. I need to feel your cock inside me."

Dare's fingers slipped out and the head of his dick pressed against him. Noah relaxed, then pressed back against the intrusion. As promised, Dare didn't rush, tormenting Noah as he slipped past the ring of muscle, then pulled back, repeating the exquisite torture for what felt like forever.

"Aww, fuck… So fucking tight. Relax for me." Dare's hands gripped Noah's hips roughly. "Ahh, yeah. Just like that… Love your ass."

Noah swallowed hard, wondering if Dare even knew what he was saying.

Dare retreated, thrust forward again. Over and over, Noah took the sweet penetration, meeting every drive of Dare's hips with his own until Dare was pounding him over and over, leaning over him and holding Noah's shoulders to keep him in place.

Dare's rough groans echoed in the small room.

"Dare... Oh, fuck... Don't stop."

"Never gonna stop..." Dare was breathing hard as he slammed into him again and again. It felt like hours passed by the time Dare's thrusts became erratic, his fingers digging into Noah's shoulders as he fucked him harder and harder.

"Come for me, Dare. Come for me, baby." Oh, God, it was so damn good. Noah never wanted him to stop, but he was going to come again, and he didn't want to until Dare found his release.

"Noah... Oh, God... Noah. Can't stop... Gonna..." Dare's body stilled above him.

Noah jerked his dick roughly, his climax slamming into him as powerfully as Dare had been fucking him.

They collapsed on the bed, and Noah pulled Dare against his side, kissing his head and holding him. He never wanted today to end, never wanted to leave this cabin. They only had a couple more days on this ship, and he wanted to spend it right here in Dare's arms for as long as he could.

Because no matter what, reality was going to come back in roughly forty-eight hours when they docked in Florida, and Noah knew that it wouldn't be like this forever. Nothing this perfect would last forever.

"Food," Dare grumbled a short while later. "Feed me, Noah."

Noah chuckled, then kissed Dare's forehead again. "Fine. Let's shower. Then I'll feed you."

"Food, not cock." Dare opened his eyes and looked at Noah. "Although I'll take that for dessert. Oh, and we're gonna need to get more condoms."

That they were.

And just like that, the easiness returned, and Noah was eager to see what the rest of the trip would bring. They still had two more nights together, so he had that to look forward to.

For now, it would have to be enough.

Twenty-Seven

Sunday, June 5th
Cruise, day eight, back in port

"DARE…"

Noah tried to break the kiss, but Dare wasn't going to let him. He wasn't ready just yet. The ship was docked, and they'd been advised to disembark, but Dare wanted to stay right here for as long as he could.

"If we don't get off this ship, we're gonna miss our flight back to Texas."

Dare slid his lips along Noah's jaw, kissing him while he worked the button of Noah's jeans open. "There'll be another flight."

"Dare…" This time the word held a warning.

Dare worked his lips up to Noah's ear, nipping the lobe. "Turn around and put your hands on the wall."

Despite his objections, Noah pivoted away from him while Dare worked Noah's jeans down his legs, then freed his own cock and suited up with the condom he'd produced when Noah had been in the shower.

"We're gonna be late," Noah muttered.

"We'll be fine. Now spread those beautiful legs for me."

Dare watched as Noah worked one foot out of his jeans, then did as instructed. Because they really were short on time, Dare opted to forego the foreplay, greasing his cock with lube before slipping inside the tight warmth of Noah's body.

For the past two days, they'd fucked more times than Dare could count. He felt like a damn teenager, his dick always hard and ready. Hell, Dare had already fucked Noah once this morning, but the thought of getting on a plane and having to wait several more hours before he could do it again wasn't at all appealing.

"Fuck…" Dare hissed when he pushed in deep. "I could do this forever."

Noah flattened his face against the wall, then reached back and grabbed Dare's hip while Dare pressed into him, thrusting slowly at first. Standing up wasn't the easiest position for them, especially since they were the same height, but Dare didn't care.

"You like that? Like feeling my cock in your ass?"

Noah nodded, his breathing ragged already.

"Yeah? Tell me. Tell me how much you like it."

"So … good…"

"Bend over." Dare needed more leverage, especially if he was supposed to hurry this along. He wasn't lying when he said he could do this forever. They'd spent the last two days fucking like rabbits and still Dare hadn't gotten enough of Noah.

Noah turned, planting his hands on the vanity counter while Dare moved with him. Once Noah was bent over, Dare grabbed his hips and fucked him harder, slamming in deep, retreating, then slamming in deep again.

"Damn… Noah… I can't get enough."

"Less talking… More fucking."

Dare chuckled, then focused all his energy on sending them both over the edge.

SEVERAL HOURS LATER, Noah was sitting on the airplane next to Dare, thankful that they'd somehow ended up on the same flight home with the rest of Dare's friends. Then again, since Milly had been in charge of all of the travel arrangements, perhaps it hadn't been a coincidence. And everyone was there—Milly, AJ, Hudson, Teague, and Roan. Well, everyone except for Gannon and Cam. Those two were off on their honeymoon. Noah recalled Cam going on and on about Gannon's first time to jump out of a plane or something. He hoped like hell Cam got that on camera.

Dare leaned over, his mouth against Noah's ear. "Good thing you let me fuck you already or we'd be joining the mile-high club in a few minutes."

A tremor raced down Noah's spine at Dare's seductive words. Maybe they were a little lewd, but it still turned Noah on. And yes, it was a good thing. Considering they'd spent the majority of the past two days doing little except fucking one another, it was a wonder Noah could still get it up.

"So you're off the hook for a few hours."

Noah smirked. "Is that right?"

Dare sat up straight in his chair, grinning like a fool. "That's right. But no promises once this thing is back on the ground."

Noah had noticed that ever since the first time they'd made love, Dare had turned everything into sex between them. Sure, they talked about anything and everything, but it seemed Dare's central focus was on sex. It was as though that was his armor, his way of dealing with this connection they shared. At first, Noah hadn't thought anything of it, but now that they were headed back home, he had to wonder if they would be able to take the next step. If Dare only wanted to keep this as a casual sexual involvement, Noah wasn't sure he could oblige.

Granted, the sex was phenomenal and he hoped it would never end, but he needed something more. And no, he didn't miss the irony of the situation. Back when they'd been together years ago, Noah had been all about keeping it physical between them while Dare was the one pushing for more.

Now, it looked as though they were trading places.

Glancing over at Dare, Noah wondered if it was something he should mention.

Dare beat him to the punch. "You working when you get back?"

"I've got another week off. Figured I'd need a vacation from the vacation."

"And do you?"

Noah smirked. "I could use some sleep, yes."

"I'll take that as a compliment."

It dawned on Noah that he didn't know whether they lived close by or not. He turned to Dare. "Where do you live, anyway? Which lake is the marina on?"

"Lake Buchanan."

Noah knew right where that was. "Not far from me, then. Thirty minutes, maybe. I'm in Cedar Park."

Dare looked at him. "So, you think we might hang out this week?"

"It's possible."

Dare leaned over and pressed his mouth to Noah's ear. "A little late to be playing hard to get now. But, if you'd like, I'll be more than happy to chase you until your clothes fall of."

Noah chuckled, trying to ignore the fact that the deep rumble of Dare's voice was making his dick hard. Knowing Dare would only keep on—not a good thing on an airplane full of people—Noah conceded, answering Dare's question. "I'd like to see you this week if possible. Maybe you can come by my place. I can cook you dinner."

Dare instantly looked away, pretending to be focusing on something outside the window. "Or you could come by my place. We'll grab food out somewhere."

Interesting. It sounded innocent, but again, Noah was already suspecting that Dare was trying to keep his distance. Still, he figured he could play along. "Sounds like a plan."

Leaning back in his chair, Noah closed his eyes. Sleep wouldn't come, but no one else would realize that. He needed a few minutes. There were a lot of ways he could see this playing out, but none of them would end well. Although he'd gone and fallen for this man twice in his lifetime, Noah was pretty sure he was the only one willing to give it everything.

And that ... that was disappointing.

Twenty-Eight

THE TRIP BACK home was decidedly less stressful than the trip to the ship, that was for sure. In fact, it had been rather pleasant. Dare had been on the same flight as everyone else, which meant he got a few extra hours to spend with Noah before they went their separate ways in the real world.

Even though he was going to be busy with the marina, covering it with Roan until Cam returned from his honeymoon, Dare was glad to be back. Although he hadn't seen Noah since their plane had touched down in Austin yesterday afternoon, he'd heard from him. They'd traded texts and even had a conversation last night that had resulted in phone sex, something Dare now was quite fond of. Especially when it came to phone sex with Noah. The man had a dirty mouth on him.

Now, as he stood behind the counter waiting for Roan to make his appearance for the day, Dare continued to glance at his phone. He felt stupid for being overeager to hear from Noah, but he couldn't help it. Their last couple of days on the ship had been mind-blowing. The only thing he had wanted to do was get Noah naked and beneath him again and again. And now it was all he could think about.

Except, last night on the phone, Noah had mentioned taking Dare on a date. According to him, it seemed to be the logical next step since they'd agreed to take things slow. Not that Dare thought fucking like rabbits was taking things slow, but apparently Noah wanted to do this the right way.

Naked was the right way, if you asked him.

Looking up, Dare noticed Roan coming around the corner and heading toward the door. Since Roan lived in the other upstairs apartment, he didn't have far to go to get to work.

He took in Roan's disheveled appearance. If Dare was right, Roan had just rolled out of bed.

The door opened and Dare waited for the chime to sound. When it did, Roan squeaked, damn near hitting the ceiling when he jumped, glancing back at the door as though it had bitten him in the ass.

"What the fuck was that?" Roan asked, glaring at him.

"It's the new chime," he said proudly. He'd set out to adjust the timing, as they'd done on numerous occasions, but when that hadn't worked, Dare had opted to add a few features. Personally, he was quite fond of it. "I couldn't fix the timing, but the new sound's cool, huh?"

"No, it's not," Roan grumbled. "Change it back."

Dare snorted, but it wasn't that he hadn't expected it. The sound of a dog growling ferociously probably wasn't the best way to welcome customers to the marina, but it was still funny as shit.

Reaching for the controller he'd placed under the counter, Dare hit a button.

"That better?"

Roan rolled his eyes. "No."

Okay, so monkeys were apparently out, too. This guy was a party pooper.

"How 'bout this?" He hit the button again.

"Dare!"

Laughing, he changed it from the hyenas to the boring chirp it had been originally. Still, he had no intention of removing the new sounds, so at least he had options for the future.

"Why do you look like you're hungover?" Dare questioned, stepping out of the way when Roan reached for the coffeepot.

"Because I've been up half the damn night," he rumbled in response.

"Your sister?" Dare knew that Roan's sister was going through a rough patch. She was an addict, and she'd relapsed at least five times in the past year. Roan was spending a lot of time trying to get her into a rehab that would keep her for longer than a week. Apparently her freak-outs were frequent and disturbing to the other patients. Since she refused not to act belligerent, they were having a hard time finding a place that would keep her. Dare didn't envy the man at all. Not for the first time, he was grateful that he was an only child.

"We got any appointments today?"

Okay, so apparently Roan wasn't going to go into the details.

"Just one," he told Roan, glancing at the calendar. "Tomorrow it picks back up, though."

Good thing Cam would be back by the weekend, because they'd be busy for sure by then. With summer temperatures officially in effect, the lake was going to be hopping.

"When's Lulu coming back?" Roan inquired.

"Tim's gonna drop her off this afternoon."

Roan nodded.

He gave Roan a minute to sip his coffee before he continued. "Oh, and I've gotta slip out at lunch."

Roan's eyebrow lifted. "Hot date with the firefighter?"

He wished. "No. I promised Grams I'd stop by when I got back. It was too late to do that last night."

"Gotcha. I can watch the place while you're out."

"Keith called earlier," Dare noted. "Said he'd be happy to help in the office if we need him." It wasn't unusual for Cam's brother-in-law to offer to help, but they usually didn't need to take him up on his offer.

"If the week picks up, we might." Roan glanced toward the back door. "You seen Teague yet today?"

"Nope." And Dare wasn't sure he would. Something weird was going on with that kid. Ever since the night of the wedding, Teague had been acting strangely. Granted, he was always standoffish toward Hudson, but this seemed different for whatever reason.

"I'll text him. I'm gonna go talk to Hudson."

Dare nodded, watching the parking lot as a truck pulled in and two guys climbed out.

Looked like they had their first customers of the day.

ALTHOUGH HE STILL had a week off, Noah had woken early that morning, geared up and ready to do something. He didn't really care what. Since his calendar was clear—he'd pushed all appointments for his roofing business to next week—he had nothing to do and he wasn't used to that.

So, the first thing he did was clean his already spotless apartment from top to bottom. He hoped to convince Dare to come over, so he used that as his excuse. Truth, it wouldn't have mattered. He would've cleaned it anyway, but seeing Dare again was definitely good incentive.

By the time he was finished doing that, it was after noon, and Noah found himself picking up his phone and checking to make sure it was working. He did that at least a couple dozen times before he realized he was becoming obsessed. Seriously, he was thirty-eight years old, damn it. Far too old to be watching his phone, waiting for a call or a text or … something. He knew how to use the damn thing.

His phone rang and he damn near fell over. He glanced at the screen to see that it was his mother. For a brief moment, he contemplated letting it go to voice mail.

Okay, fine. He couldn't do that to his mother, so he hit the button to take the call.

"Hello?"

"How was your trip?"

Noah smiled, crossing the room to the balcony doors and stepping outside. It was just like his mother to forego pleasantries.

"It was good." He got the sense she already knew that, though. "You heard from Milly yet?"

"Oh, yes. She called last night to let us know how everything went. She sent a million pictures. The wedding looked beautiful. You were so handsome standing up there."

Yeah, yeah, yeah. His concern wasn't about the pictures. Noah wondered how much Milly had shared about the trip. He hoped like hell she hadn't mentioned anything about…

"I heard Dare Davis was there. Was he in the pictures, too? Which one is he?"

Well, there went that hope.

Before he got the chance to answer her, she rattled on. "Was it good to see him after all these years? Did the two of you get to talk?"

Oh, yeah. They had talked. And then some. Not that he would tell his mother that. "We did."

"You know better than to answer your mother with two words. I asked at least five questions."

Noah chuckled. "I didn't know which one to answer."

"All of them."

Smiling, Noah said, "Then you'll have to repeat them."

"I'm looking at one of the pictures now. Which one is he?"

Noah explained which one was Dare.

"Oh. He's handsome. What color are his eyes?"

"Hazel." Shit. As soon as he blurted out the word, he realized his mother had baited him.

She chuckled, confirming his suspicion. "Yes. Hazel. So you talked? And?"

"And what?" He wasn't sure what his mother was fishing for.

"Are the two of you … you know?"

"No, I don't know." Noah hated playing this game with his mother. She had good intentions, but he always felt pressured by her when it came to relationships. He wasn't sure why that was, because she'd always been supportive of him, ever since he was sixteen years old and had come out to his parents. According to her, she wanted him to settle down. For years she had mentioned his age and how one day he would wish he'd taken a chance on love.

"Noah Jeremiah Pearson."

When all three names were used, he knew he was in for it. "It's all good, Mom. We saw each other. We talked. And yes, before you ask, I'm hoping to see him again."

Much to his surprise, his mother didn't respond immediately.

"Mom?"

"I just want you to be careful," she said softly. "I know it's been a long time, but I remember how you felt about that boy."

Noah chuckled, trying to keep it to himself. Dare definitely wasn't a boy anymore.

"I will," he assured her. "I promise."

"Okay then. I wanted to call and tell you to come to dinner next Friday night."

"I'll have to check my schedule at the station." Because he'd taken off for two weeks, he wasn't sure what days he would be on. Technically, he was supposed to be back to work on Friday.

"If not Friday, then Saturday."

"Yes, ma'am." It wasn't often that his mother asked for something, and when she did, it was only for him to stop by and visit. He wouldn't let her down.

"Glad you had a good trip and glad you're back home safe and sound. Larry said to thank you for going along with Milly."

"Sure thing."

With that, his mother said good-bye and Noah hung up the phone.

Now it was time to do what he'd been putting off all morning.

Pulling up his text app, Noah found Dare's number, which he had saved during their flight back to Texas.

He typed out a message: *Hey. What are you up to?*

He deleted it and stared at the blank screen.

He typed again: *You alive?*

Nope, he deleted that, too.

Just checking in. Wanted to see how you are.

His thumb was getting tired from hitting the delete button.

Shit.

This wasn't that damn difficult.

Can I take you out on a date?

Staring at the screen, Noah contemplated deleting the message but forced his finger to hit send instead. He had to break the ice. Seriously, they had talked on the phone last night. Hell, they'd had sex on the phone last night and it had been good. They hadn't left things weird between them, so what his issue was today, he didn't know.

Returning to the kitchen, Noah set the phone on the counter.

He picked it up and checked to make sure the text had gone.

It had.

He set it down again.

He picked it back up and checked his signal. Every once in a while, he got no reception in his apartment.

Nope, reception was fine.

He put the phone down again and decided to take a shower. At least he wouldn't be tempted to pick it up again.

For at least ten minutes.

Twenty-Nine

AFTER SPENDING NEARLY two hours with Grams, eating lunch and talking about the cruise, Dare knew he needed to get back to the marina. It wasn't easy telling his favorite person in the whole wide world that, though. And every time he saw her, the way her face lit up like it was Christmas, Dare found it just as difficult as the last time.

Then again, Grams had been the one and only consistent person in his life since he was three years old. After his drug-addicted mother had given birth to him, then attempted to be a mom for the first few years, she'd finally given up and pawned him off on Grams. Without a second thought, Dare's grandmother had taken him in and raised him as her own. He'd been one of the lucky ones. Since he didn't have a father—technically he did, but his mother didn't know who he was—Dare hadn't had anyone else to look after him. Grams had been his savior.

Even if she'd always been a tad bit kooky. The years hadn't lessened her wackiness any, either.

After he cleaned up the kitchen, Dare excused himself to go to the bathroom. His grandmother had plied him with sweet tea since he'd gotten there, and his bladder was about to explode. No way could he drive the five minutes it took to get to the marina like this.

When he returned to the kitchen a few minutes later, he heard Grams on the phone. He peeked in, saw that she was talking to someone, and decided to give her a little privacy.

"Noah Pearson, huh? That name sounds awfully familiar."

Dare stuck his head around the wall again and…

Oh, hell. Grams was on the phone. *His* phone.

"Grams? What are you doing?"

She held up her finger as though her talking to Noah on his phone was the most rational thing in the world. Then again, for her, it might've been. Since she was getting on up there in age, her wild and free spirit had gotten a little wilder and a little freer, it seemed.

"Grams? That's my phone."

She pulled the phone from her ear briefly. "I know it is. But you didn't answer it, so I did. Now give me a minute."

She sounded exasperated by the interruption, which amused him. Taking a step back, Dare stared at her in awe. He couldn't hold back his laugh.

"How do you know Dare?" she asked, once again speaking into the phone.

Since he couldn't hear Noah's response, Dare could only imagine what he was saying.

"When Dare was a teenager?" Her eyes lit up and she met Dare's gaze.

Crap.

"I remember you. You're the boy who broke my baby's heart."

Yep. Looked as though Grams remembered what had happened fifteen years ago, although he knew she wouldn't remember if she'd taken her medicine that morning or not.

"So, why're you callin' him now? You wanna play slap and tickle with him again?"

A laugh erupted from him and he bent over, gasping for air. Grams always did have a way with words.

"You *don't*? Then why're you callin' my boy? He ain't good enough to play slap and tickle with?"

He almost felt bad for Noah. He would have if it hadn't been quite so entertaining.

Silence ensued and Dare could only imagine what Noah was saying to get out of this one. Although they'd dated for more than two years back then, Dare had never introduced Noah to Grams. Somehow he'd managed to keep his two worlds separate and it had worked for him. Sure, he'd told Grams about Noah and Noah about Grams, but he'd been a little leery of introducing them. Now, he kind of wished he had.

"Yes, he's right here. And he's laughing like a maniac." Grams was scrutinizing Dare from her seat at the table. "Of course you can talk to him." She sighed heavily as though Noah's question was the most absurd thing she'd ever heard. "You called him, didn't you?"

Grams held out the phone for him to take. Dare reached for it at the same time she smiled innocently and said, "It's Noah. He wants to talk to you."

"Thanks, Grams." Dare took the phone and headed for the living room for a little bit of privacy. "Hey."

Noah cleared his throat and then his raspy voice came through the phone. "I didn't... I guess I didn't expect that."

Dare chuckled. "That makes two of us. What's up?" He remembered that Noah had texted a while ago, but he'd been talking to Grams so he hadn't stopped to text him back. "Sorry I didn't get back to you earlier. I've been with my grandmother."

"I ... uh..."

Lowering his voice, Dare moved a little farther from the kitchen. "You're thinkin' about me, aren't you? Thinkin' about playin' slap and tickle?"

Noah laughed, but it sounded a little nervous. "Something like that. I was actually calling to see if I could take you out tonight."

Dare glanced at the clock on the wall. "With Cam still on his honeymoon, I'll be at the marina until about seven. Probably not a good night to go out."

Noah didn't respond.

"I'm not blowing you off," Dare assured him. "You're more than welcome to come by the marina if you'd like. We could hang out for a bit."

There was a slight pause before Noah responded. "I'd like that. Text me the address?"

"Will do." Dare turned to make sure Grams hadn't snuck up on him. "And I look forward to playing slap and tickle with you again. I'll be the one doing the slapping."

Noah's laugh seemed less stressed that time, making Dare feel better. He wasn't sure whether the conversation with his grandmother had thrown Noah off or if it was something else. One way or the other, he would have to remember to ask him about it later.

"See you in a bit." Dare disconnected the phone when Grams stepped into the doorway.

Not wanting to go into detail about his recently reestablished relationship with Noah—although it really wasn't a relationship—Dare headed over and gave her a hug. "I really need to get back to the marina. I left Roan there all alone."

"Sure," she said sweetly, her blue eyes meeting his. "But you and I *will* be talking about this more."

"I know." And he did know. That was one thing about Grams, she wanted to know what was going on with him. She'd always been that way, and it was more of a friendship than anything else, which was why Dare had shared what had happened with Noah all those years ago. Grams was the one person in his life he could rely on no matter what. She didn't judge him, didn't look down her nose at him. And he loved her for that.

Like he'd said, he was lucky.

Dare headed to the door and Grams followed. He stepped out onto the porch and smiled back at her.

"You have condoms, right? No sense playin' slap and tickle if you don't protect yourself."

Dare felt his face heat. It took quite a bit to embarrass him, but somehow Grams always managed to. "Yes, ma'am. All stocked up on condoms."

Grams nodded. "Be good!"

"Always."

SLAP AND TICKLE.

Noah still couldn't get his conversation with Dare's grandmother out of his head, even now as he headed for the marina. The old lady had definitely taken him by surprise. Then again, she'd also managed to give him something other than Dare to think about.

Only now he was envisioning himself tickling a naked Dare.

Not nearly as romantic as he'd thought it would be.

As he pulled into the gravel parking lot of Pier 70 Marina, Noah took it all in. The sun was still high, sparkling off the water. There wasn't much wind, so the water looked like glass, reflecting back the brilliance of the afternoon sky. If first impressions were anything to go by, this place was one he would visit frequently.

After parking his truck, Noah climbed out and looked around. There were a few people scattered about, most of them down by the water. The lake itself looked empty. No boats or Jet Skis on this side at least. It was peaceful.

The door to the small building opened and he peered over. The horrendous roar of dogs growling and snarling sounded from somewhere close by, and his fight-or-flight instincts kicked in. Noah spun around looking for the threat, but he saw nothing. He heard a laugh, followed by Dare's voice. "Whatever. I'm not changin' it. Get over it. I'll be back in a bit."

Noah's eyes settled on Dare.

Have mercy. The man was … incredible.

He looked noticeably different than he had the last time he'd seen him … yesterday. Wow. Had it really been yesterday? It seemed like so much time had passed already. Gone were the jeans and polo, replaced by a pair of swim shorts and a white T-shirt with the marina's logo across the front. He was barefoot and wearing a ball cap turned backward, and he looked so fucking good it was almost painful to stare at him for too long.

That was the Dare he'd fallen in love with. Twice. Carefree and happy, with a seductively charming smile. Noah didn't think Dare realized how incredibly sexy he was.

"You caught me at a good time," Dare called out as he approached, clearly expecting him though he was early. "You wanna take a walk down to the lake?"

269

Fearless

Before he could respond, Dare got right into his personal space and … kissed him.

For a second, Noah thought his knees would give out. That wasn't a chaste greeting, that was an all-out mouth fuck, and now he wasn't sure he could pull away. He cupped the back of Dare's head and fondled his tongue with his own, devouring him right there for God and everyone to witness.

By the time Dare pulled back, Noah was out of breath, and his dick was threatening to break out of his jeans.

"Hi," Dare said softly, grinning.

"Hi." Noah barely managed to get the word out.

"Come on. We're kinda slow today. We can find a little privacy this way."

When Dare took his hand, Noah allowed him to lead him across the parking lot, then past a grassy area that was set up with picnic tables and barbecue grills. They continued walking until they were off the main path and had ventured into the shadows of the surrounding trees.

Before Noah could ask where they were going or what Dare had in mind, Dare spun on him, backing him up against a tree and once again attacking his mouth. Although startled, Noah gave in almost immediately, wrapping his arms around Dare and pulling him flush against him.

"God, I missed you."

Noah's heart kicked hard in his chest at Dare's words. "I missed you, too."

"Can't think of anything else but this." Dare's hand quickly worked the button and zipper on Noah's shorts free, and that was when the reality of Dare's statement hit him.

Dare hadn't missed *him*. Dare had missed the sex.

Dare's mouth trailed up to Noah's ear. "I need to feel you in my mouth. Wanna watch as you come down my throat."

Although Noah was a little taken aback by the turn of events, he couldn't deny that Dare's words turned him on. His dick swelled, throbbing as Dare wrapped his hand around him, stroking him firmly.

"Can I?" Dare asked.

Noah knew it wasn't really a question that needed an answer, because Dare was already dropping to his knees in front of him. He immediately pulled Dare's hat from his head so he could twine his fingers in his hair, holding him as Dare worshipped his dick. As much as he wanted to tell him they couldn't make this only about sex, it was incredibly difficult to resist Dare's wicked mouth.

Noah pressed his back into the tree, pushing his hips forward as he kept his eyes locked on Dare's face. "Fuck… I love your mouth."

Dare lapped at him with his tongue, teasing him, tormenting him, driving him out of his mind. He didn't even care that they were outside, and although they seemed to have some privacy where they were, that wasn't to say that someone couldn't stumble upon them at any time. That made it a little hotter, actually. So much so that Noah got caught up in the moment.

Reaching down with his other hand, Noah cradled Dare's jaw, halting him momentarily. "Stay like that."

Dare stopped moving, his lips wrapped firmly around Noah's cock.

"Seeing you on your knees…" Noah pushed into Dare's mouth as far as he could, then retreated. "Makes me want to come right down your throat." Noah pushed in again. "Take all of me, Dare. That's it, baby. Let me feel your throat."

Keeping his movements slow and even, Noah fucked Dare's mouth like that, slow and deep, working the head into the back of Dare's mouth as far as he could go.

Dare swallowed, compressing the head of Noah's dick. "Oh, fuck. Yes. Like that."

Noah pulled back out, allowing Dare to catch his breath before he did it again. It was almost as though he were punishing Dare. Noah wanted more than this, but if this was all Dare was willing to offer, he was going to take every damn bit he was capable of giving.

"Suck me, Dare. Don't… Ahh, yeah … don't stop." Noah wasn't ready to come yet. He craved the way the wet heat of Dare's mouth caressed his dick, but he wanted more.

Pulling out of Dare's mouth, Noah fisted his cock, stroking slowly. "Suck on my balls."

Dare took one, then the other, then both into his mouth, making Noah moan. He was relying on the tree to hold him up, because the sensations were exquisite, causing his knees to weaken.

Once again, Noah slid his hand in Dare's hair and fed his cock back into his mouth, fucking slowly at first, still maintaining control.

"Fucking suck me," he growled as the intensity overwhelmed him. He was going to come. "Faster." He continued to pump his hips forward, feeding every inch into Dare's willing mouth. "So good… Aww, shit… Dare. I'm gonna come. Gonna come in your mouth. Don't stop."

Dare didn't let up, taking everything Noah gave him until there was no holding back. He came hard, his hips bucking forward as he spurted his seed into Dare's mouth. He watched as Dare swallowed, the sight sending an additional tremor through him.

Thirty

SUCKING NOAH OFF was one of the hottest things he'd ever done. The way the man couldn't control the emotions that flitted across his face made it so intense Dare was ready to do it again. However, he didn't have time, because he needed to get back to the office to cover the phones. They didn't have a lot going on today, but Roan had been helping Hudson since Teague was noticeably absent. And since Dare had taken a couple of hours off already, he hated leaving everything to Roan.

Getting to his feet, Dare took Noah's mouth again, helping Noah fix his clothes while he did. He had to ignore the painful erection tenting his shorts while he was at it. If he'd had more time, he would've asked Noah to return the favor. Hopefully they'd get that opportunity sometime in the near future.

Nibbling Noah's bottom lip, Dare smiled. "I have to get back to work."

Noah pulled back, confusion burning in those deep brown eyes. "That's it?"

Dare smiled. "What? You want to return the favor?"

Noah frowned but then pulled away. "Is that why you asked me to come out here?"

A spark of anger ignited in Dare's gut. "What? I sucked your dick and now you're bitching about it?"

What the hell?

An unidentifiable emotion crossed Noah's face, and for a brief moment, Dare felt like an asshole. He considered what had happened since Noah had arrived, and okay, maybe he'd lacked a little in the romance department, but Noah shouldn't be complaining. Not like he would be sporting blue balls for the rest of the day.

No, Dare was the one who'd be doing that.

"I'm not looking for this," Noah blurted, waving his hand toward Dare. "That's not why I came out here."

"Then why did you?" Dare was truly baffled. He'd made Noah come in his mouth, and now the man wanted to pick a fight.

"To see you."

Dare shook his head. "Well, you saw me. *And* your dick saw my tonsils. You happy now?"

Okay, yes, he was being an asshole on purpose. The way that Noah made him feel... He didn't want to feel that way. Ever since they'd stepped off the plane yesterday, Dare had continued to tell himself that this could only be sex. He'd thought he had successfully convinced himself of that, too. Right up until he'd laid eyes on Noah in the parking lot. Then that strange feeling in his chest had ignited in full force, but he had managed to push it away, focusing solely on giving Noah pleasure.

That was the way it had to be. Dare didn't want anything more right now. Maybe not ever.

It was true, he didn't want to only be friends with Noah. He wanted more... He wanted this. The sex. For as long as it could last. But he thought Noah of all people would understand that. After all, that was the way it'd been between them before.

"Why are you doing this?" Noah was breathing hard, pinning Dare in place with his hardened gaze.

Dare shrugged. "Not sure what you think I'm doing."

"You're…" Noah's hand waved again. "Why is it all about sex with you?"

"What the fuck else do you want from me, Noah?" Dare didn't bother to hide his frustration. "We had a few good days on the ship, and now you want … what? I don't even know what you want."

Noah was shaking his head. "You know what? Fuck you."

Dare stood there as Noah spun around and stormed off.

He had to give Noah a little credit. He had lasted longer than most of the guys Dare had dated in the last fifteen years. Usually they gave up after the second date.

NOAH WAS SO fucking pissed he had a hard time focusing on the road. There was a red haze clouding his vision and a painful ache in his chest. Sure as shit, he'd been right about Dare, and now Noah was the one running away.

He hated that they'd somehow made it back to the same place they'd ended years ago, only they'd traded places. Dare was the one pushing him away and Noah was the one running.

Shit.

Fearless

Oddly, he wished his father were there so he could talk to him. Since he wasn't, Noah opted to go to the cemetery. He found it strangely comforting during times like this when he needed someone to talk to. Since he'd never been that close with his mother—at least not when it came to talking about his feelings—Noah had always relied on his dad for those heart-to-hearts. Before and after he'd died.

Half an hour later, Noah was sitting on the grass in front of his father's headstone. The cemetery was growing dark now that the sun was going down. He wouldn't be able to stay long before someone would come around to shoo him off, but he would sit there for as long as he was allowed.

He glanced at the headstone, the familiar ache in his chest returning as it always did. His dad was only forty-six when he'd been ripped from this earth, taken away from all the people who had loved him.

"Hey, Dad." Those were the only words he would say aloud because Noah wasn't interested in sharing his feelings with anyone who might happen upon him, so he lay back in the grass and stared up at the darkening sky while he thought about all the things he would say to his father today if he were alive.

He broke my heart again, Dad. But I can't really blame him this time. I should've seen it coming. Dare is different now. He's more guarded. Not the same carefree kid who loved freely and openly before. I miss that guy. I mean, I really, really miss that guy.

The past week has been chaotic. I've dealt with a lot of emotions. And it comes down to the fact that I still love Dare. I don't know how it happened, how I managed to fall in love with him twice in my lifetime. I didn't see it coming, and there was nothing I could do to stop it once it started, either. But I can't do this to myself again. I won't do this again.

I understand why he's pushing me away. It's the exact same thing I did to him back then. I kept him at arm's length, scared to get in too deep. And now the tables have been turned. I'm the one with the broken heart; I'm the one running away.

Ironic, isn't it?

Noah knew what his father would say in return. He would want to know *why* Noah was running away. He would want to know why Noah wasn't standing up for what he wanted. It was how he'd been raised. Stay and fight. That was his father's motto. Fight for the things that were important; let the small stuff roll right off.

Unfortunately, Noah wasn't strong enough to fight this time.

He wasn't sure he ever would be again.

Thirty-One

Saturday, June 11th
Six days later

"HOLY SHIT, MAN. You got a little sun." Dare smiled when Cam walked into the office on Saturday morning, a huge, shit-eating grin plastered across his face.

"Not sure we spent any time inside the whole time."

"No sex for you, huh?" Dare teased.

"Oh, let's just say the beach was secluded."

Of course it was. "I hope you put sunscreen on that husband of yours." Gannon did not have the same complexion Cam did and would've burned to a crisp.

"Trust me, I took care of my man."

"I'm sure you did," Dare told him, grinning. "And I damn sure don't want the details."

"So what the hell's goin' on around here?"

Dare looked around the office. "Nada. Did the trip affect your eyesight?"

"Okay, smart ass. You know what I meant. Things good?"

"Oh, yeah." Dare nodded toward the appointment book on the counter. "We're busy. Glad you're back to help out."

"Not sure how much I'll be able to help." Cam frowned, glancing down the hall toward his office. "I've got some accounting to take care of first."

Dare knew how much Cam loved that shit. About as much as having his fingernails ripped off one by one with a pair of tweezers. It was a good thing he did it, though, because Dare damn sure wasn't good with numbers. Okay, he was really good with numbers; he merely didn't want anyone to know that because accounting… He'd rather poke his eyeballs out with Q-tips.

"I'm sure we can handle it until you get caught up. Teague's back, so it's easier now."

"I heard about that." Cam leaned forward, facing Dare, his forearms resting on the counter. "He was sick for four days?"

"So he claims." Not that Dare had any reason to doubt Teague. The kid had been one of the most driven people he'd known ever since he'd showed up looking for a job back when he'd been in high school.

"Things still weird between him and Hudson?"

"Define weird." Dare chuckled. Things had always been weird, so he wasn't sure what Cam meant.

"They not talking to each other still?"

"Not that I know of." But that wasn't surprising. Teague had always avoided Hudson whenever possible. Somehow, they made it work. Dare had to believe that was due to Hudson more so than Teague, though.

Cam looked at Dare. "Think I should talk to him?"

Dare shrugged. "Not sure what good it'll do."

"True." Cam glanced down at the appointment book, then back up at him. "Oh, and if you see Hudson before I do, let him know the apartment'll be ready for him by tomorrow night. Gannon's making sure everything's out by tonight and he's cleaning it tomorrow."

"Will do. You talk to Roan yet?" Dare figured Cam had since the two of them were close, but with the shit Roan was having to deal with right now, it was possible Cam hadn't seen him yet.

"Yeah. Last night. I called him. He told me about his sister." Cam sighed. "He's moving in with her to keep an eye on her."

That was what Dare had heard, too. "What're you gonna do with his apartment?" It wasn't necessary for them to rent the apartments out, but it did help to have them occupied so someone could keep an eye on the place at night.

Cam shrugged. "Teague showed some interest at one point, but with Hudson moving into my old place…"

Yeah, who knew how that would turn out. "You gonna offer it to him?"

"Of course. If he wants it, it's his. I know he's been staying with a buddy of his for a while."

"You want me to mention it?" Dare wasn't sure it was his place.

"If it comes up, feel free. If not, I'll talk to him later."

Dare nodded. Cam was much better suited to have that conversation with Teague than he was. Since the kid had an issue with Hudson, Dare would rather stay out of that one altogether.

"How're things with Noah?"

Dare backed away from the counter and headed for his iPad. He could talk about the marina business all day, but this was a conversation he didn't intend to have with Cam or anyone else. Ever since last Monday, when Noah had walked away—or more accurately *run* away—Dare hadn't heard from him. He hadn't attempted to reach out to him, either.

"Man, you're seriously gonna ignore me about this?"

Dare frowned, still not meeting Cam's gaze. "Nothing to talk about." And there wasn't. Dare didn't want to think about Noah, much less talk about him.

"Tell me somethin'," Cam prompted.

Dare looked up but didn't say anything.

"Did you love him? Back then?"

"Yes."

"Do you love him now?"

"No." Dare was surprised at how easily that lie rolled right off his tongue.

"Liar."

Apparently it hadn't been a *good* lie.

"I don't love him." Dare hated that they were having this conversation, but it was hard not to. Cam was his closest friend. If anyone knew Dare better than Grams, it was Cam. He didn't share much of himself with anyone, but he was sure Cam knew the important parts.

"You mean you don't want to love him."

Whatever. Dare was not going to concede on this. No, he didn't want to love Noah. Yes, he possibly did, but if he ignored it, he would get through this.

"I'm your friend and I hope you know that. But I think you're being an idiot."

Dare didn't look at Cam. "Tell me how you really feel."

"I remember back when Roan and I had our little falling-out. You were the one sticking your nose in my business back then. I'm merely returning the favor."

"I don't need any favors." What he needed was for Cam to drop the subject.

Cam stood tall and threw his hands up. "Fine. Do whatever you wanna do. When you're old and gray and you can't get your dick up, don't come bitching to me because the only ones there to listen to you moan and complain are your twenty cats."

Dare laughed. "Fuck you." The words were said halfheartedly. He was a dog person. He would have twenty dogs, thank you very much.

Cam slapped him on the back. "I'll leave it at that. You'll figure it out. Sooner or later."

He would. He just wasn't sure whether he would like the answer that he came up with.

NOAH HAD CONSIDERED canceling on his mother, but he couldn't do it. Having dinner with her and her husband on a Saturday night wasn't his idea of a hot date, but at the moment, it really was the only offer he had.

As usual, he got in his truck and headed over a little early. When he pulled down the street, he realized tonight was going to be one of those nights. Milly's car was sitting in the driveway, which meant his stepsister would be sharing a meal and likely a dozen stories tonight. Not for the first time since he'd gotten behind the wheel, he was tempted to turn around and go back home.

Something made him stay. Noah figured he would be sorry for that decision later, but now, as he stepped into the house, there wasn't anything he could do about it.

"Hey, you!" Milly called out from her spot on the couch. "Sit. We've got wine."

Wine.

Just what he needed. Something with ridiculously little alcohol content. Maybe ten glasses would help. Before he could refuse, Milly was pouring him a glass and passing it over, urging him to sit beside her.

"Where's my mother?"

Milly smiled. "She's in the kitchen with my dad. Said she needed help with something." Her mischievous grin widened. "They're probably making out."

Noah shook his head. "That's a visual I definitely don't need."

Milly shifted so that she was facing him, her legs tucked underneath her. "So, how are you?"

"Good." It was a sufficient answer as far as he was concerned.

"You went back to work yesterday?"

Noah nodded. "At the station, yes." He didn't have another roofing job until midweek, so until then, he was going to be struggling without anything to keep him busy.

"Cam and Gannon got back last night," Milly informed him. "Have you seen them yet?"

Noah sipped his wine, using that as an excuse not to answer. Obviously Milly hadn't heard about his falling-out with Dare.

"Okay, I know that silence."

Noah laughed, choking on his wine. "How do you *know* silence? There's nothing to know."

"With you there is." Milly leaned forward. "What's going on?"

"Nothing." Rather than sip his wine, Noah downed the rest and held out his glass for a refill.

Milly obliged.

"Did something happen between you and Dare?"

Technically, no.

"Noah…" Milly dragged his name out into far too many syllables as she handed back his glass. "What the hell happened? You two looked so cozy on the airplane."

Yeah, well. "It's not gonna work out between us. Let's leave it at that."

Milly's nose scrunched, and Noah knew she wasn't going to leave it alone.

"I thought I heard you in here," Noah's mother called from the doorway, her timing impeccable. "Come on. Dinner's ready."

Getting to his feet, Noah helped Milly up, then followed her into the dining room, where dinner was laid out. His mother was a fantastic cook—a trait he'd never picked up, really—which meant there was more food than the four of them would be able to eat in a week.

"Sit."

Noah glanced at Milly, wondering what the bossy comment was for. Rather than argue, he sat.

"So, tell me about this cruise," his mother prompted.

Noah busied himself filling his plate, not wanting to talk about the cruise. Not with his mother, not with Milly … not with anyone, actually.

"You should've seen Noah with Dare," Milly stated. "They were so cute together."

What the fuck? Really?

The woman was crazy. He couldn't believe Milly was going there. She couldn't have led with how the weather was, or how cool it had been to see the beach, or hell, even how work was since she'd gotten back? As he stared at her in disbelief, he felt his mother's eyes on him.

"Did you get to spend a lot of time with him?"

Noah knew his mother's question was directed at him, but he wasn't going to answer. Unfortunately, Milly opted to fill in the blanks.

"They did."

Noah glared at her again. This time, she turned to meet his gaze, a smile on her lips.

Two could play at this game. Peering down at his plate as he prepared to take his first bite, Noah said, "Milly had an overnight guest. Why don't y'all ask her about that?"

He heard Milly's sharp inhale, and he knew he'd effectively dodged the bullet. Apparently she hadn't shared that tidbit of information with them yet.

"Is that true?" her father asked.

"Noah was holding hands with Dare," Milly blurted.

Noah choked on his first bite of baked potato. He managed to swallow, then chugged more wine. He didn't know how to respond to that. They sounded like teenage kids attempting to place blame on the other.

Then again, they were attempting to place blame on the other because the last thing either of them wanted to talk about was any significant—or insignificant—other in their lives.

"Who was this overnight guest?" Larry asked, his undivided attention now on his daughter.

Noah knew he would likely get out of this one for the simple fact that Larry was not fond of Milly dating, much less her spending the night with a guy.

Unable to help himself, Noah chuckled as he began shoveling food into his mouth, not looking up from his plate.

MILLY COULDN'T BELIEVE that Noah had thrown her completely under the bus. Then again, she had started it.

That didn't make it right, though.

For the past half hour, she had been explaining to her father (again) that she was a grown woman, and grown women tended to have sex from time to time. Even when they weren't married. For the record, her father had cringed every time she'd mentioned the word *sex*. One of the many reasons she'd used it as often as possible.

Now that dinner was over and she and Noah were in the kitchen cleaning up, she figured it was the best time to address the situation.

"Okay, spill it. What happened between you and Dare?"

"Milly…"

"Oh, cool it. You know I'm not gonna stop until you spill, so you might as well save some time and get it over with. Have you seen him since we've been back?"

"Yes." The reluctance in his tone made her smile.

"And?" Reaching for the dish he'd finished washing, Milly prepared to dry it. It would've been easier to use the dishwasher, but Milly hated the idea of her stepmother or her father having to unload it afterward, so she'd taken to hand-washing them. Not to mention, it usually gave her a little extra time to spend with Noah. Considering they weren't that close, and she really wanted them to be, she had to take what she could get.

"And nothing, Mill. There's nothing to say."

Based on his tone, there was *a lot* to say.

Men.

"Did you have a fight?"

Noah cast a sideways glance at her. That was all the answer she needed.

"I'm sorry." She really had been hoping things would work out between the two of them, but she'd promised herself that she would stay out of this one. As nosy as she wanted to be, this really wasn't her business. Had they been closer than they were, Milly would've attempted to intervene, but she knew it would only upset Noah.

"Nothing to be sorry about."

"You think things might work out between you eventually?" She took another dish and dried it.

"Doubtful. We want different things."

"Oh." That was interesting. "The same way you wanted different things the first time around?"

Noah nodded but didn't look her way. She took the last glass from his hand while he turned off the water and grabbed the extra towel to dry his hands.

"We're different people now, Milly. He wants something I can't give him."

Wait. After placing the last glass in the cabinet, Milly spun around to face him. "He wants a relationship and you don't? Please don't tell me you're going through this again. Noah Jeremiah Pearson, why—"

He held up a hand to silence her, then Noah sighed. "That's not what I said."

"Then what did you say?" She was thoroughly confused right now.

"He's not interested in more and I'm not interested in casual sex."

Oh. Well.

Crap.

She certainly hadn't seen that coming.

Milly hated that there wasn't anything she could do to help. She probably could call Gannon and get him to stick his nose where it didn't belong, but she knew how much he hated that.

Darn it.

"Don't try to figure it out," Noah said softly.

But she wanted to.

She really wanted to.

Thirty-Two

Monday, June 13th

BY THE TIME Monday rolled around, Dare felt as though he had something sitting on his chest. It was hard to breathe, but he knew it wasn't a virus. He didn't actually feel sick. Well, not that kind of sick. He felt ... off.

Which was why he was in the marina's main office, lying on the counter, staring up at the ceiling. He knew that Roan and Cam would give him a hard time if they walked in and found him there—he usually did it to rile them up—but he couldn't bring himself to care. In fact, he didn't care about much of anything right now.

For the past couple of hours, he'd been staring at his phone, wishing Noah would text him. It was stupid because he hadn't heard from Noah in eight days. One hundred ninety-two hours. The same length of time they'd been on that ship together, actually. The past eight days hadn't been anything like those on the cruise, though. However, from an emotional standpoint, it hadn't been that much different.

"What the hell are you doing?"

Dare turned his head to the side, watching as Roan walked in through the back door, Lulu trotting in behind him. "Thinking."

"And you can't think standing up?"

"No."

Roan shrugged. "You're gonna have to man up and call him."

"Call who?" Dare frowned, still watching Roan.

"Noah."

"Why would I want to do that?" It was the only thing he wanted to do.

"Because this lovesick bullshit is getting on my nerves."

"I'm not lovesick." He was. That was the only explanation, although he fucking hated it. He did not want to love Noah—well or sick.

"Well, whatever it is, you're startin' to get on my nerves."

"Starting?" Dare chuckled, staring up at the ceiling again. He didn't move off the counter.

"You're right. You've been getting on my nerves for years." Roan grinned, reaching under the counter and pulling out the appointment book. "But that's beside the point."

"Then what *is* the point?" Dare was simply trying to make conversation. Anything to keep his mind off Noah.

"The point is…" Roan stopped talking, his full attention on the appointment book.

Dare turned his head and focused on Roan again. "What's wrong?"

His friend's eyes lifted to meet his. "Nothing. Sorry."

Clearly something in that appointment book had caught Roan's attention. Dare just wasn't sure if that was good or bad based on Roan's non-answer.

"You gonna be working tomorrow?"

Confused, Dare stared at Roan. "Of course. Where else would I be?"

"I'm gonna need to take the day off, but there are a couple of appointments in the afternoon."

Okay, so now his buddy was acting all kinds of strange. However, Dare didn't get the chance to call him on it because Roan tossed the appointment book on the shelf, then pivoted and walked right out of the office, taking Lulu with him.

"That was weird," Dare said to the empty office.

"No, what's weird is you're talking to yourself."

The sound of Cam's voice scared him, making him jerk. The movement was enough to send him right off the counter and onto the floor. He managed to get his hands and one foot down before he face-planted, but the impact wasn't all that comfortable.

Apparently Cam found it highly entertaining.

"Jesus. Warn a guy, would ya?" Dare stood, dusting off his hands.

"I'll be sure to do that next time." Cam didn't sound as though he had any intention of doing so.

"You done with the books yet?"

"Yep. Why? You need the afternoon off?"

What the hell was with people today? In the ten years he'd worked at the marina, he'd rarely taken time off. He enjoyed being there more than he enjoyed not being there, so it wasn't a hardship.

"Why would I need time off?"

Cam shrugged, the response very similar to Roan's earlier. "Thought maybe you'd want to head into Austin. Stop at a particular fire station. Like, you know, Station 45."

"You suck at hints, Cam." Dare hadn't known what station Noah worked at and he hadn't come up with a way to figure it out, either, without being way too obvious. Now he knew.

"Maybe. But it gave you all the information you needed, right?"

"I don't need any information." He repeated the station number in his head.

"Suck it up, buttercup. You're in love and you're starting to act like a pussy. We don't like pussies around here."

Dare nearly fell over, a laugh bursting out of him. It was the truth. Which made it even funnier.

When he finally stopped laughing, Cam was watching him, still smiling.

"What?"

"I thought you also might want to know that a particular fire station is doing a boot drive this afternoon."

He was familiar with the Austin boot drive to collect money for the Muscular Dystrophy Association. They did it every year.

"So?" Was Cam telling him he needed to make a donation?

"Might not hurt to slip a note in the boot along with your money. And don't be skimpy on the donation, either."

Dare shook his head. "You really do suck at subtlety."

Cam chuckled. "Man, subtlety was lost on you a long time ago. I'm starting to think a two-by-four upside the head might be our only hope." Cam's attention turned to the parking lot. "Now, go. Take the afternoon off while I spend some time up here."

Before Dare could argue, Cam took him by his shoulders and pushed him toward the door.

"Fine. I can take a hint," Dare grumbled.

"Yes. Because that's what I've been doing. Hinting." Cam laughed. "Bye, Dare."

"PEARSON!"

Noah spun around and headed back toward the kitchen when he heard one of the guys call his name. "'Sup?"

"Looks like you've got an admirer."

Noah moved closer, hesitant when he saw a small sealed envelope.

"Whoever it was attached it to a hundred-dollar bill. Generous, huh?"

Yep. Generous. Noah didn't know anyone that generous.

Taking the note with him, he headed for his bunk. He wasn't sure what the note would say, but he needed privacy regardless. Sitting on his bed, Noah stared at his name written in block letters across the front. It was sealed and for that he was grateful. The guys would give him a rash of shit, regardless of what it said. He wasn't worried that they would learn that he was gay, because he'd never kept his sexual orientation a secret. Since heteros didn't go around proclaiming they were straight, Noah had never felt the need to announce he was gay. It was who he was, not what defined him, and as with everyone else in the house, no one really gave a shit. To each his own.

Sliding the tip of his finger beneath the flap, he unsealed it and pulled out a folded sheet of paper. His hands were shaking, but he had no idea why. He wanted this letter to be from Dare, but he had no reason to believe that it would be.

As he opened it to the note portion, Noah closed his eyes and took a deep breath.

Please be from Dare.

When he opened them, his gaze strayed to the bottom of the note first. When he saw Dare's messy scribble there, he nearly cried. Not something he would ever be able to live down at the station, though, so he managed to refrain.

Noah,

Fearless

*It's a long shot, I know, but I'd like one more
chance. I wasn't lying when I told you the last
relationship I'd had was you. I don't know
how this works, so I'm probably going to keep
fucking it up. But, if you're up for it, meet me
at the marina tomorrow night around seven.
I'll even treat you to dinner.*

Dare

Taking a deep breath, Noah tried to calm his
pounding heart. It wasn't much, but Dare had made the effort.
Noah had been the one to walk away, but Dare was the one
reaching out. He didn't know what to think. Eight days had
passed since he'd last seen Dare, and his heart still ached the
same as it had that day. Although they'd reconciled such a
short time ago, he had somehow fallen in love with the man
all over again. This time, far more intensely than the first.
Likely that was due to the time they'd spent together years ago
and the feelings that he'd buried.

He needed some time to think about this, to process
what the potential outcome could be. He was a planner; that
was what he did.

The alarm sounded and Noah shoved the note
beneath his blanket before heading out to the bay to grab his
gear. A call wasn't a bad thing right now. It would give his
mind a little break and his heart some time to reinforce itself
for what he knew would be inevitable.

Tomorrow night, Noah would go see Dare.

He only hoped that it wouldn't be for the last time.

Thirty-Three

Tuesday, June 14ᵗʰ

BY THE TIME six thirty rolled around, Dare was beginning to drive himself crazy. Ever since he'd dropped that letter into that boot yesterday afternoon, he'd been waiting for some acknowledgment from Noah. Something to let him know that he'd gotten it, and that he would or would not be stopping by. Since Dare had mentioned seven o'clock, there was still a little time before he had to panic, but his nerves were already rioting.

Everyone else had bailed on him about an hour ago. Cam had insisted that if he was going to pace the office, then he could handle any walk-ins. He had even offered to take Lulu back to his house for the night so Dare could get a break. Teague had told him he needed to get laid before someone punched him. That was Teague, prone to violence. Hudson hadn't had anything to say, but that was because Hudson didn't have to be around him. And Roan … well, Roan hadn't been there all day, but he had shown up about half an hour ago to check on things before he'd once again headed out.

Hopping up onto the counter, Dare dangled his legs and waited, drumming his fingers on his thighs. He stared out at the parking lot, sucking in air every time he saw a car pass by on the main road. Since Noah drove a truck, it was a stupid reaction, but something he couldn't seem to control.

Shit.

He should've told Noah to message him one way or the other. This waiting game was bullshit. He was antsy and irritable.

And fucking hungry.

He had skipped lunch because his stomach had been churning since he'd woken up that morning. Now, he could hear it rumble over the sound of tires crunching on gravel in the parking lot.

Wait...

Tires crunching on gravel.

Dare focused, realizing he was looking at Noah's truck pulling into a parking spot.

He'd come.

Holy fuck.

A huge bubble of emotion built in his chest.

Dare hopped off the counter and grabbed his flip-flops from behind it. He slipped them on and then made his way to the door. Should he greet Noah at the truck? Or should he let Noah come to him?

Fuck.

Why the hell was this so hard?

Because he couldn't stand still any longer, Dare flipped the open sign to closed, stepped outside, then locked the door behind him. When he turned around, he saw Noah rounding the front of his truck.

God, the man looked good.

Better than good.

The faded jeans he wore showcased his muscular thighs while the black T-shirt hugged his fantastic upper body.

Screw dinner. Dare no longer wanted food, he wanted...

"Hey," Noah greeted, his tone flat.

He couldn't produce a single word in response as he moved closer, eliminating the space between them before crushing his mouth to Noah's. No greeting, no warning, only a mind-blowing kiss that stole what little air was left in his lungs. Dare cradled the back of Noah's head in his hand, holding him to him. At first, he thought Noah was going to resist, but his lips parted and his tongue danced into Dare's mouth. They were both attempting to take control, though it was clear neither of them could. This thing between them, it was stronger than either of them and more powerful than both of them combined.

Dare finally managed to pull away, remembering he wasn't supposed to make this about sex, although that was his first reaction. With any man he'd come across, it had always been his first reaction. No strings, nothing serious. Only sex.

Except for Noah. Noah had been the exception, but he had also been the reason. After Noah had shattered his heart, Dare had refused to allow anyone else to do so again. And it had worked.

Right up until Noah had reappeared in his life.

"I wasn't sure you were gonna come." Dare forced his hands down to his sides even though he didn't want to stop touching Noah.

"I wasn't sure I was, either."

Dare didn't like the sound of that, but he'd learned to roll with the punches long ago.

"You hungry?"

"I could eat."

Forcing himself to relax, Dare managed to smile. "Good. I know the perfect place. Come on."

NOAH FELT AS though he were in a dream. The moment his feet had hit the gravel, his heart had started pounding. Now, as he stood face-to-face with Dare, after another soul-stealing kiss that had rocked him in his shoes, he wasn't sure what he was doing.

Oh, right.

Dare had just offered him food and had started to walk away, which should've been his cue to follow.

"Wait. Here?" Noah glanced around. "We're gonna eat here?"

"Sure." Dare nodded toward the building he had emerged from. "We've got a small restaurant down by the water. Nothing fancy, but they serve good burgers."

Noah glanced back at the lake, once again taking it all in. The sun was low in the sky, blazing across the still water, adding to the ethereal effect. It was as though Noah had done this before, although he knew that wasn't the case. The last time he'd been here had been much different. However, eerily the same.

Dare touched his arm. "We could even eat outside. Watch the sun set."

Okay. Yes, he'd go for that.

Noah nodded, then allowed Dare to take his hand and lead him down one of the wooden piers to another small building that sat right on the water. It only took a minute to place the order with the big guy behind the counter, then Noah followed Dare outside to the deck that overlooked the lake.

"This is incredible," Noah mused, watching the glittering orange of the sun on the water.

"Didn't think you were much into the water."

Noah glanced at Dare, then back at the lake. "I enjoy it. Just don't have nearly enough time to."

"We'll have to take the boat out one of these days. Let me get you naked out there."

For some reason, that statement caught him a little off guard and Noah blushed. It wasn't that he was embarrassed, but he hadn't expected it, although he should have. Dare was still drawing the sexual tension tight between them. It had started on the cruise and ended a week ago when Noah had walked away. For some reason, he had hoped tonight would be different.

"So, how was the boot drive?" Dare prompted when they took a seat at a table.

"Good." He didn't want to talk about the boot drive and he could tell Dare didn't, either.

"How's your mom?"

It looked as though Dare was attempting to make conversation, but it felt a little awkward. Still, Noah answered. "She's good. I had dinner with her a couple of days ago."

"Yeah?"

Noah nodded. "And your grandmother? She doing okay?"

"As kooky as ever," Dare said with a smile.

"And Cam and Gannon? They get back okay?"

Dare nodded, then turned to face him more fully. Noah could see that Dare was as uncomfortable as he was. "What do you say we chill for a bit, eat some dinner, then go back to my place?"

Without thinking, Noah agreed. He didn't particularly want to go back to Dare's place for the simple fact that privacy would be too much temptation for him at the moment. Since it was clear they were both edgy, neither of them knowing what to say, sex would likely be the next item on tonight's menu, and he wasn't sure he was ready for that.

Leaning back in his chair, Noah sighed as he took it all in again. Looked as though he would have to be on his game to keep up, because this certainly wasn't what he'd expected.

He only hoped that Dare didn't intend to make this only about sex. If he did, then this would end up being a wasted trip for both of them. Noah could only handle so much before he broke. And he was dangerously close already.

Thirty-Four

DARE COULDN'T WAIT to get Noah naked and beneath him, there was no denying that. From the moment he'd seen him standing in the parking lot, he'd wanted to strip him naked and rub up against him like a cat. Hell, he'd almost done just that with the kiss he'd planted on him. A kiss he was still reliving almost an hour later.

Now that they'd finished dinner and suffered through some rather uncomfortable conversation, Dare was ready to get on with the rest of their evening. It was clear by their less-than-stimulating conversation that something a little more intimate would likely break the ice. Which, if he had anything to say about it, would involve the two of them very naked in the very near future.

"Follow me back to my apartment?" Dare asked when they reached the parking lot. The sun had gone down, and the only light was the one buzzing in the parking lot far above them, but it provided enough for Dare to see by, enough for him to watch Noah's expression.

Noah didn't respond at first and Dare realized he was considering his options.

"We can talk," he clarified, not wanting Noah to back out on him.

Noah breathed in deeply, then nodded. "Sure. You live close?"

"About five minutes away."

As Dare had predicted, it took right under five minutes to get back to his place, and that included getting in his truck and getting out. The apartment he lived in had been his primary residence for the past decade. Because of how small the town was, there weren't many options, and since Dare refused to commit to buying a house—he actually had a long-standing issue with commitment of any kind—he had only one choice. In order to be close to Grams and the marina, he had opted for a complex between the two. Since it was just him, he'd picked one of the smaller units—a one-bathroom studio—and he used the money he saved to do what he loved to do. Water sports.

Well, that and his savings account had a pretty damn nice buffer, as well, in the event he ever did decide to do something as crucial as settle down.

Since Dare hadn't had a place of his own because he'd lived with Grams back when he and Noah had been dating the first time around, he wasn't sure what Noah would think. He'd always spent his time at Noah's, and at the time, they'd both been young. Noah's apartment had been nicely furnished— thanks to the fact his parents had money—but it hadn't been fancy. Nicer than Dare's place, though.

Apparently his insecurities got the best of him, because before they even reached the door, Dare started explaining. "I don't have a lot. I'm not usually here. Only to sleep. I spend most of my time at the marina." He stuck the key in the deadbolt and twisted. Once it was unlocked, he turned the knob and opened it. "It's kinda small, but more space than I need, actually. I—"

"Dare."

Dare turned to look at Noah.

"It doesn't matter to me. This place is great."

Well, he wouldn't go that far, but it was home. He had just enough furniture to fill the space and still leave room to move around. In the far corner, he had a full-size bed (which he'd never once made since he'd gotten it) and a nightstand. In the beginning, for many years, actually, he'd slept on a lumpy futon that had doubled as a couch. Eventually, his old ass hadn't been able to take it anymore, so he'd bought a bed.

To the left of the bed was the bathroom. On the floor just outside, a clothes hamper was overflowing, coughing up his dirty laundry. Oops.

On the left side of the open room, closest to the door, was a small kitchen that he hadn't used once since he'd moved in. Cooking was not his thing, and he refused to do it. Needless to say, he'd had more than his fair share of hamburgers from the marina restaurant over the years. That or pizza. Speaking of … an empty pizza box sat on the counter above the trash can.

He did have a table that had become a sort of catch-all, a place to put his wallet and keys so he didn't lose them, but he'd never eaten a meal on it. He probably should've cleaned up a bit, because there was also a couple of magazines, a pair of scissors, some Q-tips, an opened package of razors, and… Shit. He'd left the brand new box of condoms and the lube he'd purchased sitting right there for the world to see.

Too late now.

Flipping on the light, Dare stepped back and let Noah inside before shutting the door and locking it. He had a nosy upstairs neighbor who had been known to walk in from time to time. It was sometimes downright creepy, but up to this point, the old guy had simply been curious, probably lonely, too, so Dare hadn't seen the need to do anything about it.

"I guess you don't need a tour." Dare was attempting to make light of the situation because he was nervous.

Noah smiled, then moved right up against him and put his arms around him. The gesture was comforting. Not to mention distracting.

Exactly what he needed right now.

"It's nice. It definitely makes me think of you."

"Are you saying I'm small and not well furnished?"

Noah's hips moved forward, brushing against Dare's semi-erect cock.

"There's nothing small about you."

Ahh. See, that was the exact direction Dare was hoping this evening would go. After what had transpired between them by the lake, he hadn't been sure which direction it would take. Worst case, he figured they would spend the whole night talking. Best case... Well, this was the best-case scenario.

This he could do. Changing the subject to sex was always his specialty. It made things easier, less intense. And Dare was ready to get to that phase of their impromptu date.

Sliding his hand up the back of Noah's shirt, Dare ran his palms over smooth, warm skin. Leaning in, he brushed his lips against Noah's. "Wha'd'ya say we get you outta these clothes?"

Noah pulled back, seemingly studying Dare's face for a moment. For a second there, Dare thought Noah was going to turn him down, but then Noah smiled and his eyes dropped to Dare's mouth.

"I won't complain about naked."

Well, then.

Dare backed Noah up until he was against the wall, his body pressing intimately against Noah's. God, he felt so good against him. Needing to get closer, Dare fused their mouths. He loved the feel of Noah's lips against his, that exquisite, skillful tongue searching his mouth, seeking, tormenting. It was almost as good as sex. Hell, it *was* sex. The way Noah worked his tongue, fucking into Dare's mouth … it was a wonder he didn't explode. Good thing he'd jacked off that morning or he might've been pushed to the edge before he was ready.

Pulling his mouth from Noah's, Dare ran his lips over Noah's jaw. "Let me show you the bed."

It was time to get this show on the road.

YES, THIS WAS already headed in the direction Noah hadn't intended for it to. However, he couldn't seem to stop it. Something was off with Dare, but Noah wasn't sure what it was. Something about Dare's insecurity made him want to comfort him, made him want to go against his entire reason for being there tonight.

He got the sense that Dare was trying to set things right between them, but sex was his go-to in order to relieve some of the tension. Noah had planned for them to be hands-off, but now that he was alone with Dare, he couldn't seem to stop. He had missed him so much, and the proximity gave him comfort.

Sure, Noah felt the intense need coursing through his veins, a desire to be with this man so strong it was almost painful, but that wasn't the only thing on his mind. Seemed that it was something that Dare was definitely battling. Which was the reason that Noah was pushing for the intimacy so quickly. Part of him wanted to talk a little more the way they had during dinner, only without the nervous tension. He wanted to get to know Dare, learn what he'd done for the past fifteen years, but, as they'd learned back at the lake, that hadn't gone over so well.

However, the kissing was certainly doing a good job at persuading Noah to forget all about the talking. When Dare reached for Noah's shirt, tugging it from his jeans before lifting it over his head, he sucked in a breath. Dare's warm hands slid up his torso slowly, causing his heart to beat a little faster, a little harder.

"You work out," Dare noted, chuckling as though he had just noticed Noah's body.

"Every now and then." Noah worked out most days, but it wasn't something he focused his life around. He did it for work mostly because he needed to be in the best possible shape for his job.

Dare's tongue slid across Noah's collarbone, causing him to groan while he held Dare's head, his other arm wrapped around his back. The heat from Dare's mouth caused goose bumps to form on his skin. And when Dare's mouth latched on to Noah's nipple, he growled.

"Like that?" Dare continued to torment him.

"So fucking much." He liked everything Dare did to him. His body came alive, reliving everything Dare had done to him when they'd been on the ship, making it nearly impossible to think about anything except the way it felt when Dare touched him.

Before Dare could work Noah's jeans open, he managed to toe off his shoes, then help Dare out of his shirt. He damn sure didn't want to be the only naked one here. Although Dare seemed to have a one-track mind, Noah wasn't interested in quick tonight. He had spent the entire day thinking about Dare, obsessing over him, trying to figure out how to make this work. Since it was inevitable that they get naked and on that bed, Noah intended to ensure they took their time getting there.

Noah grabbed Dare's wrists when he once again reached for Noah's jeans. "Slow down. We've got time."

Dare met Noah's gaze, and for a few seconds, they held each other's stare. It was intense. Despite Dare's attempt to keep this simply physical, Noah detected emotion in his eyes. Noah could see the battle warring there, knew Dare was distancing himself from whatever he might feel, he just didn't know why. Noah had picked up on that during their time on the ship.

Placing his hands on Dare's sides, Noah slowly slid his palms upward, over the smooth skin, the tense muscles. He flattened his palms and glided them up Dare's chest, spreading his fingers and pausing when he had the nipple piercings between them. Leaning down, he licked one nipple, then the other. Returning to the first, he took the piercing between his teeth and tugged gently.

Dare's hands covered Noah's, which were still flat on his chest. The intimate contact made Noah's head swim. He continued to fondle Dare's nipples, enjoying the soft moans and groans that rumbled up from Dare's throat.

Noah wanted to relearn everything that drove Dare wild.

"You drive me crazy when you do that."

Noah smiled to himself. That was the plan.

Fearless

While he continued to fondle Dare, they managed to remove the rest of their clothing, tossing each piece on the floor before they found their way to the bed. Noah once again fused his mouth to Dare's, trying to slow things down. They'd been in the apartment all of ten minutes and already they were naked. He knew he shouldn't be complaining, but this wasn't exactly how he'd seen this night going.

It took some effort, but Noah managed to gain the upper hand, getting Dare onto his back while Noah lay at his side, partially covering him with his body while he stared down at him.

"What am I going to do with you?" He didn't expect an answer to his question, however, Dare seemed eager to give him one.

"Whatever you want."

Noah wanted a lot of things, but only part of that involved sex.

As much as he wanted to push for a little conversation, he got the impression it would push Dare in the opposite direction.

So for now, he would settle for getting his fill.

If that was even possible.

Thirty-Five

DARE WAS STARTING to have doubts.

Not about Noah but about himself.

About what he wanted. What he expected out of this. Sex.

That was what he was supposed to want; that was what this was supposed to be about. Hell, he'd given himself that pep talk a dozen times since the morning he'd woken up in Noah's arms on the ship. He didn't want more than that. He didn't want anything that involved emotions. He wanted pure, unadulterated sex.

Fun sex.

Sexy sex.

Kinky sex.

Noah could give him that, of that he was certain.

So why the fuck was he continuing to screw this up by thinking about more?

"Dare?"

Dare opened his eyes when Noah pulled back from their kiss. He found his lover staring down at him, worry creasing his forehead.

"Hmm?"

"You okay?"

Shit, he was better than okay. He was naked. Noah was here. They had an endless supply of condoms … well, at least enough to make it through the night. What more could he ask for?

Don't answer that, he mentally warned his subconscious.

Knowing he would never stop thinking if he didn't start doing, Dare smiled up at Noah. "I'm better than okay. In fact, I'd be fucking fantastic if you were the one lying here and I was tormenting you for a bit."

Noah shrugged. "Do your worst."

Laughing, Dare flipped their positions and returned his lips to Noah's, kissing him as though his life depended on it. His dick got with the program as he ground himself against Noah's thigh, the friction sending pleasure coursing through him.

Yes, this was more like it.

He slowly worked his way down Noah's chest. He was almost where he could take Noah's cock in his mouth when Noah shocked the shit out of him by jumping up from the bed and strolling across the room to the kitchen.

Okay, so *that* wasn't supposed to happen.

"What are we doing?" Noah asked, thrusting his hand in his hair.

Dare watched, awestruck by the gorgeous, naked man now pacing. *What the fuck just happened?* One second they were making out, the next…

Looked as though Noah's conscience was speaking to him.

"I was thinking we were getting to the point where you screw me senseless." Dare sat up. "Maybe I was wrong?"

Noah stopped at the end of the bed, then stared down at Dare. Holding his breath, he hoped Noah would join him once again, because he knew where this was headed and he did not want to go that route. It was enough that he'd spent every waking moment since he'd stepped off that airplane—after he and Noah had gone their separate ways—thinking about this man. And it hadn't all been about sex, either, which wasn't the norm for Dare.

"Why are we doing this?" Noah questioned, still watching him.

"Because it's fucking awesome?" Dare wasn't sure what Noah wanted him to say.

"Fine. I'll give you that. But that's…" Noah dropped his gaze to the floor, then turned and picked up his jeans. "That's not why I came over tonight."

"So you're saying you don't want to fuck me?"

Noah pulled on his jeans slowly, not looking at Dare when he responded. "That's not what I'm saying. I think about it more often than not, but I'm not looking for that right now."

Dare was royally confused. "Right now, *right now*? As in this minute? Or are you being purposely vague? Because I'm not following, and I don't know what the fuck you want from me."

Okay, so he hadn't meant to get angry, but this felt like rejection. And since Noah had already rejected him once in recent days, Dare had expected that if they did see each other again, they could and would pick up where they'd left off.

Noah turned to face him, his jeans not fastened. "Is that all you want?"

"Considering I'm naked and my dick's hard"—Dare glanced at his dick—"or rather, it *was*, I thought it was a good place to start." Dare couldn't contain the frustration in his voice.

"That's not what I meant and you know it."

Dare sighed, then flopped back on the bed. "What the hell *did* you mean, Noah? You're making this so damn complicated. One minute, I'm giving you a blow job and then you're running away. The next minute, I ask you to give me another chance, and it looks like you're about to do it to me again."

Noah stared back at him but didn't say anything.

Dare continued. "I can't keep doing this. Did you think we were gonna pick up where we left off fifteen years ago? Did you think I was going to fall in love with you in a matter of a week and want to shack up and take your name? I'm not that guy anymore."

And he wasn't. Or he hadn't been, right up until Noah had walked into his life and turned it upside down and sideways. Yes, deep down he wanted all of those things, but he knew he shouldn't. They'd been down this road before. Dare wasn't willing to jump into something again. Noah might not have been affected by their breakup or the ups and downs of the past week, but Dare had been devastated. He wasn't putting himself through that again.

"That's not what I'm expecting." Noah's voice held a hint of emotion. "But I'm not interested in a once-in-a-while fuck with you, Dare."

"Then why the fuck did you come over?" Dare lifted his head and met Noah's gaze. "If I recall correctly, that's how you roll, right? I remember trying to push for more and being brushed off like I didn't matter."

Shit. Open mouth, insert foot.

As soon as the words were out, Dare wanted to take them back. He knew he couldn't hold what happened between them a long time ago against Noah forever, but for some reason, he wasn't ready to let go.

Rather than argue, Noah grabbed the rest of his clothes, tugged them on quickly, and then walked right out the door.

Fuck. This was beginning to get old fast.

As he stared at the door, Dare couldn't do anything more than sit there, too stunned to move.

NOAH WAS AN idiot.

Not for walking out on Dare, but for thinking that they might've had a chance at something again. He should've known that Dare wouldn't be able to get over their past long enough to try. That was what Noah had wanted. He'd wanted a chance to talk it out, to even apologize for how things had ended up, but he would never get that now. It felt as though Dare was attempting to punish him, and maybe that was all his fault. He shouldn't have gotten his hopes up again.

Noah had just opened the door to his truck when he heard Dare shouting his name. He peered over to see a half-naked Dare coming toward him, wearing only his boxers. He looked pissed.

"Don't walk away."

He sounded pissed, too.

"I'm only doing what you want me to do, Dare." Noah wasn't sure that was entirely true, but he knew Dare was still looking for a fight, and Noah was itching to give him one. It wasn't the way they should've been handling this.

"I don't…" Dare walked right up to Noah, putting his arms around him and pulling him close. It was a move that shocked the shit out of him. "I don't want you to go. Come back inside and we'll talk."

Fearless

Noah didn't think that was a good idea. Dare had told him how he felt, and Noah wasn't interested in beating his head up against a brick wall. They weren't looking for the same thing, and whether Dare knew it or not, Noah had been punished enough for what had happened all those years ago. The downward spiral had started the moment he'd woken up to find Dare gone. It'd grown out of control from there.

Shaking his head, Noah tried to push Dare away. Granted, he didn't put much effort into the move. "I don't think this is a good idea. It's clear we don't want the same thing."

"Please don't go." Dare's voice was so low, had he not been talking into Noah's ear, he wouldn't have heard him. "Don't do this to me again."

Noah sighed.

"What happened to taking things slow?" Dare asked.

Noah couldn't see his face because he still had his arms tightly wound around Noah.

"I don't think screwing each other's brains out is the right way to do that."

"Maybe not." Dare pulled back and looked him in the eye. "But right now, I don't have any other suggestions. Come inside, please. I don't need my neighbors knowing my business."

The safe thing would be to hop in his truck and head home, to forget this had ever happened. Except Noah knew he wouldn't be able to. He would spend the next few days sulking about this until he pissed himself off. At least if he went inside, they could hash it out and either move past it or walk away with some closure.

He damn sure wasn't looking forward to the latter.

"Fine."

Dare closed Noah's door for him, then took his hand and led him back into the apartment.

Once inside, Noah didn't know what to do or say. Since Dare didn't have a couch, the only place to sit was on one of the two chairs at the small kitchen table or on the bed. Noah didn't feel comfortable sitting on the bed—the risk of them getting naked again was far too great—so he opted to lean against the wall.

He was tempted to tell Dare to put some clothes on because seeing him standing there in only his boxers was a distraction he didn't need. In fact, what Noah needed was a way to turn back time to fifteen years ago so he could change the conversation he'd had with Dare *that* night.

Much like this one, if he'd only said the right thing, they wouldn't be here now.

Thirty-Six

IF THEY'D BEEN in the movies, this would've been the part when shit got real. Dare had no idea what had spurred him to go after Noah, but he knew that letting him walk away wasn't an option. Not until they aired things out between them.

Funny how it seemed their roles had been flipped. Noah was now the one wanting something more and would run away if things got tough, and Dare had become the one who didn't know how to express himself.

And yes, he could accept he had faults. He had many. However, he also had feelings. For this guy. The one standing in front of him, looking completely unsure of himself.

Dare knew how that felt. He'd been there before.

"I don't know what to say," Noah muttered.

"I do."

Noah's eyes widened as Dare crossed his arms over his chest and stood only a few feet away.

"Yes, it's true," he admitted, "I want to fuck your brains out. I want to fuck you a million times in a million different positions. I want to feel your skin on mine, Noah. You do that to me. You drive me fucking crazy. It's no different than when I was nineteen years old." Dare dropped his arms. "And no, this isn't usual for me. I've been attracted to guys over the years, but never have I felt this…" He didn't know how to explain it. "This unruly need to fuck you senseless."

Noah continued to stare back at him, a line creasing his forehead. Clearly he wasn't listening to what Dare was trying to tell him. Or it could be that Dare really sucked at this and it wasn't coming out the way he wanted it to. Taking a deep breath, he tried to gather his thoughts, tried to order them so that they made sense.

When he opened his mouth to speak, he shocked himself as much as he did Noah. "I love you, Noah."

Noah stood up straight, the defensiveness in his posture draining. "What?"

"You heard me." Dare wasn't sure he could say it again. Hell, he wasn't sure he'd said it the first time.

"You love me?"

"Please don't make this awkward." Dare took a step back when Noah took a step forward.

"Tell me again, Dare."

Swallowing hard, he forced the words past his lips. "I love you, Noah. I loved you then, and I love you now. If you ask me, it's too fast, but—"

Noah put his hand over Dare's mouth. "I don't think fifteen years is too fast."

Dare pulled Noah's hand down. "Now, let's get something straight. I haven't loved you for fifteen years."

"Liar."

Whatever.

"And maybe you haven't," Noah continued, his hand coming to rest on Dare's cheek. "But I have. I've loved you from the moment I met you and through all of the years between then and now."

"I lied," Dare said quickly. "I loved you all that time. I win. I loved you longer."

Noah chuckled and some of the tension eased out of Dare's shoulders.

"It's not a competition."

Of course it wasn't. "I still win."

"How do you figure?" Noah's eyebrows shot downward.

"'Cause I said it first."

Noah didn't respond immediately, and Dare suddenly felt incredibly vulnerable standing there. And it had nothing to do with the fact that he was only wearing boxers, either.

"Is this real?" Noah finally asked.

Dare didn't know what was real anymore.

Noah took a step back, then turned away completely, and Dare felt his stomach plummet. Maybe he should've answered.

"I know I hurt you, Dare. During a time when you were open and honest with me, I kept myself closed off." Noah turned to face him. "I was scared at the time. I knew that I loved you, more than I'd ever loved anyone. And I knew that you loved me, too."

"Yet you pushed me away." The pain of that time echoed in his chest.

"I did. I was selfish. I thought I could keep you there without having to commit completely. I took you for granted, so when you disappeared, it felt as though you'd ripped my heart out of my chest."

Dare knew the feeling. He'd experienced that then, as well, and it had been the reason he'd walked away.

"I'm sorry, Dare. I'm sorry for all the pain I caused. And I do love you. I never stopped. Even when I hated you, I loved you."

That didn't make any damn sense, but Dare kept his mouth shut.

"I should've come after you." Noah's gaze dropped to the floor. "I probably would have … eventually … if my father hadn't died."

Dare felt a sharp pain pierce his insides. Noah's father's death was his fault.

When he met Noah's gaze again, Noah was shaking his head. "Don't you dare blame yourself for that. I don't. I don't blame you, and I don't blame myself. What happened was tragic, and I miss my father every single day, but he didn't die because we broke up."

Dare wanted to believe that, but he didn't know how Noah could look at him every day from here on out and not think about how his father might still be there if Dare hadn't walked out.

As much as he loved Noah, as much as he was willing to walk through fire for him, he wasn't sure they'd ever be able to let go of the past.

Not completely.

NOAH HAD COME here with the intention of getting things out in the open between them, but he hadn't expected Dare to tell him that he loved him.

That had changed everything.

It had changed everything fifteen years ago and it changed everything now. The only difference was that Noah wasn't too young to be grateful for what he had. He wouldn't let Dare go again. Not if he had any say in the matter.

But he could see the concern in Dare's hazel eyes. He could see the pain and the fear. The man he had known back then had always worn his emotions on his sleeve. This Dare... He hadn't changed all that much. And what had changed was only for the better.

Once again closing the distance between them, Noah wrapped his arms around Dare's neck and held on tight, burying his face in Dare's neck. "I love you, Dare."

"I love you, too." Dare's words were so soft, his body so rigid.

Noah knew Dare was scared. But so was he.

Lifting his head, he leaned back enough to look Dare in the eyes. "Nothing can change how I feel about you. I damn sure don't want to spend the next fifteen years hoping someone will come along and make me feel the way that you do. It hasn't happened yet." Leaning forward, Noah rested his forehead against Dare's. "I remember the first day on the ship, I wondered if you were single or not. I assumed you were, but then I realized how stupid that was because some guy should've snatched you up by now."

"Oh, they tried," Dare said, a small smile on his face.

"I'm sure they did. And then after that first dinner, when I saw you talking to Hudson's brother, I lost it." He hadn't known that was Hudson's brother at the time.

Dare pulled back, frowned. "That's why you ran out of there that night?"

"I was jealous." It was hard to admit, but he knew he had to. "I couldn't stand the thought of another man having you. Even that day, it killed me to think of you with someone else."

Dare's fingers slipped through Noah's hair. "I've tried. Trust me on that. But I've never wanted someone the way I want you."

Noah couldn't even describe how good that made him feel. "So can we start over?"

When Dare pulled back quickly, Noah dropped his arms and stared at him.

"No." Dare was shaking his head.

Noah wasn't sure what to think.

"Okay, yes," Dare added. "If by starting over you mean you'll get naked again, then yes. Otherwise, no. I've spent fifteen years without you. I'm not willing to go backward this time. I don't want to start over. I can't pretend not to love you one day and then admit it the next. I want us to start from right here. And the next step is for you to get naked."

He couldn't help himself, he laughed. Dare thought he'd meant they could start over completely.

"I think naked is good." To prove himself, Noah pulled his shirt up but didn't remove it because he was distracted by the heat in Dare's eyes.

"Oh, fuck," Dare whispered harshly, his gaze raking over Noah's chest. "Naked is really good."

"Come here."

Noah waited until Dare stepped into his personal space before he wrapped his arms around his neck again and leaned in for a kiss. He kept it gentle at first, wanting to linger for a few minutes. He knew where they were headed, and he was no longer scared to go there because he knew this wasn't the end. It was the beginning. Their second chance.

Dare's hands cupped his face, holding him still while Dare's tongue did wicked things inside Noah's mouth. He tried to keep the contact, but Dare was teasing him, pulling back enough to make Noah beg for more.

"Touch me, Noah. Put your hands on me."

Fearless

Noah slid his hands up Dare's sides, pulling him closer, letting the warm, smooth skin caress his palms. Wrapping his arms around him, Noah glided his hands over Dare's back, feeling the muscles flex with every move. He dipped his hands into the back of Dare's boxers and cupped his firm ass, kneading the muscle and listening to Dare moan into his mouth.

Dare nipped Noah's bottom lip. "I want to feel you against me. Skin to skin."

Noah freed his hands long enough for Dare to remove his shirt. Their chests came together, heated flesh against heated flesh. Remaining upright became too difficult, and somehow, without releasing Dare's mouth, Noah managed to guide them both to the bed. He urged Dare backward, crawling over him, never breaking the kiss.

"Noah…"

The way Dare said his name made his body heat. There was so much emotion in that single word.

"We're gonna do this," he assured Dare as he stared down at him, "but we're gonna do this my way this time."

Dare frowned, his hands gliding over Noah's chest. "What way is that? There're are only so many holes."

Fuck. The man unhinged him.

Smiling, he leaned in and pressed a kiss to the corner of Dare's mouth. "For every question you answer, I'll give you more of what you want."

"Deal."

Noah smirked. "You don't even know what questions I'm gonna ask."

"Doesn't matter. As long as you keep touching me."

That he would do.

Noah trailed his mouth over Dare's cheek, then down his jaw, licking and kissing him while he humped Dare's thigh. His skin was tight, his emotions on rapid boil. The only thing in the world that he needed right now was to feel Dare against him. Holding him. Kissing him. Loving him.

"Why'd you get your nipples pierced?" He took one piercing in between his teeth and tugged gently.

"I dared Cam to do it," he explained breathlessly. "I told him that if he did, I would. Bastard went through with it."

Noah tugged on Dare's nipple once more before sucking the piercing into his mouth. Dare groaned, his hand going to the back of Noah's head. He tortured each of them before sliding his mouth lower, running his tongue over Dare's ribs.

"And the tattoo? Why that one?"

Dare didn't respond right away, so Noah lifted his head and waited.

"I needed a reminder that I couldn't stop living because my heart had been broken."

Noah frowned, lifting his head higher. "But you said you didn't do relationships after me."

Dare's smile was wicked. "I should've gotten it tattooed somewhere I could see it."

Shaking his head, Noah chuckled, then dropped his mouth back to Dare's skin. He worked his way lower, kissing Dare's stomach, his sides, loving the way Dare moaned as he did. Rather than go lower, Noah reversed and starting working his way back up, tormenting Dare's nipples once more.

When he paused to look at Dare, he saw the way his eyes narrowed. He was clearly growing tired of this game.

"I'm no longer enjoying this game," Dare admitted, his hands sliding to the back of Noah's head.

"No?"

Dare shook his head. "I need more of you."

Noah nipped Dare's chest lightly, working his way back to Dare's mouth. "I'll never get enough of you," Noah whispered against Dare's skin. "Never."

Dare's hands traveled over his back, his fingers digging into the muscle as he held him. Noah could hardly focus with Dare's teeth nipping at his shoulder, the pinpricks of pain exquisite.

As much as his cock desired attention, Noah didn't want this to end. He never wanted to stop touching this man … feeling him. For the first time in fifteen years, his heart felt full, all the cracks mended, all the pieces put back together.

And he knew, in this moment, that this was it for him. Dare was it for him. No matter the obstacles they might encounter, there was no way Noah could ever let him go.

Thirty-Seven

DARE WASN'T SURE what he was feeling, but he was overwhelmed by everything. The feel of Noah's lips on his, Noah's hands gliding over his body, the warmth of his skin … it was driving him mad. He needed more… He needed *something*.

"Fuck… Noah… Please."

"Please what?" Noah asked, pressing his forehead to Dare's. "Tell me what you need."

"You. I need you."

"I'm right here. You've got me. All of me."

He hoped like hell that meant they were through with the questions, because he wasn't sure how much longer he would last. He would gladly tell Noah anything he wanted to know … *after*. Dare reached between them, working the button on Noah's jeans free. He needed to feel all of him. There were too many clothes in the way. Too much still separating them.

Noah obviously took the hint, because he was up off the bed, removing the rest of his clothes while Dare shoved his boxers down his legs and kicked them off.

Fearless

When Noah returned, Dare wrapped his arms around him, pulling him against him. Chest to chest, thigh to thigh, shin to shin. He made sure he could touch every inch of Noah with his body while their mouths melded together, their tongues exploring, owning, claiming. The kiss was intense, reflecting the adrenaline now pumping through Dare's veins. He'd never been this turned on before, never needed to feel someone as much as he needed Noah. It was as though the man could anchor him, and he needed that because the storm raging inside him was quickly getting out of control.

The electricity crackled between them. The tension growing, making it hard to breathe, much less think. A nearly debilitating sense of urgency consumed him.

"Want..." Dare kissed Noah's mouth, holding his head roughly. "Need..." He couldn't bring himself to break away although he wanted to get the words out. "Need you, Noah. Need you now."

Noah lifted so that he was holding himself up with his arms, staring down at Dare. While he was suspended above him, Dare tried to catch his breath. The beautiful man hovering over him offered too much temptation.

"I want to take this slow." Noah lowered himself back down on top of Dare. "I want to tease you until you can't take anymore."

Dare was almost to that point already and they hadn't done anything yet. This was so much more than physical, though. The emotional intensity was searing him from the inside out.

Noah's lips traveled over Dare's chest, pausing to tease his nipples again. He kept his eyes open, his attention on everything Noah was doing to him. He loved watching him. He was so fucking beautiful, so damn perfect...

"Aww, yes," Dare hissed, his hand reaching for Noah's head as he guided him lower until the heat of Noah's mouth was surrounding his cockhead. "Lick me."

He felt like a caged animal, trying to hold back, trying to keep within his emotional restraints, but it wasn't working. He figured this was how Bruce Banner felt when he turned into the Hulk. Without the whole giant green part.

His body temperature soared as Noah held his cock in his fist, using his tongue to torture him so exquisitely. It wasn't until Noah's eyes locked with Dare's that he took him fully into his mouth, robbing Dare of the rest of his sanity.

Sitting up, he held Noah's head, guiding his mouth down, forcing him to take all of him. He ran his hands over Noah's back, clutching at him, needing that touch to keep him whole.

"Fuck... Love when you suck my dick." Dare lifted Noah's head by his hair, then guided him back down. He continued the motion while he reached around Noah and gripped his dick, stroking him at the same pace Noah was blowing him. "Oh ... yeah."

Somehow Dare managed to get up on his knees, holding Noah's head as he continued to fuck his mouth, driving his cock in deeper. Noah shifted so that he was turned sideways, giving Dare better access to his cock.

"Take all of me..." Dare forced his cock to the back of Noah's throat until he gagged. He then pulled Noah off him, tugging his hair until Dare could crush his lips to Noah's. While he feasted on Noah's mouth, Dare repositioned so that he was on top once again. He wasn't ready for this to be over, but he couldn't relinquish control right now. He needed this and he could tell that Noah knew that.

Straddling Noah's chest, he fed his cock into his mouth once more, thrusting his hips forward and back, fucking past those sweet lips. He continued to use Noah's mouth for long minutes, watching as his dick tunneled in and out, in and out.

Using his thigh muscles to lift him, Dare knelt beside Noah's head, freeing his cock from the warm cavern of Noah's mouth to fist it himself while he dragged his balls over Noah's lips.

"Lick." Dare stroked himself while Noah's head disappeared between his legs, his lips closing around his nuts, warm and wet and so fucking good. "Oh, yes."

He worked his way around so that he was aligned with Noah's body. Shifting over him, Dare pressed his full weight against Noah, pushing him into the mattress as he ground his cock against Noah's.

"Want to fuck you."

Noah nodded. "Want that, too."

"Bare," Dare added, kissing Noah's mouth. "Want to feel you." He could hardly breathe for wanting it so badly. "Never been with anyone bare... No one except you."

"Yes." Noah lifted his legs at the same time he grabbed Dare's ass and pulled him forward. "Bare. Want ... you."

Dare sucked Noah's tongue into his mouth, trying to calm himself enough that he wouldn't shoot as soon as he felt the tight heat of Noah's ass strangling his dick. Releasing Noah's mouth, Dare sat up, planting his palms on the backs of Noah's thighs to open him. Dare pushed him higher as he scooted down, using his tongue to lube Noah's ass. Using his saliva, he slicked Noah as best he could. He knew it wouldn't be the same as lube, but he couldn't seem to stop long enough to get it.

"Inside me," Noah groaned.

Dare spit in his hand and lubed his cock more as he guided himself into Noah's ass, once again claiming his mouth as he worked inside him inch by slow inch.

Noah groaned.

"Too dry?"

"No... Don't care..." Noah grabbed Dare's head and pulled his mouth down to his while Dare impaled him, working in deeper.

Lube would've helped, but this felt ... different.

Noah groaned into his mouth. Buried inside him, Dare thrust his hips against Noah's ass, not retreating, simply adding friction as he fucked him deep. "Wanna come in your ass and fuck you again and again."

Noah moaned, his arms wrapped around Dare as he held him close. Focusing only on the pleasure, Dare continued to penetrate Noah over and over, fucking into him until he knew he was going to come. He couldn't hold back, but that didn't matter. It wouldn't be the first time he would come tonight; of that he was certain.

"Gonna come in your ass," he warned Noah.

"Come for me, baby."

The endearment did him in. Dare pumped his hips over and over until he was coming, filling Noah's ass, lubing him enough that he could fuck him harder. He couldn't stop. Didn't want to.

He only hoped Noah would catch him when he fell, because there was no doubt about it, he was going to fall and it was going to be life-altering.

Fearless

NOAH FELT DARE come in his ass, the pulse of his cock as he buried himself deep. He never let Dare go, never stopped holding him, kissing him, mumbling whatever words tumbled out of his mouth.

"Don't stop," he pleaded. "Fuck me harder, Dare. Harder, baby."

Dare lifted his upper body, grabbing Noah's legs and forcing them toward his chest. The position bordered on painful, but he didn't care. The friction in his ass, the way Dare's thick cock brushed his gland made him whimper. He didn't want to come yet, fearful that he couldn't match Dare's stamina, so he urged Dare to continue until they were both covered in sweat and panting.

When Dare fell on top of him, his cock still hard inside him, Noah took his mouth again, slowing the kiss, bringing things down a notch. He had felt Dare's eagerness, knew he'd needed to be in control, likely unsure of the emotions churning inside him. Noah was okay with that; he would do anything for this man.

Anything.

As they kissed, Dare's dick softened until he was pulling out of him.

In order to give Dare a second to come down from the high, Noah slipped into the bathroom, cleaning himself quickly before returning to the bed. He remembered seeing lube on the kitchen table, so he retrieved it before crawling back over Dare once more. While Dare continued to breathe deeply, still worked up from that intense moment, Noah lubed himself up and rubbed against Dare's puckered hole.

"You ready for me?"

"More than ready."

Noah wasn't sure *he* was ready. The last time he'd had sex without a condom had been with Dare. Fifteen years ago. In fact, Dare was the only person he'd gone bare for ever. The only one he'd ever loved enough to go bare for. Which meant Dare would be his first and last … always.

Pushing the head past the tight ring of muscles, Noah watched closely as Dare's ass gripped him.

"Oh, fuck…"

Noah glanced up at Dare's face. "Am I hurting you?"

Dare shook his head and gripped Noah's thighs. "Need to feel you all the way."

Noah pushed in more, taking his time, pressing his hips forward until he was balls deep. He leaned down and brushed his lips against Dare's. "Perfect… That's how this feels. So damn perfect."

Dare cupped the back of his head, kissing him softly as Noah pulled his hips back, then pushed in again. He kept the pace languid, not wanting to rush this. He continued to screw Dare deep, shifting their positions so that Dare was on his side, Noah spooning him from behind, allowing him to hit that spot that made Dare moan. Minutes passed as he continued to torment them both until finally Dare was on his stomach with Noah behind him. His pace quickened as he thrust his hips forward, then retreated.

"Harder," Dare growled, his face against the mattress.

Noah slammed into him once, retreated, slammed into him again. He picked up a rhythm that made his eyes cross, fucking Dare harder and deeper with every stroke. When Dare reached back with one hand and gripped Noah's thigh, he leaned forward, pressing his chest to Dare's back.

"I love you," he whispered in Dare's ear as he continued to pump his hips against Dare's ass.

"Love … you … too…" Dare moaned long and slow. "Need … more."

Noah gave him more. He gave him everything he had.

Unsure how much time had passed, Noah got lost in the sensation of being inside Dare, covering his body, having him so close. Before he knew it, the electrical current shot from his spine to his groin, and he groaned, his release barreling down on him.

"Coming," he said on a harsh whisper against Dare's ear. "Fuck... So good."

"Yes," Dare hissed. "Come for me, Noah. I've got you."

Dare's ass clenched around his dick, making Noah groan as he shot deep inside him. It was so much more than a fuck, though. This... What had transpired between them just now was a claiming. Dare belonged to him and he belonged to Dare. Nothing and no one could ever come between them again.

Thirty-Eight

Wednesday, June 15th

BY THE TIME morning arrived, Dare was sore all over. After the first time last night, he'd taken Noah in every conceivable way possible. Not that he wouldn't be thinking of some new ways in the near future. He most definitely would.

Before he opened his eyes, he curled up against the warm body practically wrapped around him. He did not want to get out of bed, but he had to. He had to get to the marina.

"Your phone alarm went off," Noah whispered against his ear before pressing a kiss to his temple. "I was going to give you a couple of minutes, then wake you."

"It's set to go off early. I tend to oversleep."

"That much hasn't changed." Noah chuckled softly. "Neither has the fact you tend not to unpack."

Dare peered over at the suitcase he'd brought back from the cruise more than a week ago. He had yet to unpack it. Not like he would be wearing jeans or polos, so probably didn't matter anyway.

Fearless

Rolling over, Dare hugged Noah to him, a tiny bit of anxiety flaring up inside his chest. When they had finally given up and gone to sleep, Dare hadn't been sure how the morning would go. Last night, he'd been swamped by emotion, spewing words in the heat of the moment. Sure, he'd meant them, but that didn't mean Noah had meant the words he'd spoken.

"You have to work today?" Dare asked, practically wrapping himself around Noah.

"At the station, no. Next shift is tomorrow. I worked a double last weekend to adjust my days."

"Twenty-four on, forty-eight off." Dare repeated what Noah had told him before.

"Yep. Then I've got a roofing job scheduled the day after." Noah kissed his nose. "What about you? What days do you work?"

"All of them." He smiled when Noah's eyes widened. "Because I want to. There are four of us. It's not necessary, so I can take off when I need to."

"Sounds like we're both spending too much time working." Noah smiled, but it didn't quite reach his eyes.

"So when do I get to see you again?" That was the real question he was trying to get at. And yes, it did sound like their schedules would collide more often than not, but Dare was willing to do what was necessary to spend more time with this man.

"Well, you've got me for the day. Thought maybe I'd hang at the marina, watch you work." Noah pulled back and looked Dare in the eyes. "If that's okay with you."

Cupping Noah's cheek, Dare smiled. "I'd love that. But don't think I'm not gonna put you to work."

Noah's eyes softened, but before he could lean in for a kiss, Dare untangled himself and bounced out of bed.

"I plan to kiss the fuck outta you," he told Noah as he headed toward the bathroom, "but I get to brush my teeth first."

Noah chuckled. "I beat you to it already."

Dare stuck his head back into the room, toothbrush dangling from his mouth. "I know. I smelled your minty fresh breath." Tossing a quick smile at Noah, he then stepped back into the bathroom and proceeded to brush his teeth.

When he returned, he was disappointed to find Noah had gotten up and pulled on his underwear. Probably for the best, though. Dare could've easily spent another half hour or so driving them both crazy with lust, but then he would be late for work. Since he'd slipped out a little early last night, he didn't want to be late.

Not that Cam, Roan, or Teague would care. That was one of the benefits of the four of them owning the place. There was always someone who could fill in. And they were lucky because they each had a strong work ethic, wanting to be at the marina whenever possible.

Walking up behind Noah, Dare wrapped his arms around his stomach, pulling him back against him. Although he had learned his lesson before, Dare had a couple of things on his mind that he needed to share with Noah. Since he refused to live in the past, he wasn't worried they'd have a repeat, and he refused not to speak his mind.

"Thanks for not leaving last night."

Noah turned in the circle of Dare's arms. "Thanks for coming after me."

"I had to. I couldn't let you go. The past week has been hell."

Dare noticed the way Noah swallowed hard, his eyes roaming Dare's face. "We need to talk about where this is going."

Yes, they did. But Dare knew right this second wasn't the right time for that. "We will." Loosening his hold, he put a little more space between them. "But right now, I've got to get to work. If you're really nice, I'll even stop and get you breakfast."

"How chivalrous of you." Noah moved closer, his hands cradling Dare's face. "What do you consider really nice?"

Dare didn't get the chance to respond because Noah inhaled him, their mouths melding together, tongues dancing. It was sweet and sexy at the same time.

But he feared if he didn't press pause, neither of them would make it anywhere, because he was about ten seconds away from his dick making nice with Noah's prostate one more time.

SOMEHOW, HE AND Dare managed to get out of the apartment and over to the marina without getting naked again, but it had been close there for a minute.

Now, Noah was getting schooled in how to get the equipment set up for the day. Not that he was learning much, but that was mostly due to the fact that he was spending all of his time ogling Dare. The man was... There weren't words for how utterly fuckable the guy was. And when he was working, he was even hotter. Not only was Dare's body a work of art, but the way he laughed and smiled, talking to everyone he came into contact with as though he'd known them his whole life...

Yes, it was safe to say, Noah was a little jealous.

Jealous that Dare had established such strong friendships over the years, and was doing something he loved to do. More so, Noah was jealous that he hadn't been a part of that, jealous that nothing Dare had established for himself was because of Noah.

Granted, it didn't bother him that Dare was happy. He simply wanted to be a part of it.

"Come on, slacker!" Dare hollered from one of the Jet Skis. "Get your ass in gear so we can check these out."

Noah made his way down to the dock, then climbed onto the Jet Ski Dare pointed him to.

"You ever ride one of these?" Dare questioned, watching him closely.

"Once or twice." He didn't bother to tell him it had been a while. Like, at least ten years. Maybe more.

"Here!" Dare tossed a life jacket his way before pulling one on.

Noah was a little shocked to see Dare taking such precautions. He'd assumed he would be more of a daredevil.

"What?" Dare's forehead creased, but Noah couldn't see his eyes behind his sunglasses. "You think big boys don't wear these things?"

Noah chuckled, pulling the vest on and clicking the straps together. "I always thought you were fearless."

"Oh, I am," Dare nodded, starting the engine. "I'm just not stupid."

With a sexy-as-fuck smirk, Dare took off, leaving Noah straddling the machine and wondering how he'd managed to get so damn lucky.

Fearless

By the end of the day, Noah was exhausted. Dare had worked his ass off, and he got the impression the man had doubled up on his responsibilities on purpose. He had managed to do everything Dare had instructed him to and then some. And as he stood here on the pier, staring out at the sun starting its slow descent in the sky, he had to admit, he felt good.

"You wanna take the boat out?" Dare asked, coming to stand beside Noah.

Noah turned around to face him. "I thought for sure you'd want food."

Dare grinned and Noah saw the twinkle of mischief in his green-brown gaze. He was in for it, he was sure of it.

"Oh, I'm hungry, all right."

"Of course you are."

"But not for food."

It was Noah's turn to grin. "Then what're you waiting for?"

Noah followed Dare down the dock to a boat slip that held a decent-sized boat. It was nice, though not too fancy.

This time, Dare didn't put on a life vest, but Noah noticed they were on board.

Wanting to be close to Dare, he stood behind him, holding his hips while Dare maneuvered the boat out into open water. The guy looked so damn good standing there, both hands resting on top of the steering wheel, the muscles in his back flexing when he steered one direction or the other.

Noah wanted to kiss him.

Taking a step closer, he closed the gap between them, pressing his chest against Dare's back, sliding his hands around him, keeping them low. There was no one else on the water—in the spot they were in, anyway—so he wasn't worried about someone seeing them. And even if they did...

What was the point in being fearless if you couldn't be a little wild at times, too?

"Lower," Dare instructed, taking Noah's wrist and guiding it to his crotch.

"You're not in charge right now." Noah smiled to himself, then sucked the warm skin on the back of Dare's neck into his mouth, enjoying the way Dare moaned.

The boat slowed and then stopped. Noah glanced around to see they were in a small cove, a good distance from the shore and from the open water. Definitely a private spot.

As soon as the motor turned off, Dare was turning around to face him. "Then I'm at your mercy."

"Definitely like the sound of that." Noah leaned in and stole a kiss, taking it from zero to intense in a matter of seconds. He allowed his hands to roam over Dare's back, memorizing the feel of those muscles tensing against his palms.

"You're not worried someone might see us?" Dare asked as he tilted Noah's head to the side and trailed his tongue downward.

Noah helped him along, shifting to give him better access while he pulled Dare closer. "I'm not worried. You?"

"Nope." Dare's smirk was naughty and sexy. "Fearless, remember?"

Oh, he remembered, all right.

Thirty-Nine

"SO, TELL ME this, Mr. Pearson." Dare dragged his lips over Noah's sun-warmed skin, inhaling him. "Would you like me to drop to my knees right here and suck you off? My mouth wrapped around your dick while you fuck my lips? Out here in the open where anyone could see?"

Noah groaned, his fingers digging deeper into Dare's back.

"You would like that, wouldn't you?" Although Noah had told him he wasn't the one in charge, Dare wasn't so sure that was the case. It didn't really matter to him who was in charge, just as long as someone was.

"I would," Noah confirmed. "I'd love to see my dick tunneling in and out of your mouth."

Dare remembered last night and the way he had fucked Noah's mouth. So damn hot.

Without waiting for Noah to provide instructions, Dare dropped down to his knees, kissing Noah's stomach while he held his shirt up. He had never done this before. On a boat. In the open. For some reason, he had never seduced a man while out on the water. Perhaps because this was his sacred place. He didn't care to tarnish it with one-night memories.

But Noah wasn't a one-night memory for Dare. He never had been and he never would be.

Tucking his fingers beneath the waistband of Noah's shorts, Dare eased them down enough to free Noah's cock. He was iron-hard and silky-smooth. And beautiful. Noah had a cock that Dare wanted to worship from sunup to sundown, every day of the week, every week of the year.

Noah pulled Dare's hat from his head—a move that Dare really, really liked—and twined his fingers into his hair, pulling him down so that Dare's lips were a breath away from the thick, swollen head.

Dare licked the tip, looking up at Noah, who was watching him, one hand holding up his shirt, the other in Dare's hair. To his surprise, Noah didn't get bossy, he didn't tell Dare what to do, and that was perfectly fine because he wanted to get intimately acquainted with Noah's dick. He wanted to explore him with only his tongue.

So he did.

Trying his best not to rush things, Dare took Noah in his mouth, slowly working his lips down the shaft, taking all of him, stretching wide to accommodate him.

"Oh, yes." Noah's fingers tugged Dare's hair as he held him in place. "Dare... Your mouth... It's so fucking hot."

Dare met Noah's gaze while he slowly bobbed up and down on Noah's dick, hollowing out his cheeks to apply more suction. He wasn't trying to send Noah over. In fact, he wanted to relish this for as long as he could, wanted to give Noah as much pleasure as he could stand.

Noah held Dare's stare, his hips rocking as he began acquiring the control, taking what he wanted from Dare, and shifting the momentum so that Dare became the outlet. Watching as it happened was sexy as fuck. Dare wasn't even sure that Noah knew he was doing it, taking control, becoming the aggressor. It made him want to give in to Noah, to do whatever he wanted, however he wanted it.

"Use your hand," Noah commanded, his fingers tugging on Dare's hair, pulling his mouth away from Noah's cock. "Jack me off. Make me come."

Dare sat back on his haunches, wrapped his fist around Noah's cock, and did as Noah instructed. He tightened his grip, jerking Noah slowly at first, then faster. He watched Noah's ab muscles contract as the pleasure swamped him. He was magnificent.

"Put me in your mouth," Noah rasped, his voice tight. "Want to come in your mouth."

Dare put the head of Noah's cock in his mouth and continued to fist fuck him until the grip Noah had on his hair became almost unbearable. Noah's hips jerked forward, a long, deep growl escaping as he came, his come splashing against Dare's tongue.

While Noah caught his breath, Dare cleaned him with his mouth, then adjusted Noah's shorts and got to his feet.

"That was my first blow job on a boat," Noah told him, cupping Dare's face in his hands as he pulled him in for a kiss.

Dare smiled against Noah's lips. "My first time *giving* a blow job on a boat."

Noah's kiss was sweet and gentle but too short as he pulled back and stared at Dare, confusion marring his features. Dare knew Noah wasn't sure whether or not to believe him.

"It's true," Dare explained. Nodding his chin toward the water, he added, "This has always been my place. I knew one day I'd bring someone here and be able to share it with them. Turns out that person is you."

Noah pulled Dare's face back toward him and pressed a kiss to his lips. Even in the sweet gesture, he could sense Noah's approval and that … that was what made this moment worth all the years of waiting.

NOAH WASN'T READY for this to be over. After Dare had given him the most erotic blow job of his life right there out in the open, they had relaxed on the deck, lying back and watching the sun move lower in the sky. Neither of them had said much, but that was probably the best part. Noah had spent that time reflecting on what had happened between them last night.

They'd admitted their love for one another. And that had changed everything.

"You ready to head back in?" Dare mumbled from beside him.

"Not yet." Noah wanted to take advantage of this moment one more time before they had to return to shore.

Dare turned his head to the side, concern etched on his face.

Noah smiled. He loved that look.

"Something wrong?" Dare questioned.

Noah shook his head as he got to his feet. He then held out his hand to help Dare up. He led Dare to one of the seats. Before he allowed Dare to sit, he pushed Dare's shorts down his hips, letting them pool on the floor. Only then did he force him to sit.

Dare smiled up at him. "I like where your mind wanders when you have time to chill."

"Me, too."

Noah dropped to his knees between Dare's splayed thighs, watching him closely while he worked Dare's dick until he was hard. He used his hand at first, then his tongue, even gently scraping his teeth along the sensitive shaft, relishing all the grunts and groans rumbling in Dare's chest.

When Dare was good and hard, Noah stood, retrieving a small packet of lube he'd stolen from Dare's bathroom.

"You little sneaky bastard," Dare teased, reaching forward and yanking Noah's shorts down before pulling him forward.

Noah laughed as he stumbled, managing to straddle Dare's legs and not fall.

Dare cradled the back of Noah's head and pulled him forward, crushing their mouths together while Noah lubed Dare's dick between their bodies. He teased him until Dare was panting, begging him for more. Only then did Noah lift himself up and readjust his position so that Dare could work his dick into Noah's ass. He impaled himself on Dare's cock, taking him inside inch by inch.

"That's it, baby." Dare groaned. "Ride me."

Noah held on to Dare's shoulders while Dare fucked his ass so superbly. He never hurried, chuckling when Dare would grunt, begging for more.

When Dare gripped his hips and stilled him, Noah prepared himself for the fucking of a lifetime.

And he wasn't disappointed.

When Dare Davis took control, the only thing Noah could do was sit back and enjoy the ride.

An hour later, as Noah was heading home from the marina, having left Dare a short time ago, he couldn't stop thinking about the man. Years' worth of memories and heartache consumed him, but they seemed trivial compared to the feelings he had right this minute.

He loved Dare. That was all there was to it.

He loved his smile, he loved his positive outlook...

He loved the way he wore his ball cap backward and refused to wear shoes…

He loved the sexy rumble of his voice, he loved the reverberation of his laugh…

He loved his delicious body, he loved the strength he felt when Dare held him…

He loved the fact that all these years later, Dare had been put in his path, and though their past was riddled with the obstacles of being too young and too naïve to know what was good for them, and the oversight of thinking that they had all the time in the world, Noah was right where he was meant to be.

Noah felt lighter, more in control of his destiny. There was only one thing he wanted in this world, and that was to spend the rest of his days with the man he loved.

As of last night, he had accepted that this second chance was more than a blessing. They still had to figure out a way to move forward, but Noah had no doubt that was possible.

With Dare, anything was possible.

Forty

Saturday, July 2nd
Two and a half weeks later

DARE WAS AWOKEN by the sound of a knock on his front door, combined with Lulu's disgruntled bark. He rolled over, noticing the sun was up. For the first time since he'd gotten back from the cruise, he had taken the day off, hoping to sleep in a little. Apparently, that wasn't going to happen today.

Lulu barked again, the sound the equivalent of an air horn in the small space.

"Lulu... Chill."

He managed to roll out of bed and saunter to the front door. Without looking through the security hole, he pulled it open, rubbing his eyes.

"Morning."

Dare came awake almost immediately. "What're you doing here?"

Noah stepped into the apartment and gave Lulu a pat on the head. "Couldn't stay away."

"Did you come right from work?"

"I did."

Dare closed the door and locked it, not wanting to risk another neighbor visit. It had already happened once in the last two weeks. Luckily he and Noah had been watching TV and not getting their freak on at the time. He still remembered the shocked look on Noah's face when the old man had come waltzing in as though he owned the place.

"I brought donuts," Noah announced, effectively defogging his brain.

"Have I mentioned how much I love you?" That made up for Noah waking him up during the dream he'd been having. The kinky dream. The dream that had involved Noah strapped to the bed while Dare did devious sexual things to him.

"Not today, no." Noah placed the box of donuts on the table.

It took a minute for Dare to remember what he'd said. Oh, right. Love. Yes. "Well, I do. More than…" Dare didn't waste any time, flipping the lid open and grabbing a donut for each hand. "I'm pretty sure I love you more than donuts, but I'll have to eat a couple to be sure."

Noah chuckled.

After downing two, Dare grabbed a glass and the gallon of milk out of the refrigerator. "What brings you by so early?" Dare smiled. "Not that I don't want to see you every minute of every day as it is."

Noah's grin widened. "You said we were having lunch with your grandmother today."

"Oh, shit." Dare downed his milk. "You're right. We are. What time is it?"

Noah peered over at the alarm clock beside Dare's bed. "Ten thirty."

"Oh, thank God. We've still got time."

And now that Dare realized that, he was coming up with ideas for how they could spend the next hour and a half. Allowing his gaze to slowly travel the length of Noah's body, he came up with a damn good idea.

"Slow your roll, Romeo," Noah said on a laugh. "You're not getting me naked just yet."

"What?" Dare frowned. "Why not?"

As it was, he hadn't seen Noah in two days. They'd finally gotten into a routine, and because of their schedules, they were finding it was difficult to spend much time together at all. Between Noah working at the station, plus his side gig with the roofing business, Dare wasn't getting to spend nearly enough time with him.

"I want to show you something first."

Dare's eyes dropped to Noah's crotch.

Noah barked out a laugh. "Nope. That's not the surprise."

"Damn."

"Get dressed."

Pretending to pout, Dare headed for the bathroom. He didn't bother shutting the door as he stripped naked, brushed his teeth, then took a quick shower. Because his apartment was so small, he knew Noah would get a peek of his naked body. If the guy could refuse him after that, then he clearly had more willpower than Dare did.

Fifteen minutes later, Dare was dressed and ready. He was pretending to pout as he searched for his phone. Unfortunately, Noah had been able to resist him, which only made Dare want to work harder to tease him.

"Where're we going?" Dare grabbed his ball cap and pulled it on backward.

"Get in the truck and I'll show you."

"Do I need shoes?"

Noah chuckled. "Yes. You need shoes."

After grabbing his flip-flops, Dare did as he was instructed, hopping into the passenger side of Noah's truck. He did his best not to ask questions as Noah drove. Since Dare recognized the area, he couldn't contain his questions.

"Are we going to Cam's?"

Noah shook his head.

"Do you have friends who live over here?"

"Nope."

Dare watched out the window as they drove down a tree-lined street dotted with houses that backed up to the lake. Unlike Noah, Dare did have friends who lived over here. Cam and Gannon had bought a house here recently. Cam's dad also lived on the lake, as well as Cam's sister and her husband.

Noah stopped in front of a decent-sized ranch-style home with huge windows on the front and a long, narrow yard. There was a car parked in the driveway in front of the two-car garage.

"Where are we?"

"Get out."

Dare's head snapped over at Noah's firm yet playful tone. He sighed dramatically as he climbed out of the truck and stood on the curb. Noah came around to stand beside him, taking his hand.

"Trust me?"

"No. I don't." Somehow Dare managed to hide his smile. "If you're planning to break into this place, you should know, I've got some money you can borrow."

"Not breaking in." Noah tugged on his hand and pulled him to the sidewalk, then led him to the front door.

The door was open. The only thing separating them from the interior of the house was the glass storm door. Rather than knock, Noah opened the door and stepped inside.

"What're you doing?" Dare tried to pull him back out.

"Relax, babe. It's all good."

An older woman appeared, dressed in a pencil skirt and a silk blouse. Her smile was radiant as she greeted Noah. "Mr. Pearson. So good to see you again."

Again?

What was going on here?

"Feel free to look around."

"Thank you."

Noah didn't release Dare's hand as he led him toward the back of the house and right out onto the back patio. The yard was beautiful, with tall trees and thick, green grass. Bushes and flowers lined the back of the house and the deck leading to a stone walkway that ran all the way down to the water.

"What is this place?"

Noah turned to face him, blocking his view of the lake.

"I know this might seem sudden," Noah began, taking Dare's hands in his. "But these past couple of weeks have been fantastic." Noah smiled. "With the exception of us being apart so much, that is. I thought maybe we could solve the distance problem…" Noah swallowed hard and took a deep breath. "I thought we could solve the problem if we were to move in together."

"Here?" Dare peered over Noah's shoulder to check out the lake again.

"Here." Noah nodded toward the house behind Dare. "It's three bedrooms, three baths, plus a study and—"

Dare placed his hand over Noah's mouth and smiled. "You had me at 'here.'" The relief Dare saw on Noah's face made him laugh. "You want me to move in with you?"

Noah nodded.

"But what about the station? And the roofing jobs?"

"The station is only half an hour away. Since it's not an everyday commute, that's no problem at all. And the roofing business..." Noah looked slightly unsure of himself. "It's something I did in order to occupy my time. It's not a necessity for me. I make enough to support—"

Again, Dare cut him off. "We."

"What?"

"*We* make enough." Dare pulled Noah forward and kissed him. "I'd love to move in with you. Wake up to you every morning." He lowered his voice. "Go to sleep every night after banging your brains out."

Noah's arms slid around his waist and he held him close, their lips brushing together. "Oh, thank God."

"You like the idea of me banging your brains out, huh?"

Noah smiled against Dare's lips.

Dare chuckled. "Did you think I'd say no?"

Noah pulled back and looked at him. "Actually, I thought you would tell me you found a better house somewhere." His smile grew wider. "I know how competitive you are."

It was true. Dare was competitive. And yes, Noah had beat him to the whole moving-in-together thing. But he knew there was one thing Noah hadn't beat him to.

And now seemed like as good a time as any...

Fearless

NOAH HADN'T BEEN sure how Dare would react to him bringing him here. It wasn't as spur-of-the-moment as it seemed, though. They'd had a couple of conversations in recent days about moving in together. Because their schedules didn't mesh, and the thirty-minute drive made it difficult to merely drop in, he and Dare had tossed around the idea of finding a place.

Since they hadn't gotten into the logistics, Noah had simply been browsing for real estate when he'd stumbled upon this house for sale. As soon as he'd seen the pictures, he'd known he couldn't pass it by. At least not without mentioning it to Dare. Last week he had scheduled an appointment with the realtor, snuck over, and checked it out. He'd fallen in love with it instantly, and something—maybe the lake view—had told him Dare would love it, too.

For the past two weeks, they had made as much time for one another as they could, but it was never enough. Noah had convinced Dare to have dinner at his mother's house, which had been far less stressful than he'd expected it to be. Sure, it helped that he'd convinced Milly to come along to provide comic relief. Didn't matter, Noah's mother still loved Dare, the same as she'd loved him back then. They acted as though not a minute had passed since the last time they'd seen one another. Hell, even Larry had taken a liking to Dare.

Because Dare had to be at the marina every morning, they hadn't stayed at Noah's apartment at all. On the nights they did spend together, Noah made the trek out to Dare's. And he wasn't complaining about where they slept, merely that they didn't get to sleep together enough. Noah hated being away from Dare most nights, even if they'd mastered the art of phone sex. That was great and all, but Noah knew he had to do something to bring them closer together.

As far as Noah was concerned, they'd spent the last fifteen years apart, and they had a lot of time to make up for. He didn't want to wait any longer. He didn't care about the whole dating thing. He and Dare had long ago done that whole song and dance. The only thing he wanted was to fall asleep with Dare in his bed every night and wake up with him every morning. Well, most nights and most mornings. He would still be working at the fire station, so there would be those to take into account.

Dare pulled back, and Noah searched his face to try and determine what he was thinking.

"Why are you looking at me like that?"

There was a mischievous gleam in Dare's eyes when he released Noah's hands. Dare took a step back, peered around once more before meeting Noah's gaze.

The next thing Noah knew, Dare was dropping down on one knee…

"What are you doing?" Noah rasped, reaching for Dare to pull him back to his feet.

"I've loved you my whole life," Dare began, dodging Noah's attempt to grab him. "Stop. Seriously. I have something to say."

Dare was grinning from ear to ear while Noah's heart was pounding like a bass drum inside his chest. He stopped reaching for Dare and stood up straight.

Dare continued. "The only regret in my life has been walking away from you. I want to spend the rest of my life with you, Noah Pearson. I want to be hyphenated."

Noah laughed. That was Dare. "Hyphenated, huh?"

"Marry me?"

Before he could respond, Dare shocked him when he reached in his pocket and retrieved…

"You did not!" Noah couldn't contain his laughter.

Dare pulled out a silver chain, which had a ring dangling from it. Noah's high school class ring. The one that Dare had worn back when they'd been together the first time. High school had been far behind Noah at the time, but Dare had found the ring in Noah's dresser and insisted on wearing it. Although Dare had done it as a joke, Noah had secretly enjoyed seeing it around Dare's neck. For the two years they'd been together, Noah had never known Dare to take it off.

"I can't believe you stole that from me." Noah had wondered what had happened to that ring. He hadn't been sure whether Dare had kept it or ditched it somewhere along the way.

"Marry me," Dare repeated, his tone serious. "We can be Davis-Pearson."

"Why not Pearson-Davis?" He was teasing Dare. He honestly didn't care; he was merely buying time to keep from crying. This was more than he'd ever expected, more than he probably deserved.

"Fine. We can be Pear-vis."

Noah cupped Dare's cheek, still staring down at him. His heart smiled. "Of course I'll marry you."

Instead of putting the chain around Noah's neck, Dare put it around his own.

"Ask a guy to marry you and *you* get the ring, huh?"

"That's the way it works," Dare noted.

Helping Dare to his feet, Noah pulled him into his arms. "I love you. Even if you are crazy."

"Speaking of crazy…" Dare chuckled. "It's time to go meet Grams."

Forty-One

DARE WAS GIDDY. It was a strange feeling, one he hadn't had in years, but he couldn't help it. As he directed Noah on how to get to Grams's house, he was practically bouncing in the seat, likely driving Noah crazy. They were buying a freaking house. Together.

And they were going to be hyphenated.

Holy shit.

"Since we're offering full asking price, you think we'll get the house?" he asked Noah.

"Let's hope so. The sellers seem eager, so hopefully it won't be a problem."

"Are there any other offers?"

"Not that she knows of."

Dare wanted that house. Mostly because Noah wanted that house. Oh, and also because it was on the lake.

"What is your grandmother going to say when she finds out you're engaged to be married?"

Dare glanced over at Noah. He forced his expression to be serious. "Well, I'm sure she's going to sit you down and ask you a million questions. I'm sure she figures she has the right to interrogate the man I'm going to marry." It wasn't true, but he loved seeing the panic etched on Noah's face.

"Like, what sort of questions?"

"Oh, she'll want to know what your intentions are, how much money you make, how long you've been a firefighter, where you see yourself in five years."

"Those aren't too bad."

"That's only the beginning." Dare fought to keep from smiling. "She'll want to know about your family, whether you've ever owned any animals, if you prefer to be on the lake or on the shore. She'll ask your penis size."

Noah's head snapped over, his eyebrows slanting.

Dare laughed, feeling even lighter than before.

"You're fucking with me, right?"

"Oh," Dare sobered. "And she'll also want to know how many times a day you plan to play slap and tickle with me."

Noah snorted.

"I think you should say at least three, but more than likely four." Dare reached over and took Noah's hand. This time, he responded seriously. "She'll love you, Noah. As much as I do. You have nothing to worry about."

"Thank God."

"As long as she took her medication."

Noah grimaced.

"Kidding." Dare didn't bother to tell him that she really would probably say slap and tickle at least a dozen times while they were there. He figured he'd let that part be a surprise.

When they pulled into the driveway, Dare noticed Grams sitting on the porch, a huge grin growing on her aging face as she recognized them.

"God, I hope she likes me," Noah muttered as he got out of the truck.

Dare knew she would like him. Hell, she would love him.

Didn't mean she wouldn't give him a hard time. After all, Dare hadn't been born with his witty personality and wicked sense of humor. He'd gotten them from her.

Knowing Noah was nervous, Dare took his hand as they made their way up onto the porch. Without releasing him, Dare leaned down and planted a kiss on Grams's smooth cheek.

"Grams, this is Noah. Noah, this is Grams."

His grandmother's blue eyes raked ever so slowly over Noah as she took him in. Dare figured she was trying to determine her first impression.

"Nice to meet you..." Noah trailed off, glancing over at him with an expression of terror.

"You can call me Grams," she said, drawing Noah's attention back to her. "No need for formalities." She nodded toward their clasped hands. "If you're good enough for my boy to bring you here to meet me, you're good enough to call me Grams."

Dare smiled. Not once in his life had he ever introduced his grandmother to a guy he'd dated. Not even Noah. So, she was right.

"It's a pleasure to meet you, Grams." Noah's voice shook with nerves, which was oddly endearing.

"Nice to finally meet the boy who's been playing slap and tickle with my Dare."

Noah turned several shades of red. Dare couldn't help but pull him close and kiss him quickly. "See, I told you she'd love you."

"Now where's my food?" Grams asked, watching the two of them closely.

Another horror-stricken look took over Noah's face. "You didn't tell me we were supposed to bring food."

"She's kidding," he assured him, laughing. "Come on, Grams. Let's feed him before he has a heart attack."

Dare helped Grams get to her feet, then followed her inside.

"While I get the sandwiches ready, why don't you show this sweet boy your old bedroom."

"Grams…" He drew the single word out into a whine. He had absolutely no intention of showing Noah that room. Shit. He'd forgotten all about it.

"Hush that. Go show him."

Crap. She wasn't asking, she was telling, and Dare knew better than to ignore a command from Grams.

Now Dare was the one feeling a little awkward, while Noah was grinning from ear to ear.

It was definitely better when he wasn't the one in the hot seat.

BASED ON DARE'S horrified expression, whatever was in that room was a doozy. Noah wasn't sure he'd ever seen Dare that panicked before, which only made him want to know why.

"Seriously, we don't have to do this," Dare muttered as Noah followed him out of the kitchen. "You can pretend you saw it and she'll never know."

"That's not happening." He had to know what was hidden in that room, what Dare didn't want him to see.

Noah couldn't hide his curiosity as Dare led him down the dark, narrow hallway toward the doors at the far end. As soon as Grams had mentioned the bedroom, Dare had gone a little pale. Now he wanted to know why.

Before Dare opened the door, he turned to face Noah.

"Keep in mind, I moved out of her house right after you and I broke up. I couldn't bring myself to sleep in this room anymore. Plus, I needed some space from everyone. She has never changed anything about my bedroom in all the time I've been gone." Dare's hand tightened on the doorknob. "In my defense, that was fifteen years ago."

Noah smirked. "What? Are you embarrassed?"

"You don't know the half of it."

Dare opened the door and allowed Noah to walk around him into the room.

"Holy shit," Noah whispered. "Obsessive much?"

"Shut it."

Dark blue curtains covered two long windows, while a twin bed sat in the far corner, the comforter neatly covering the mattress—he figured there were some things Grams had changed about the room in the past decade and a half. The carpet was clean, as were all the surfaces. A small television sat on top of the dresser and a lamp sat on the desk.

Those weren't what caught Noah's attention, though.

He stepped farther into the room, taking it all in before he turned back toward the desk. Covering nearly every bit of wall space above the small desk were pictures of Noah. Some including Dare, others of only him. There were so many that it was clear Dare had taken a lot when they'd been together. Noah couldn't remember Dare ever having a camera, but clearly the guy had.

It was a trip down memory lane. There was a picture of them at the party where they'd met. Others of them playing whatever sport had attracted them at the time—soccer, football, baseball. There were smaller pictures of only Noah, some of him standing around, a lot of them in his apartment. He could probably relive all the months they'd been together if he took the time to look at each and every one.

He was about to give Dare a hard time when he leaned in closer, noticing that the largest of the pictures—the one pinned in the center of them all—had words written at the bottom.

There was an arrow pointing toward Noah's face and red ink scribbled inside a circle: *This guy. The man I intend to spend the rest of my life with. He makes up for all the love my life has been lacking. And then some.*

Noah felt the pressure of tears on his sinuses.

He turned to look at Dare. For the first time in his life, Dare appeared to be embarrassed. He was staring at the floor, and he looked so incredibly vulnerable in that moment that Noah couldn't stop himself from grabbing him and pulling him close.

"God, I love you. I'm so sorry for all the pain I caused."

Dare buried his face in Noah's neck but didn't say anything.

Noah knew that Dare's mother had abandoned him. He remembered the conversations they'd had about how Dare felt he wasn't good enough for her to stick around. In fact, Noah had always argued that he was wrong, but the fact that Dare's mother had never been a part of his life was the proof that Dare had always said he had.

"This isn't why I brought you here." Dare pulled back and looked at him. A small smile formed. "If I'd known Grams would suggest this, I would've gutted the room before you had a chance to see it."

"I'm glad you didn't." It was a reminder that Noah had taken Dare for granted back then. He'd known at the time that Dare was the greatest love he would ever know, but he'd been too immature to grab hold of it and never let go. And to think, he'd thought Dare had been the immature one.

Luckily, he'd learned his lesson and someone up there was looking out for him. He wanted to believe it was his dad.

"You boys better not be playing slap and tickle back there!"

Noah laughed, but his face heated instantly.

"We're not!" Dare assured her.

"We should probably go—" Noah didn't get to finish the sentence before Dare had pushed him up against the door, his mouth coming down over his for a brutal, all-consuming kiss.

"Oh, we're gonna play slap and tickle, all right." Dare sounded extremely confident. "I just hope you can keep the noise down, because I'm not gonna lose the opportunity to screw you senseless in the one place I spent nearly two years dreaming about."

Noah curved his head to the side, allowing Dare's lips to trail over his skin. "Here?"

"Right here." Dare sucked on Noah's neck, making him groan. "Now turn around and put your hands on the wall. And remember, you have to be quiet. Grams'll never let you live it down if she finds out."

Noah peered around the room once more while he contemplated what would happen if he gave in. Never in his life had he known a love quite like this one. As he took in all those pictures on the wall, he knew there was no way he would hold out on Dare.

After all, Dare made him feel the one thing he'd hadn't felt in fifteen years … fearless.

Only now, Noah knew what that meant. And he wasn't about to let the greatest love in his life go.

Not now.

Not ever.

However, he really hoped they wouldn't get caught.

'Cause that would just be awkward.

Fearless

Epilogue

Friday, August 5th

"DARE! I'M HOME." The screen door closed behind Noah at the same time Lulu bounded toward him, tail wagging, tongue lolling. She looked as though she'd settled in already. As he greeted her with a rub on the head, he glanced around his new house for the first time.

Well, the first time since they'd officially moved in. While Noah had been at the fire station yesterday, Dare had incorporated the help of his friends, and they'd managed to unload the storage unit that had held Noah's furniture for the past month, along with everything from Dare's apartment.

As soon as they'd received the news that the sellers had accepted their offer, Noah had put in his notice with his apartment complex. Instead of waiting for his lease to be up, he had moved his things into storage, then moved in with Dare in the interim. And since that day, they'd been counting down until they could move in here.

Noah had hated not being able to help them, but Dare had insisted. From the second they'd put ink to paper and officially closed on their very first house, Dare had been overly anxious. Noah hadn't been able to make him wait, so he had relented.

Fearless

Now, as he dropped his bag in the entryway, he looked around. He fought to keep his OCD at bay, knowing he would get the chance to clean and organize as soon as he saw Dare.

It was already a little after nine in the morning because he had stopped by his mother's house before heading home, needing to pick up a few things she had set aside for them. Mostly extra dishes—matching, of course—as well as some extra towels and sheet sets she had stored away. Noah had informed her that they didn't need them, but she'd insisted and he hadn't been able to tell her no. But, as he'd learned when he arrived at her house, the dishes and sheets hadn't been what she'd really wanted to give him.

His mother had been almost as excited as Dare that they'd decided to move in together and were planning to tie the knot, although they hadn't set a wedding date yet. Dare had promised they would sit down and figure that out once they got settled into the house.

When he'd arrived at his mother's house, she had offered him coffee, then led him into the kitchen. It was there that he'd had his first breakdown in a long, long time. Waiting for him on the kitchen table was a shadow box that held only one thing … his father's shield. His mother wanted him to have something that was his father's for his new house.

He'd wanted to say that the tears had broken loose because he hadn't been expecting it, but he knew that wasn't true. For the first time since the day his father had died, he'd actually felt whole again. He still missed the man, but having Dare back in his life had righted things in a way he hadn't expected. And for the first time, over coffee, Noah had talked with his mother about his father. By the end of that conversation, he might've still been shedding a tear or two, but he was no longer shouldering the guilt he'd carried for the past fifteen years. And his mother had agreed, it was probably his father who had manipulated things so that he and Dare would find each other again. It was something he would've done when he was alive. He simply loved Noah that much.

However, they had both agreed not to share that with Milly, because she was already taking all the credit for bringing the two of them together again.

On any normal day, Noah would've assumed Dare was asleep—the guy was not prone to getting up with the sun—but he doubted Dare had slept much, if at all, last night. Based on the fact a lot of the boxes were already unpacked, the empty ones tossed haphazardly in the breakfast nook, he figured he was right.

"Where are you?" he called out, smiling as he noticed the video game system set up in the living room. Dare said he rarely played, but Noah knew differently. In the past month and a half, he'd learned a lot of things about Dare, including his secret video game obsession.

As he made his way toward their bedroom, he heard the shower water running. The thought of seeing Dare in the shower sent a frisson of awareness through him. Rather than barge in, Noah stopped in the doorway, taking in the view of Dare's sleek, naked body through the glass shower doors.

Holy fuck. Not in a million years would he ever get tired of seeing that beautiful man. He stole his breath every time as though it were the first.

"You gonna stand there and watch?" Dare turned to face him, pushing one of the glass doors open and offering a better view. "Or you think you might want to join me?"

"This watching thing…" Noah noticed Dare's hand slide down his stomach before grabbing his dick. "It's kinda hot."

"Yeah?" Dare's crooked grin said he agreed.

Noah went into the bathroom and pulled off his shirt, but instead of undressing completely, he leaned against the vanity counter and watched Dare.

One of the greatest things about this house was the oversized shower. Whoever built it had been thinking more than one person should be in there at a time. It ran the entire length of one wall and was as deep as it was long. Between the double shower heads and the tiled bench, it wouldn't be difficult to spend an afternoon right there.

Or morning. Whichever.

Dare snapped his fingers. "Hey, Pearson. My eyes are up here."

"I'm not interested in your eyes right now."

"Why am I not surprised?" There was amusement in Dare's tone. "I always knew you liked to watch."

"Oh, I definitely do." Noah's eyes were fixated where Dare was teasing his dick with one hand, the other sliding down and cupping his balls. The water was raining down over him, slicking his sun-bronzed skin. It was like a freaking porno, right here in his own bathroom.

"You like when I jack myself off?"

Noah met Dare's gaze. "Depends. What do you think about when you touch yourself?"

Dare took a step back and leaned against the wall, spreading his legs wide as he fondled his balls.

"I think about you," Dare explained, his voice raspy. "I think about your hot fucking mouth wrapped around me. Or your hand stroking me."

Noah released the button on his jeans and lowered the zipper. He slid his hand inside.

Dare's eyes immediately dropped to where the action was. "Show me yours."

Standing up straight, Noah pushed his jeans down his hips, pulling his cock out so Dare could watch.

"Now stroke it."

Noah loved when Dare got bossy. It was sexy as fuck. He leaned his bare ass against the counter and leisurely glided his hand up and down his dick, watching the show in the shower. Dare reached up and retrieved the shower wand. Spreading his legs farther, allowing Noah a fantastic front-row view, he turned the spray toward his balls.

"Oh, fuck…"

Unable to look away, Noah watched every move Dare made. From the way his eyes drifted shut and his head tilted back to the way his abs contracted as he pushed his hips forward. He continued to aim the water directly at his balls while he fisted his dick, his hand working faster than before.

"I wanna watch you come."

Dare's eyes opened. "Yeah? Right here?"

"Right here." And then Noah intended to join him, but first, he wanted to watch Dare bring himself pleasure.

"Then you'll fuck me?" Dare closed his eyes.

"Absolutely."

Dare's hand started moving faster, his grip tighter. "I want to feel you in my ass."

Fuck. If Dare kept that up, Noah could possibly be the one blowing his load.

"Oh, fuck…" Dare opened his eyes and met Noah's gaze. "I want to come in your mouth."

Noah toed off his shoes and shucked his jeans, hopping on one foot to get his socks off as he neared the shower. Without hesitating, he stepped inside, pulled the door shut, and dropped to his knees in front of Dare, staring up at him while he stroked himself.

"Yes … fuck yes…" Dare's hand was a blur as he jacked himself roughly. "Now, Noah… Oh… Fuck… Gonna come."

Noah wrapped his lips around the head of Dare's cock as he was coming. He sucked the head hard, making Dare hiss as he unloaded in Noah's mouth, his hips jerking wildly. Noah didn't move until Dare relaxed.

Gripping Dare's hips, Noah urged him to turn around. When he was facing the wall, Noah spread Dare's ass cheeks, burying his tongue between them while Dare pushed back against him.

"Oh, yeah…" Dare groaned again. "Fuck me with your tongue. Lick my ass… God, yes."

Noah tongued him for long minutes, wanting to calm down enough to make this last.

"Fuck me… Want your cock inside me," Dare pleaded, reaching over and grabbing what appeared to be lubricant that he'd stashed on the shelf.

Noah got to his feet and took the bottle. "Prepared, are you?"

"Oh, you just wait. I've hidden that shit all over this house."

Of course he had.

"Plan to be doing more of this?" Slicking his dick up, Noah then guided himself into Dare's ass, pushing in slowly.

Dare grunted. "In every room of the house. Twice a day."

Noah groaned when he bottomed out in Dare's ass. Gripping Dare's hips, Noah pressed up against his back, holding him still. "Is that all?"

"We've also got a hot tub." Dare moaned when Noah pulled out and pushed back in. "Oh, God, Noah. Fuck me. Please… Fuck me hard."

"Did you miss me last night?" he grumbled against Dare's ear.

"So fucking much." Dare grunted again with Noah's next thrust forward. "Did you miss me?"

Noah nipped Dare's earlobe. "More than you can imagine."

"Show me," Dare insisted. "Show me how much you missed me."

Noah pulled Dare's hips with him as he took a step back. "Bend over."

Dare reached for the bench, planting his palms flat while Noah began screwing into him. He tried for slow and easy, just to torment Dare a little, but he couldn't last. The heat of Dare's body gripping him was too much. Their combined moans echoed off the tiled walls as Noah impaled him over and over, slamming in deep, retreating, then slamming in again. He lost himself to the sensation, his hips colliding with Dare's ass as he gave him everything he asked for.

"Oh, fuck…" Dare cried out. "I'm gonna come again. Fuck me…"

Noah wanted Dare to come. Hell, he wanted Dare to come a million times just like this.

Dare's cry of release bounced off the walls, triggering Noah's climax. He stilled his hips as he pushed in deep, coming harder than he'd ever come before. Luckily they were in the shower already because Noah wasn't sure he had enough strength in his body to clean up. He would've been content to remain just like that for the next … well, forever.

Half an hour later, after they'd lingered in the shower until the water turned cold, Noah and Dare were lying on the couch, a movie playing on the television. Noah had been drifting in and out while holding Dare in his arms, enjoying every single second of being right here with him. It was similar to that night all those years ago, and here they were again. In their new house, their new life.

They'd officially come full circle, back where they were both meant to be.

Together.

It still seemed too good to be true. Only a short time ago, Noah had only wondered what Dare was up to, what he'd made of himself while he immersed himself in work, doing whatever he could to forget the past. And now ... now he was sharing a life with the only man he had ever loved.

"What're you thinking about?" Dare mumbled groggily, rolling onto his back.

Noah inched deeper into the cushions so he could look at Dare. "You."

Dare smirked. "What about me?"

"About how lucky I am to have you?"

Dare's smile softened. "See, I was thinking the same thing about you."

Noah locked eyes with Dare. "Yeah, but I was thinking about it first. So I win."

"I'll let you believe that," Dare mumbled, leaning over and kissing Noah softly. "Since winner gets to make lunch."

Leave it to Dare to turn this into a bet *and* to let Noah win, yet still he got to do all the work. "What were the odds of that happening?"

Dare chuckled. "Not sure. But I'll be glad to look up the statistics *after* you feed me."

Noah shifted, crawling over Dare and crushing him into the cushion. "Oh, I'll feed you all right."

Dare laughed, his arms wrapping around Noah as he held him tight. "God, I love when you make promises like that. It's so damn sexy."

Noah shook his head. He had no idea whether Dare was talking about sex or food, but he knew, either way, it wouldn't matter.

One way or the other, they'd be having both before the afternoon was over.

♥□□□□♥□□□□♥

I hope you enjoyed Dare and Noah's story. Fearless is the second book in the Pier 70 series. I started writing their story shortly after I finished Reckless, however, I put it away for a little while. On morning, I woke up and Dare was right there, ready to go. Turned out, his humor was exactly what I needed at the time and I had so much fun writing this book. You can read more about the sexy guys in charge of the marina by checking them out on my website.

Want to see some fun stuff related to the Pier 70 series, you can find extras on my website. Or how about what's coming next? I keep my website updated with the books I'm working on, including the writing progression of what's coming up for the Pier 70 series. www.NicoleEdwardsAuthor.com

If you're interested in keeping up to date on the Pier 70 crew as well as receiving updates on all that I'm working on, you can sign up for my monthly newsletter.

Want a simple, *fast* way to get updates on new releases? You can also sign up for text messaging. If you are in the U.S. simply text NICOLE to 64600 or sign up on my website. I promise not to spam your phone. This is just my way of letting you know what's happening because I know you're busy, but if you're anything like me, you always have your phone on you.

And last but certainly not least, if you want to see what's going on with me each week, sign up for my weekly Hot Sheet! It's a short, entertaining weekly update of things going on in my life and that of the team that supports me. We're a little crazy at times and this is a firsthand account of our antics.

Acknowledgments

I have to thank my family first, for putting up with my craziness. From my sudden outbursts when I think of something that needs to be added or when I question why one of the characters did what they did, to the strange hours that I keep and the days on end when I'm MIA because I'm under deadline or just engrossed in a story… Y'all are incredibly tolerant of me and for that, I am forever grateful. I love you with all that I am.

My street team – The Naughty & Nice Posse. Ladies, your daily pimping and support fills my heart with so much love. You are a blessing to me, each and every one of you.

My beta readers, Chancy and Denise. Ladies, I'm not sure thanks will ever be enough. However, not only are you the ones who catch the weird things and ask the bigger questions, you've both become my friends and you keep me going.

My copyeditor, Amy. Punctuation and grammar… well, that's not my strong suit. But it is yours and you are truly remarkable at what you do. You simply amaze me and I am so glad that I found you.

Nicole Nation 2.0 for the constant support and love. This group of ladies has kept me going for so long, I'm not sure I'd know what to do without them.

And, of course, YOU, the reader. Your emails, messages, posts, comments, tweets… they mean more to me than you can imagine. I thrive on hearing from you, knowing that my characters and my stories have touched you in some way keeps me going. I've been known to shed a tear or two when reading an email because you simply bring so much joy to my life with your support. I thank you for that.

♥••••♥••••♥

About Nicole

New York Times and *USA Today* bestselling author Nicole Edwards lives in Austin, Texas with her husband, their three kids, and four rambunctious dogs. When she's not writing about sexy alpha males, Nicole can often be found with her Kindle in hand or making an attempt to keep the dogs happy. You can find her hanging out on Facebook and interacting with her readers - even when she's supposed to be writing.

Nicole also writes contemporary/new adult romance as Timberlyn Scott.

Website
www.NicoleEdwardsAuthor.com

Facebook
www.facebook.com/Author.Nicole.Edwards

Twitter
@NicoleEAuthor

Also by Nicole Edwards

The Alluring Indulgence Series
Kaleb

Zane

Travis

Holidays with the Walker Brothers

Ethan

Braydon

Sawyer

Brendon

The Club Destiny Series
Conviction

Temptation

Addicted

Seduction

Infatuation

Captivated

Devotion

Perception

Entrusted

Adored

The Coyote Ridge Series
Curtis

The Dead Heat Ranch Series
Boots Optional

Betting on Grace

Overnight Love

Also by Nicole Edwards (cont.)

The Devil's Bend Series
Chasing Dreams

Vanishing Dreams

The Devil's Playground Series
Without Regret

The Pier 70 Series
Reckless

Fearless

The Sniper 1 Security Series
Wait for Morning

Never Say Never

The Southern Boy Mafia Series
Beautifully Brutal

Beautifully Loyal

Standalone Novels
A Million Tiny Pieces

Inked on Paper

Writing as Timberlyn Scott
Unhinged

Unraveling

Chaos

Naughty Holiday Editions
2015

Made in the USA
Middletown, DE
22 April 2016